THE RETURN OF THE CAVALIERS

Biography of M. Fethullah Gülen

The Pioneer of the Cavaliers
Who Emerged from the Invisible Realm

Farid al-Ansari

New York

Published by Blue Dome Press
244 5th Avenue, Suite D-149
New York, NY 10001, USA
www.bluedomepress.com

Translated by Amany Shalaby

Library of Congress Cataloging-in-Publication Data
al-Ansari, Farid.
[Riwayat 'awdat al-fursan. English]
The return of the cavaliers: biography of M. Fethullah Gülen: the pioneer of the cavaliers who emerged from the invisible realm / Farid al-Ansari; translated by Amany Shalaby.
pages cm
"Originally published in Arabic as Awdatu'l-Fursan, Dar al-Nile, 2011."
Summary: Novelized account of the life of M. Fethullah Gülen.
ISBN 978-1-935295-60-0 (alk. paper)
1. Gülen, Fethullah--Fiction. 2. Muslim scholars--Turkey--Fiction. I. Shalaby, Amany. II. Title.
PJ7814.N745R5913 2014
892.7'37--dc23
2014032341

ISBN: 978-1-935295-60-0

Printed by
Imak Ofset, Istanbul - Turkey

Table of Contents

CHAPTER 2
BETWEEN BOOKS AND SHEEP

CHAPTER 3
THE STATION OF UNVEILING
AND VISIONS

CHAPTER 4
THE CONQUESTS OF EDIRNE:
FROM RETREATS TO REALIZATIONS

CHAPTER 5
ENDURING THE MANDATORY
MILITARY SERVICE

CHAPTER 6
RETURNING TO THE RURAL AREAS
OF THRACE

CHAPTER 7
THE MAIN MIGRATION TO IZMIR:
THE FIRST UNION WITH
THE HORSES OF CONQUEST

CHAPTER 8
OPENING UP TO THE WORLD AND
THE CAVALIERS' VICTORY

In the Name of Allah,
the All-Merciful, the All-Compassionate

Dedication

I dedicate these pages to you
Oh youth of the Muslim world
In hope that together we can see
The primary place of the Muslim nation;
To be able to navigate the right direction
Towards restoring the spirit that we lost.

The one who cares for you,
Farid al-Ansari

Epigraph

*A*s the world turns round, it is shifting toward its real orbit, getting ready to come to a new equilibrium day by day. But I wonder if the true *Inheritors of the Earth*[1] are ready to reclaim the inheritance they lost and which others have taken!

Having initial possession of the truth is one thing, becoming a rightful claimer by continual representation is another; for if the truth is not represented in practice as its true worth deserves, it may be taken from its possessors at any time and given to other people or groups, and it will continue to change hands among those who might be capable of representing certain aspects of its goodness until the true representatives of the Truth arise.[2]

---

[1] Gülen's use of the allusive phrase of "the Inheritors of the Earth" is derived from the verse (which means), "…*My righteous servants will inherit the earth*" (Al-Anbiya 21:105). The expression in the verse would be more understandable when it is considered along with the verse (which means): "*God has promised those of you who believe and do good, righteous deeds that He will most certainly empower them as vicegerents on earth, even as He empowered those that preceded them…*" (An-Nur 24:55). (Ed.)

[2] Except from Gülen's article, "Yeryüzü Mirasçıları" (The Inheritors of the Earth), *Yeni Ümit Magazine*, Vol. 3, Issue 19, 1993.

Preface

This text which I am offering today to the readers might be considered a novel, a biography, a poem or a history book. I am not exactly sure what it should be considered, but I know that it is a story of a spirit in anguish, an existential heartfelt experience of a nation bleeding. It is a flood of pure longing for salvation from the heart of a man from Anatolia whose radiance has abundantly flowed upon the whole world!

There is something I should mention here about this book. I began writing it at Sema Hospital in the metropolitan city of Istanbul in 2008. Later, I wrote more at my house in Meknes, Morocco. But it was decreed that I would finish writing it one year later at the same hospital back in Istanbul.

Before I finish this preface, I must thank the Turkish brothers who exerted their utmost effort to translate the excerpts of the journalistic dialogue titled *Küçük Dünyam* (*My Small World*) in which Mr. Fethullah Gülen mentioned a great deal about the stages of his life. This became the main resource for this text. The Turkish brothers also offered me many other texts that aided my writing. For years I stayed in touch and had fruitful discussions with them; they supplied me with precious information concerning important historical facts and the circumstances that surrounded all faith-inspired services in Turkey which could not have been found in books and documents. These were indispensable references.

Farid al-Ansari
Istanbul, Sept, 23, 2009

Chapter 1
Searching for the Spirit's Enlightenment

A Man of Secrets

ethullah[1] had a secret that he could not speak of!
Fethullah had a secret that the whole world was waiting for but he could not tell anyone about it!

Fethullah carried within his heart that which could not be endured and that is why he continuously wept until tears were perplexed at its death!

Fethullah inherited a secret. If a high mountain carried such a secret it would be utterly demolished from its top down and the pillars of its foundations would perish out of awe!

Fethullah was a relentless cavalier whose determination never wavered and his will never weakened. The echo of his voice was louder than the roar of thunder! He strove in the morning until the sun would melt into the bleeding ocean, and when he was alone at night with agonies he would weep!

---

[1]   The author makes insistent use of Gülen's middle name "Fethullah" alone throughout this section, thus demanding attention to its meaning. The given name of "Fethullah" (or Fathu'llah) is built from the Arabic words *fath* and *Allah*, meaning "Conquest of Allah" or "Opening the Door to Divine Mercy and Benevolence." (Ed.)

He was like a leaping lion, with acute vision like that of a falcon. His silence inspired awe like that of an ocean. When he was silent he delivered a speech and when he would speak he would ignite passion! When he wrote he was as transparent as fine glass!

People know Fethullah and people have heard of Fethullah Gülen but no one knows what Fethullah wanted! His secret was kept within his chest, laid in his innermost being like hidden pearls! Who knows? He might have been a cavalier whose light has not yet reached our time! His time has not yet arrived! How difficult for a human being to live at a time ahead of his time and to mingle with people who are not of his time!

Nevertheless, Fethullah continued to draw the features of the past on the canvas of the future, then he would blow and it will become a reality by Allah's leave! Whenever he would write an article or deliver a speech his words would form vivid images of the noble Companions' convoys and of Mehmed (or Muhammad)[2] the Conqueror's troops, emerging marching in ranks from beyond the dusty clouds like rain pouring from the sky of Anatolia upon the whole world!

Fethullah only owned in this world his old clothes, carrying a suitcase full of sadness wherever he traveled or stayed. However, in that case he kept three ancient keys. The first key was the key for "the High Gate"[3] in Istanbul. The second key was the key of "Exoneration" (*miftah al-Hittah*) at the Masjid al-Aqsa, or the Farthest Mosque, in Jerusalem. The third key was the key of the Cordoba Mosque in the Andalus of agonies!

---

[2] The proper name Mehmed is the most common variant of the name Muhammad used in Turkish. (Ed.)

[3] The High Gate (or Bab-ı Ali) is a term used in Ottoman-Turkish to refer to the seat of government in Istanbul. (Ed.)

Alone, he listened to the moaning of the old walls, the whimper of the departing wind between Tangier and Jakarta and the cry of seagulls at beaches left empty of the beloveds' ships, the beloved who lived a long time ago and there has been no trace since then of their sailing boat rising! He would listen and weep!

Alone, he listened to the neighing horses coming from beyond the clouds and to the call of the veiled unseen, feeling its influential vibration upon the shore of his chest urging him to cry out from his podium, "Oh horses of Allah, ride! Oh swords of lightning, strike!" He used to see that which was not seen by others and weep!

Fethullah's life is a story of tears! His family name is Gülen which means "the laughing one" in the Turkish language. What an irony of opposites! The weeping of all the pious at that time was marvelously synchronized! He did not weep but to put a smile on the face of the future so that springs will bloom in the children's gardens. I have not seen anyone whose tears flowed more easily than his nor have I seen anyone enraptured by love more than him. It is as if all the tears of the past history had been gathered into rivers flowing from his eyes.

Those who thought that he wept out of weakness or fatigue were mistaken; for he was a mountain whose rocks cracked revealing a spring of overflowing vigor which caused him to weep!

Admonishment was one of Fethullah's secrets and that is why he would always weep whenever he attended a sermon of admonishment, and for his weeping all the birds in the world would also weep! I've seen him weeping as a child and as a youth, then as an adult and as an old man; for he was always weeping. His springs never dried or stopped gushing with his warm tears. Fethullah watered all of Istanbul's forests and quenched the thirst of the horses. It fed the poor at night and from the barrages of his tears he watered the world's deserts! I have always wondered which mountains of the world his springs were gushing from?

I traveled back to his childhood so that I could find how and when he started to receive the extraordinary gifts of the secrets and oh gentlemen, I found a marvel! The honeybees used to feed on his streaming tears and then form many cells everywhere!

* * *

My illness augmented my fatigue but I once saw in my dream honeybees at my window and in another dream I saw myself eating honey so I realized that I was called! Thus, I rode my longing out and threw myself into the departure's embrace!

Stations of Transformations

Here is Istanbul! Here is the passageway of the Conquerors to all directions of the world!

Whenever I dwelled in Istanbul's minarets my heart would feel ecstatically hopeful! But whenever I would approach the Bosporus Bridge I would feel anxiety! The seagulls seemed to bustle irritably in the sky! I was not sure if the bustling was for a wedding or was it mere wailing? And who really knows!

Did that dove cry? Or did it chant upon its dancing branch?

This was the stage of change and the time of transformations has an impact like that of earthquakes upon houses! The world was turning at a rate of a different nature where rays overlap between sunset and sunrise! The wind was blowing bitter coldness and the swarms of doves and seagulls were trying to escape under the pillars of minarets and domes to protect themselves from the severity of such coldness.

I was sitting by the corner of the ancient city walls of Constantinople close to the school gate waiting for the schoolmaster to come. When the storm reached its climax Master (*Ustadh*) Bediüzzaman Said Nursi leaped about and looked from above the domes of the city. He then stretched his great wings around its walls until he encompassed all the gates to the city! He remained there for some time alone, battling against the gusts of wind all alone! Whenever he would look under his wings he would see the nightingales, silent behind the domes and his tears would stream out into the wind and he would cry out amidst its severe current: O Said! Be humble like soil so you would not pollute the purity of the *Risale-i Nur* (*The Epistles of Light*). When the storm calmed, he recited the Qur'anic chapter of *al-Fath* (the Conquest) and then he opened the gates and left!

I called him with the loudest voice, "Oh my Master! Will the Last Cavalier[4] return?"

He looked at me and his frown drew a gesture of denial upon his revered face and he threw at me a glaring light from his luminous eyes and said, "Woe to you! O wakeful one! Do you not know that every age has its own particular cavalier?"

I said, "But who will close the gates in the face of the gusting wind when it blows all anew?"

He said, "My son, this is the stage of conquest and there will be no closed doors to its time!"

I said, "Oh my Master, what a wonder! How could there be a conquest at a time when the wind would neither spare our gates nor the walls of our old minarets?"

---

[4] The author alludes here to his other biographical novel on the life of Bediüzzaman Said Nursi, titled *Akhiru'l-Fursan* (Last of the Cavaliers). (Ed.)

He said, "Oh my son, how ignorant you are of your time! Raise your head a little and look at the highest horizon and you will see the sun of hope rising little by little from beyond sorrows and you will see the words of the First Light (i.e. the Noble Prophet) illuminating a rainbow between its hands and embroidering its message upon the ocean waves! If you are one of those who are fluent in the language of water, then read: 'First, Constantinople will be conquered then Rumiyya (or the Roman) will be conquered.'"

I said, "My Master, may my father and mother be sacrificed for you, what is Rumiyya?"

He said, "Rumiyya, my son, is an alluring woman that lives within our own ribs! It is the great capital of Satan! Its four pillars are plunged into the ocean of darkness! Across the world it has fires and smoke; for every day it burns one thousand birds and one thousand doves! Nevertheless, the 'army' of Light has devoted itself solely to confront it with weapons made of the sun's glare! And the prince of the 'troops' of Light is reciting the Qur'anic chapter of *an-Nasr* (Succor) for help coming from beyond the Unseen! This is the end of suffering for weakened ones. Very soon, you will see marvels! Today, the 'army' of Light, across the world is gathering strength from the niche of the fruitful night in order to progress! Oh my son, look for your share of the fruitful nights!"

I asked, "What then are the characteristics of its prince?"

He said, "My son, do not tire yourself looking for titles! He is but a phantom, a meaning, or a spirit! Nay! He is more of a heart that comes from the glowing light! He is an army of a glowing sun! He is a longing in the heart, a chanting of a spirit, a resistance of a love whose wound is still bleeding from a yearning heart. He is the moaning of a nostalgic sentiment that rises between bowing and prostrating forming a cloud in a sky that is painted in rainbow colors and is full of pure goodness and blessings! It rains all over the continents of the earth! If you wish, you can watch for its meadows no matter where it travels; for you will always find its flowers blooming with fresh dew drops!"

I asked, "But what would his lineage and his location be? Where and when will he be born?"

He said, "Woe to you, wakeful one! The possessor of this time (*Sahib az-Zaman*) has two births! The first birth is within a place. And what happened, happened! As for the second birth it is within time! So watch for the time when the wound hurts the most! When the wind is moaning; for indeed there is no birth without pain! Thus, acquire the second birth, may you prosper through poverty! Oh my son, if you attain such circumstances, you will be one of those Conquerors!"

I said, "Can I be one of their vanguards?"

He said, "But right before arriving at their houses, there is a secret password that is hidden, concealed within the maw of a bird."

I asked eagerly, "O Master, which bird?"

But the visions came to a halt!

After such visions, I spent a whole year waiting for more to come but there were no more visions. I returned to my home in Meknes waiting for permission to depart one more time to the City of Light.

* * *

Between Tangier and Gibraltar lies the strait of sorrows! Every evening, the strait's seagulls still moan while telling the story of the Moors' misery! Nothing is causing the strait to change its habit! Its dreams send a signal towards the north but the pains return it broken towards the south! Whales are there between going hungry and returning fully fed on the flesh of the human being!

I was a captive with bare feet between Tangier and Tetouan trying to attentively listen to the cooing of the carrier pigeons; for I was told they had been here since Granada's last prince crossed the strait after he was repulsed out of his Garden! The marvelous pigeons mourned him and carried to him the treasures of the secrets of wisdom! I was told that such pigeons coo when they release their longing, which when heard, the rocks on the shores shake, the seagulls cry and the waves become agitated!

I said to my youthful companion, "Woe to you! This is what we are pursuing! It is the secret password! Return us so I may gain its signs or I may solve the puzzle or I may be able to read therein the birth of Andalus in a new location! I still preserve its image within my heart since the sun set atop its minarets but the image caused other visions! The cavalier of the new era has been illustrating the features of its Gardens within my heart flower by flower, preparing the spirit of longing whose mosques have remedies for the pains of the world. It was said that the sorrow of the strait would not be soothed except with the echoes of its minarets!

Thus, we returned tracing our pains searching between rocks and trees for a sign of a nest or a feather but we found no trace of the bird that morning!

The wind was blowing with a spring breeze and the sun rays were rising slowly; to the brightness of the morning drawing unlimited rainbows upon the mist of the sea! Suddenly, gentlemen, the pigeons began cooing from all around. I could not define their exact pain! Their cooing had the rhythm of the call to Prayer! I tried many times to figure out its direction but I could not! As for the mosques, they had Andalusian architecture. The cry was Turkish in its style of chanting and the moaning returned, echoed from Istanbul's minarets and its bays where the mosques of Fez drink sip after sip and weep!

I received the sign and I saw a marvel! I then entered into a state of wonderment (*maqam al-hayrah*)! The Master said to me, "This is the time of the death of geography and the birth of history! Oh my son, the secret password is within a fertilized drop of Light (*nutfah min Nur*) which will emerge out of the Prophet's Household in the east of Istanbul in Eastern Anatolia, so depart!"

Here is Istanbul again! A passing sad thought called me and said to me, "Your place is where Allah has chosen for you. Oh wakeful one, there is no place for you today except in the state of seeking His forgiveness!" As soon as I heard that, I started to hear from the depth of my consciousness a voice rushing to arrive at the shore of my tongue: "O my Lord, forgive me! O my Lord, forgive me!"

I was being taken in an ambulance, extremely sick, but fully conscious of what I was hearing and what I was witnessing! I became conscious of everything! This is the major highway in the middle of Istanbul. These are its domes and its minarets are to the right and to the left, shedding their lights in all directions. This is the great suspension bridge which was newly built on historical bases between Asia and Europe and it is the new arch for passing new Light to the future! And this....Ah! This is the hospital Sema (literally, "Heaven") again! At this point I realized my place! I knew I had failed in the first trial! Thus, I resumed my studies in the School of Job[5] anew!

---

[5] According to the meaning of the verse, "*So he (Joseph) remained in prison some more years*" (Yusuf 12:42), Prophet Joseph, upon him be peace, is usually accepted as the patron-saint or guide of prisoners, and

Oh gentlemen, I stayed for a whole year running between sunrises and sunsets! A whole year thinking I was washing the soul's defilements off my body but now I discovered that I had never left my space! Thus, I returned burdened by all my sins! I had followed the wrong way then! Thus, it was decreed that I must retake the lesson from the beginning! Oh Allah, please bestow Your mercy! Oh Allah, please bestow Your mercy!

The hospital bed was lined up in the *qibla* direction and the big windows were embracing the Marmara Sea. The five islands were standing before me like edifices! The sun was about to set beyond my feet and its rays were weaving a quilt, a memorial for all the sorrows sending to me chants of evening invocations recited through the leaves of the sycamore tree standing right in front of my window! When the day was ending I saw my funeral rising before my eyes on the horizon above the disappearing sea! I remembered my Prayers so I prayed the Sunset and Night Prayers united and shortened racing towards the moment of connected Prayers (*wasl*)! By that time, the night had raised its lamps shimmering across the islands amidst the sea. The shores' lamps seemed to be dreaming about something! I was overwhelmed with nostalgia for my special collection of litanies and invocations (*awrad*) and once I started to recite them waves of mercy flew, hitting me one after the other! Yes, I just described it as mercy even though it was hitting me! And oh gentlemen, the pain was so intense!

---

the prison is seen to be a kind of "the School of Joseph," where Prophet Joseph continued his mission. Similarly, the hospital is called here "the School of Job." There is, therefore, an allusion to Prophet Job (Ayyub) who patiently endured all the illness and afflictions that befell him. With this use, the author refers to his remaining steadfast to Allah in the Sema Hospital where he stayed for some time for treatment. (Ed.)

Then I remembered...Ahha! I digested the lesson: there is no birth without pain! "Pursue the second birth so you may prosper through poverty!" Thus, I called in the night of the still ocean, "Oh gentleness! Oh gentleness! Oh what a wonderful prince of gentleness! And what a wonderful army of gentleness!"

Did the Master not say to me, "This is the point where geography ends and history is born?" Yes, but please be gentle with my heart that is too weak to fly! It is my situation to embrace the present place stage after stage, so that I may be able to free myself from it towards the stages of time! This was what my present incapacity demanded; since for a seeker like myself there's no way but to sit as a student with good manners!

Such were the passing visions of Light (*tajalliyat an-Nur*) whose creeks are flowing now between your hands, oh wakeful one! Thus, carry your stick on your shoulder and depart towards the soul's enlightenment seeking its original springs so that you may enter the time of the conquest and discover the secret of Fethullah's weeping and then you will be healed.

My room in the hospital used to open to another room that my companion occupied. He was not an ordinary companion but he was a possessor of spiritual states. They introduced him to me as a language translator but he was a spiritual translator. He had mastered the language of signs and allusions and he had the ability to untangle the puzzles of navigating the Path! I have never seen a young man who had more depth than him. Yet he was too humble to admit it even to himself! If anyone just looked at him outwardly he would certainly miss a precious treasure and what a treasure he was!

He had eastern features with noble sadness breaking upon his handsome face. His eyes were traveling into the ocean of the Unseen, radiating dignity and demanding reverence! He had visions during which he would sometimes be fully present and at other times utterly absent and his location could not be fath-omed! Between his black eyes and black hair his white forehead was shining with light like a dawn with truthful features, ever giving glad tidings of blessings and goodness regardless of his suffering and sadness.

With his subtle receptivity, he could have heard the scream-ing of my silent spirit as I made a hidden call from the depth of my conscience to the Prince of Conquest! Who knows! He just opened my door and asked politely my permission to enter. The night had just revealed its beauty with its phantoms and imagination. Beside my head was a small lamp pulsing light slowly around the room radiating marvelous colors accompa-nied by sorrows!

He asked me, "Do you need anything?" I looked at his sad face and noticed traces of fresh tears in his eyes. I realized that I had just interrupted his deep diving into his spiritual chanting and I felt regret. Embarrassed, I offered some apologetic words and asked him, "What did the doctor say?"

He kept silent for a moment then murmured some words which I could not understand. Then, he stared far away through the window gazing at the shimmering lights of the islands. Half of the night had almost gone and silence had its revered author-ity over the world. I looked at his departing eyes and asked him once more silently gazing at him without allowing the words to slip through my tongue – sorry, what did the doctor say?

His innermost being stormed strongly but he did not utter a word! But indeed oh gentlemen, I heard all the words flow-ing from his innermost being as if they were the echo of a call-er descending upon me from a loftier realm.

He said to me, "Oh wakeful one, your body is very disturbed as if it were a broken image of the broken spirit concealed with-in you. The physicians are just dealing with your pottery-like clay, but it is the wounds of your soul. Regarding the one who is navigating the way within you towards the soul's wounds, O wakeful one…Ah! The navigating way of the spirit towards the cause of your pains, O wakeful one…Ah!"

He became silent! After he exhaled deeply out the window, he said, "As far as the first misalignment, it is from there!"

Oh gentlemen I was terrified. Then I said, "May my father and my mother be sacrificed for you oh strange one! Tell me where my remedy is and how and when I can find it!"

He traveled into the horizon once more as if he were departing from this world and he sent a scorched moan with burning exhalations flowing in a deep breath. He said, "Your remedy, oh sick companion, is in finding the pearl of your secret?"

The pearl of my secret! What is the pearl of my secret? How could I know?

He said, "There are pearls within emerald shells! They grow within the depth of the lake of secrets!"

I said, "By Allah, your words perplex me! How can I know the lake of the secrets?"

He said, "It is a lake whose water is assembled from the tears of the sincere and truthful ones who did not reach the protection of its wetness. There are seven beautiful mountains that look at it and each mountain has seventy peaks! From ancient times, the tears of the disciples have visited it as well as the longing of the noble Companions, the sufferings of the pious, the expiration of 'Uways al-Qarani, the weeping of Hasan al-Basri, the sobs of Abi al-'Aliya ar-Rihani, the secrets of Imam al-Junaid, the breath of Bishr al-Hafi, the pains of al-Harith ibn Asad al-Muhasibi, the admonishments of 'Abd al-Qadr al-Jilani, the efforts of Shaikh Ahmad Zaruq al-Fasi, the anguish of 'Abd al-Wahid ibn 'Ashir al-Andalusi and the visions of Bediüzzaman Said Nursi. In each era, a sincere friend of Allah or a martyr is informed of the lake from the weeping of passionate longing!"

The guide said to me, "Today, there in its protected valleys on the right shore Fethullah stands! Behind him are thousands of thoroughbred horses which spend the night with heads dropped down lowering their white necks towards those who were buried in silence, piercing through the standards of time and the stages of the hours! From time to time, you can see these horses in the fold of pure darkness standing on their hind legs raising their front legs high. Sometimes they dip their legs in the lake. Every dawn they gulp the water of life and they send their warm tears in peace and delight to the world, listening attentively with their delicate ears awaiting the call to the Prayer. They are surrounded by thousands of phantoms diving within the depth of the lake searching for emerald shells while others stand by the shore opening the shells which God gifted them with, picking up the secrets found within!

"Oh wakeful one, devote your determination towards passing the Path's mountains which have many hardships and many destructive obstacles! To cross the Path safely, you must look within yourself for your heavy burden and unload any excessiveness and reduce the load of impurities and know that you will not be able to do so except by cutting the ties to your lower desires and by liberating yourself from the captivity of misalignments and by exiting the narrow passages of your habits. Sincere repentance will pick you out of past failures and it will raise you to the degrees of what is becoming so that you may become worthy of flying with the wings of the unburdened ones! There is no crossing for the form that still carries the fat of lower desires which clogs its arteries!"

I looked at my companion and said imploringly, "Where is the direction then?"

He said, "Is there any Light rising except from the East?" He raised his hands up and pointed! Then he said to me, "There, you will find a ride to the lake of life in this era and you will find the spiritual leader of all those who are walking towards it in this era! The spiritual leader is made to lead and no one is informing you except one with experience! Thus, rid yourself of your mud, Oh wakeful one, and depart!"

The Spirit's Nectar

The fragrance of Eastern Anatolia is something else! It was said to me: "Your remedy is there; for there is a beautiful lake there called Van. Its two wings are the meeting point of the two bodies of water for those in quest of wisdom. It is also a place of washing for the sick and the low-spirited!"

The Lake of Light is the dominion that embraces ancient history. Through its gardens, it teaches the chanting birds the spirit's songs which were enriched with the Prophets' anguish! Its small towns are still concealing secret treasures: Van, Tatvan and Ahlat. Not too far towards the southwest there is a city covered by solemnity and decency; the small village of Nurs is concealed by its beautiful veil!

There is a lake that is different from any other lake. It is a Sign emanating beauty and majesty! It swirls from the west towards the east in the form of a legendary bird that tells the legend of the dinosaurs' era and the saga of the phoenix! Its head carries a tall crest like that of the peacock rising towards the orient looking at the Muradiye Waterfall nearby, watching it cascade from the beautiful high grassy rocks while the lake beyond flaps its wings ready to fly far away to settle on top of the snowy mountain; the glorious Ararat!

Here, with the ancient East, Turkey's surface rises and Anatolia's head rises high! There are wild and rugged earthly pathways and native mountains! Heights tell the ancient prophetic stories, the tales of tribal heroism of different nations. Endless stories!

Everything here is distinctive and its distinction tells of its uniqueness! Nonetheless, the uniqueness of Ahlat is something else! It is located on the northwestern shore of the lake, curved with innate allure towards its blue water as if it were the eyebrow of a beautiful lady's eye! Safeguarded and precious! Its buildings are erected between the snowy mountainous pathways. These characteristics made it historically a natural bridge between the East and the West for generations because of the caravans of many diverse nations, and invaders that have passed by since the era before Christ until the Ottoman era. All of this made it a record of the many periods of the history of humanity! Because of its beauty and richness, many nations and empires squabbled to control it until it fell in the Muslims' hands in the first centuries after the Prophet's Migration and since then it has started a new history; for it was a new birth to it and until now it continues to gradually ascend to the loftier place of meanings and stations of the spirit! Thus, it became a new rich resource of an ever renewed life!

Ahlat is still a harmonious mixture of nations and a mosaic, decorated with diverse colors and different languages: Turkish, Arabic, Persian, Kurdish, Armenian as well as many languages of the jinn that are cast adrift by the wind as it plays the melody of its melancholy passing through the mountains!

What unites all the marvelous diversity is that Spirit which crossed towards Eastern Anatolia coming from the springs of the universal message of Prophet Muhammad, peace and blessings be upon him! There, in the oasis of Yathrib, the City of the

Messenger, its lights rose upon the proud mountains! Since then, its high waterfalls continue to flow and cascade with guidance and light upon all of Turkey. From there, the arteries of faith extended and reached Constantinople and passed to Eastern Europe up to the walls of Vienna!

Since the first centuries after the Migration of the Prophet, doves and hawks migrated from the Prophet's Household avoiding the conflicts in the Arabian lands from its Syrian region to Iraq until it settled between the rugged pathways of Anatolia. Then, many people from the family of the Prophet, may Allah be pleased with them, inhabited its mountains and valleys seeking a safe refuge which no eye could reach from Bani Umayya and Bani Abbas!

The righteous generations of the Prophet's Household inoculated the mighty Turkish tribes! As certainty of faith united with the majestic mountains, a new Turkish people emerged as the victorious people conquering the hearts! The Turkish people united the visions of beauty both in heart and in sentiment and the visions of majesty in Prophetic determination and in form! This is how the Ottoman Empire arose!

In the depth of this history, a gamete from the Way of the Prophet's family kept migrating from exile to exile until its flower bloomed within the Turkish Gülen family! From an original seed that had a tree with high branches centuries ago, here in the small beautiful town of Ahlat the tree of the Gülen family was steadily erected and it continued to stand tall until the time of the disorder arrived and fights emerged between that family and other families. This took place in the nineteenth century CE. One of the daughters of Gülen's great-grandfather was kidnapped and her brother, Khalil Ahlati, fought on her behalf until he defeated the usurpers and he executed whoever was worthy of being executed! This bore heavily on the tribes and they demanded the intervention of the state authority. The verdict was to exile Khalil Efendi and the rest of his family to Hasankale which was a small town of Erzurum in the north. Nonetheless, Khalil Efendi did not stay there for too long, for he migrated to a village named Korucuk where he settled with his family and once again they planted their roots deep in its soil!

This is why the ancient lineage of the Gülen family is usually known to be in Erzurum and more specifically in Korucuk; for generation after generation the Gülen family lived there and they had forefathers and great grandchildren there. The Gülen family did not leave their favored village except for two periods. The first was when most of the people of Erzurum were displaced at the time of the Russian attack in the late nineteenth century. At that time the family migrated to the Sivas province in the middle of Turkey. After the war ended the family returned to Korucuk. Then, the family left Korucuk again after the fire of the First World War was lit. This time, the family migrated to a village near Yerköy in the province of Yozgat and they stayed there for several years until the war ended. They returned to their favored village in Erzurum – Korucuk. The family then continued to climb lofty stages of knowledge and righteousness and precious places of ethics, asceticism and chastity generation after generation. Many of its ladies and gentlemen were beacons of guidance and edifices of virtues.

Then Fethullah Arrived!

Here is the village Korucuk, one of the beautiful villages of Erzurum. Here the Arabian blood still propagated full of the sadness and happiness of its history. Such blood is still the fragrance of Prophethood and is emitting from its arteries with its wounded rising in affirmation of its lineage that goes back to the family of the Messenger of Allah, peace and blessings be upon him. It is a blood that is still carrying the bleeding sorrow and the terror of manslaughter and the pain of exile! Here is a waft of light concealed and well-guarded, transported through the lineage of the Gülen family from long ago! It was not decreed for it to arrive to the lower realm until the first third of the twentieth century had passed. At that time, the earth rebounded when it was at a level of ignorance that portended the emergence of Dajjal, the great imposter!

This time the wind blew from western veins! It was freed from the icy mountain of denial of the Truth that was armed with the claws of the wolf and the teeth of the invaders' lions and the venom of the snakes' descendants! Blue death swept all of our cities and tore up our bodies!

On the eleventh day of the eleventh month of the year 1938, Mr. Ramiz Gülen had an appointment with Divine Mercy; for on that day his son, Muhammad Fethullah Gülen was born and with his birth a new meaning for life in Anatolia was born! And one day before that, Kemal Ataturk passed away!

Fethullah grew up ascending the stages of conquering, passing through a life that was very far from ordinary! His life was full of marvelous circumstances and he passed through many stages of spiritual strife and heroism which remind us of the *karamat al-awliya*, or the extraordinary gifts and wonders of the great friends of Allah, the legendary princes and the heroes of ancient history.

When the boy attained adulthood the Ottoman mosques embraced him everywhere and their domes pulsated with his deep cry! Birds and sparrows followed his prayers and the chanting of the remembrance of God. The seagulls used to carry the echo of his weeping throughout Anatolia waking sleeping souls and freeing the spirits imprisoned in their physical bodies created from clay! He continued to ascend in his spiritual homes until events started to speak to him with the language of Divine Signs and doves started to carry warnings and good news to him! Then, the Bosporus flew from between his fingers branching into springs that watered the whole world!

All the signs prove that it was he! It is he who is the possessor of your Path, oh heart! Seek then the secret password and seek when and how you can receive it. Seek within the one whom he had deposited and entrusted it to and seek when he deposited it so that you may gain and decipher the code of the symbols you saw in your old vision! Fethullah has a secret that he does not reveal but if you meet the one who accompanied him you may receive a clue from him! Fethullah is a man who has special times. Thus, accompany his shadow, oh wakeful one, so you may see marvels; and if you find the sycamore seed you would own its forest! Be patient then concerning the obstacles on the road and go ahead!

Spiritual Incubators

The narrator of sorrow told me that the incubators of childhood are the farms of secrets! In the incubators' soil, the seeds of Light were planted as well as the map of the coming conquest and the appointed times for the new era! Who knows? You may learn from Fethullah how to truly become a human being! He may even give you from his childhood a hint about the time of the march of the strong horses from beyond Istanbul's clouds! He might also give you the time for being all over the world and for crossing the gulf to the sorrowful Andalus and for sailing into other seas during the painful night! Rumiyya's body is still suffocating the Palestinian birds! There is nothing between the jinn's entrance into the bottle and the rising of dawn except secret words! Maybe you will be there, oh wakeful one!

He also told me that the incubators do not appear to everyone; for they were prepared by the Divine Decree for whomever He willed to give a measure of His Command! No saint or spiritual reviver came but by a measured decree; for no river flows except after the rain pours! Thus, get your walking stick and get ready for your journey, oh my son, and depart; for no wayfarer travels into the great souls but returns a great soul himself!

The First Incubator: Accompanying the Grandfather and the Historical Suffering

Snow is the king of all seasons in the districts and villages of Erzurum! Winter there extends and swallows the rest of the seasons except for a short summer! There is nothing that can overcome the severe coldness of the winds. Nonetheless, there is one wind that is capable of transferring the rough snowy mountains to warm tears as they weep from their sorrow! Such mountains submit to their springs in the middle of winter! What cold can stand the warmness kindled by the begging of spiritual human beings? How can such coldness stand against the fire of the love of the Substitutes (*Abdals*) in the midst of darkness?

Korucuk was there, an extraordinary village! Therein, the spiritual incubations of Fethullah were formed and therein the flower of the new era bloomed and therein the cavalier mounted the saddle of Light racing to the encroachment of darkness!

The house was one and the family was big; for there were seven children and a number of grandchildren, all as branches of one and the same tree which was supported by one root.

Nonetheless, he was distinguished as a vigilant cub within that big assembly of family giants! There were father, grandfather and grandchild. The grandchild became attached to his grandfather before he became attached to his father! He dwelled in his huge wing in marvelous spiritual company which had a great effect upon his prominent personality.

The narrator looked at me and said here, the narration would not be able to describe the glorious stage! Nonetheless, let us leave the barren stories and words and let us knock on the door of "witnessing"! Lift the veil of the words, o wakeful one, and look, here is Şamil Agha (also spelled Shaamil), a name so appropriate for the named! Indeed the grandfather had such a complete personality that it contained all the realities of a subtle and gentle spirit and all the rigor and firmness of a knight's cavalry. He was strong and august even when he became elderly. He continued to wrap his big turban majestically like Sultan Osman Ghazi, the founder of the Ottoman Empire. Sultan Osman (or Othman in Arabic) never took the turban off his head and no one, even from his family, ever saw him bare-headed. In his longing and states he was a marvelous man from the other world, full of deep meanings!

Fethullah, the child, used to watch his grandfather carefully and caught glimpses into his inner states which helped tailor his early manhood. He remembers that he never saw his grandfather laugh, he would only smile. He was greatly revered and held in dignity by the people of the village. No one dared to touch the wall of his sanctuary nor approach his retreat or dishonor him.

By the same high and serious standards he would evaluate the scholars and the shaikhs. He would show great respect to those who were sincere among them and despise the shaikhs who were concerned with getting invited to feasts and he used to call them "the companions of rice." Şamil's father, Mulla Ahmed, was the grandson of Khalil Ahlati, who was his fundamental reference for the meaning of sainthood and asceticism; for he was a man of knowledge and a possessor of a lofty position of certitude (*yaqin*). No one could easily emulate his behavior; for he never used his knowledge and righteousness to make money and he never asked people for anything. He did not even accept gifts. He used to fast and spend the nights praying. He used to eat little, a few olives were enough for him, even though he was one of the richest people; for Allah had enriched him with a wealth he inherited from his father. He inherited a lot of gold which was divided between him and his brother and it was the talk of the city at the time! Nevertheless, the lower realm did not affect his stern asceticism.

Mulla Ahmed, who was the great grandfather of Fethullah, had a strong stature. He was tall and had a dignified look. He was a role model in piousness. In the last thirty years of his life he fully devoted himself to Allah to the extent that he never stretched his body on a bed to sleep. Whenever slumber would overcome him, he would put his right hand on his forehead and take a short nap for a few moments! After that he would go to work on the farm or to perform acts of worship or he would immerse himself in his large library to read and contemplate for a long time and no one would dare to ask him to come out. He would leave the library on his own when he heard the call for the Prayer.

These were the stories told to Fethullah by his grandfather Şamil Agha regarding his great grandfather. A grandfather whose effect influenced the whole family and led their asceticism which led Fethullah, the youth, to witness the virility of the possessors of the lofty states!

Şamil Agha's standards were so high that he would not permit the pseudo saints and pretenders of righteousness any excuses and he would not waver in applying his high standards in
evaluating them. "The companions of rice" and the "shaikhs of
loafs" failed to pass his exam and so none of them were recognized by him. In this way, none accompanied him on the
Path towards Allah except for a very few among the people of
knowledge and piousness. One of those righteous people was
the Imam of the village, Shaikh Mehmed Efendi who was a truly
pious man. He spent about forty years leading people in prayers
there. In Şamil Agha's heart he had a special place; for he loved
him and had great respect for him. This is because the Imam
was a man of relinquishing (*takhliyya*) and adorning (*tahliyya*).[6]
He was a man of visions and he was truly favored with extraordinary divine gifts! Grandfather Şamil told his grandson the
story of when the great earthquake hit the area before the First
World War and how all the houses in the area were destroyed.
The whole village was ruined and people used to sleep outside
from the fear of aftershocks! For many days and nights people lived in such fear until winter arrived and threw its snow
in every corner. Wolves were howling everywhere and the situation became so hard on people that they turned to remembering Allah, invoking His Name and supplicating Him to
keep their hearts warm. They covered their children with the
embrace of remembrance to protect them from the severity of
the cold weather in the wilderness. This situation remained
like that until the good news arrived! Şamil Agha was on his

---

[6]   *Takhliya* means purifying the self from every bad characteristic Allah
       does not approve nor accept and *tahliya* means adorning the self with
       the beautiful virtues. (Ed.)

way to his family's tent when Imam Mehmed Efendi stopped him and asked him, "Master Şamil, where are you going?"

"To the tent," Şamil Agha replied. The Imam smiled and said, "Good news! There will be no more earthquakes after today, God willing. O people return to your houses and sleep safely and if even a small stone falls on you, you can throw it on my head later!"

Şamil Agha marveled at the Imam's certitude and he asked him, "O Imam, how are you so certain?"

With these words, the Imam's smile faded away and was replaced by reverence and majesty and he gazed at his friend's face for a while and then he started to tell him about a vision he had with deep faith in its truth.

Tonight, Allah's Prophet, Muhammad, peace and blessings be upon him, came to the village and behind him came the four Rightly-Guided Caliphs, may Allah be pleased with them all. Our Master Ali, may Allah be pleased with him, was carrying some stakes. As soon as I saw them I hurried to them. I approached them and was two bow lengths or closer to them so I turned to the Messenger of Allah, peace and blessings be upon him, and he said to me, "Mulla Mehmed!" I responded, "Here I am to serve you, O Messenger of Allah!" He said, "Is this your village?" I said, "Yes, O Messenger of Allah!" The Prophet, peace and blessings be upon him, went towards our Master Guide Ali and said, "O Ali, drive a stake in this village as well." Thus, our Master Guide, Ali, may Allah honor his face, established one of the stakes there in this location so that the earth would stop shaking here.

Imam Mulla Mehmed woke up after that feeling peace and tranquility. People then entered their ruined houses and they were safe.

Grandfather Şamil repeated this marvelous story many times and he would comment that, "Mulla Mehmed Efendi is one of Allah's people who received true Signs from the spiritual realm and then reflected its Light through the mirrors of their pure hearts! Today, I know none of them except him!"

This is why Şamil Agha did not easily believe those who would speak to him about their unveilings and the realities of the spirit until he investigated their state and place and became certain of their righteousness and piousness. The afflictions and the bitter experiences he had in his life had probably made him a sharp critic who strongly rejected the slightest falsehood and dishonesty. In addition, the consecutive displacements that his family experienced due to world wars and regional conflicts as the Russians and the Armenians attacked the region, including the city of Erzurum, and cruelly treated its people, ruining the country, made him as if he were a solider!

Painful Displacements

When spiritual alienation unites with displacement, sorrows transform to a severe storm striking the heart with lightning that is a mix of light and fire, causing the new generation to inherit intense yearning for the eternal voyage! This storm instills within the hearts a longing to migrate towards the unknown so that they are not attached to the dusty forms except by a thin attachment which keeps a small lamp in all the places that they migrated to. Whenever walking takes them to the shore of sunset they fuel the fuse of their lamp by the ember of sadness which guides them to cross the surrounding darkness to arrive at a new dawn!

Şamil, the grandfather, used to sit in the midst of his family at night looking at them with eyes appearing from under a big turban. He would tell stories to his children and grandchildren bringing the characters to life as if they were watching the images of the great ancestors moving in sadness. He would tell them the stories of exiles and displacements which his family had bitterly experienced since the exile from Ahlat in eastern Turkey during the time of the first grandfather, Khalil, until the migration out of Korucuk village at the time of Mulla Ahmed, the great grandfather. He would then tell them about the war with the Russians and how they had to go to Sivas and settle there for a while.

The grandfather, Şamil Agha, was a young child at that time nearing adolescence. This is why he remembered and could not forget the poverty and the difficult situation they suffered during this migration. He did not forget what he witnessed in Korucuk after the war and how the Russians destroyed it until there was not even a wall left there. The great grandfather, Mulla Ahmed, Şamil's father, passed away eight years after returning to Korucuk. His sons continued working very hard to restore their wealth. Allah bestowed upon them a great favor and abundant blessings and they were able to buy other properties. But as soon as their condition improved and they had almost restored their wealth the First World War started and people started to leave Erzurum once more until Korucuk was almost empty.

The grandfather, Şamil Agha, who was the head of the family at the time, carried everything the family had in five or six carts pulled by cows and he migrated with his family to the village of Yerköy in the province of Yozgat where they settled for many years until the war ended. This time, however, they returned to Korucuk without any food, luggage or farm animals. They used everything they had during their exile and nothing remained of their wealth except two donkeys. Fethullah's grandmother mounted one of them and she put the youngest child in the family on her lap. On the other donkey the family put their luggage while they all, including the women and the children, walked on foot led by the grandfather, Şamil Agha. It was a long distance that they had to walk on foot!

Their village, Korucuk, was ruined and there was no trace of houses or gardens or even stables and no trace of life! They spent a very difficult time there without food or drink, struggling with severe poverty. The resolve of grandfather Şamil did not waver and his hope was never shaken. He stood and lined up his sons to battle poverty and hunger. They all worked so hard here and there to build their wealth anew until Allah enriched them once more as a Favor from Him. Şamil Agha was a man whose manhood manifested itself during hardships and through managing crises.

When he used to talk, his grandchild Fethullah's spirit would be engulfed by the spirit of the grandfather and would travel therein towards the past until he witnessed the events themselves! There, he would suffer the exile with his family and experience the hardship they went through. He would drink the sadness caused by such afflictions of those times even though during those afflictions he was not yet born. He walked on foot during a migration he did not physically live and he would experience the feeling of hunger, the tiredness of the journey and the taste of bitterness that displacement and poverty causes and he would feel the horror of fire and wars. He would spiritually live it and look admirably at his grandfather and he understood how he became such a majestic revered man. All of these experiences made Şamil Agha behave in a very serious manner concerning his relationship with his family and his relationship with people in general. No one ever saw him laughing out loud and no one can claim to have seen him weeping either, except once! It was a rare experience which occurred with his grandchild Fethullah. It was a secret of the secrets that made the youth discover a vaster realm within his grandfather's heart that he had not discovered before! This is why their love intensified and was refined to the level of spiritual intimacy and spiritual union.

The grandfather loved his children and grandchildren deeply but he never declared this love to any of them except to Fethullah! He even used to beat them sometimes or scold them harshly. The grandchild would remember how the grandfather once had beaten his father, Ramiz, right in front of his eyes! Şamil was a rigid man to a degree close to cruelty. This is how it seemed! This is why any gentle attention he gave to any of them was considered a great mercy on his behalf and they would never forget it. In spite of that he had a unique affectionate relationship with his grandchild, Fethullah. However, it was a concealed affection. Its depth was not expressed outwardly and it was not easy for others to notice it except the one who was meant to grasp it, which was Fethullah, the grandchild. Şamil Agha's gazes at him would carry deep spiritual messages that would not manifest outwardly except on rare and special occasions that took place only two or three times. These gazes expressed the depth of the feelings that swelled within the heart of the grandfather which opposed the stern outlook he was known by. However, Fethullah received all the messages, and in spite of their rarity, were enough to unveil his grandfather's reality and which enabled Fethullah to dwell in full spiritual union with him! The grandchild was so familiar with his grandfather in such an extraordinary way and to such an extent that he felt he would not be able to live without his presence or without listening to him.

A Mountain Explodes into Rivers

Alvar is a small village in Erzurum only a few kilometers from the village of Korucuk. It had no imam to lead the Prayers so its people asked Fethullah's father, Ramiz Efendi, to fill that vacuum. It was an opportunity for the young man to experience something new and he did not hesitate to pursue that opportunity. So, Ramiz Efendi decided to go to Alvar after asking permission from his father, Şamil Agha. Thus, he took his small family and went to his new settlement while the grandfather remained with the rest of his children and grandchildren in the family's big house in Korucuk.

Şamil Agha had seven children. Only one of them was a female whose name was Durdane. The six sons were: Fethullah's father Ramiz, Rasim, Nureddin, Enver, Sefer and Seyfullah. All of them were distinguished by their loving and courteous characters. Their relations with each other were based on respect and the great reverence they had for each other. They were sympathetic, sincere and willing to sacrifice themselves for each other. This is why their family was legendry in Korucuk.

Only one week passed after the departure of the small family to Alvar but when the physical time inhabited the spiritual time, it seemed to Fethullah as if it were one year. He was about nine years old but his consciousness was that of mature men. He remembers how he was so happy when his father instructed him to go to Korucuk to bring some branches of the willow tree from the family's garden so that they could plant them in front of their new house to remind them of their old house in Korucuk.

The child's longing for Korucuk was so immense that once his father finished his words, Fethullah ran towards his beloved village feeling as if he were flying. He felt energetic and light and hurried towards the place of love which lifted for him the veil of secrets!

Fethullah entered the family's garden unnoticed and he lurked among its trees! Suddenly the passage of time stopped; for the ecstasy of meeting has the eternal moan of love within the hearts of enamored lovers! Fethullah's eyes opened wide sipping from the nectar of the flowers and the roses moving from one flower to another until he dwelled in a spiritual realm beyond time while it was only a few minutes of earthly time! Then, he saw his grandfather Şamil standing right in front of him like a glorious mountain in the garden. Their eyes locked in a spiritual retreat! Then there was what was!

The grandfather took a few steps towards his grandchild and no one could fathom which visions led him to move; the visions of beauty or the visions of majesty! One cannot possibly know what swam within his deep ocean and whether there were whales or corals! The ocean does not reveal its secrets until its rolling waves arrive at the shore! He came nearer until he was two bow lengths or closer! His eyes were radiating both eeriness and charisma! But when the mountain could no longer contain its rushing water the rocks exploded into rivers! The consecutive visions flew, destroying all the grandfather's fortresses and he fell down upon his grandchild thunderstruck! Then, he embraced the child with both hands and burst into tears! All the stones were moved by the power of the flow of a deep inhalation that shook the very core of birds and trees! Indeed, the weeping of the grandfather stimulated awe, and what awe! Their weeping caused all the sadness in history to drift. It agitated all the ends of what had died in one's life and triggered the misery of one's past! Who can stop the flood when it rises from every river and valley?

The wind was exhaling awe between the top of the mountains! The child stood perplexed! His wounded mind was shocked to see his grandfather Şamil crying. To him, the surprise was like a thunderstorm or like a flash of sudden unveiling where the heart is overcome with light so that it does not know how to react! His perplexity did not last for too long, for the little birds in his heart could not stop the echo of weeping from entering into his heart and he did not know how or when he tucked his face into his grandfather's chest and indulged in pouring his pain out in loud weeping! The blood of history united with the tears of the new era! O doves of lamentation be silent and listen! Here is the wise old man painfully engraving his lament, throwing it from his passing time of sad history into the time of the grandchild, full of thousands of painful wounds! His sobbing exploded from Erzurum and traveled with the wind until its longing echoed on the minarets of Istanbul in the northwest of the country!

The grandfather continued to repeat verses of sad Turkish poetry which engraved upon Fethullah's memory an ecstatic pain that he never forgot.

> *The rose has left the place*
> *And the nightingale departed!*
> *No laughter can keep us warm*
> *And sobbing does not help us!*

The Second Incubator: A Gnostic Grandmother

When a woman becomes a teacher all natural sciences fade out and depart, picking their broken foundations. Assimilating into the realm of true teaching, such sciences throw their waste into the garbage basket. When the mother leans towards her child, birds fly chanting, each in a unique way, and all tender twigs produce beautiful roses and spring rejoices!

The mother or the grandmother or the maternal aunt or the paternal aunt is a princess sitting on the throne of the children's hearts. She is a nest made of delicate feathers rocking the dreams of beautiful *bulbul* songbirds! Let her be present here and it would be enough! It does not matter if she speaks or keeps silent; for she fuels the space around her with glowing radiant lamps! Lamps lit with a light without fire fueling them! This is why all beautiful butterflies surround her in the blessed nights! Tender hearts receive the lessons of love with a signature of virtues and the original universal values! Intuitive lessons that achieve their goals completely by their natural flow! The full success of a female teacher and a student cannot be explained by any natural science even though it follows the natural way!

Munise Hanım, Fethullah's grandmother, was not an ordinary woman. She possessed lofty spiritual states and stations! During her life's journey, she accompanied her husband and shared his pain during exile, migration and displacements. She drank the cups of patience and resilience from the well of the Emigrants until she ascended to the station of the speaking silence; of knowing Allah. Thus, her simple presence in a place was the cause of the descent of tranquility and overwhelming mercy.

She used to weep abundantly as an act of true worship. She was mostly silent and always in a contemplative mood. She was well-regarded and respected by all scholars and prominent shaikhs of the town. She had a noble personality and she was the first to open the Path to Fethullah to navigate the Way towards knowing Allah! He drank from her silent beautiful fountain a spiritual ecstasy that he did not drink from any other source.

He drank the joy of hope and reverence! From her, he learned how to connect with Allah. In her deep silence he saw visions of Light that only belong to those who navigate their way to Allah.

She never frowned at the face of her grandchild and never scolded him with a harsh word. On the contrary, she was lenient and gentle, possessing a smile that would rise as light upon her facial features! Her words were gentle, distributing flowers of mercy and beauty, sprinkling dew drops and beautiful fragrance upon everyone she would meet!

Her grandchild never saw her recoil out of the ocean of her tranquility except one time. It was a very sad day, for his father, Ramiz Efendi felt anger towards his wife, Refia Hanım, and he moved towards her as if he were about to attack her but the grandmother jumped off her seat yelling strong words at him saying, "Beware Ramiz! Stop or I will not grant you forgiveness as is my right as a mother." The lion immediately retreated broken-hearted, moving slowly in fear, apologizing and feeling regret. The rain fell abundantly upon the burning gardens until they were washed of their disease by the droplets of peace!

The Third Incubator:
Paternity Exploding into a Fountain

Ramiz Efendi was a man of his time and a master in his place! Feeling the present time is a state that not everyone attains; for becoming dull emotionally and infertile spiritually deprives the heart from witnessing the motion of time that flows within things with its indicators escaping from the Orient to the Occident morning and evening! The number of compulsory migrations which displaced Ramiz's family during his early childhood delayed his pursuit of knowledge for thirty years! Nonetheless, during these thirty years, he learned the most important lesson in life which is his deep consciousness of time! This is why as soon as the situation settled the man hurried to memorize the Qur'an and he was then a head of a household. He devoted his time to pursuing knowledge side by side with his son, Fethullah, and he never felt ashamed of that. Allah opened for him a clear door and he was able to attain tens of spiritual stages in a short time. In an exceptionally short time he was able to cross a large distance and in a few years he belonged to the group of the contemporary prominent scholars of his city.

Ramiz Efendi was gifted with a very sharp memory and an intellect that had a remarkable capacity to comprehend. He had passion and a lofty spirit that was always connected to Allah. At times he would attain moments of high spirituality and proximity to Allah during his Prayers. Whenever he entered the Prayer niche He was there! His eyes were always wet with tears. He never knew empty time and never had spare time in his entire life. Whenever he returned home after working the whole day on the farm, he would start reading a chapter or a few chapters of a book even before he took off his shoes! He would be immersed in the book until food was ready for him. For him, reading was a daily function, an intellectual joy, a spiritual ecstasy and a resting time after hard work in the field.

Even on the way between the farm and the house, he would spend his time as if he were at school; revising what he memorized and memorizing what he had not memorized. His mouth would never stop revising what he had recently memorized of the Qur'an or from reciting Ottoman-Turkish, Arabic and Persian poetry that he had learned. His son, Fethullah, had received a lot of knowledge from him and memorized it by listening to him repeating it over and over. Through this method, Fethul-

lah memorized the Burda Poem[7] of al-Busiri in its full length
as well as many Arabic, Turkish and Persian poems. He also
memorized his father's sermons and admonishments which he
often delivered in the mosque.

Fethullah still remembers Shaikh Halil Hoja who came to
visit them in Korucuk. He also remembers the shaikh spend-
ing a few days in their house. He was a great scholar, well-re-
spected by the elite scholars as well as by ordinary people.
Ramiz accompanied him all the time and never left his gatherings and received from him Islamic knowledge and Qur'anic
sciences.

When the glorious Shaikh left Korucuk and went to the village of Maslahat, Ramiz followed him and he was away from
his family for two years! At that time Fethullah was not even
five years old! He felt like an orphan, especially during winter
when the days were extremely cold!

During that time the father studied both Arabic and Persian
and increased his knowledge remarkably. After he returned to
his village he devoted all his time to practicing the *tajwid*—the art
of the recitation of the Qur'an, under Shaikh Sulayman Efendi.

Ramiz Efendi continued to immerse himself in the realm
of knowledge and gnosis in quest of wisdom. He always wrapped
himself with the garment of dignity. When Fethullah's youthful consciousness opened, Allah made him receptive to his
father. His father was thirty-five years old at that time. He used
to wear an upright turban that appeared majestic on top of his
head. He never saw his father without the turban just as he
never saw his grandfather, Şamil Agha, without one. Nonethe-

---

[7]   The Burda is an ode of praise for the Prophet, peace and blessings be
      upon him, composed by Imam al-Busiri in 10 chapters and 160 vers-
      es all rhyming with each other. (Ed.)

less, his father had a sense of humor which was the result of his marvelous intelligence and quick intuitive wit. His forced displacement taught him great wisdom that was manifested in his speech. He never spoke without a just assessment; all the shaikhs would marvel when they conversed with him. He had accurate expressions, beautiful articulation, lofty ethics and honorable manners.

Ramiz had strong determination and intense endurance; for he lived through stages of turbulence and the disturbing transformation of Turkey from the Ottoman Empire to the modern secular country. He loved these afflictions and what they entailed. In that era, the Arabic language was sentenced to death and the rich Ottoman-Turkish was annihilated. Teaching and learning Arabic and memorizing the Qur'an posed a risk of great danger for both teachers and students. It was considered a crime equal to drug trafficking! Nonetheless, with his great determination, Ramiz learned to read and write Arabic. This was the case of many Turks at that time; as many of them were displaced, and found themselves in the midst of wars. But in spite of all such dangers and difficulties, Ramiz mastered the art of Qur'anic recitation and entered the circle of the scholars and the shaikhs, drinking from the spring of spiritual mysteries and sciences. Moreover, Ramiz made his house a meeting place for the shaikhs. Most of his guests were shaikhs and his house was rarely without their presence.

Beside most of the houses of Eastern Anatolia, where severe coldness sucked the veins of water and blood, there were stables for horses and a special room for guests. Both the stable and the guest room surrounded the house in a marvelous geometric architecture that transmitted the warmth of the stable into the whole house, especially the guest room.

In the long days of winter, which can last nine months in Erzurum, people used to always burn coal or wood logs in a stove in the middle of the living room. The pot of coffee and coffee cups were always put beside the stove and made handy for all visitors and guests.

Ramiz's house was always full of people. It was a house that melted the icy climate with its warm hospitality and by the warm embrace of all the guests, especially the shaikhs and the scholars. They all loved to meet at that house whose lineage was pure and kind and it left its trace on Fethullah's personality. He used to sit with his father and the scholars, receiving at a very young age subtle knowledge and many sciences that were beyond the capacity of many of his peers. Beside the scholars, there were imams of mosques who were honored in that full house. Many of them built their houses on Gülen family's land and became part of their province.

During the years when teaching the Qur'an was forbidden, Ramiz Efendi dug a secret tunnel in his stable that opened at the nearby house of the imam! Through this secret passage Ramiz and his children would go to the imam's house to learn the Qur'an and then they would return home through the passage they came from. Ramiz used to conceal the tunnel's entrance with straw and animal dung.

Ramiz's act had a great impact upon his son, Fethullah. Seeing his father at that age endure such difficulties in quest of knowledge made the son's intellect mature very early; so much so that he never accompanied his peers during his childhood and adolescent years. He did not know children's games or the fun of youths; for he always accompanied the adults. Thus, the chivalry, strength and characteristics of manhood were imprinted on him while he was still a young child.

There is no doubt that his father Ramiz was behind Fethullah's acquisition of such traits; for he let his son accompany him on his difficult path in his quest for knowledge. He let him sit around the same nourishing table which one can never have enough of, especially sitting around the table of Muhammed Lutfi Efendi, the Imam of the village of Alvar. Even though Fethullah could not at that time understand everything the old man said, he would always memorize whatever the wise man uttered! After every meeting he would return to his mother, grandmother and his uncles' wives and tell them every word the Imam of Alvar had uttered; for he felt an ecstasy that cannot be described and experienced a joy that never ends!

Thus he inherited the love of the noble Companions, may Allah be pleased with all of them. His family was a Sunni family. Ramiz had obtained a station of comprehension and lofty love for the Companions. He also revered all the prominent Islamic scholars and jurists as well as the great Imams. Regarding his noble love for the Companions it led him to experience ecstatic epiphanies that blew his mind away! He used to read their biographies often and reread them without experiencing any boredom. He read them so often that the pages were worn out from their extensive use! Whenever he would talk about any of the Companions during family gatherings he would become absent in the realm of witnessing! He would fly away with his spirit and ascend with his innermost being to a lofty dimension to the extent that his eyes would look up as if they were following his spirit seeing another realm! He would then tell his children what he grasped of this lofty realm and what he witnessed so they would all feed from the nectar of pure love for the Noble Messenger's Companions who were the fruits of the Prophet's guidance and nobility. Thus, the presence of the Companions within the children's hearts became a "live reality" and their names where often mentioned by the children as if they were family members!

On the path of pursuing knowledge, a friendship between the father and his child formed. It was a friendship whose current did not reach the rest of the children even though he still overwhelmed them with love and kindness which made their spirits attain the station of pious and faithful children. For Fethullah, however, his father had a secret love concealed within his heart; for he found in him a great fondness for memorizing the Qur'an and acquiring knowledge. Thus, the father would treat him as he treated the spiritual masters and shaikhs. When they used to sit together in a room, he would put a warm pillow underneath Fethullah to keep him warm and would thus raise him to face him as he would do for his spiritual teachers. If there were other people in the room, he would still secretly put the warm pillow underneath Fethullah.

The relationship between Fethullah and his father was that of fellowship on the path of knowledge. He must have seen in Fethullah the characteristics of a genius and had great hope in him. He must have seen a marvelous future for him with his insight and so he cared about guiding the talents within his son so that they would grow. At the same time Fethullah would be sitting to memorize his daily Qur'an lesson, the father would sit to memorize his own lessons to encourage his son and make memorizing the Qur'an even more appealing to him. It can't be described how the child used to acquire from him such energy and a lively attitude. Fethullah would feel ecstatic when competing with his father and trying to memorize his lessons before him with a feeling of playful joy and the ecstasy of winning the race!

In spite of the playful attitude he and his father had together, Fethullah does not recall that he ever saw his father deviate from his sublime state and respectful attitude and so he never dared to act impolitely with his father nor with his brothers. His father was always in between two states of expressing love and sentimental appreciation, radiating beauty, and expressing toughness, radiating majesty.

Disciplining the Self

Fethullah would never forget the holy lesson he received one day from his father's lofty position in the form of a flogging silence of burning visions! It would have been easier on him if these burning visions were replaced by one hundred physical floggings! He was around fifteen years old when he smoked to emulate some of the men in the village; for it is a natural tendency for youngsters to try to emulate what they think characterizes manhood and virility. Fethullah started to smoke cigarettes as rich men do! He continued to smoke for a whole month until his father discovered signs of imbalance in the smart youth. He did not scold or punish him but he chose a spiritual method to discipline him which deeply shook the youth from within!

In one of their private meetings, while the son was sitting in front of his father, the father sat crossed-legged with a condescending attitude that was not his usual manner. Then he took out of his pocket the same box of cigarettes that the youth had hidden under his pillow and lit a cigarette with the youth's lighter and pretended that he was about to smoke it; and he was not a smoker. The son fell into heavy silence and he started to sweat until his entire shirt became wet and he felt great shame. He was so embarrassed and felt a deep regret that he had never experienced before in his life. He wished to be swallowed by a sinkhole. He never imagined that he would sit in front of his father in this disturbing situation. He saw his father imitate the fake and cheap pretensions that do not befit the majestic characteristic of a knowledgeable man with a beautiful soul. This practical lesson was enough to make the youth make an immediate decision to never smoke again.

The Fourth Incubator: A Mother Profiting from Qur'anic Sparks at Night

At the time of alienation, the Qur'an radiates a peculiar Light! Whoever holds onto its verses its embers would burn his sorrows! But who can risk swimming against the current in the middle of a severe storm? Such was Fethullah's mother, Refia Hanım, the Qur'an teacher who taught the women of the whole village. She took the vow of throwing herself in the burning bosoms of the Qur'an lovers!

She inherited her passion for the Qur'an from her father, Mulla Sayyid Ahmed. He used to finish the Qur'an every three days. If something would delay him he would finish it in a week. He often established night vigils and fasted. He lived far from the cities and their adornments. He would go to the city only for a necessity as he witnessed a lot of corruption in his time and in his people. He lived with Allah during all of his states. His pious image remained alive in the memory of his daughter, Fethullah's mother. Thus, she herself became a symbol of enduring life by the Qur'an, especially when the "modern" nation state started to exile the Qur'an reciters and even violently annihilate them.

Midnight was the appointed time for the exiled bird; for there was no chance to recite aloud during the morning! How could the bird chant in the morning when the snipers' guns had directed their terrifying mouths towards all the green trees, looking to hear a single song in order to treacherously stop the beautiful voice of love with thousands of gunshots?

Fethullah was four years old when he started to sit as a student in the middle of the night repeating the melodic Qur'anic verse that sat upon fueled hearts with glowing tears within his mother's eyes.

The snow was striking the besieged land, accumulating on windows and doors, dispatching a bitterly cold anger as a storm circulating through all houses, disposing of trees and stones. Bodies curled under heavy covers, terrified of its fierce canines except these two guests who were flying with the fueled sentiment of mother and child! The heat of longing and the fire of sadness lit with their hearts were enough; for it was stronger than winter with its bitter coldness! Their warm breath was circulating around the room blocking the cold tongue from sneaking through the cracks of windows and doors, and repulsing the coldness back on its tracks as it evaporated under the fire of alienation!

The mother recited her chant and with each breath the lessons from the verses of the Qur'an became obvious. The child was receiving one breath after another. The longing of those who were weakened was ignited in the sky of the sad night as hope flying with wounded wings. The four year old child completed the recitation of the entire Qur'an within thirty nights of earthly time which perpetually connected to Heaven's blessings, like reaching the *Sidrat al-Muntaha*—the Lot Tree of the furthest limit, of the Qur'anic Ascent!

His father announced a celebration for finishing the Qur'an and invited the whole village to a dinner in honor of his wonderful son. Fethullah still remembers how one of the guests joked with him saying, "O boy, this is your wedding feast." Fethullah was drowned in shyness, as he was a child raised in a house of modesty and chastity. He could not contain his feelings and he almost cried. It was an evening whose beauty and majesty he would never forget! Until now, it continues to supply him with longing for the Qur'an and its lights whenever the Caller calls him to travel in a spiritual ascent towards the stations of the lofty assembly! Since then, the doors of extraordinary spiritual gifts of relief have opened for him whenever the arid earth narrowed its passage in his face throughout all the tribulations of his life. His mother is still standing behind him with her pious personality providing him with signals of openings, blowing on him the spiritual good news whenever the siege is intensified around the houses.

This was how the night often was. When the morning would come the mother would stop unveiling the wounds, preparing to give her utmost effort for the morning duties. She would go to help her husband on the farm and she would milk the cattle then return to the house to cook for a family of fifteen to twenty members. When sunset approached she would go to the women of the village who hid themselves behind the veil of sadness. She was challenging the watchers who were armed with iron and fire. She would go to teach these women the Qur'an. One cannot but wonder in perplexity how much patience she had and how much effort she exerted at this difficult time!

In the village of Alvar her efforts intensified and she was always sick with pains that would not leave her day or night. Why was she often sick and in pain? She was responsible for raising eight children from among eleven stars she gave birth to one after the other. Three passed away, but eight survived. What added to her strife was that she had to leave her older daughter in Korucuk as a helping hand to the grandmother. She had favored her pious mother-in-law over her own self. Since that time, Fethullah took his older sister's role and became his mother's best helper; for even though he was only ten years old, he was the second oldest child in the household after his older sister. He used to knead the bread dough, cook food, wash dishes and clothes and he would still do his Qur'an homework to memorize the Noble Qur'an. He probably did not realize at that time that destiny was preparing him for a special life in which he would find himself alone and in need of using the skills he mastered at that age.

Refia Hanım made her son a man who became the possessor of Divine Secrets, with their night appointments and morning concerns! She made of her generation and her daughters' generation mothers who raised lions and cubs. They became the offshoots of the Clear Conqueror in the battle of the new age!

The Fifth Incubator: An Elder Teacher Whose Secret Is in His Lofty Shadow

He was the Imam of Alvar, who was a spiritual leader and a guiding teacher who had knowledge and visions and possessed spiritual states and stations. His orbit was around the station of the heart (*maqam al-qalb*). His star was flowing in the orbit of the Perpetual Divine Presence. Meeting him was receiving some of the abundant gifts! The Gülen family was very deeply influenced by him. Mentioning his name roused the remembrance of Allah and opened the hearts to pursue the spiritual ascent. All conditions allowed Fethullah to be attached to that revered scholar. His heart was directed towards his holy embrace, receiving from him knowledge and gnosis. He was connected to him as a student and accompanied him to the extent of being one with him spiritually. The words that would disperse from the Imam of Alvar would be received by the youth as inspirations descending fresh from the Unseen Realm!

Whenever the old teacher would speak of the realities of knowledge and gnosis, the hearts would be impressed with his lively conversation and clear explanations. His words were not the same as anyone else's; for he would speak as if he were seeing what he was describing not as one who remembers and thinks. People would be all ears listening to him and receiving the heavenly realities as if they had just descended to earth. The hearts would fly with their sorrows out of fear and hope. The seeping sorrow of the gathering would gradually be lifted until everyone saw the Light and drank from the fountain of direct knowledge of Allah, of the realities of faith which pour out of the ocean of certitude.

The spiritual guide was a rare pivot point in his time. He was one of those who were granted the balance between reason and revelation, between the hearts' findings and the tasting of the soul. This is why he had a great effect on those who pursued him for guidance.

The Imam of Alvar lived a giant spiritual life with rare sincerity. He did not fall into the folkloric sufism which was widely spread in his time. He was not afflicted with the disease of pretense and forging knowledge. He lived as if he were the legendary guarding bird who has a shadow on earth but none can ever see its body.[8]

---

[8]   It is a legendary bird often described as having two emerald green wings. It sometimes resembles a dove and at other times the birds of Paradise. It is believed to live on high summits of mountains and so none can see it because it flies at a very high altitude. Its presence can only be known by seeing its shadow on earth. Therefore, it has always been used as a metaphor for the realities that can be known by witnessing their traces without fully comprehending their essences, the realities whose characteristics can never be fully described. (Ed.)

The youth accompanied the old teacher during his childhood years until he attained adolescence. The teacher passed away while the seeker (*al-murid*) was sixteen years old. Nonetheless, the connection between both of them was something else! The old teacher embraced the student not only as a spiritual guide and educator but with an overflowing love like that of a mother's unconditional love! Fethullah still remembers how his teacher was irritated when he learned that the family was planning to send Fethullah to another teacher in the cosmopolitan city of Istanbul in order to learn Arabic. The teacher withdrew and let his student dwell in his spiritual presence and embrace. He then spoke to him loudly, "By Allah, in Allah and with Allah, if you go, you will be torn to pieces (in a big city alone)." He was like a mother whose son is about to be taken away from her and so she holds him tightly!

Whenever the teacher would wipe his pursuer's head he would say to him, "My student, my student." And immediately the child would feel the pious gifts flowing to his melting little heart! His love for his spiritual teacher and the teacher's love for him would increase and cause a marvelous sensation and a feeling of peace and security to flow in his body and it would overwhelm him as if he were supported by a trustworthy Pillar.

The feelings he felt during these spiritual transmissions of spiritual gifts would continue to fill his heart for the rest of his life. He has not yet felt anything like the subtle and gentle touch of his old teacher's hand as it massaged his ear with a softer touch than that of silk! He still hears the echo of his loud voice saying to him, "I will tie your ears shut until all the doors of your consciousness open."

The old teacher was revered for his majestic qualities which reflected his honored origin and noble character and the originality of his spiritual roots and his spiritual epiphanies. The youth continued to sit in the spiritual gatherings of transmission looking at his revered face trying to read his marvelous features. With his spiritual youthfulness he would touch the light of the old teacher's forehead, the glow of his cheeks and the lines of his eyebrows then he would drown within his eyes that overflowed with secrets trying to reach something by reading these apparent and hidden features. Many times the youth would ask himself, "I wonder how much this man with beautiful revered features resembles the greatest grandfather Muhammad, who was the most noble human being, may the peace and the blessings of Allah be upon him."

To this extent, the student admired his old teacher and loved to seek that which is beyond the spiritual springs, trying to hold onto what the teacher was holding onto to know it. The spiritual attraction of the teacher and the readiness of his student's soul would meet and embrace each other, intimately conversing and leading the youth to experience spiritual states that was a delicious existential experience full of visions with vivid and rich colors!

The Sixth Incubator: Vehbi Efendi, the Leader of Silent Knowing

He was the Imam of Alvar's brother and was older than him and he had spiritual characteristics different than his brother. He possessed unique godly states and marvelous states of faith. His silence was speech and when he spoke, he was silent! He was as an ocean in his vast patience, he was magnanimous with a great ability to comprehend and include people regardless of their levels. He would treat everyone with what suited him, seeking the protection of his lofty fort. He would not leave his station except on rare occasions. If he left it, it would be to utter a wise saying or a witty gentle allusion which would take only a few moments after which he would dive again into the depth of his silence! Silence was the state that often overcame him and the Sultan that manifested its power upon him! With his mysterious stages he would weave the spiritual lives of people around him!

The youth had drunk from the cups of his silence which overflowed with abundant secrets of the realities and the meanings that fed the contemplative gift in his soul and lit the purified ember of reflection in the flow of his life.

* * *

The sum total of the spiritual transmission of such an assembly had produced Fethullah's first feelings and sentiments which shaped his spiritual personality in his youth, then as an adult and an elder. By this great spiritual power he established the offshoots of Conqueror under the domes of Edirne's mosque and later upon the mats of Izmir's schools at the night gatherings and in the summer tents. Later, he arranged its lined up horses listening to the echo of Istanbul's minarets and the rushing water of its bays leading them towards the thresholds of the rising lights in Anatolia, from Erzurum to Van Lake and the boundaries of Mt. Ararat! When the trees grew everywhere and were well established on their trunks, the Conquering Youth called by a deep spirit, "O horses of Allah, march!" The forests, the beaches and the bays repeated his call, "O horses of Allah, march! March! March!" It was a heated echo striking the peaks of the mountains like lightning. The minarets would reflect it back towards the cities as spring rain, quenching the thirst of other domes and minarets! The horses' neighs would race the horses' crests as they galloped like the pollinating wind! They ran towards all the earth's continents, raising the flags of Light and peace! Look! Look, my friend, here and there! Do you not see? Those who can see witness its sparks sweeping everywhere!

Chapter 2

Between Books and Sheep

From the Window of the School of Job
I Used to See Him

Every evening the narrator used to tell me about Fethullah. I was a resident in the School of Prophet Job (i.e. the hospital) at that time and the healing place overlooked the Marmara Sea. The sea was reflecting the Lights of the All-Beautiful Names of God day and night! The night held marvelous visions, dazzling the eyes of those who can truly see! As for the day, it was full of chanting and conscious invocations. At night, I would receive visions of the hero of Light, the one who inherited the secrets of wisdom!

On many evenings, while lying on my sickbed, I would be totally immersed in the company of my visitors, the pioneers of Light and the porters of its torch. I would drink the beauty of the eloquent literature which is soul-delighting and ecstatically healing.

Every morning, I used to take a walk tracing the footsteps of Fethullah whose shade extended over the country of Light. I used to attentively explore all the steps of this extended distance, counting them one by one. I almost heard the echo of his weeping under some of Istanbul's domes! I felt that I was so close to gaining access to his presence. I was about to arrive and my heart was deeply trembling within my chest! I coveted unveiling the cause of his weeping and finding the key to his heart and intellect in order to witness how he used to kindle the fire of his luminosity and tirelessness so that I may find guidance in such fire!

But what a pity! I had exhausted the time permitted to me in the country of Light! Thus, I had to return empty-handed. Carrying nothing except heavy pain, I returned to the town of olives, Meknes, in my home country with the hope that I could soon resume receiving instructions in the school of Light! But destiny delayed me a year or a little more!

When I left Istanbul's airport I felt that I was carrying the pain of the whole world in my very being; for I had not yet succeeded in finding my secret cure! I held my head between my hands, leaned forward and put my head on the back of the chair in front of me. I closed my eyes in an attempt to relax and I felt sleepy. Out of the corner of my eye, I looked at the shore of the Hereafter, and all of my past deeds were demonstrated to me and I realized my terrible state. I wept.

Disturbed, I left home in my mournful country crawling towards my mosque. I saw my old platform and I trembled, yearning for the good old days! And behold I could not contain my longing before my visitors so I threw myself wholeheartedly between the lofty arms of my nostalgia! To quench my thirst I started to drink from the springs of a small Qur'an opened in my hands, sprinkling with its water the green stalks of wheat in front of me. The moist stalks were emerging from underneath the mosque's mat and its beautiful leaves were clustering around the walls and the pillars of the mosque filling the whole place with green foliage that was leaning towards the *qibla*—the direction of Prayer!

But how sorrowful! Not many days passed until the platform crashed under my feet and I fell on the ground thunderstruck; for I realized that I was just an unauthorized preacher! Thus, I returned to my sickbed heartbroken! However, that year did not snatch days of my life span without the wind of traveling blowing again, pulling me to leave. Thus, I collected my pains and departed for Istanbul again.

All flights of the world travel in the sky except Istanbul's flight; it is a time-travel flight! Whenever I landed at the airport of the vicegerent's home I found myself living in a completely different time! The loud noise of the technological era with its industrial advancement did not succeed in veiling from me what is truly real!

I easily mingled among the horses of the vanguards and I witnessed the throngs of the troops of the Companions and their followers as waves flowing up to the old city walls of Constantinople. Their chanting and glorifications echoed all around the space bringing glad tidings and Light.

I approached the throne of Sultan Murad II and listened to his night vigil and determined invocations. I could hear the nickering of the horses of his son, Sultan Mehmed the Conqueror. I approached Mehmed the Conqueror and his face became clear to me, it resembled a beautiful full moon. He was a nineteen-year old youth equal in age to Usama ibn Zayd when the Prophet, peace and blessings be upon him, appointed him to become the leader of the Companions' troops during the battle against the Romans. I had seen him once in the city of Edirne[9] while he was lining up his troops in preparation to open Constantinople. He was so close to me and I would have loved to

---

[9] Situated in the farthest northwestern part of European Turkey, Edirne was the capital of the Ottoman Empire until the conquest of Constantinople in 1453. (Ed.)

greet him and kiss his hand, but only the fact that I was not authorized prevented me from doing so.

I kept mingling between the time of the Seljuk Turks in Anatolia and the Ottoman era, the glorious representation of Islam. I witnessed the waves of history flowing live in front of me and I followed the movement of the openings from the midst of Europe to the farthest edges of China!

I would prepare for the nights by fueling myself with perseverance in order to be able to enter the era of the ugly grey wolf! I witnessed the diminishing of the last Ottoman sultans as they fell into the trap of the foreign enemies! I would hear the cries of pain ascending from the depths of Istanbul's hills, from the waterfalls of Turkey and from the moaning of the agonized in Palestine.

I followed the ring of Turkish wisdom as it passed between the heirs' fingers and settled wherever it could find rest. I found it after the falling of the Sultan's minaret—settled in the hand of Bediüzzaman Said Nursi until he passed away. I then saw Fethullah placing it in his ancient treasury box! I continued to gradually ascend from one station to another through the ages until I arrived at the door of my healing place! There, I realized that I had just reached the current era to climb up the near branches that were dangled from melancholy and thus delved into the nest of my sorrows!

* * *

When I used to receive the lessons of wisdom at the hands of the narrator of sorrows his eyes used to sail, escaping into a setting sun. He would continue to narrate until all Marmara's ghosts left their hiding places and spent the night lying down in complete darkness, piercing it with light luminous lamps of small boats sailing there while islands cast their dim lights upon the water's surface.

He said to me, "O wakeful one! Accompanying the sheep in the theaters of seclusion is the first runway of the Prophets towards the lofty station of connecting! It is the way of the Substitutes to receive spiritual states. There is no other passage for the lover of Light but that way! Thus, carry your rod on your shoulder and depart alone to the valley of the spirit. All the obstacles of the self are Sinai and all of its longing is the Mountain of Tur and the Mountain of Nur (Light)! O wakeful one! You will not catch the sparks of good news until after you continuously walk on the thrones of the night, taking care of the sheep while they graze and walk between the valleys towards their promised appointment! When the sheep speak in an understandable language know that you have attained your *maqam*, or station. O wakeful one, there you have to take off your shoes and throw away your stick. Then, witness on the dark horizon the light of connection like lamps made of drooping clusters of love! Pluck whichever cluster you want; for with every heartbeat you will have a light and a fire! Regarding the light, it is your food when you return to their cities and regarding the fire...."

As he said this, the narrator paused a while and I was waiting anxiously to hear his wisdom but he did not utter any further word. Thus, I said impatiently, "Let both my mother and my father be sacrificed for you, oh narrator of the spirit's story, what about the fire?" He was looking towards the sunrise in silence. He was looking at the coming light of dawn on the far horizon and he pointed with his hand towards its magnificent springs! So I looked and beheld! There was Fethullah. He was walking barefoot upon burning pebbles and lightning was sprouting from between his wings, illuminating the horizons. He was in pain from his plight. He was not even realizing how the Light was flowing out of the fire of purification that was burning all the dust leaving only his pure essence. I then knew my way and I followed the traces of the sheep; for such is the fuel of the luminous Light burning in their pastures!

* * *

Fethullah was now a young shepherd caring for his sheep in the heat of his village. Under his arm, he kept a book whose secret he embraced! But Fethullah will never divulge it to anyone! He was still in shadowy childhood, secretly ascending in his navigation! I followed him like his shadow so that I might find the door to his ascent as I followed his footsteps so that I might find the box in which he hid his keys!

He told me he was an Imam who graduated from the schools of his incubators tightly attached to the pathway of love, passionate about knowing the realities of the spirit, and connected to its lofty behavior. He had always performed his Prayers since he was a child. He did not miss a single Prayer since he started learning from his mother. Then he continued to gradually ascend through his childhood when the stinging fire had also begun!

When the first elementary school opened in the village, he joined only as a listener for three years; for he was not allowed to officially enroll because of his young age, which was below the legal age of enrollment. Nonetheless, he proved to be the most intelligent and understanding student among his peers. He continued to perform his Prayers regularly on time during his school time with an amazing determination.

Prayer was a great trial for those who performed it at this difficult time in Turkey's history. There was an army of teachers who were alienated against their belief in modern secular schools and were dispatched into the whole country from the east to the west to raise children on the basis of ultrasecularism and rejection of spiritual realities. By coincidence the teacher who taught Fethullah's class was one of them and he tried to prevent him from performing the Prayers. He used to chase him to prevent him from praying even during break times. The more the teacher mocked religion and its people and the more he besieged the innocent quiet child, the more Fethullah held onto his Prayers and insisted on performing them on time until he frustrated the teacher's attempts. He defeated the spiritual army of modern Turkey with all of its intimidating weapons. This triggered the teacher's anger and increased his wrath so he started to mock the youth and ridicule him in public. This only increased the youth's love for the Prayers and increased his passion towards his unique spiritual ascent and he disregarded the cruel and blunt attempts to annoy him.

There was one teacher, however, that was really nice. Her name was Belma and she was a secular lady who came from Istanbul, but when she saw the child she discovered in him the early signs of genius and she gave him special attention. His polite manners and lofty ethics made her love him more and she held him in high esteem. She continued to treat him nicely, gently and lovingly until he left the school. Sometimes, she would look at him and speak to the whole class pointing at him, "One day, he will be a great officer and will proudly walk on the Galata Bridge." Galata is a well-known historical bridge which was built on the Golden Horn of Istanbul, the city of beauty and dreams!

All pundits, writers and poets used to meet at the cafes around the lower deck of the bridge. They sat on chairs put on both sides of the lower deck or walked back and forth across its top deck. Belma, Fethullah's teacher, would close her eyes and imagine that genius child as a grown man who had finished his education, and as a soldier ascending the ranks until he attained the highest rank and became the head officer. Through her imagination, she would witness the youth leaving his small distant village to become one of Istanbul's elites. She had a prophecy that this child would have a bright future in which he would become one of the edifices of Turkey's intellectuals and leave a great mark on this culture. Her prophecy came true!

Fethullah would never forget the day the students made much noise and chaos in the classroom and the teacher summoned them for punishment. He found himself among them while he was not one of them. The teacher struck them one by one and when his turn came to receive the punishment and he stood in front of her she said, "Even you!" Then she gently pulled his ear and let him go. These two words, however, were enough to cause him great suffering and pain that was harder on his heart than all the hits that the other students had received.

Belma was later so sad when she missed the child in her class. His family departed to Alvar when his father became the Imam for that new village. The child left the class while he was in the middle of the third grade.

One day, Fethullah visited his old village where the rest of his extended family continued to live. The teacher saw him and called him appealing to him, "O Muhammad! I've promoted you to the fourth grade, would you not then like to resume your studies?"

This was without even testing him and without his finishing the third grade curriculum. She wished that her dream would come true because of the genius she saw in him but her effort was in vain because the youth had chosen another path and this was his last date with official schools. He did not follow the way of obtaining degrees and finishing official curricula but he only obtained the elementary certificate which he later pursued in Erzurum.

* * *

Between helping his mother with house chores and helping his father to care for the sheep, Fethullah, the youth, would embrace his books intimately with overwhelming longing when he retreated alone in the house or in the field devouring with his pure soul one page after another; inserting one book after another in his heart! What was truly marvelous was his mastery of reading and writing Ottoman-Turkish in Arabic script which was the official language for all publications and writing at that time in the Ottoman Era. What makes it marvelous is that he does not know how he learned it or who taught it to him. It was not proven that he had learned it through any of his family members or anyone else he knew and the school at that time was teaching Latin script, which was enforced by the secular government after it had forbidden using the Arabic script years before Fethullah was born. It seems that as far as he could remember he knew how to read and write the Ottoman-Turkish language!

In spite of all of this, the youth continued to memorize the Qur'an by heart. The father was so keen on deeply entrenching Allah's Book into the heart of his son. He used to read with him one surah after another and let him recite it back to him until Fethullah was able to keep the whole Qur'an in his heart. The father taught three other students with his son, helping them all to recite the Qur'an. Fethullah's ability to memorize the Qur'an was very remarkable. He would race time during winter in fear of when summer came he would be busier doing house chores and farm chores. Thus, he started to memorize half a *juz'* of the Qur'an daily so that when summer came he had finished his goal and had memorized the whole Qur'an. He also did not deprive the sheep or the house of their due rights upon him. He was still a child but within his chest he had the heart of a man and so he was treated as men were treated even though he was still only ten years old!

Schools of Traditional Education and a Journey of Suffering and Pain

All the gardens of Anatolia's schools were burnt! All the books became fuel for the fire since the Caliphate was besieged by the furious storm! No attendee remained in the scholars' lectures which had only a faint smoke that kept slowly departing on the set horizon from one mosque to another!

Fethullah was envisioning his future in the top of a mosque's minaret! He saw the horses waiting for him on the other side of time's shore on a morning that its birth had not yet been announced. Nonetheless, he was certain of its appointed time! First, he had to receive the wisdom of thousands of books in hope that he would someday be crowned the prince of the Conquest Time! Thus, whenever he would see even a faint trace of smoke of the burnt gardens he would follow it!

The Narrator said: At that time there were neither true schools nor true institutes for spiritual and religious sciences in Erzurum and its surroundings. This was partly because the ultra secular regime had eliminated all religious education and partly because the truly educated scholars started to disappear! The succeeding generation was not at the same level of knowledge and it became rare to find a truly knowledgeable scholar. There were only a few imams left to teach the religious sciences at that time and they were dispersed everywhere in different villages and areas. In addition, many of them did not carry any knowl-

edge but rather they carried fake items. In addition to other fac-
tors, Fethullah did not settle down with any of the shaikhs he
went to. He would usually stay a month or two then he would
carry his stick and depart again looking for an authentic spiritual
guide. He experienced great sorrow searching for what seemed
impossible! He would travel to different places without provision
and so he resorted to quenching his thirst by himself through
reading different religious and spiritual books. He would study
them and evaluate them until he actually excelled in knowledge
beyond many of his contemporary scholars even though he was
still between childhood and adolescence.

The journey was difficult on all levels, psychologically and
socially. After his father taught him the basics of the Arabic
language and he was assured that he had mastered the recitation
of the Qur'an, he decided to send him to Hajji Sıtkı Efendi in
a little town called Hasankale in Erzurum which was seven miles
or more away from their village. The youth flew to it happily
racing the wind, longing to meet Hajji Sıtkı Efendi. Sıtkı Efendi was well-known as a teacher of the art and methods of the
Qur'anic recitation (*tajwid* and *qira'at*) as well as other religious
sciences. But the trouble was that the child could not find a place
for him to sleep so he continued to travel back and forth every
single day from his village to the teacher's place on foot.

Hajji Sıtkı Efendi was a merchant and he had a dry goods
store. He could, therefore, teach his students only when he had
spare time, and he would not charge money for this considering
it a duty he did for Allah's sake. He was a generous and compassionate man, may Allah bestow His Mercy upon him. He
used to prepare food for his pupils every day in his house.

Fethullah's father was not content with his son's situation
and one day he instructed him to stop going to the lectures of
Hajji Sıtkı Efendi because the time that was wasted on the road

each morning and evening was more than the time he spent with the teacher. It was, however, another chance for Fethullah to embrace his books and freely tour the horizon of knowledge and the spiritual sciences.

The Imam of Alvar interfered later and suggested that the father send the youth to his grandson Sadi Efendi, the Imam of the Kurşunlu Mosque which was in Erzurum. The young Imam took a very small room in the mosque and made it into a school where he taught the religious sciences. The school was so small that it only contained two small mats. Its roof was made out of wood that did not protect the place well from rain and snow. But in spite of this, the Imam used to sleep there and teach five students and Fethullah became his sixth student.

The youth started going to the new school and learning at the hand of a young Imam who was only about five years older than him. Even though Sadi Efendi had mastered the sciences he had no experience in how to pass on knowledge and teach others. He insisted that Fethullah must start from the beginning even though Fethullah had already mastered the basics. It was a repetition for Fethullah and so he finished after two and a half months and the Imam had to move him to the circle of the advanced class, which had started to learn grammar and language two years before.

Fethullah had a difficult time at Sadi Efendi's school and it would not be erased from his wounded memory. He used to put all of his belongings in a small box that he always carried with him. His father could not afford to give him any extra money so he could buy a piece of bread because he needed to support his other children on his limited income. This was after the financial situation of Ramiz Efendi, Fethullah's father, had changed when they left their original village Korucuk and they lived on a very tight budget.

Fethullah would never forget the time of the bitter and continuous cold, for Erzurum with all of its surrounding villages and
cities is the home of everlasting snow and coldness – more than
any other place in Anatolia. Its summer is warm and its winter
is annihilation of activities for both human beings and animals
alike. Everything there would be covered with snow and its
people would meet through tunnels and trenches which they
dug under hills of snow during the winter season. They went
out only for their necessities and quickly returned to their nests,
seeking the protection of the heat lit by the families before their
flesh and blood would freeze.

In these difficult days, the youth would sometimes have to
wash with very cold water when he would use the school's toi-
let. It was torture for him. He still remembers how his feet
would slip on the frozen water he had washed with just a few
seconds before. The water would immediately freeze under
his feet and his feet would slip on that freezing ice so he had
to exert some effort to raise his feet to walk. He would never
forget the shiver he would feel when such cold water ran down
his body from head to toe. If Allah had not provided the youth
with such a strong body he would have surely perished.

Painful Loss

Orphaned but not as an orphan who lost both of the parents!
Sadness but not as the sadness of the two species![10]
Absence but not like the setting of both the sun and the moon!

The Narrator said to me: When the youth was at school he was
immersed in reading a book in morphology and the students
around him were whispering to each other! From their ges-

---

[10] i.e. the human beings and the jinn (ed.)

tures, he understood that they were trying to hide some news from him. He then heard from one of them that both his grandfather, Şamil Agha, and his grandmother, Munise Hanim, had passed away that same day within an hour or so of each other in the village of Korucuk. The youth's heart lept out of his chest and the earth underneath him shook with strong commotion. He felt as if the whole world were destroyed on top of his head and every cell in his body had also perished. The tragedy became even greater when he arrived in Korucuk and found out that they had already been buried and everything ended.

The youth wept abundantly and could not believe that his beloved grandfather had left this world for good nor could he believe that his pious grandmother had followed her husband, leaving this world without a farewell word! His love for them was extraordinary and his relationship with his grandfather was unique; full of spiritual language and sentimental feelings. It was so hard on his young heart to experience such a painful separation from them that he would supplicate Allah, "Please take my soul so I can see my grandparents."

The bond of love among the family members was so strong, but Fethullah's relationship with his grandparents was something else! When they passed away he felt a loss of a special spiritual provision that always energized his spirit and implanted within him a feeling of beauty in life. What was really strange is that both grandparents passed away at the same time as if they had made an appointment to leave together. The grandfather passed away first then the grandmother passed away one hour after him in the room next to him. They departed together and were both buried together while Fethullah was still on the road coming from Hasankale with a heavy heart torn by sadness and anguish. When he arrived home, his heart felt empty like the emptiness felt by Prophet Moses' mother. The shock was doubled and he continued to weep for days until many family members reminded him that he had to resume his studies at school.

When grandfather Şamil passed away, Fethullah felt that his pathway to the ancient time had closed forever. He felt that he had to open a new pathway within his wounded heart and find a door to the new era. When he climbed the emerald hills of his heart, he found his grandfather's commandment written on a rainbow. It was in a form of a map of light that would help him to navigate the way to the treasures of the spirit. It was his heritage of the secrets of wisdom which unveiled to him how to balance the cycle of history. Thus, the youth carried his sadness on the shoulder of patience and departed to his distant school again.

The Story of the Young Preacher

The Narrator said: It was the custom during the annual festivals and religious occasions to return to the village and join his family and they would have a family reunion with all the uncles and aunts in Korucuk. In the village a celebration has a special beauty that the people in the cities do not know about. On Eid al-Adha (the Feast of Sacrifice), some people asked Fethullah to give them a sermon in the village mosque. It could have originally been Ramiz Efendi's idea. He loved to train his son in how to be a spiritual teacher from that age. The youth hurried to his books, reviewing the biography of the Prophet, upon him be peace and blessings, for a short time then he went to the mosque. The preacher's chair was so high and its stairs were too high for the young preacher to climb, but the few moments of embarrassment did not last long. Within a few seconds he found himself being carried by one of his father's friends who picked him up and put him on the chair, which caused many people to smile.

Fethullah chose a lesson that showed how the Messenger of Allah, upon him be peace and blessings, had experienced hardship for the sake of conveying the message. He started to tell the people the story of Allah's enemy 'As ibn Wa'il who labeled the Prophet, upon him be peace and blessings, *al-Abtar*— the one who would not have offspring. Fethullah made a mistake in pronouncing the man's name; for when he reviewed the story right before he entered the mosque he mixed up the name of the hadith narrator with that of Allah's enemy. He did not know how it happened but it was implanted in his mind that the name of Imam Abu Salih from the second generation of the early Muslims was the name of Allah's enemy. Moreover, he did not even remember the title 'Abu' (i.e. the father of) while he was delivering the speech and he only mentioned Allah's enemy by the name Salih, attributing to him the worst of qualities. What made the situation worse is that there was a man in the village whose name was Salih (meaning "pious") and he did not have any pious qualities but he had an evil disposition, a bad attitude with others, and he would never acknowledge any good in others or prohibit anything that is naturally abhorred. He didn't use to attend the Prayers except during feasts and this year it was his fate to sit right in front of the young preacher during his lesson of admonishment, listening to a type of scolding that he had never heard before in his life.

The youth started attacking Salih thinking of him as the Messenger's enemy and he yelled loudly from his tall chair, "O stony-hearted Salih! O sly-tongued Salih, O glum-faced Salih! Evil-motivated Salih!" and many other strong phrases of admonishment and satirical expressions, repeating them one by one from his tall chair.

Such phrases descended upon the other Salih's head as thunder claps because he was sitting close to the platform. When one of the missiles of the innocent child hit his head, his eyes would become red and his cheeks puffed up as if he were about to explode. What could he do or say because such a young child was telling the biography of a noble Prophet, upon him be peace and blessings. By the time Fethullah finished his admonishment Salih's anger was about to suffocate him.

Many attendees were aware of the situation and they felt happy with every thunder clap that fell upon Salih's head. They were relieved that finally someone was able to scold him in that way. They realized that all the descriptions that the young preacher said fit their Salih who was rough and cruel. They felt that Allah had appointed someone young to discipline him in a way none of the adults dared to do. What happened happened and the youth felt heated and sincere and he had good intentions. He was fully immersed in his topic and with his innocence he was defending his beloved Messenger, upon him be peace and blessings, without being aware of whom he was actually knocking down and defeating!

After the Prayer finished, the young preacher returned home. As soon as his father saw him he burst into laughter which was not his usual way to laugh. He almost rolled on the floor laughing so hard. The youth was astonished by his father's strange attitude. After the storm of laughter passed the father told his son the story and how he had flogged the village bully with an unintended mistake!

The Death of the Spiritual Father and the Tragedy of Displacement

The tight relationship between the Gülen family and the family of the Imam of Alvar was a very distinctive one. The grand-

son of the Imam of Alvar, Sadi Efendi, could not keep its purity. He had failed in treating his student Fethullah well and the
youth was disturbed for days. After that he was forced to leave
the school and returned to his village. He was free to enjoy his
reading.

One day, while Fethullah was sitting on the couch in their
small living room in Erzurum, stretching his legs and relaxing,
he heard a voice clearly whispering in his ear, "Efe passed away."
He jumped from his seat terrified. Efe was the title of the
Imam of Alvar. His full name was Muhammed Lutfi Efe. The
youth ran quickly to the house of his beloved spiritual guide.
When he arrived he realized that the voice had spoken the
truth. There he found many neighbors gathered but the news
had not yet spread in the village. The youth felt that the village
had lost its spirit by losing its wise guide! Fethullah once more
burst into tears just as he wept when he lost his grandparents.
Just as he was saddened by the bleeding of the kinsfolk, he was
saddened by the bleeding of his spirit caused by his greatest
teacher's death.

After the passing away of the Imam of Alvar, Ramiz Efendi realized that there was no room for him to stay in the Alvar
village; for it was Muhammed Lutfi Efe who had appointed him
to be the imam of the Alvar Mosque and he had some envious
fellows from among the deceased imam's sons and grandsons.
Ramiz felt protected by the respectable Imam of Alvar himself
and no one in the village was able to harm him or attack him
because the Imam of Alvar was his shelter. When he passed
away the shelter was demolished and Ramiz realized that it
was time for the Gülen family to depart again regardless of the
great respect he enjoyed among the villagers. He had experienced cruel treatment and trouble with the Imam of Alvar's
sons and their supporters and he was the foreigner in the village

without supporters or extended family members to protect him. He was wounded by many offensive words that would pierce his ears and cause his heart to bleed. The position of an imam was a position many aspired to have and people envied the one who had it. Anyone who memorized part of the Qur'an aspired to become the imam.

Fethullah was deeply hurt by the situation for he could not bear to see his beloved father in this humiliating position. There was no other solution but for the Gülen family to move. But to where?

Naturally, they first thought to return to their home village where the old house and the extended family were. This was very difficult on the youth's heart for going back meant returning to farm work and taking care of the livestock. He loved to see his father leading the people and teaching them the Qur'an. Fortunately, Allah made it easy for his father and he was given another chance to work as an imam in another village that was not too far from where they were. Thus, the family moved to the little village of Artuzu and settled there for some time without suffering.

Displacement in the Nights of the Hurricane

What remained from the spiritual gardens except its ruin? What remained of the gardens except its ashes? The seekers of knowledge were in a state of misery searching for a single paper or a notebook in the ruined Islamic schools so that they might find in the burning fire a trace or a nest that had not yet been touched by the flames so that they might throw themselves in the embrace of the broken ribs, so that the birds may return!

But alas for the spring time! Alas! Due to the ultra secularist antidemocratic regime in Turkey, millions of Islamic books and rare Arabic documents were sent to be torn up outside Turkey and many others were burnt in ovens. Regarding copies of the Noble Qur'an, their possessors executed them violently. It was said that some made boxes for their Qur'ans and buried them in the depth of their houses or that they got rid of them by leaving them on top of the mountains or in caves. Woe to the one who was found guilty of having a paper or a notebook that had a trace of the Arabic or the Ottoman-Turkish languages on them! Children's and teacher's fingers were arrested and chained in Latin letters in Anatolia.

All the religious schools that existed in the Ottoman Era were closed or were transferred to secular schools teaching ungrateful laicism after the ultrasecular republican regime took over. Those who sought religious knowledge had no choice but to go to far away villages and secluded places in which they hid in small rooms which were made into schools far away from the authorities' eyes. Most of the time, these rooms were attached to mosques in which those teachers would sleep, eat and teach.

The longing for learning and receiving from the spiritual guides was stirring within Fethullah's heart. His hope went high from time to time to the extent that it almost revealed his secrets. The youth could not endure its storming any more so he asked his father's permission and carried his small suitcase in which he had gathered everything he owned of clothes and books and he departed once again to Erzurum. There he enrolled into another school near a mosque called Kurşunlu Camii that taught the ancient knowledge, but he found the place as small as the other school and it could not hold more than five or six students. Some of those whom he met there were from the Alvar village. Their families were friends of his family. He joined them, again as the sixth student in the group. The school was so small that if one of them would have a guest, another student had to remain standing or sitting the whole night!

Fethullah spent most of the nights sitting, just taking short naps; for there was no room for him to stretch his legs. He still remembers an incident which reveals a lot about his personality. His sensitive feelings and gentle attitude are so refined that he seems transparent so that one can observe the blood rushing through his arteries. One night the friends went to bed and each of them stretched his legs comfortably. Fethullah too went to sleep like them on his spot but he soon noticed that his feet were almost touching the head of his classmate. This disturbed Fethullah a lot for he considered it impolite, so he tried to change his position. He noticed that if he did, his feet would be facing the *qibla* direction and that too disturbed him. He tried a third direction but he found that his feet were almost touching the religious and spiritual books and he was not comfortable with that either. He then stretched his feet in the direction of his village Korucuk but he thought that was impolite, what if his father were sleeping there now. He had such great respect and reverence for his father that he could not stretch his legs in front of him, even if that were only a mere possibility. In the end, he spent the whole night sitting.

After six months of staying in such discomfort, the oldest student decided to leave the room. However, he made a secret deal with the caller to Prayer in the mosque to let him keep the room key so that he could join it to his house. So all of a sudden, Fethullah and his peers found themselves homeless.

Fethullah left his small suitcase at the school temporarily and went to a mosque called Taş Mescid that was not too far. He tried to see if he could enroll in its school and if he would be welcomed there. As soon as the imam, who was one of the deceased Imam of Alvar's in-laws, saw him he yelled, "This is

Ramiz Efendi's son! Do not allow him to come here from now on." So the young student left with a broken heart and hurt feelings.

The lodging problem was difficult to solve in a place like Erzurum. At that time, accommodating a bachelor was considered inappropriate and scandalous. But one day a man informed him that a shoemaker was ordered to enroll in the army and he had a small shop that he was seeking to rent. When Fethullah looked at the shop he found it so small that it couldn't hold even one bed and one had to sleep sitting. But the youth told himself, "Let it be, for I am now in desperate need of a home." He had an agreement with the shoemaker to rent the shop for five liras per month. He then happily returned to his small school and took his small suitcase and went towards the shop of the shoemaker, but when he arrived the man told him coldly, "I have changed my mind regarding renting the shop. I am not going to rent it to anybody." Blood froze in the youth's veins and he stood still in the middle of the street with his eyes wide open. He became as motionless as a statue. He was still carrying his small suitcase and the wind was galloping between his legs. Sadness slapped him on his right cheek and on his left cheek. He became truly homeless. There is nothing more intense than the alienation of the pursuer of knowledge when the wind swipes him and displaces him in mazes. A child from a small village looking for a place to protect him from the bitter coldness and the swords of tragedies and no helping hand there to even tap on his shoulder or to peacefully wipe his hair which was disturbed by the wind of alienation at a time when the effect of alienation was stronger on the soul than the darkness of the sterile night! How painful for a human being when he finds himself alone on the journey of suffering and anguish, lost between the abandonment of an envious neighbor and the rejection of an unreliable stranger!

The spirit's lamp in Anatolia was besieged by a wind striking back and forth between Istanbul and Fez. The rooster's call faded in the middle of the hurricane's thunder and the howling of wolves that were angered by the weeping of the diminishing light. There was no one to disclose the lamp to a little bird. Fethullah spent time; he could not even count walking on the streets aimlessly. Sadness was building bridges to allow him to walk to the time of unveiling. It was arming his soul with the slashes of patience and the thorns of wild roses. There, where the door was opened for his pain, his body was striving strongly against the severe storm of cruelty. With his revolutionary anger, he was delving into the darkness of alienation challenging with his faith the plots of evil and the storm of bitter coldness.

All the conditions of suppression, the canines of poverty, and the lashes of displacement were pushing him to return to his village so that he could disappear into the nest of his family in the company of the poor so that the hope for the conquest within his arteries may die, but Fethullah endured. If one is inhabited by the secrets he cannot turn away from the front line facing the fire.

Fethullah remained in that condition until Allah bestowed upon him the gift of the reunion of soul and body. His determination was lit again and he started to search every mosque for a place to lodge. As he was crossing in front of one particular old mosque he noticed that its *mihrab*, or prayer niche, was separated from the main building and that a small opening led to the outer space. He asked for the reason behind that and he was told that a man in the past had made this opening to lodge there and he later deserted it and left it ruined like that. The youth entered the mosque and found its wall almost falling

down, to the extent that when someone raised his voice a little bit, pebbles fell from the ceiling from the echo. It was a der-
elict mosque called Ahmediye and it is a very important historical site. It was built in the Seljuk era and it was originally
a very modern school but days passed and it lost its importance
as many other mosques of the Sultans' era until it deteriorated to its current state.

Fethullah's gaze was fixed on the ruined niche and it did not
take him but a few seconds to decide to lodge there. He went
to a friend of his, Zinnur who was still in the stage of memorizing the Qur'an and was like him – homeless. He offered him a
place to sleep in the niche with him. The young man accepted
without hesitation, and together they worked to repair it. The
youth did not waste any time and right away started building a
wall inside it facing the mosque. His friend helped him until they
raised the wall to six meters and they finished it with metal
wires until it reached the mosque's ceiling. Then he added a
small door that led to the outer space.

The mosque niches in Turkey used to be really high, as high
as the mosque ceilings themselves. Some of them were as wide
as a small room. This niche was one of those wide ones that
could comfortably fit two students.

Later, Allah eased the way for them to find a small heater
that radiated beautiful warmness around them. They lived there
happily as if they owned the whole world; for now they had a
home and a place to sleep which they had built with their own
hands and no one could kick them out of it. Some people
warned them that their place or the whole mosque was about
to be demolished but the two youths did not care. They used
to sleep there feeling absolute tranquility. They stayed there
as long as their studies in Erzurum lasted. Then they left the
place to other students who were looking for lodging. The

mosque stayed in this condition until the country smelled the fragrance of freedom and opening and the authorities considered repairing the ancient mosques from the Sultans' era. The mosque was repaired and its niche was joined back to its prayer area.

Osman Bektaş: The Teacher of the Sterile Time

Since the youth left the school of Sadi Efendi, the grandson of the Imam of Alvar, he joined the circle of Ustadh Osman Bektaş, who was a master of Arabic language, Islamic jurisprudence and its principles as well as other religious sciences. The Mufti of the city used to consult Osman Bektaş and invite him to his office whenever a challenging issue came up. In spite of the fact that Osman Bektaş was very busy, he gave special attention to Fethullah; for he saw his distinctive qualities and extraordinary gifts. He used to teach him the curriculum of the advanced class until Fethullah mastered the linguistic and rhetoric sciences, Islamic jurisprudence and its principals (*usul al-fiqh*). His genius opened to a wide horizon and his intellectual comprehension ascended to lofty degrees. By tutoring the newcomers in the basic lessons and thus reviewing them in different classes, knowledge was firmly established within him. He also gained experience in education and teaching.

Ustadh Osman Bektaş is the only teacher whom we can say that Fethullah graduated from his school and that he was the one who mostly trained him in spite of the short period Fethullah accompanied him. If we could gather all of what Fethullah had learned from the teachers of the ancient knowledge, we would find the total sum of years he spent with them was about two years. Nonetheless, the few months which he spent with Ustadh Osman Bektaş were enough to send him out into the ocean of knowledge all alone. With his accurate understanding of the secrets of rhetoric and a linguistic foundation and with his reception of the science of jurisprudence and its principals, the treasures of the ancient knowledge had opened to him, especially when he joined that with the curricula he studied before. Afterwards, Fethullah would pour knowledge from within his heart and intellect, feeding himself as he was getting fed. He made use of all of the sciences in ways that his own teacher, Osman Bektash, did not make use of. And why not? "There could be a listener who comprehends more than the conveyer." The Path became clear to Fethullah and he was dispatched.

At that time Allah made it easy for Ramiz Efendi, Fethullah's father, to be appointed as the imam of one of the central mosques in Erzurum. He moved there and settled with his family forever. This marked a new beginning in the youth's life. He was no longer worried about finding his food and lodging in small ruined places. He would no longer be subjected to displacement. Thus, he did not busy himself with anything else except pursuing knowledge and understanding spiritual mysteries. This was mostly facilitated through individualized schools found in books. He realized the sterility of the educational curricula of the teachers of ancient knowledge at the time. Such curricula focused only on making the student memorize some texts and grammar and rhetoric rules which the students never understood. How could they have understood when their own teachers who were supposed to teach them did themselves not understand? In addition, they were not capable of elevating the students to the level of interpreting the Qur'an and the Sunnah through internalizing them so that the genius of a student would allow him to be one of the *mujtahid*s, or attentive interpreters. The teaching was rigid and frozen and committed only to memorization which cannot lead the student to any horizon. But Allah had taken Fethullah away from all of these dead end pathways which consumes lives in vain. Thus, Fethullah directed his whole attention into transforming himself by himself.

After a long journey of pursuing education, the student realized that Ustadh Osman Bektaş was himself limited in knowledge. He had no ability to deduce rules even though he had studied the theoretical knowledge of jurisprudence and its principals. Fethullah still remembers when he once returned to Erzurum after a long four year journey which he spent between being an Imam in the city of Edirne in western Turkey and being drafted into the army for the compulsory military service. At that time he paid a visit to his teacher, Osman Bektaş, and the teacher asked him about the books he had been reading. Fethullah told him that he had been studying with a group of fellows *Sahih al-Bukhari* as interpreted and commented by Imam al-Qastalani. The teacher felt hurt and asked him, "But who do you think you are to study *Sahih al-Bukhari*?" The reason behind his annoyance was the fact that he had not studied *Sahih al-Bukhari* well and did not like to hear that a group of young students had been studying it. None of the scholars in the area had studied *Sahih al-Bukhari* or even leafed through its pages. He had never seen a copy of the collection in his entire life and did not know all the books that were written to discuss and interpret it, and he was the head of the scholars there and the most learned among them. He was the Mufti of the city! He was limited in the resources available to him after the furious attack of the secularist tyrants on the ancient knowledge in Anatolia. They caused the disappearance of many resources and forced many great scholars to escape the country so nothing remained for the students of religious sciences except some texts to memorize.

A Deserted Course

The youth realized his time's crises which convinced him that he needed to establish a new course in pursuing knowledge and wisdom. He had to break the chains of rigidity and mimicry which imprisoned the teachers of his time. To navigate the path towards Allah he had to exit the lethargic darkness of the then Sufi lodges and retreat centers (*Zawiya*s and *Tekke*s) to the light of the horizons and the expansion of the soul. He had to let the water gush forth out of the stones and to demolish the boundaries of fatal illusion.

He found the Muslim community lost in the wild desert and he watched the ruin of Istanbul's domes, minarets, the threshold of the High Gate, and the historical city walls which were demolished by the host of the new Goliath. They had burnt all the storage of love and all the scrolls of the secrets. They threw their ashes into the water of the Bosporus and the weakened Istanbul wept for the burning of its doves' nests!

Only Fethullah could hear the howling of the sea gulls, the whimper of the night, and the breath of the Devil. He would weep and weep. Nonetheless, he would see the horses of triumph waiting in lines on the shore of the Unseen! But the horses were without cavaliers. Fethullah would weep and weep. Between retreats and visions, Fethullah would secretly study the map of Constantinople. He used to read in the morphology book how to mutate the Turkish generation in accordance to the Qur'anic scales. He would look at the grammar books for how to repair the break (*kasra*)[11] and how to raise the heads

---

[11] By making use of the basics of Arabic grammar through this paragraph, the author articulates the broad vision Fethullah Gülen had even when he was in his teenage years. *Kasra* (literally "breaking") is one of the basic diacritical signs used in the fully vocalized Arabic texts in order to

high everywhere. He would look how to treat the verb (i.e. act) that has no subject so that it may cross the established bridges for the Conquest upon the Bosporus, so that the doer might be liberated from the passive act and so that one day it will know its subject. Then, the horses will meet their cavaliers and the nation will rid itself from building the passive tense!

Fethullah busied himself with studying modern sciences and their men, trying to remedy the bleeding wound of the nation's body and healing chains of transmissions that were not conscious of the niche of Prophethood. If this could be healed, the nation would be fully cured and the cloud would lift discarding the darkness. Fethullah used to spend the night evaluating men in accordance to the balancing scale of al-Bukhari. He would choose of his narrations the closest to the words of the Prophet, upon him be peace and blessings; for the ocean of darkness cannot be conquered except by the "army" of the lofty chain of transmission.

He used to deduce in jurisprudence the rules to heal the birds' wounds, the rule on how to nurse them from the nectar, the rule on how to repair the heedlessness which occurred during the prostration of the heart without a focal direction of Prayer—the *qibla*. He would deduce new limits that the rice-scholars and the bread-scholars could not see.

In the biographical books on the life of the Noble Prophet he would read about the witnessed triumph, and he would measure the distance between the two victories: the Conquest of Mecca and the Conquest of Constantinople, so that he might

---

help the learners to articulate the Arabic letters correctly while reading religious texts and children's literature. So the word "kasra" is used here as a play on words. (Ed.)

find how long was left to walk towards the third Conquest of Rumiyya.

From the books of logic, Fethullah would learn the secret logic of birds, the language of the wind, the speeches delivered by thunder, and the secret of the concealed weeping rain. He would memorize the hymns of the humble mountain and the chanting of the night and he would weep and weep.

In the scent of the spirit, he would receive through the transmission of the pure chain of inspirations, "My heart told me, receiving it directly from my Lord, that there is no sunrise except through the purification of the night's tears." He would then weep and weep!

But in spite of fully busying himself with the quest for religious knowledge, moving from one old school to another and from one master to another, Fethullah never neglected to quench his thirst by attending the gatherings for the remembrance of Allah. He never forgot to pour from the spirit's fountains. His first role model on that pathway was the Imam of Alvar, may Allah bestow His mercy upon him, whom he intensely loved. The gatherings with the Imam of Alvar were the first and main incubation for him during which the child's spiritual gifts opened and matured in his sincere findings. Therefore, whenever he would visit Alvar village he would not return to his school unless he had taken provision from sitting with the Imam, a provision that would fill his heart's longing to attain the lofty stations of the spiritual ascent. After the Imam's death, may Allah bestow His mercy upon him, the youth continued to sit in the gatherings of another shaikh in Erzurum. His name was Rasim Baba. When the Shaikh noticed the youth he admired him and was impressed by his manners, his character, his intelligence, and open mind; so he brought him closer to him even putting him to his right side even though he was just a young student. As time passed, people spread a rumor that the Shaikh intended to wed Fethullah to his daughter. When Fethullah heard this, his enthusiasm about attending those gatherings diminished and he stopped going.

After he attained the station of the firmly established knowers, Fethullah became certain that the balance between studying the religious sciences and attending the circles of remembrance (*majalis adh-dhikr*), which he intuitively followed, was what enabled him to gain a comprehensive balanced perspective concerning the law and the reality of religion. This is why he never became one of the dervishes who would pursue their quest by wearing rough patched clothes; he would rather pay attention to his clothes and care for his hygiene and his elegance. He would iron his coats and pants and he would never neglect cleaning his shoes. If he could not easily find an iron he would stretch his pants under his mattress and sleep on them so that in the morning he would find them wrinkle free. He would not leave his room unless he was assured that he looked beautiful and elegant. Allah gave him a handsome look and increased the light of his eyes that glow with majesty and demand reverence.

Many of his friends could not understand the relationship between his two states and could not comprehend the harmony between them. What was popular at the time was that the sufis were those who attended the Tekkes and Zawiyas and who would wear weird clothes that went against elegance and beauty. One of them scolded him one day saying, "Do you not feel ashamed of yourself? Show piousness, even a little of it." He was saddened by the remark for a long time; for his friends could not understand his behavior. He too could not understand the relationship between his ironed clothes and negating his piousness.

Some of his friends would marvel at his diverse states and stages; for they would witness his hankering for the lofty spiritual stations, his keenness to attend the circles of remembrances and his drifting into weeping loudly during admonitions, but they would also witness his expanded taste of beauty in the way he would choose and handle his clothes and care for his outer look. They could not understand his love for nature and observing life's beauty from a lofty state.

Fethullah was a youth who loved to explore and he had an unusual enthusiasm for discovery. He never neglected his physical exercises; for Allah had gifted him with an energetic spirit, a strong body and expanded knowledge. He was in the beginning of his youth full of energy, overflowing with vigor and vitality. He did not understand why he loved retreats, the highest and most diverse adventures. He would just find himself racing towards the unknown!

He had lived a different life from that of ordinary teenagers which made him love examples of heroism and chivalry. He loved to face challenges and destroy the walls of fear that surrounded anything and everything.

He loved to walk at night on the shores of awe inspiring rivers rushing through the valleys. He would intentionally put his feet in the tip of the river while it was rushing and sweeping away trees and dust. He also loved to climb high trees and soaring minarets. There was a high willow tree close to one of the mosques in Erzurum and no one dared to climb it because the height of its branches inspired fear, but Fethullah quickly overcame its overlapping branches. Once he set his foot on one of the branches, people saw him sitting on the highest branch in no time. Only a very few of his peers dared to climb just the lower branches of the tree. He would then sit and look at the far horizon observing the city and its suburbs, quenching the thirst of his love for nature and its hills. He passionately loved looking at the world from a higher place. He would climb the tall minaret and walk on the edge of its highest balcony which instilled reverence in the hearts of those who observed him doing it. They could not tolerate watching him walking around the minaret balcony's outer wall knowing the danger involved. He would not notice anything because he would be looking at the far horizon, enjoying the beautiful scenery; for to him it all looked like a wide panorama worthy of looking here and there so that a glowing spark might cross the horizon pointing to him the landmarks he was waiting for! When Fethullah would climb to that height he would be like a dove carrying a message soaring to the horizon, defining a direction, setting his focus on the journey's destination and flapping his wings in the right direction.

He was a brave youth to the extent that courage itself would be in awe of his bravery and valor itself would distinguish his daring. He would compete with other youths in sports and none could defeat him. He would win a wrestling competition in the blink of an eye, leaving his competitors astonished at how and when they fell. He was the foremost in everything. He was an elegant youth with handsome looks and a strong body, catching the attention with his cleanliness and beautiful manners. Nonetheless, he kept his secret within, concealing the reality of his essence and walking as an ordinary youth among his peers, flowing under the shadow of his generation until the right moment comes and time gives its permission!

Chapter 3
The Station of Unveiling
and Visions

From the Concealing Darkness
to the Light's Ascending Tracks

stadh Bediuzzaman Said Nursi had lit the lanterns of Light across Anatolia after the doves' nests were demolished, after the cooing of the pigeons suffocated in their throats and after the lamps had been broken on the heads of the vigilant worshippers at night. The sun had eclipsed out of sadness for losing its moons and darkness spread everywhere. Ustadh Bediuzzaman left his bed at night and went out in the midst of the severe storm, distributing candles among the houses of the poor!

The darkness had crept into the country and swept away all the lamps in the city turning them off. Laws to confiscate the lights (i.e. *The Epistles of Light*) had been issued. One storm after another blew and left the country in complete darkness. Mosques had no right to pour the tears of light or to embrace the inflamed ire. Small schools had no right to offer nests for its little birds so they could chant the Qur'anic promises to the whole nation. Arabic letters had no right to be inscribed on the spiritual tablets to illustrate the hearts' bleeding wounds. All the turbans were shot by the snipers of treachery in the war for hats. The imams, spiritual guides and even the callers for the

Prayer were slaughtered and the echoes of the remembrance chanting (*dhikr*) were dispersed beyond the oceans. All the keys of sufi lodges and retreat centers were confiscated. The sea gulls and the dove flocks were kicked out of their towers and their nests were demolished between the minarets and the domes. The heart and intellect of the city became empty. The call for the Prayer (*adhan*) had no right to weep.

The darkness had allowed the night ghosts to roam freely in the country, abducting the children and youth, tearing the veils to dishonor the believers. The darkness taught the crows to sing curses and insults in the ears of those who were weakened. The trees abandoned their leaves out of sadness and the birds migrated to the unknown and never returned to their nests. Faces became pale as the promising glow diminished in the streets. How can they smile and where is the good news when all the scholars of the country have been annihilated or displaced?

Only Bediuzzaman (literally, "Wonder of the Age")[12] remained there alone, providing people with the good news of coming rains and light. In his exile, he would scoop from the oceans of the Qur'an and send the clouds with good news to the sad cities and villages. He continued to write the collection of the *Risale-i Nur* (*Epistles of Light*) in exile and prisons, letting it escape with the wind to the houses of the poor and the miserable until the hearts became full of longing and sparks. The rain fell.

---

[12] Said Nursi was given the title "Bediuzzaman" (or Badi' az-Zaman in Arabic), meaning "Wonder of the Age" due to his extraordinary intelligence and capability of learning that he showed at a tender age when he was a very brilliant student at the school of Mulla Fethullah of Siirt. (Ed.)

Bediuzzaman Said Nursi had realized with his Qur'anic insight that this era is the time for rescuing faith and for providing hope in people's hearts. The duty of the time is to confront atheism and infidelity and to frustrate the plot of making the country sink into ignorance. Thus, he dedicated his time to teaching the young birds the Qur'anic chapter of *al-Fath* (The Conquest).

When the wolf attacked the shepherd and was now in charge of the flock, Bediuzzaman started to fight to snatch the young sheep from his hands. When people were escaping to their shelters, he was teaching the young sheep to escape to the shelters of the Qur'an. In the *Epistles of Light*, he illustrated the landmarks, showing the way to exit the darkness of fatal despair. He was digging a small opening through the stones of the dark cave from which they can see the sun rising upon the future.

In this way, Nursi led the hearts of the Turkish people while the sword was in the hand of the Devil; for the Devil is unable to defeat the Power of the Qur'an. Ustadh Bediuzzaman had rescued his sheep from between the canines of the wolf, leaving him angrily howling atop his hill.

Such was a special stage of calling for the Light which Nursi made reach the threshold of migrating. But between Mecca and Medina is another journey with another type of longing that needed to be lit so that the nation of being humanity's witnesses can be established. Nonetheless, Nursi left his message to the youth who could hold the secrets and he then departed. For each era, there is a particular possessor and there is no candle that can burn twice by its light. O wakeful one, have glad tidings; for none graduates from the Qur'anic school except a leader who is permitted to lead.

The Narrator of sorrows told me: When Bediuzzaman was struggling against the darkness in his eighties; Fethullah was climbing his adolescent years. He became familiar with the *Epistles of Light* in 1957 when he was nineteen years old.

Nursi had taken a mighty step in dragging the carpet of tyranny from under the feet of the Devil. He plowed the land and fertilized it and spread the seeds everywhere. He left for his students the epistles on the secret of farming and its characteristics and he then disappeared. But Fethullah came.

When the youth found the *Epistles of Light* he realized that he was the one addressed by it and he knew that he must take the next step. He must care for the seeds until they produced fruit. He realized that the farm land could not be watered except by the tears of the passionate servants and he continued to weep until his eyes swelled. The fields became green from his tears and the fruit would ripen from his deep breaths. The wind would blow slowly, humbled at the door of his mosque, and would not hurt his noble sprouting trees and fruits!

When Nursi's grave was grabbed and he lost it, he secretly lay in Fethullah's heart. The youth went out speaking to people with Nursi's tongue. But people ungratefully rejected him. He wept and wept and continued to weep until the earth vibrated and swelled and delightful pairs of fruit of all kinds sprouted. Then, trees grew and birds came. People's eyes were delighted and hope was chanted everywhere. Nonetheless, Fethullah continued to weep! How marvelous!

This is because Fethullah has a secret that he cannot reveal! Fethullah has a secret the whole world is waiting for but he cannot divulge it to anyone! Fethullah carries in his heart what he cannot bear and that is why he is weeping until tears were perplexed by its death. Fethullah inherited a secret that if a magnificent mountain would inherit, the stones on its peaks would fall and its very foundation would crumble out of reverence!

When Fethullah found the *Epistles of Light*, the map for the universal Conquest was unveiled to him. He touched the case where he kept his keys and he was fueled with his longing. Then, he entered into the niche of night all alone, following the map!

Mehmed Kırkıncı was the pursuer of knowledge and Light. He learned with Fethullah in the circle of Osman Bektaş. He was older than Fethullah and was in the advanced class. Fethullah was just a new student but when Osman Bektaş realized his genius he moved him quickly to the advanced class where he became the youngest student.

Mehmed Kırkıncı knew about the *Epistles of Light* of Ustadh Bediuzzaman Said Nursi, may Allah bestow His mercy upon him. At that time, Nursi was departing from one exile to another and one prison to another, besieged by the ghosts of the Intelligence Department night and day. Thus, joining his group was a risk one had to take, considering the possibility of easily being thrown into an undisclosed prison. Those who belonged to his group agreed to hold the live coals in their hands to distribute warmness and light to all the weakened people across the world.

One evening when sorrow was heated, Kırkıncı came to where Fethullah was sitting with his classmates, Hatem and Selahaddin, and told them that a man would soon be coming to Erzurum from Ustadh Bediuzzaman's group and that there would be a gathering in the city at night where the man would deliver a speech. Kırkıncı made the idea of attending the gathering appealing to them so they all stood up enthusiastically ready to go; as Bediuzzaman's name was on every tongue during that period but none had seen him except a very few. Fethullah's heart was beating fast as if he were racing with time for the meeting so that he could see the man who had actually met Ustadh Bediuzzaman. Why not? At that time Bediuzzaman was already a legendry hero, and a piercing light in the hearts of those who were impressed by him across Anatolia. Was he not the one who defeated the British by his *Al-Khutuwat as-Sitta* (literally, "The Six Steps")[13]? Was he not the one who disregarded the threat of execution and challenged the Russian Commander-in-Chief when he was just a captive in their country? They killed him but he did not die! Was he not the one who besieged the fires fueled by the Devil in his home country and was he not the one who put them out with the simple words he threw on the flames that are forever diminishing? Was he not the last cavalier who was still carrying the flag of the Ottoman army and tracing the path of light to save the world in an era of turmoil and collapse? Why wouldn't the hearts love him and be attached to him and why wouldn't the souls long to see him?

When the time came, the students were already at the meeting place, the tailor shop of an ordinary man named Mehmed Şergil. The tailor shop was small and could only hold a small number of people. The night swallowed movement from the streets and cut off the noise of salesmen and markets. The streets were almost empty except for a few pedestrians.

The attendees sat in an intimate circle as if they were one family that had met after a long period of separation, even though many of them had just met for the first time. They were all brought by their common friend Mehmed Kırkıncı. It was a small gathering of some students and professionals, but they all had a role in shaping the history of bringing the Light back. Fethullah had found the pollination of his soul, the lightning

---

[13] With this short treatise he wrote and published, Bediuzzaman spoilt the fearsome plan of the commander of the British occupation forces in Istanbul who tried to prepare the ground for the defeat of the Turkish Army in Anatolia through sowing strife among Muslims, even deceiving the Shaykh al-Islam and some leading scholars. (Ed.)

of his cloud, the wind of his rain and he wept. Who could have imagined that this warm gathering would kindle the spark of the Conquest in the youth's heart? Who could have imagined that this gentle youth would be the one to mount the horse of Sultan Mehmed the Conqueror, and cross the ocean of darkness in its saddle?

A Man Traveling across Time

When Bediuzzaman's student Muzaffer Arslan sat quietly in the circle of Light all eyes were fixed on him. He was Nursi's messenger to Erzurum. He was one of his first students who shared with him the hardship of exile and imprisonment but their determination to convey the Message of Light was never weakened even when they were besieged by the touch of darkness.

Muzaffer was a humble, quiet and easy-going man. Bediuzzaman sent him to tour the east of Anatolia. He stopped by many of its cities and villages. He stayed in Erzurum about fifteen days.

The gathering of the first night was a strange mix of merchants and students and some members of the army. All hearts were yearning to listen to the words of the guest so that they might know the secrets he was carrying. All eyes were contemplating his calm features, fixing their gazes on his lips to hear what he would utter. Fethullah was spiritually thunderstruck and his eyes were wide open. He was impressed by the outer appearance of the man before he even spoke!

The man said a few words about his teacher, Bediuzzaman, then he took some papers of the *Epistles of Light* out of his pocket and started to read *Hucumat as-Sitta* (literally, "*The Six Attacks*"). The listeners were all ears; for this was the first renowned table stretched for them on the first night. On the second night, the man threw upon them sparks from *The Fifth Ray*. This was a chapter from a book titled *Şualar* (literally, *"The Radiant Rays"*). It was an exegesis of the Signs of the Hour and a comparison of the *dajjals*, or satans, of the era to the greatest Dajjal (the false Mesiah or anti-Christ), explaining how the destiny of imposters is absolute defeat. The radiant rays were rising to renew life and to open the doors of hope for millions of weakened people.

As for the short treatises of *The Six Attacks* and *The Six Steps*, the former was a clarification from Bediuzzaman concerning the inner struggle and it brought awareness concerning faith while the latter was a defensive plan against the British for the time they occupied Istanbul. It was spiritual steps to frustrate the psychological warfare and the propaganda that the media were spreading. It was reviving the spirit of resistance within the people.

Some of the students who attended the first gathering had hearts that were buried under the barren educational system that blinded their eyes and so they could not see the light that was flowing out of the man's lips. His simple and old attire added another layer to their blindness, for he did not look like the well-known scholars. He did not have the same attitude like that of most scholars and sufi shaikhs of this barren time so they started to interrupt him, objecting to a phrase he uttered or a case he made in their attempt to divert the class to that darkness of vain conjecture. Thus, Allah turned their hearts away from witnessing the waterfalls of Light that were rushing calmly from the mouth of that poor man who renounced the world.

However, Fethullah was fully attentive to the man from the first night. The few words which he read for them had captured his heart and immediately he felt that he had left the state of confusion to the state of certainty. His beguiled soul exclaimed, "Just now, I've just found the Way. Just now, I've found myself. Just now, I've found the Light I was searching for in vain between the dervishes and the Sufi lodges."

Muzaffer Arslan was a poor man. His coat was worn out; it had holes in the sleeves and elsewhere. When he sat, the patches of his pants appeared. His clothes revealed how long they had been used. Nonetheless, his clothes appeared clean in spite of their patches and holes. The patches seemed elegant without faking elegancy and how many a scholar was destroyed because of his pretense and conceit? The man appeared so simple but he was very spiritually deep. The one with insight could see the shining pearls in the depth of the ocean of his calm eyes.

Fethullah looked at him and he could see the traces of traveling on him, but it was a lofty journey he had traveled, different from a physical journey. His was not a journey of distance and miles and crossing places but it was a journey of piercing beyond the layers of all eras and crossing the intermediate realm of time. Muzaffer was a man who descended on earth from the era of the Companions, carrying the good news of the coming clear Conquest. He was calling all the youth: O chivalrous cavaliers! O horses of Allah, march!

Who else loved the Noble Prophet's Companions more than Fethullah? On that night, Muzaffer brought to him a glimpse of their states and their great station.

When Muzaffer Arslan talked about the sparks of Light, his calm voice would gently flow tracing the caravan of the Beloved Prophet from the Era of Bliss. His eyes would radiate a glorious spiritual ray that almost illuminated the whole place. Fethullah fixed his gaze on him, concentrated in listening to his words with full presence. He forgot the darkness in his depressing

time because of the light he saw in Muzaffer's radiating luminous eyes. He also saw his deep sincerity in his eyes.

In his speech, Muzaffer would travel to what he was talking about describing it in a way that made people see him there!
What a marvel! They would even smell the fragrance of the
Prophet's time filling the whole place. They would see the
smoke of the Companions' campaign when they stopped by a
valley in the evening. They would feel the dust of their running
horses when the morning came! Fethullah saw the army of the
Conquest besieging the old capital of the Romans, and the one
who sees is distinguished from the one who just hears. His hair
stood up out of reverence and humbleness when he saw Muzaffer there. He might have tied his horse's bridle at one of the
city's entrances and hung his sword in one of its trees then he
entered Erzurum without her inhabitants taking notice of him!
What a marvel!

There, Fethullah became determined to accompany him to
his place and to travel with him to his time. He felt the call for
migration filling his lungs so he sighed and wept.

The news about Muzaffer's visit reached the scholars of the
barren education in Erzurum, especially to Sadi Efendi, the grandson of the Imam of Alvar and Ustadh Osman Bektaş. Some
of these scholars were not in agreement with Bediuzzaman
Nursi's call. This was either due to their ignorance of his reality or out of jealousy, seeing him as a competitor who may attract
some of their followers. But indeed, he was not an adversary.

Nonetheless, these two scholars spent their time trying to
push the youth away from Muzaffer Arslan and from studying
the *Epistles of Light*. They warned them of the consequences
of following a man who was being chased by the government.
They made them fear reading his books and spreading his *Epis-*

tles, explaining how this can expose them to the danger of being arrested or exiled.

It was very hard on Ustadh Bektaş to lose his most intelligent student, Fethullah, so he persistently pressured his student to leave the company of Light. But the youth, who loved his teacher deeply, respected him, and held him in high esteem, could not listen to his teacher's request and was not convinced of his explanations and warnings regarding following Bediuzzaman. The youth was like a man traveling on a long journey and he was extremely thirsty in the middle of the desert and he was about to perish but Allah sent to him relief and all of a sudden he saw a green oasis that had cool water and shade. What kind of explanation can then deter him from ascending as fast as he could to the sources of water?

Fethullah saw with his clear insight and pure conscience the visions of Light upon those in quest of the Light and he could not help but be attracted to the glow of the brilliant Star. He continued to circle Its orbit until he was completely burnt by Its heat. In spiritual navigation, burning is the condition for penetrating and without it the navigator would continue to be veiled from the heaven of arriving!

The youth received Ustadh Bediuzzaman's lessons seeing his fingerprints to educate and discipline in live motion, beating with a live pulse in the arteries of his students and fellows. He could not go anymore to the Tekkes and Zawiyas as time had issued its verdict for their death.

The scene of Muzaffer Arslan praying captured Fethullah's heart and his whole being. Once the man would immerse himself in Prayer by saying "Allahu Akbar" (God is the All-Great) the springs of ecstatic findings would rush forth into Fethullah's heart. Their abundance would overflow through his pure tongue and lips, calmly going to its Lord with deep humbleness and quietness such that the youth had never witnessed before; for praying had diminished at that difficult time and it had become a fast paced Prayer with restless steps that were empty of meaning far from being an ascension to heaven for a worshipful servant. The purpose and the goal were polluted and had become rotten. Veils were pulled down and the doors were closed. Then, flies fell upon the rotten piece turning it to dust.

But the intelligent grocer, Zeki Efendi, would raise his hands supplicating Allah in fear of experiencing the anguish of the hell fire. He supplicated as if he were seeing the place of the Final Abode which filled his heart with reverence to the degree that his words were moans inside his mouth and his wings shook in strong commotion so much that no one would dare to sit beside him when he was inundated in such a state. If anyone sat beside him he would be overwhelmed with fear and awe! Fethullah continued to ride with the cavaliers of the Conquest!

Fethullah continued to visit Muzaffer Arslan in his temporary house in Erzurum taking provision from his words and states until his departure arrived. After saying farewell, Fethullah stood on the train station's platform with five other pursuers of Light, looking with eyes full of hope and empathy at a man who descended upon their hearts with his wings, kindling within them the lamps of love before he flew!

Unusual Message

There is nothing more beneficial for the soul than having a spiritual connection that can kick loneliness away and can keep one in a state of spiritual intimacy that energizes one's walking towards Allah! Whenever such a connection is weakened, longing becomes less intense and ecstatic results become less frequent and one tumbles in his walking and in this state it is feared

that the navigator of the Way to Allah might go into the mode
of separation! Thus, spiritual gatherings have a provisional effect
upon the caravan of the devoted; for it energizes their walking
and lessens the distance towards the Beloved's House.

This is why Bediuzzaman would not neglect a student of his
no matter how many students he had and no matter where they
were scattered and that included the students whom he saw
and those whom he did not see. The souls' eyes have rays that
stretch between the devotees and their spirits are disclosed to
each other in spite of the thousands of miles between them.
The hearts can still embrace each other and that which is pursued occurs!

Fethullah was in the company of his friends in one gathering for *dhikr* when one of them informed him about a message
which Bediuzzaman Said Nursi had sent to the gathering of
students in Erzurum. Such was the same group of students who
used to secretly gather and sit under the protection of the night
in a small shop. Joy, happiness and ecstasy shook the students
when they heard this. Fethullah felt himself very close to
Bediuzzaman in an unusual way. The road marks became very
clear in front of his eyes. The navigation of his wise teacher during the time of storms became clear to him. The message was
read to everyone. Necks were lowered while listening and hearts
were raised to receive its contents word by word in complete
silence that hid the thunder of the enamored ocean whose high
waves crashed upon the shores of their chests!

Then, there came a surprise that had a great effect on everyone, but especially on Fethullah! At the end of the message,
Nursi sent his greeting of peace for everyone he was informed
of. When Fethullah's name was uttered, it descended upon his
longing heart as lightning strikes trees. The radiant Light was
pulsing within his heart, illuminating the whole place! Fethul-

lah still lives the moments of his ecstatic pain and joy, the intensity of which his soul could not bear; for he does not remember living such joyful moments except a few times. What could make his heart, which was longing for Light, to rejoice more than at receiving the greeting from the reviver of the religion in Anatolia? This indicates how much his heart was longing for this revival. Thus, no matter how many years passed, he would never forget Bediuzzaman saying, "And give my greeting to Fethullah."

This was a gate of permission for you, O youth, so march forward!

Agonies of Beginnings

There used to be an annual tradition in Erzurum of reciting the whole Qur'an a thousand times by a group of people, then invoking a comprehensive supplication at one of the city's mosques where people gathered. Many people volunteered to recite the Qur'an, staying up all night long or a major part of the night. They recited what they were committed to recite until the Qur'an was recited one thousand times. After the Imam led the Dawn Prayer, he would recite the comprehensive supplication then people would leave. This was one of the ways to resist the sneaking ultrasecularist oppression against the believers that was overwhelming the country. There was a ban on reciting the Qur'an for many years, preventing the birds who were taken by the Noble Messenger's love, from chanting day or night.

On that night, Fethullah went early to join the gathering at the mosque to attend this occasion of reciting the whole Qur'an. That year the time of the occasion came on the night of the middle of Sha'ban. At times like that, Erzurum mosques were so crowded with people that there wasn't enough room for all of the attendees. People would be prostrating on top of each other's backs. This meant that whoever came after the Night Prayer would not find a place to pray inside the mosque at dawn.

Therefore, the youth went early and sat in the middle of the mosque and prayed the Night Prayer in congregation. In such a spiritual environment, the whole of his heart started to shake and ascend! The trees were growing from beneath the earth at an unusual fast speed! Here is a sprout, here is a small tree and here is a great garden! The branches kept stretching towards the lofty heavens to the degree of piercing the veiling clouds! While he was raising his hands begging Allah, Fethullah was attracted without being aware of it to the Lofty Domain. He was begging, begging and begging. The ecstatic revelations tore his soil open and a forest with high trees rapidly grew. Longings struck it with lightning and hurricanes and the night unveiled glowing flames through which the youth saw what he saw and he trembled in anguish out of ecstasy. Hot tears streamed from his eyes until he could not see the outer sensual realm of shadows and his eyes opened to witness the spiritual realm. On that night, the youth was annihilated and he could not hear the noise or see the crowd and he only existed there in the Divine Presence!

There, in his spiritual ascent, he witnessed how the pursuers of Light had already taken their places. His tongue became a creek pouring out pure supplications that have not become stagnant and their radiance has not ceased to radiate: Oh my Lord! Make me one of them! Make me one of their troops marching as they marched carrying the lanterns of Light until I meet You! Let me enter through the door of servitude and accept me as Your servant! Here I am, I've tasted and seen so please do not ever deprive me of this gift! Oh my Lord, I seek refuge in You lest I enter from one door then exist deprived from another door! Make my heart steadfast; so that it can travel through the fire in coolness and peace! Make my soul an eternal gift that is forever dedicated only to You! To You only.

He continued to beg while the wind was blowing the trees until not a single leaf remained! Then water poured down washing all the naked branches from every trace of blemish. Fethullah wept and wept and continued to supplicate.

The voice of the caller to the Prayer exploded from the minaret and echoed in the intermediate realm that is between the spiritual domain and the birds' cities. Fethullah was surprised to hear it for he was completely absent from the earthly time until morning arrived and he stopped the permissible weeping. The youth spent the whole night praying and he did not sleep for even a moment or a blinking of an eye. How could he have slept when his heart was taken to the balconies of a wakeful station? It was a single night in his life which he had never lived the like of before! It was a crossroads in his walking in his small world and a station to launch into his major journey.

Before leading the Dawn Prayer, Imam Sadık Efendi stood on the platform and he delivered a speech. His words were gentle and it triggered people's feelings. He wept and made everyone weep, including those who do not easily do so. Sadık Efendi was enamored by the love of the Messenger, upon him be peace and blessings, to an extent that cannot be described. Every time he would utter the Noble Prophet's name he would say, "Our Master Guide" or "Our Beloved" then he would stop to hold his tears and slowly utter the name of the Prophet, upon him be peace and blessings, as if he were sipping a delicious drink and he would then say, "Muhammad! How sweet his name is!"

In general, the Turkish people are enamored with the love of the Messenger, upon him be peace and blessings. For his sake, the Turkish people indulged in battles of longing and anguish; if they would be distributed among the people on earth, it would overwhelm them all with love and peace. The Turkish people inherited a love for the Noble Messenger that is truthful and sentimental. They also love the members of the Prophet's Household and all of his Companions. Their love for the Prophet, upon him be peace and blessings, his Family and Companions was augmented, especially after the time when peace and love were abducted from the hearts of the weak in the time of suppression and tyranny. Their love for the Noble Messenger was kindled into flames of longing. Nothing can move the hearts' hills and shake the trees' branches except a strike of lightning in the middle of the dark night. The horizons poured abundant rain!

Fethullah listened to the Imam's supplication and wept and then he participated in reciting the supplication for ending the Qur'an trying to bring the ray of Light he experienced earlier. After the Prayer and the supplication ended, Fethullah started to massage his joints to relief his pain and tried to lift his limbs one by one until he was able to stand and he left the mosque at sunrise.

Hatem, Fethullah's friend and fellow in studying and attending the gathering of Light, stood at the mosque door looking at people's faces as if he were counting the people who were leaving the mosque until his eyes saw his friend. He hurried to him and threw a shirt of glad tidings on him. Fethullah said, "O my friend, what is the matter with you?" His friend said, "Tonight I saw my master Bediuzzaman Said Nursi in a dream. It was about you. I saw him sending you a message. It was his biography accompanied by a jar full of almonds. That was it. The dream then ended!"

The passionate lover was wandering in the mazes of the desert walking towards the Beloved's house! He knew that there was danger in the mazes of the desert; for death inhabits its mountains and dust! Yet the passionate lover was captured by stormy mad longing! He had no control over his faculties and could not prevent them from riding on the journey of madness. His throat was so dry out of thirst and his stomach was shrunk out of hunger. His clothes fluttered in the wind and he was dragging his feet in the dusty hills! But when the breeze of the Beloved blew, its fragrance called him, carrying to the enamored youth the good news of his imminent arrival. His neck stretched to enable him to look beyond the hills and when he saw a glimpse of the Beloved's tent, he fell on the ground out of intense joy!

Fethullah's tears were running all night long, longing and yearning. By morning, he received the good news of the arrival. All the hills of patience were demolished under the heat of longing. He wept again but this time it was tears of joy that soothed his heart. Oh soul, rejoice in the good news and feel tranquil in the synchronicity and beauty of the extraordinary Divine gifts and wonders!

The youth continued to mutter words as if he were rambling! But he was in fact reciting a few verses of poetry that the Imam of Alvar used to recite whenever the Divine Subtleties would overwhelm him with generous gifts. He was just a servant at the beginning of the Path and such extraordinary gifts took his breath away! How can his pupils bear looking at the intensely bright sunlight?

> *It is a matter beyond my limits*
> *And I am just a weak servant,*
> *Who is not worthy of such generosity.*
> *Why all of this gentle benevolence*

Throwing to me rains of grace?

Fethullah wondered about the symbolism in this dream and tried to ask interpreters of dreams about the meaning of seeing a jar of almonds. Most of them said it meant traveling. As for Nursi's biography, it meant a coming station. Fethullah wondered about the meaning of the whole dream that his friend saw especially on this special night when he had stayed up all night turning on the fire in his heart and washing it off with his heated tears.

Nonetheless, what settled within his heart that this dream along with the other signs he was shown, such as the personal greeting from Bediuzzaman, meant that he had permission to pursue the Path of Light. In fact, his spiritual experience and Hatem's dream eventually convinced him that he was not only permitted to pursue the Path of Light but he was ordered to pursue it. The veils were lifted from the secrets and hearts flew to hearts. The ustadh's heartbeat and the student's heartbeat pulsed with the same pain! Whoever is afflicted by the unveiling of love cannot forsake his intimate friend! Otherwise, he would be among those who would perish!

My fellows, are you the best in the eon or the worst?
Be as you want but I am this intimate friend!

The Seeker of Light

To be the seeker of Light in the time of darkness means that you have to enroll as a spiritual soldier and give yourself out to the niche of the poor to take you as a lamp which you kindle by the fire in your blood. Who knows? You might carry on top of your head some bread from which birds can eat! Or the sun may purify your heated longing so that you may become a moon traveling to lofty orbits!

To be a seeker of Light means to go out alone at night in the storm and to face the severe coldness with a bare chest! It means that you have to walk in empty tracks to distribute heated pulses in cold hearts hidden in hollow caves! Nothing would conceal you from the night snipers except Allah's decree!

Thousands of scholars were tortured or put to death by hanging on the gallows erected there. Others spent nights sitting on swings threatened by the blowing wind to lament the doomed weddings! Their bloodied turbans testify to the sun's eclipse at a time when the devil veiled the sunrise of the spirit with his pale face. His guns besieged all the minarets of the country, confiscating the longing of the poor and banning papers sealed by the tears of the full moon! Banning the images of the joyful birds of dawn and silencing the chanting of the birds who were expressing its anguish in the middle of the night!

The Narrator of sorrows told me: When Nursi passed away he did not leave anything except a small basket that had a worn out garment, a pocket-watch by which he used to count the sorrows at night and messages he kept for a spirit he saw coming after him! As for Fethullah, Allah sent him all the tears of the world, the wounds of history and then said to him: It is time, Fethullah! Arise!

Huzayfa ibn al-Yaman was a unique type of Companion. He used to ask the Messenger of Allah, upon him be peace and blessings, about evil out of fear that he may be there when its time arrives! There is much news concerning the battle with evil in the last era. When I asked the narrator about it he just added to my tiredness!

When Nursi threw the message of sorrow to Fethullah, he wept but then he drew for it the sword of the Qur'an whenever he secretly experienced its pain. He witnessed the cutting of the sycamore trees everywhere! He saw the Light's chicks burning in the hell of darkness! His speeches took the form of storytelling full of examples and deterring lessons. Fethullah would open the locks to show its reality and receive its funerals with a bare chest. He would then weep and weep.

Oh Fethullah! This is your time! Such is your destiny! Thus, carry the stick of your sorrows and depart towards your Tur; for you have arrived as it was decreed and you have no choice! You have never been the seeker but you are what have been sought! Whoever is called by the Glowing Face and blasted by its Light has no choice!

Fethullah looked to the burning fires in his doomed time and saw Satan's smoky flames blocking the road and delaying the appointed time! Nonetheless, he carried on his shoulder the tear sprayer and entered in the midst of fire.

The Narrator of Light told me about the epic of sadness saying: The spring of 1924 was a spring without flowers; for all of Turkey's gardens had burned. Its rivers carried poisonous ashes towards all Muslim countries. Such was the year of the greatest doom by a declaration to separate Turkey from its historical roots. Anatolia entered the time of fire and hurricanes. The stories of ladies weeping behind their veils became thousands in number!

The Story of the Sad Muezzin

Shaikh Mehmed Efendi was the *muezzin* (the caller for prayer) of a small mosque and he taught the Holy Book in its warm prayer niche. When the news of the sultan's expulsion and abrogating the Islamic Caliphate spread, Mehmed Efendi looked at his young students and wept. In his eyes he saw the greatest epic going through storms blowing in the middle of a coming night! He saw rivers of blood running within their arteries, burning their Qur'anic books with fire. He kissed each one of them and asked them to take good care of the mosque and he left and never returned.

A few days later, a law was issued banning the teaching of religion in Turkey. Chains tied the wings of chanting birds on top of Istanbul's minarets, cruelly suffocating the throats of young chicks which used to mummer the Qur'anic letters, closing in its faces all spiritual windows. Many honey bee hives were destroyed, suffocated or drowned in their bitter honey!

When Mehmed Efendi arrived at his small house, he found out about a law that forced the imams, muezzins and caretakers of the mosques to wear European hat and to chant the *adhan* (the call for prayer) in the Turkish language. The Arabic language was banned from the Friday sermons at the mosques. Mehmed Efendi realized that the time to migrate had arrived. Its time was determined by the lightning that struck through the cloudy dark horizon! Before a shameful dancing party between a mix of men and women was announced for the first time in Turkey's history, Mehmed, the muezzin, had already carried his light luggage and secretly migrated to Damascus.

The Story of the Jailed Preacher

Bayram Efendi, the Imam, found himself all of a sudden without a job. He was not able to do his job as a spiritual guide and imam and he could not do the legal documentations for marriage and divorce, or to counsel people regarding their share of inheritance. He used to perform these functions in his small office every evening. But the modern country had revoked the Islamic Ministry and all the Islamic courts and issued laws that prevented the Islamic laws of inheritance and instead permitted marriages in accordance to the Western ways without the need for guardians (*wali*) or dowry. Women had the right to marry themselves to whoever they wanted, even to non-Muslim men. All religious laws were canceled and replaced by Italian and Swiss laws. The phrase "Islam is the official religion of the country," was eliminated from the constitution. The Name of God was removed from the oaths of office for anyone serving in the government and other prestigious jobs.

Imam Bayram was imprisoned in his house for twelve years, during which he repeatedly recited the Qur'an secretly. He could not leave his house and could not look from the window because he was embarrassed to wear a hat in accordance to the new laws which forced people to wear black western hats. How could he have taken off his great turban and worn the hat?

All the scholars who could escape out of Turkey did, while many others were martyred when they were shot dead in the middle of main streets and public squares. Bayram, however, could not escape with his five girls for fear that they might be raped on the road. Thus, he chose to jail himself forever. The family lost its income; for the mother and the daughters sewed scarves and veils for women before the new laws banning the wearing of veils.

To step out of his house, Bayram Efendi had to wear western attire. Otherwise, he would be risking his life at the hand of the tyrant snipers who would shoot the head of any imam or muezzin who would not wear the western hat on his way to the mosque.

In this way, the blood of many weakened Turks was shed for sixty years during which Shaikh Bayram did not leave his house until the doors of his house opened to take him to his burial place covered in sadness.

The Story of Yusuf, the Calligrapher

Yusuf Özcan was a proud man in a chain of professional teachers of calligraphy. On the wall of his office he hung his certificate which the Shaikh of all calligraphers had issued him in
the Diwan, or Privy Council, of the Sultans. Calligraphy was not
only a source of income for Yusuf but it was also a spiritual provision. Calligraphy was a shade under which his soul found rest.
He used to enjoy exploring with his pen the curves of the beautiful letters adorned by faith. When he would start a piece he
would enter the prayer niche made of letters and become absent
from the outer realm as he responded to the spirit's call. He
would be upset with clients who would attempt to talk to him
during his immersion in his masterpiece or if he were working on designing a title for a book.

When the law of banning the use of the Arabic script was
issued, people were forced to use Latin letters instead of Arabic, and exchanging books and documents written in Arabic
script became a danger so people had to do it secretly. Tons
of books were sold at a cheap price to Europeans while other
books were sent to paper factories. Within one day all magazines and books were printed in Latin. All commercial signs had
to also be replaced by Latin signs. Even street names and towns
were changed into Latin. Teaching Arabic and trading Arabic
books were banned. Governmental officers spread everywhere
confiscating the Qur'an copies and chasing those found teaching the recitation of the Qur'an under the mosque domes or
in the privacy of their homes and they would be dragged in
chains and thrown in prisons.

People surrendered to the law of banning calligraphy under
the threat of swords of fire except Yusuf Özcan. He declared
civil disobedience. He continued to paint his masterpieces open-

ly but found no client willing to buy. To abandon calligraphy was equal to him to committing spiritual suicide. It was a painful spiritual death. Thus, he continued to paint his masterpieces, illustrating an *ayah* or a phrase of *dhikr*. The colors and the intricate designs expressed his spiritual longing and sorrows which led those who can feel deeply to weep. He would present his masterpieces to the pedestrians passing in front of his office. People would secretly glance at them fearing that Satan's watchers might see them. They would marvel at the courage of the daring calligrapher who had gone mad. After he felt satisfied with his public presentation Yusuf would carry his masterpieces to one of the city's mosques and hang them on the high walls.

This did not last for too long; for soon the police officers raided his office and pointed their guns at him and within a few seconds he was chained and dragged to jail. In prison Yusuf used to climb on the back of one of the strong inmates and paint on the highest wall in the prison, "*Oh my two prison companions, which is more reasonable and better: having multiple lords or having Allah, the One, the Irresistible?*" (Surah Yusuf 11:39).

The Story of the Distinguished Teacher

Mustafa Arslan was a powerful teacher. He graduated from the school of education which was established especially to prepare secularist teachers. Thousands of teachers graduated from such schools and were dispatched everywhere to teach children, adolescents, and teens the theory of evolution and other philosophical concepts based on secularism and speculative philosophies of the heretics. They taught them things contrary to the spirit of the religion and they tore down the religious and social fabric of the country. They spread everywhere in Turkish society starting from its European side to the farthest eastern part of

Anatolia. They focused on small cities and villages where people were still holding onto their beliefs and lofty ethics.

Schools officially continued to teach irreligious theories at all levels of education. Experts came from communist Russia and Western Europe to help them spread this education. Sunday became the official day off instead of Friday. This was associated with a vigorous media campaign dedicated to spreading the concept of the western culture which calls for an era of assertive secularism. This became the trend of modernized intellectual thinkers.

Mustafa Arslan was a different type of teacher. His father was an ordinary farmer in eastern Anatolia. He raised his son to love his religion and his shaikhs. He graduated from the modern school of education in which he was exposed to brain washing techniques. Nonetheless, such exposure did not have any effect on his faith in Allah. Instead, it actually increased his conviction concerning religious realities. He observed modernity with a critical eye and continued to search for the reason modernity was without religion.

New magazines and newspapers raced to praise the heresies of modernity and its symbols. They started to publish types of indecent pictures and encourage the concepts of sexual freedom. At that time, the first beauty pageant for Muslim women was announced for the first time in the history of the Islamic world!

The government reduced the number of mosque caretakers from two thousand one hundred to less than two hundred. In Istanbul alone, seventy mosques were closed. All Islamic schools, Sufi lodges and retreat centers were shut and their belongings were confiscated. The historical Aya Sophia Mosque was transformed into a museum. The Fatih Mosque, built by Sultan Mehmed the Conqueror, was used for storage and other major mosques were used for stables for the police horses or for night clubs that offered wine.

This culminated in the farce that planned for all mosques to replace carpets with chairs and to put musical instruments in every mosque so *Tajwid* classes could be accompanied by music. However, no one dared to execute that decision. Allah must have saved His Book from being humiliated.

In Mustafa's mind the plot of the hellish chain became clear. He realized that his country was sick and that it had been captured by a giant dark octopus that was seeking to swallow it. He was certain that such dark smoke would turn to fire one day!

Thus, one day when Mustafa entered his classroom he found himself reciting loudly, *"Bismi'llah ir-Rahman ir-Rahim"* (In the Name of Allah, the Universally Merciful, the Singularly Compassionate). The words were coming from the bottom of his sad noble heart. It had a great effect upon the souls of his students. When he stood in front of them he saw that they were surprised and a strange silence crept between them. Finally, a courageous student asked, "Would you please explain to us the meaning of such beautiful words?"

Within the blink of an eye, the teacher led his students onto the ship of longing in the spirit's ocean! He did not wake up from his vision until he heard the bell ringing announcing the end of the class.

When Mustafa went to his school the next day he found the principal waiting for him at the door, standing still as if he were a statue made of stone. When the teacher approached him he made a gesture with his hand and all of a sudden police officers surrounded the teacher. The principal then handed him a document stating that he was fired from his job.

The Exit Door
Between Said Nursi and Shaikh Said Pirani

Both men were named Said (spelled also as Saeed or Sa'id, meaning "happy"). While Said Pirani is a Shaikh preferring to apply to the sheer force, Said Nursi is Bediuzzaman (or Badi' az-Zaman, meaning "Wonder of the Age"). In the early stages of the terrifying eclipse, Shaikh Said Pirani (a.k.a. Shaikh Said of Piran) started his major revolution in eastern Anatolia. He prepared an army of the best among all the tribes accompanied by many clan leaders. He declared civil disobedience. The government met that with destructive weapons and the air force. They chased the leaders of the revolution into the mountains and caves. It was a terrifying massacre and thousands of people were killed as well as many women and children. Dead bodies were found in streets and valleys in a way that was never seen in Turkey before, not even during the First World War.

Shaikh Said of Piran was arrested and executed along with forty of his assistant leaders. This took place on the 29th of June, 1925. After this, courts were set up across the country to terrify people and plant fear within their hearts. Gallows were set up to hang many scholars and spiritual counselors.

Bediuzzaman saw all the horror with his intuitive insight which he had anticipated happening even before the rebellion. This is why he objected to the revolutionary way of Said of Piran and he even sent him a message advising him and explaining to him how his attempt for a military confrontation would go in vain at a time when everything was being destroyed. The way that Bediuzzaman proposed was to reconstruct the society to build it anew by educating and training people on how to save their faith.

Nursi got burnt by the fire of Shaikh Said of Piran's rebellion even though he was in a retreat in a secluded area in the mountains in the eastern part of the country to which the government had exiled him to keep him away from society. This enabled Ustadh Bediuzzaman Said Nursi to start writing his first *Epistle of Light* in 1928. He would send it secretly through some of his first faithful students from the small village he lived in. They would then hand copy the *Epistles of Light* and distribute them everywhere.

The *Epistles of Light* was a call to return to the spiritual orbit during the time of modernity. It was a movement to actually live in the spiritual orbit of the Prophet, upon him be peace and blessings, which the seekers of Light pursued and to live by the pain of its suffering and the joy of its hopes. It is to resume the historical motion of the global Muslim community and a renewal of the magnanimity of the Islamic Call from the house of the Prophet's young Companion Ibn Arqam to the valleys of Mecca to the Conquest of Mecca! It is to surrender to the trials of the Qur'an and to be patient concerning its rulings and verdicts and to walk in accordance to the balance of its stages and the results of its actualizing within the self and within the society by gradual progress in awe and desire until Allah permits the migration!

The sufferings that Nursi experienced for the sake of serving the Divine Call, is a different story! He continued to carry the secrets of his findings in his small basket until he threw it to Fethullah in a dream and then he departed!

The message within the biography of Nursi was revealed and its symbols were unveiled as they manifested in Hatem's dream. Bediuzzaman was in his late years. He did not live more than three years after the age of eighty. His message, glimpses from his biography, was sent to Fethullah. He sent to him his life's experience, the fruit of his inner struggle and the harvest of his entire life. He threw his heavy burden upon the youth's shoulders in one basket! Fethullah responded the morning after the message was delivered, "Oh, the Diamond Sword of the Light, Here I am!"

From the minaret in Erzurum, the youth spread his wings in the wind and he flew. Oh ladies and gentlemen! I saw him flying across the horizon, striking the horizon with a shimmering and scorching passion towards the darkness of the far west!

Chapter 4

The Conquests of Edirne:
From Retreats to Realizations

Journey, Oh Messenger of Allah

A retreat is contemplation while a vision is remembrance! Between them, the ascension of the soul is erected! None can arrive at its runways unless he journeys on earth until he arrives at the union of the two seas! The Path has obstacles; for climbing the mountains is exhausting and the desert has a scorching heat. He who walks between them ascends and descends between a state of concealment and realizations. He finds ecstasy in striving and he is fed by the exhaustion. Whoever thinks that arriving at the water of Madyan can occur without traveling is wrong and is deluded. Thus, carry your provision on top of your staff, oh my heart, and depart! On the shore of the secure neighborhood the houses, or stations, of the loved ones exist!

Anatolia is the land of everlasting travel! Everything there is migrating and on a journey: human beings, birds, animals and fish. Every land and marine track is inhabited by a wind that has continuously blown since the first dawn of history upon the hearts pushing them to journey on. Whenever their longing is kindled they submit their wings to the wind and fly off. From early centuries birds gathered on top of the mountains in the eastern areas between Van and Bitlis up to Mt. Ararat. Others gathered in the western area between Istanbul's domes and Izmir's shores. Others settled in the north on top of the mountains across from the Black Sea. Others gathered in the south between the lakes of Isparta and the province of Antakya. Nonetheless, when the Caller called, "O horses of Allah, March!" all flocks here and there took off and began striking the sky with their wings in one rhythm. Their longing ignited by the spirit's call!

Awliya Çelebi was a famous Ottoman-Turkish traveler who lived in the seventeenth century. He once saw the Messenger of Allah, upon him be peace and blessings, in a dream entering one of Istanbul's mosques. He approached him and kissed his hand. He wanted to ask for his intercession (*shafa'ah*) on the Day of Judgment but being overwhelmed with excitement and awe he said instead, "O Messenger of Allah, journey (*sayahah*)." The Noble Prophet smiled and invoked Allah for him to grant him safety in all of his journeys!

Since then, the echo of Awliya Çelebi's inflamed outcry has been pollinating the trees of Anatolia, feeding the traveling wind with agitation so that it knocks on the shores and the mountain caves. Every morning the falcon chicks inhale some of its crossing essence which causes the feathers in their wings to grow until they become ready to leave their nests, shouting: Journey, Oh Messenger of Allah. They then fly off into the lofty sky!

Ramiz Efendi saw that Fethullah must leave Erzurum. This had been his desire for a long time. But the youth's mother found that difficult. She pitied sending him to the mazes of Anatolia. How can she do so in such difficult times? The sword was pointing to the chests of the faithful believers! Nonetheless, the father realized that Erzurum cannot contain the intellectual potential of his genius son nor was it vast enough for his shimmering spirit. He realized that if he did not let him go, his precious seed would be wasted in the arid soil. Thus, he continued to convince the youth's mother until she softened and agreed.

To Fethullah, this was another indication concerning the long and difficult journey ahead of him. It was the culmination of the signs of Light which started when illuminating his fruitful night during the gathering in the mosque! As soon as Fethullah received his mother's consent he realized that his time to travel had arrived and he shouted silently from the bottom of his innermost being: Journey, Oh Messenger of Allah!

He hastened to the train going to Edirne which consumed four thousands kilometers departing from the farthest eastern part of Turkey to its farthest western city! In the beginning, the wisdom of going to that particular city was not so obvious except that his mother's cousin, Huseyin Top Hoja, was living there. His mother wished that Fethullah would live under his care. However, time revealed that he had gone specifically to Edirne for a known decree! The base of his lofty ascension was not but this scorched city! This is why he left and never returned even though in the beginning he was thinking that he would stay in Edirne only for some time after which he would return to Erzurum. But the journey's call was more powerful than his will. It ousted him high up to the lofty ascensions of the soul. Since then he has been migrating towards Allah, traveling from deep sentiment to deep sentiment and from ache to ache, healing sores with open wounds, and dressing the wounds with agonies in an everlasting journey!

To Fethullah, train stations seemed like major cities, places to rest from the exhaustion of traveling. It was a chance for him to knock on the doors of other cities with the magical wand of his spiritual journey. Ankara was the first place that attracted him in his youth. He stayed there for a few days. He knew of the time when the Directorate of Religious Affairs administered a test for the scholars and speakers. During his stay he used to frequently visit a district where some of his friends lived. He admired the district a lot because of its unique spiritual characteristics due to the presence of the spiritual educator and glorious ascetic Hajji Bayram. The youth loved him intensely.

There, Fethullah visited one of parliament's representatives. His name was Mustafa Zeren. He was one of his father's relatives. He spent one night with him in one of the upper-class neighborhoods.

In this way, Fethullah was able to see Ankara's diverse characteristics. After that, he resumed the sentimental journey!

Istanbul was the second city Fethullah stopped at on his way to Edirne. It was a must that the youth get to know Istanbul. He stayed there for a few days in a small motel in a neighborhood called Sirkeci because it was very popular among the people in Erzurum who recommend it to each other. Most of them would stay there when they visited Istanbul. It was in fact an ordinary motel or even less than ordinary. But it was the most suitable motel for the poor inhabitants of Erzurum. Its sheets and pillows were worn out. Its cracks were places for flees and cockroaches and many other tiny insects. It was noisy night and day. At that time it was categorized as a three-star motel. The youth could not sleep at night, itching, tossing and turning.

The Exhaustion of Arrival

The train left Istanbul after midnight and it was supposed to arrive in Edirne at a very late hour. Most of the travelers fell asleep as soon as they sat comfortably on their chairs. Fethullah fell asleep too and he continued to sleep until the train arrived at the last station of Edirne. The officers started to wake people up to leave the train. When the travelers left the train they found themselves in a remote area and they were forced to walk a long distance towards the city while carrying their heavy luggage.

The youth entered the city unnoticed by its people! As soon as he found a suitable motel he went in and fell asleep; for he needed to rest. In the morning he found himself in a motel very close to a historical mosque, which was named after its elegant "three-balconied minaret"—the *Üç Şerefeli* Mosque. At that time he did not know that he would later become the Imam of that mosque.

The youth started searching for his mother's cousin Huseyin Top Efendi. When he met him, the man welcomed him and found him a temporary place to stay in a mosque called the Yıldırım Beyazid Mosque at which Huseyin Efendi worked as the imam and preacher. Fethullah understood that to be hired for a religious job he must obtain permission from the Mufti (Grand Jurist) or from the Mufti's representative. But the problem was that there was no Mufti, or Grand Jurist, in Edirne.

Huseyin Efendi took Fethullah to the Mufti's representative who disregarded Fethullah seeing that he was still a young man. He did not trust his abilities and knowledge and he proposed to test him. The youth accepted the challenge immediately. The representative gave him a book on *fiqh*—the Islamic jurisprudence that he opened randomly and instructed the youth to read the page in Arabic. Fethullah read then translated what he read into the Turkish language. The representative was fascinated and impressed by Fethullah but he controlled his expressions and as soon as Fethullah finished reading and translating he instructed him to leave the office. After a little while, Huseyin Efendi came to him flying with joy and told him the good news that the representative admired him a lot and complimented him with great words, saying, "This youth is still young but it seems that he built his character very well." These words made Huseyin Efendi happy but to Fethullah they were signs of arrogance and conceit.

A few days later, Fethullah was hired as the second imam for a mosque called Akmescid and he continued to lead people in Prayers and deliver lessons until the time for the scholarly test, which was organized by the Directorate of Religious Affairs in Ankara, came. Fethullah traveled to take the test. Their relative, the parliament's representative, called him and said, "My nephew, let me kiss your forehead; for you have passed the test. Congratulations!"

As much as this good news made Huseyin Efendi happy, it was heavy on the Mufti's representative who felt somehow threatened by it. This was because Fethullah sent an application to the Directorate of Religious Affairs requesting to become the Mufti (Grand Jurist) of Edirne which only had a representative. However, he was denied the job. The reason cited for denying him the job was because he had not yet finished the military service; for he was only sixteen years old according to his identification card which meant he was not required to do his military service yet and it also did not allow him to work in any governmental jobs. Fethullah did not give up and he went to court asking to correct his identification card to his actual age which was eighteen years old.

The Jurisprudence Department arranged a competition to fill the empty spots for imams in different mosques across the province. Fethullah won first place and he had the right to be hired as the Imam of the historical Üç Şerefeli Mosque. However, Ibrahim Efendi, the Mufti's representative, said to him, "Even though you got the highest mark on the test, you have not yet done your military service and this is why we are going to consider you equal in qualification to the one who came second in the test. Thus, we are going to draw a lot to see who should be hired." The lot's result was disappointing to the representative and Fethullah was hired as the Imam of the Üç Şerefeli Mosque.

At that time, the Imam's salary was 200 liras but when Fethullah went to get his salary he found that it was reduced by thirty liras! What could the youth do when he lived at a time of alienation, out of place, especially considering his modesty and humbleness and his renunciation of worldly pursuits? He did not leave Erzurum in pursuit of money, jobs and wealth but he left Erzurum in quest of raising the flag of Light atop the minarets and domes and to serve faith in remote areas and for this reason, Fethullah accepted his reduced salary.

The Test of Words and Overcoming Obstacles

For the worshipful slave to rightfully attain the station of spiritual leadership (*imamah*) his cuts must be inflamed by testing words that burn him one by one. When he passes these tests, then he becomes a spiritual leader for the people. Otherwise, he would just become one of the followers. What is meant by "words" here is not a mere word but an actual provocative action, a volcanic obstacle and a difficult trial where feet are walking on the edge of a sword and where hearts burn by the fire of abandoning one's lower desires (*takhliyya*) and adorning one's self with the pious qualities (*tahliyya*). Many in this world just mimic and follow but very few are the spiritual leaders and the revivers.

In Edirne Fethullah found himself meant to occupy that station of spiritual leadership and he realized that he had to be worthy of that or he would have no room in this station. This station required a unique ability for it is a very critical position and he had no choice but to move forward; for never in his life had he known how to move backward. He would also take double steps forward. Why not? He had just made a pledge weeping, "Would he not overcome the obstacle? Would he not overcome the obstacle?"

The testing words started to pour on his head one after the other. Whenever he existed from a fire, he would find himself faced with another fire. Nonetheless, the rescuing rain would wet his inner being with a cooling and peaceful effect increasing his faith and strengthening him to face the fire. It would make him more determined to overcome the flames of one obstacle after another!

The First Obstacle: Edirne's Wounds

Edirne has a story in Turkey's history. Edirne is the house of devils! Edirne is the cradle of those who struggle for the Divine Cause! Edirne is the sinners' abode! Edirne is the capital of the conquerors! Edirne is the meeting place of the fallen! Edirne is the ascension of the navigators of the way to Allah.

Edirne is an unusual city in a strategically important location in the farthest western part of the European section of Turkey on the boundaries of the Balkans where Greece and Bulgaria are. The lights and buildings of other cities in different countries can be seen from Edirne!

Edirne, with its geopolitical location is a reminder for any Muslim who has an insight into history. Any truly faithful believer who enters Edirne should feel sorrow striking his back and shoulders! It is a city guarded by Allah. Its domes and minarets are like piles of iron preventing the commotions of history and

the flood of geography; for beyond its boundaries in lands owned
by others are cities and villages inhabited by Muslims in Bulgaria
and other neighboring countries. The call for Prayer is still called
there, deriving its sad tone from the Abbasid lady who screamed
for help in the land of the Romans where she was taken captive.
Pleading in an emotional tone to Caliph al-Mu'tasim in his
absence, she said, "Wa Mu'tasima!" (O my grief, Mu'tasima!)
Anatolia echoed her scream, "O my grief! O my grief!" Could
it be possible that Edirne too is captured in the deadly painful
dungeon? What a blessing then for the worshipful servant to
enter Edirne today safe and secure? What a powerful blow he
receives today realizing that he is a weak inheritor who has no
mastery! Why is the Selimiye Mosque crying out to Allah out of
pain? Why when it calls for the Prayers through its minarets,
does it cry, "Everyone alive come feel the wounds! Everyone
alive come feel the wounds." And why is no one ministering
its wounds?

Edirne is the capital of spiritual strife! It is the den of lions
and cubs. Therein, the good news which was prophesized by the
Messenger, upon him be peace and blessings, came true – Sultan Mehmed the Conqueror, conquered Istanbul. The best of
armies is Edirne's army and the best of princes is Edirne's prince!
History testifies that the vision of Prophet Muhammad, upon
him be peace and blessings, had come true; for he is the truthful one on earth and in heaven! So, may the peace and the blessing be upon you my Master Guide, O Messenger of Allah! From
that time on, Edirne should be proud of its erected marquee; the
cradle of the good news brought by the Messenger, upon him
be peace and blessings!

The capitals of the early Ottoman Empire were the places
on the way of striving for the sake of Allah. The thrones of its
rulers were their horses' backs. When the Sultans became indul-

gent in the luxuries of palaces and thrones Allah removed them from leadership and denied them victory. Then other nations started to snatch the resources of the Ottoman capital and the blood of God's representation, or vicegerency, flew causing hearts to bleed everywhere.

Satan has a concealed hate for Edirne and an old desire for revenge; for it was the birth place of Mehmed the Conqueror. He was raised and educated in this early capital of the Ottomans. From its hills he was dispatched to besiege Constantinople which he snatched from between the Roman's teeth just as his great grandfather had snatched Edirne from them. After the vicegerency (*khilafah*) was torn down, Satan invaded it and removed its veil by force and raped it!

Afterwards, Edirne became a farm for grape wine, and bars competed with mosques everywhere. The smokestacks of its factories exhaled into the polluted bellies of the drunk in a way that was never known before in Turkey! Many evil individuals occupied Edirne and spread their corruption through the country and people by promoting bad habits. They would dance, drink and steal. Edirne became the home for many Muslims who had escaped the Balkans. They brought with them their moral decay. Because the city has boundaries with western countries, it became the pathway for tourists who were coming to visit Turkey. This added to the city's afflictions. Its people lived a difficult time after the fall of the Islamic caliphate experiencing moral decay in all of its forms until its youth woke up in the 1960s hearing the call for religious revival.

Fethullah was highly disturbed by what he saw in the city; the religious scholars were ignorant about religion. Those who were in places of authority misused the power which they had been given, instead of protecting people's rights they violated people's rights. The courtyards of some mosques became places for indecent acts. Streets and markets competed with Europe in lewd activities. The imam's daughters or the muezzin's daughters were those who won the first prizes in dancing contests; for religious leadership had become a job void of meaning and had nothing to do with worship. Some of the muezzins—those who would call for the Prayer, did not even pray. They would rush to call for the Prayer then hurry out of the mosque to meet the tourists and take them on a tour inside the mosque in return for a few liras. He would then return to the mosque just as the imam was about to end the Prayer so that he could recite the *adhkar* and *tasbihat* for the ones praying. He would not be involved in advising people to do what is good or prohibit them from doing evil.

The western side of Turkey was collapsing. The minarets of the Üç Şerefeli Mosque were powerfully spinning around themselves so that they might shake off the shame that was surrounding the whole country. Surrounding its corners was the spirit of the Sultan of saints and the saint of Sultans, the Ottoman Vice-regent, Murad the Second. He was sadly touring the mosque, weeping as he witnessed the state of the mosque he had built with stones that are always blessed with the running water of the ablution fountain. His son and the inheritor of his secret, Mehmed the Conqueror, was looking at the far horizon and crying out in consciousness of the time to start a new conquest!

The colossal dome of the Selimiye Mosque was shaking as if it were a spiritual being, pointing with the tips of its four towering minarets as if it were an eagle about to take off! The great Ottoman architect Sinan's weeping was echoing with each phrase of the call for the Prayer lamenting the masterpiece which his hands had carved in the form of longing for Allah! Alas for you, Oh Capital of the Conquerors! Oh city of Allah's friends. What a devil who threw you into a dirty swamp that you are drowning in. O my grief! O my grief! The echo continued to repeat the cry until Fethullah arrived!

The beginning was difficult for the youth; for imagine how a religious person coming from a city like Erzurum, which is very conservative, would feel. Erzurum observed the values of decency and ethical behavior to the extent that people would not rent their houses to a bachelor visiting the city. Imagine a youth coming from this conservative community, arriving at a city that had lost the virtues of modesty and chastity to the extent that many of its ladies would harass men with lewd words in the streets worse than the usual way of debauchery in history.

The Second Obstacle: A Trial like Joseph's

When the financial situation of the youth became relatively stable he started looking for a house to rent. He rented a house for fifty liras per month. It was a small beautiful house with a small yard. He was determined to study and rejuvenate his spiritual energy. He did not know that the house was surrounded by snake burrows. It was located on a narrow dead-end street and its door was the last door. It was summer time when heat affects everything. Along the sides of the street women spent their time there standing around in the morning and even late at night. They would pose vulgarly! The youth soon realized that he had been put in a critical place! To go to his house he had to cross the road where they were standing around and he would feel as if he were stepping on scorching coals. The eyes of the companions of Joseph (Yusuf) would follow him, throwing tempting arrows from all directions. Sweat would flow from the tip of his head to the tip of his toes until he arrived at his house drowning in his sweat as if he had just taken a shower.

This state continued for fifteen days after which the ladies gave up breaking his steadfastness. Some of them dared to call him provocative names that he could not bear to hear and he would hasten his steps to his house, burning between the fire of sadness and the flames of shyness! He would not be able to sleep afterwards out of sorrow for the city of the pure ones, which had fallen into a dirty swamp! He would go out before dawn and come back after midnight to avoid seeing these women. He continued to do so until the end of the month. He suffered the hardship of sleep deprivation; for he would not sleep except for two hours, then he would have to wake up before dawn to go lead the people in Prayer. He found himself paying rent without benefiting from the house. In addition, he had to walk a long distance to the house. Thus, he gathered his little suitcase and went to the Üç Şerefeli Mosque. He looked at its corners and pillars weeping and asking for help.

One of the windows seemed to welcome him so he threw himself on it with a wounded heart that was tired of walking in rotten places. When he entered through the window and closed its door he felt its wall kindly and warmly embracing him as if it were a loving and caring mother. The windows of the mosque were huge and vast as if they were doors. This was one of the characteristics of Ottoman architecture of the Sultan mosques. The outer door of the window was about two and half meters high and its ceiling three meters high. Its width was two meters and the depth of its threshold was a meter and a half. Its exterior frame was strong solid iron. Its interior was made of wooden frames with squares filled with transparent glass to allow the sun rays to fill the mosque. From the inside, the window had wooden doors so it was like a small room or chamber.

Fethullah kept all of his belongings there: two blankets, two plates, one spoon and one cup. This is all that he had when he left Erzurum. He thought that he had saved himself from the snake burrows and their sudden sting. But snakes are snakes and they act in accordance to their nature. What would prevent her from creeping into the mosque? Fethullah did not ever think that the fire he escaped would follow him. One day, after he finished the Prayer and people left the mosque, he sat behind the muezzin's room drinking from his contemplation in silence. After a short time a seductive woman stood in front of him with her flames. She tried to seduce him with her beauty and with a tongue flamed by mesmerizing allure. He realized that she was dragging him into trouble and his spirit silently leaped, crying out from the depth of his innermost being. No ear heard him screaming, but the pillars of the mosque and the heavens heard him. Within a blinking of an eye, the youth jumped through the window behind him and closed its door. He said to the poison snake: death to you!

This action was like a slap on her face and she felt humiliated and how cheap she was. She retreated swearing at the sincere youth: so stay as you are, miserable and lonely until you die alone. Stay away!

She was a poison snake sent by Satan to Fethullah so she could sting his purity and burn his secret. Fethullah had a secret that he could not divulge. If Satan would have broken the box of his pearls he would have perished but the sincere one was saved. He closed the window of his infallibility in the face of the smoking fire. He threw the water of his ablution on Satan and was saved!

When his mother's cousin Huseyin Efendi knew that Fethullah was using the window as a house, he called the electric company and asked them to extend light to the interior part of the window. The technician arrived at the mosque when there was no prayer and started to work. When he was about to put a light bulb inside the small widow chamber Fethullah saw him and asked him what he was doing. When the technician explained, Fethullah felt upset and prevented him from putting in the light bulb and started to remove the wires himself, saying, "This electricity belongs to the mosque and it is paid for by the money of donors and so it is not permissible for me to use it. I am not in need of it; for I have my candle."

Whenever people left the mosque after the Night Prayer (Salat al-'Isha') Fethullah would turn off the light, go to his chamber and light his candle. Its dim ray was his way of navigating his journey in time. He would share in the scholars' gatherings of past eras or at times he would deliver his lessons to spirits of individuals gathering in the future.

Fethullah spent two and a half years safe and secure in his lovely chamber. It was a place for his retreats, his ascension, his resting place, his restaurant and he would sleep there, and welcome his guests. He never thought to change it until he was summoned for the military service.

The Third Obstacle: Accommodating Guests in the Window

Nothing troubled him about lodging in the window chamber except accommodating guests there. His brother Sıbgatullah visited him once so Fethullah had to let him sleep in the chamber while he slept on the mosque floor. The next day, he had to let his brother go back to Erzurum and he had to borrow seventy liras to buy him a train ticket.

He also still remembers when the prominent preacher, Salih Özcan, visited him. His visit left a great impact on the youth's soul which he would never forget. He came at a critical time when Fethullah was in great need of someone to give solace to him and sooth his pain. Salih Özcan was a man from east Anatolia. He was a member of the Arabic tribes migrating from Medina. He met Bediuzzaman Said Nursi and he dedicated himself to serve his cause. He had an effective role in publishing the first editions of the *Epistles of Light*. He was imprisoned a few times during the difficult times of the seekers of Light. He is credited for being the first to make Nursi known to the Arab world by spreading his *Epistles of Light* in the early printing of it.

The hearts of both ordinary people and those of the elites opened easily for him in a marvelous way. He even befriended some kings like King Faisal, may Allah bestow His mercy upon him! He also befriended many of the popular people, political leaders, and scientists from the East and the West such as Shaikh Muhammad Mahmud as-Sawaf, the poet 'Umar Baha'addin al-Amiri, Ustadh Allal al-Fasi, Shaikh 'Abdullah Kanun, 'Allamah Muhammad ibn Tawit at-Tanji. He did not leave a spot on earth without visiting it! He had a daring political and traveling attitude. Bediuzzaman used to joke with him saying, "You are my minister of Foreign Affairs."

Fethullah was generous with him as much as his capacity would allow. He prepared the window chamber for him to sleep while he slept on the floor as it was his usual manner to leave his bed for the guest. In the morning, at the train station, as Salih Özcan was saying farewell to Fethullah he embraced him warmly and said to him, "You are absolutely a hero." These words that were spoken from this great man were enough to renew Fethullah's vigor and energy in his young soul. It was as if he had snatched him from a state he had been caught in for many days. He returned to his window in a joyful mood, feeling an energizing faith exploding anew within his innermost being.

The Fourth Obstacle: Spiritual Adventure

Fethullah as a young man was full of vigor and energy. He was handsome and had a beautiful character and good manners. He liked to wear elegant clothes. He had a beautiful and majestic outlook that was augmented by the visions of the spirit. Such adorning qualities tired him and made him face difficult situations full of temptations in an environment raining alluring memorization! For how long had he been patient? Whenever he closed the door on the face of Joseph's companions, other doors opened for him. Even when he lived inside his narrow private chamber behind the window, plots were planned in the streets to tempt him! How can a green branch live in the midst of a forest full of burning logs without the fire reaching him and trying to consume his trunk and drink his dew drops? Where should he escape?

Fethullah well-realized his critical position and his difficult path. He contemplated the issue then decided to resort to the unusual path of spiritual practices, striving against the lower self until its desires would be defeated. He went to escape so he walked on a sword edge and he suffered immensely. He forced himself to ascend spiritually beyond this world. He raised himself one hill after another! He dwelled in station after station! When he arrived at the threshold of the expanded horizon, he sought to knock on the door but he did not find any trace of a door. But, lightning struck his chest, tore his flesh asunder and his blood flowed! Thus, he realized that he had mistaken the Path so he wept! He slumped down on the beginning tracks searching for the door of ascension!

His spiritual practices were meant to besiege his commanding lower self so that it would be weakened in the hands of the mesmerizing temptations. It probably had an unconscious revengeful attitude towards the spiritual void which polluted the city of the striving ones who strive for the Divine Sake.

His behavior was out of the ordinary! He would sleep but little and he would eat but little and he would speak but little! He did not own anything except two blankets. During the severely cold nights he would lay one of them down to sleep on and cover himself with the other. Edirne has cruel nights which cause her inhabitants to long for the extremely cold mornings! Fethullah slept embracing hunger for many long nights. He would not sleep but for two hours; for how can a body escape the canines of coldness and sleep? He would curl himself up so he could fall asleep. He abandoned eating delicious food until he lost a lot of weight and his face became pale!

Fethullah's spiritual practices increased in cruelty until he tasted their tyranny. Nonetheless, he continued to walk on their disliked thorns; for he is a man who does not give up!

Hayriye Hanim was a pious woman whose retired husband had passed away. He used to be a colonel in the army. She was the only one who knew Fethullah's state. She realized how much he was suffering. She would treat him kindly as she did her own children. She had empathy for him, seeing how much he starved himself. She came from a righteous lineage and had lofty ethics and polite manners. She became concerned about him and decided to take care of him. She served him as a caring mother would. She saw how his ribs seemed frozen from the cold so she brought him an extra carpet and she spread it in his chamber in spite of his objection. From time to time, she would bring food to him which he had to eat. He held her in high esteem, respected her and appreciated her favors.

Nonetheless, the youth continued his strange spiritual practices to the extent that he felt alienated from people, especially those who ate all types of food and meat; for in his eyes they appeared as wild beasts.

One day while he was between sleep and wakefulness, his self appeared to him in the image of a cat which he kept chasing until it escaped. He continued in his spiritual exercise and this time his self appeared to him in the form of a bear which he struggled with until he woke up from his slumber without one of them defeating the other! In another vision, after more spiritual exercises, his self appeared in the form of a giant gorilla! He was terrified and escaped seeking protection behind high fences!

The ardent seeker's body became so weak from hunger, cold and sleeplessness that illness crept to it and he fell in his chamber lying down for days and later staying half a month in the hospital under medical care. When he was in the hospital he received the news of his father's serious illness and his state deteriorated. This was an occasion to review his path of reclusiveness.

The strange states and stages he had experienced during his spiritual exercises were like lightning sparking from merciful warnings. It would descend upon him with water, coolness and snow to turn off the burning flames in his soul in hope to straighten any step that turned away and return it to the straight path of the Noble Prophet's ascension which leads to Heaven's gate!

Fethullah realized that his ego had confused him and dressed falsehood in the garment of the truth! It was drawing him to clear destruction. When he entered the intermediate realm that was mixed between absence and presence, and he was perplexed until he was about to become lost, the lightning of the Divine Law struck his sky suddenly, making him realize that his ego had taken him far into the paths of mazes!

Finally he found the door to exist! The landmarks of his new path became clear; as clear as the sun is clear during the middle of the day! It was a path through which he found what he wanted and much more! In it, he found protection from mesmerizing temptations, security from going astray, safe walking and a grant to arrive at the Divine Presence by Allah's leave!

Fethullah realized that striving against one's ego and disciplining it cannot occur without being involved in social work and without drowning in social life based on sharing people's sadness and pain. Absolute spiritual isolation is rather a risky spiritual adventure and its results are not necessarily granted! He had existentially experienced how disciplining the ego and mastering it can be through walking the Path of calling people towards Allah, through serving the Way of Allah, through supporting His cause during hardship and calamities. It is the greatest guarantee to achieve spiritual balance and to protect the soul from slipping into the detours of the abyss!

The Fifth Obstacle:
The Way of Calling People to Allah

The youth started to come out of his seclusion and he tried to connect with ordinary people. In the beginning, he only got to know some of the youth of his age so he started to think of new ways in which he would be able to dig a hole in the satanic wall that had been besieging the city!

So one day after he had finished leading the people in Prayer he did not go to his window chamber as usual but he left the mosque and went directly to the café. There, he sat sipping his tea and conversing with people about the concerns they had for religion and the country.

A few minutes into the conversation the youth had taken the lead of the conversation pulling the attention, ears and eyes around him. Out of the flame heated within his spirit, he lit warmness which all the attendees gathered around. When it was time to leave, there was longing to meet him again. It was a different and enjoyable day. His religious enthusiasm was fueled and the credit of faith greatly increased in his heart! The tracks of the new way manifested to him with clear landmarks and he knew that he was not created but for that path!

His spiritual invitations started to produce its fruits by Allah's leave! In the beginning, whenever he finished the Prayer he would hasten to the café. Later, he was able to convince one man to accompany him. After a few days, he was able to convince two more, then three and four. The extraordinary spiritual gift to guide started to move as clusters in the café until the group of those who were performing the Prayer was strengthened. The tree started to produce!

He then started to confront some of the bad habits in the society such as smoking. Many of the faithful believers' mouths started to be purified by the water of repentance. Fethullah would never forget a man named Halil who was moved by an eloquent admonishment by Fethullah so he took his cigarette box out and tore it into pieces then threw it away. That day was the last day Halil would taste such accursed poison in his life again.

The Narrator of sorrows told me: Religion was about to be absolved in Thrace—part of Turkey located in Europe! One day, a man from Diyarbakır, which is located on the farthest eastern side of Anatolia, visited Fethullah and said to the youth, "I've toured the whole Thracian part of Turkey and did not find anyone still practicing Islam except two individuals. One of them is you and the other is the Imam of the other mosque in the city of Kırklareli. After a few days, the mentioned Imam came to meet Fethullah. This meeting began good cooperation between them. It was very rare to find someone with religious sentiment at that time and if you found one, you would have to travel at least two hours to meet him. This was the landmark of religion in western Turkey.

Nonetheless, the youth started to carve into the stone and was able to attract two youths in high school. Then, later he attracted a few more college students. He started to arrange for them an Arabic class in an environment where learning Arabic was a risk, exposing one to danger as if he were a drug dealer!

But gradually the youth's spiritual invitation started to progress and invade many circles in the society. He openly unveiled the secret of his being in Edirne and the reality of the Divine duty which Allah brought him for. Fethullah started to love Edirne and found his soul united with it. He sympathized with its sorrows and started to moan when it moaned and weep when it wept. His young heart expanded and grew until it contained all of its inhabitants and he loved them all. He would embrace its pious ones and treat its sinners kindly. He would feel pity for those who had gone astray and for the dissolute. Edirne became part of his life and a cornerstone within the pillars of his formation. Some of the habits he formed there became part of his nature and the manners he learned there became established traits in him and accompanied him on his path towards calling people to Allah and achieving social transformation.

He continued to have an everlasting nostalgia and a perpetual longing for Edirne. Whenever he crossed the Bosporus Strait, which separates the two continents of Europe and Asia, he wished that the strait would rise above the earth and that Edirne's soil would unite with Anatolia forever! Edirne and the rest of the Turkish cities located on the European side are no more than good roots for a good tree whose branches stretch high in heaven! The tree spread horizontally until its branches hung down everywhere in Anatolia! The branches are now hanging down under the domes of Istanbul and swaying around Konya's minaret. It stretches by the power of the spring to the extent that its green branches intertwine in the provinces of Urfa, Bitlis and Van in the farthest eastern part of the country. Why then should the passionate loving youth be angry at the Bosporus? It is one garden underneath which rivers are flowing. Doves tour the place with the passionate devoted ones, cooing out of love and sorrow. Its flocks have been soaring beautifully between its eastern and western regions, spawning eggs in Urfa and Mardin on its southern border and chanting on the balconies of Edirne!

The youth accompanied some spiritual masters who lived in the past era and who witnessed the Balkan War as well as the First World War and the late days of the Ottoman Empire. He received from them the sorrows of the past and its pain, but he would illustrate with its blood the future of his hopes. He became popular in the city and known for his speeches, sermons and admonishment. He was known to have the beauty of eloquence and the logic of reasoning. His connections evolved little by little and their branches reached even the elite of the city and even some of the police officers and military. He gained the admiration of the Head of the Military Recruiting Department. He was a kind man from the Black Sea region.

He was a colonel and he loved Fethullah a lot. He used to tell him, "You cannot be from Erzurum; for your features are like ours. You are a son of Edirne."

Fethullah also had a friendship with the Head of Security, Resul Bey. He also had a good relationship with some judges and general attorneys. This took place at a strange stage in the history of the Republic of Turkey. It was quite odd for an imam to have good relations with bureaucrats. To meet with governmental officers, police officers, and judges was quite exceptional. It was an extraordinary spiritual gift more than we can understand with our minds!

The Narrator said: At this stage, some religious people started to publish faith-inspired magazines and newspapers. The spirit was resurrected in this kind of media and some of these publications reached Edirne such as *Büyük Doğu* (*The Great East*) magazine which would send two copies. Another newspaper, *Hür Adam* (*The Free Man*) used to send twenty-five copies. There was also a magazine called *Sebilürreşad* (*The Way for Spiritual Maturity*).

Hür Adam (*The Free Man*) was a weekly newspaper at that time and it was the only voice for Muslims in Turkey, besides the two other magazines mentioned. Fethullah used to order forty copies of that newspaper and pay for them out of his pocket then he would distribute them for free. Sometimes he would pay his whole salary for publications like *The Risale-i Nur* (*The Epistles of Light*) collection and some other books that he believed would be beneficial, and then he would distribute them for free. Sometimes he had to borrow money for this cause or he would starve himself.

One day, when he was about to ascend to the platform to deliver his speech he felt great pain in his stomach; for he had not eaten well for a few days. He looked for something to relieve him of the pain, at least during the time he would deliver the speech. He remembered an empty jar of honey that he used to have and he tried to take the scoop that was stuck in its very bottom. When he stood on the platform and started to deliver the speech, he felt the honey moving his stomach upside down and he felt severe nausea which increased the pain he was trying to reduce. He continued to suffer until the end of the lesson.

One day he was walking on the street hungry and it was raining and all of a sudden he found five liras on the ground. He took it immediately and entered the mosque, finished his Prayer then hurried to a restaurant and ate to his fill and managed his affairs with it for the next few days. But when he received his salary he took the five liras out and added to them five more liras and gave it to the poor. He would never forget the five liras he found when he was battling severe hunger. It was a great subtle gentleness from Allah. Fethullah did not abandon his habit of buying Islamic books and magazines and distributing them freely. The burning in his heart for religion made him forget the burning in his stomach.

The books from the collection of the *Epistles of Light* were sent to Fethullah from Erzurum through his tailor friend, Mehmed Şerkil; for he did not know anyone he could trust in Istanbul or Ankara to send them to him. At this difficult time in Turkey, doing these actions was not easy. It was considered a crime that could send the person to prison. This is why whenever Fethullah would like to give someone these publications he would first invite him for a cup of tea and have a conversation with him and he would then give it to him with extra caution to make sure that none of the devils were looking. Because of the strict ban on the *Büyük Doğu* (*The Great East*) magazine Fethullah would hide it inside the *Cumhuriyet* daily that has given full support to the ultra secular regime and would not give it to anyone except in an absolutely vacant place.

The youth put his entire self into the major battle. He stepped forward to fight in the frontline. It did not befit Fethullah but to achieve clear victory! His sparkling nature did not permit him to be in the back. He still remembers when he was just a little child in Erzurum, he would rock vigorously to the right and to the left while memorizing the texts as if he were battling someone! He would remember the intensive deviation that occurred to the nation and the rejection of religion and his soul would be inflamed and his motion would increase in force, wishing to put the entire earth under his forefinger so that he could move its events in the right direction! It was the *Epistles of Light* that balanced his flames and put the bridle on his horse of emotion which tended to strain. Without the *Epistles of Light*, his horse would have thrown itself in a fire that would have destroyed him.

The Sixth Obstacle: Police Harassment

Across the road from the mosque there was a man who used to sell watermelons and watch those who went to pray one by one. He used to throw blazing gazes at the faithful believers as if he were a devil from among the jinn. Fethullah's movement between the mosque and the café was not a secret from him; for he would record everything. At one point, there was a local election and the government at that time prevented publicity in the media. One time, the man saw Fethullah sitting in front of the café with two men. He quickly arranged a plot to arrest him. As soon as the youth returned to his window chamber he heard gunshots and terrifying noise. Suddenly, the lights in the mosque were turned on and the police invaded

the place. They looked directly towards the window. Fortunately they did not see the books and magazines beside him because
there was no light inside the window. They saw the youth sitting alone and they immediately arrested him. On the way to
the police station, one officer continued to curse and insult him.
The youth was not one to bear such insults and he would return
every insult with an equal insult and every curse with equal
cursing. The officer tried to shut him up and terrorize him but
that increased the determination of the youth. He was so angry
at the tyrants who forced him inside the police station. They
took him upstairs to an area where if a man were pushed, he
would fall right away and his skull would be broken. A secret
officer, a lame man with an ugly face and terrifying features
snuck in as if he were a snake. He provoked the youth and insulted him and the youth could not accept that so he gave him what
he got. The officer's anger intensified and he attacked the youth
physically pushing him towards the abyss at the end of the
stairs. But suddenly, the Head of Security surprised them as he
arrived at the right moment and yelled for them to stop.

This was a terrifying event in the youth's life that he would
never forget. It was like a movie and it was Allah's Clemency
that protected him from falling into this abyss. Resul Bey loved
the youth so much and he rescued him. The tyrannical officers
did not know that he was a close friend of his and that the man
used to attend Fethullah's gatherings. Nonetheless, in this critical situation Resul Bey asked him sharply, "What are you doing
here?" The youth politely answered, "These officers arrested
me on a false accusation that I was involved in political publicity but I am innocent." The head of the officers replied sharply, "So go out of here quickly." He had saved his friend while
they were unaware. The youth left seeing the shame on the
faces of the tyrannical officers while the seller of the watermel-

ons was standing behind them with his mouth wide open in disbelief!

This was the first time that Fethullah was arrested, and even though it passed peacefully he returned sad to his window and stayed there for a few days in retreat. This time it was not his intention to seclude himself from people, but he was contemplating how to wrestle with the dark spirits without letting any candle of light go out from his hand!

Yaşar Tunagür Hoja:
The Falcon of the Islamic Call Landed in Edirne

Yaşar Tunagür entered Edirne as the Mufti, or Grand Jurist, of the city. His arrival at Edirne was a great provision for Ustadh Muhammad Fethullah; for Yaşar was an employee in the Religious Affairs Department but he was a different man than all other governmental employees.

Yaşar Hoja had great experience and he was an expert in the field of inviting people to Islam and he had a marvelous ability to communicate with ordinary people. He had a deep understanding of the conditions in his era. He had a refined intelligence in how to communicate with people, and even with people in authority. His courage was rare and he became a role model for the preachers and those who confronted oppression. He had an adventurous way of opening a siege that was set around a mosque. Many faithful believers remember the story when they gather.

The Narrator of sorrows said: Yaşar's father, Shaikh Ahmed Hoja, was one of the prominent scholars. He settled in Istanbul with his family in the last period of the Ottoman Dynasty. He used to live in Bitlis in the east of Anatolia. Sultan Abdulhamid II employed him as a clerk in his bureau and he hired two of his in-laws as personal body guards. Both men were martyred in two failed coups. Thus, Yaşar's family became one of the aristocratic elite in the last era of the Sultanate.

After the abrogation of the Islamic Caliphate and after the secular Republican People's Party gained control over the country the social position of Yaşar's family changed. Yaşar continued to strive at this difficult time with deep faith, firmness and patience. Thus, in spite of the ban set against learning and teaching the Noble Qur'an and the religious sciences, Imam Yaşar never stopped doing it. He used to meet his students secretly hidden under the wing of night where he handed them the trust which was betrayed by those involved in the coup. By the end of the 1950s, Yaşar Hoja became the Grand Jurist of Balıkesir which is located next to Bursa, south of Istanbul.

The Narrator said: It was then that the military coup took place against the government of the Democratic Party. This took place exactly one month after the death of Ustadh Bediuzzaman Said Nursi in 1960. It was another great storm in Turkey's difficult history. As a result, the Prime Minister, Adnan Menderes, was executed along with two of his faithful ministers. This was because of the great service his government had offered the country and for religion such as permitting calling the adhan in the Arabic language and abrogating some of the bans that were forced upon the society. There, the good people were once again slaughtered or exiled and displaced. Turkey entered new layers of darkness one atop the other. Martial law was enforced and guarded by deadly sickles and a curfew. Guns were pointed in the streets to shoot the head that dared to get out of its house. No one dared to open a window or even to look through the door's peephole except one madman, Yaşar Tunagür. He wore the best of his clothes, opened the door wide and went out.

It was Friday but in a country placed under curfew and ruled by fear it was not like any other Friday; for any mass meeting or congregation was not allowed. All mosques were closed and a group of soldiers were watching every move in any direction that might lead to a mosque in front of Yaşar's road. When they saw him opening the door with a daring attitude and walking firmly towards them they marveled among themselves and were perplexed. One of them speculated that he could be an important man from the government. The others believed the speculation; for after all the man was walking with confidence and did not seem to be afraid of anything.

When Yaşar arrived at the house of the mosque's imam he knocked on the door, then he instructed the man to come out and he walked with him towards the mosque. They opened it by force and entered. Yaşar quickly held the microphone and started to announce the adhan which echoed loudly everywhere. When people heard it, they left their houses and went directly to the mosques in large groups. Within minutes, the minarets echoed the adhan everywhere. The soldiers were confused and did not know what to do. They started to wonder if the curfew had ended but none of them dared to shoot the people hastening to the mosque en masse or to disturb the sacred glorifications by the sound of a prize gunshot. The curfew was breeched and failed; for people returned to their ordinary activities after that.

As a result, the struggling Imam, Yaşar Hoja, was arrested and exiled to an area close to the boundaries of the Balkans to work as a jurist and a preacher in the old Selimiye Mosque in Edirne.

Because of his experience and good communication skills with all types of people he succeeded in establishing good connections with the bureaucrats in a short period of time and even with the mayor himself. He had a wide range of audiences among ordinary people as well as those who went to pray in the mosque and to listen to his Friday sermons at the Sultanate Selimiye Mosque, which has the most glorious dome in comparison to all of Turkey's mosques. He had a strange habit whenever he would go to pray the Friday Prayer; he would wear the best of his clothes and hang a sword on his left shoulder referring to Edirne which was a trench of the struggling trenches on the western boundaries. Yaşar was the man who returned dignity in the eyes of the public and the elite alike to the Religious Affairs Department in Edirne. Thus, its employees were energized and became active.

Yaşar was a faithful believer who strove for the cause of Allah. As soon as he met Fethullah and observed his condition of living in the window chamber, he loved him and embraced him. He would argue in his defense with the high officials in the district. He succeeded in getting him acquitted of many accusations. He had a highly intelligent way that would take people by surprise. One day, he was asked by the governor about his opinion of the Imam of the Üç Şerefeli Mosque in the presence of a man called Rakım who used to be one of those who liked to speak bad of Fethullah and get him in trouble by suggesting to the authority that Fethullah was a dangerous man. Yaşar naturally answered, "Imam Fethullah is a fine example of a virtuous man with lofty ethics, but sir, how can you ask me when there is a man more qualified than me to ask. Rakım is here and he knows better than me how sincere and honest that youth is and that he has a noble character." Rakım could not say a word. How could a lowly spy like him lie in front of the Grand Jurist of the city, especially if this Jurist was a revered man like Yaşar Hoja?

Thus, Rakım was obliged to agree with the Grand Jurist and praise Fethullah while his heart was full of envy and anger. That day was a day of triumph for Fethullah; for he gained the admiration of the governor. Thus, he was free to preach, teach and establish personal ties with people.

His relationship with Ustadh Yaşar was strengthened and he used to consult him concerning everything he did. Thus, he gained a lot from his wisdom and experience. When the news of the execution of the Prime Minister Adnan Menderes was announced, Fethullah's soul entered a stage of continuous agitation and this state lasted for a few months. It was very difficult for him to tolerate the great oppression that took the life of Menderes and his companions. He suffered great anguish from this terrifying event and he started to tell himself that he must respond in one way or another, even in ways that might be contrary to the doctrine of the school of Light which he embraced. When he informed Ustadh Yaşar how he felt, consulting him about what to do, Yaşar calmed his anger with his wisdom. Fethullah was convinced by his logic and never doubted his sincerity, or his honest advice. This is because Ustadh Yaşar did not lack courage or boldness; for he was a spiritual leader who would sacrifice himself to redeem his country and religion. Thus, his advice had an effect on the youth like that of cold water on a flame of fire!

The Seventh Obstacle: The Last Incentive

A great affliction fell upon Fethullah when he was appointed to be the Spiritual cleric of those on death row. This job made him live and witness that which he never imagined. He lived the experience of watching people executed while he was not yet twenty years old. This experience left a great spiritual effect upon him that helped him to cut his ties with dust and to live flying in the spiritual ascent forever!

In the first year of being the Imam at the Üç Şerefeli Mosque a man came to him and told him in a rough tone that the judge, Gani Bey, wanted him. The youth remembered that he had met this judge once in one of the gatherings and he gave him some of his books and the judge seemed suspicious of Fethullah's preaching. Thus, worries overtook Fethullah as he wondered what would have prompted the judge to request meeting him. When he appeared in front of him, the judge said, "Fethullah, we have a criminal who was sentenced to death and we would like to have a spiritual cleric to counsel him at the time of execution and we have appointed you to perform this duty."

Fethullah is a very sensitive and emotional man to the extent that his heart would explode out of empathy and feelings for others. But when the judge firmly told him that he was chosen for the job, he accepted it without thinking, especially because he felt relieved from the other worries he had.

At that time, executions used to be done in public squares so people could see them and crime would be deterred. Thus, after the Afternoon Prayer, (*Salat al-'Asr*), the court van stopped in front of the mosque door and the Imam was called. He came out and rode with them.

Fethullah was informed that the man who was sentenced to death was a dangerous criminal whose name was Rasim Dik. When they entered the prison cell the youth looked at him and saw that his hands were chained. He was a strong and angry man and that was why people assumed that he would attack whoever approached him. The list of his crimes was long and one of his crimes was that he had robbed a house of someone who they thought was rich. They killed the owner and his wife. When the criminal heard the barking dog, he split the head of the dog with his axe. When they found the money box they found three hundred liras only! The bitter fact was that the man they had killed was a poor man whose work was polishing copper vessels in return for a few coins.

When the criminal read in the newspaper that the parliament signed his death sentence he lost his mind and started hallucinating. The young Imam tried to urge him to repeat some supplications but all his efforts went in vain. The man kept repeating, "Ataturk will come and we are going to go home together!"

After a while some guards came and dressed him in a white garment and they hung around his neck a paper that had the horrible crimes he had committed. The gallows was set in the square across from the mosque. Fethullah looked at the people who were crowded in the street and none seemed to care. To them, the scene resembled a market place or a carnival. Some sellers were selling pistachios and walnuts to the audience while others were selling drinks as if no execution was about to take place. Hearts had hardened from a long time ago, except for the Muezzin Ibrahim Efendi's heart. He used to teach the Qur'an in the Kuşcudoğan Mosque. He was in his fifties and he was the only one whom Fethullah had noticed with a sad expression on his face. It was as if he were the one to be hung on the gallows. He was deeply troubled by having to watch someone being executed, so much so that he could not pass by that square for a few days after the execution had taken place.

Fethullah made the last plea, urging the man to declare the Oneness of Allah but all his efforts went in vain. A policeman then took him straight to the gallows. The Judge, Gani Bey, approached the criminal and asked him, "Do you have a last request?" He answered, "Ataturk is coming and we will go together to the house." The Judge stepped back and the executioner directed the man towards the *qibla*. He put the rope around his neck and executed the man immediately. The man's tongue hung from his mouth. The corpse immediately blackened in a terrifying way and turned facing the opposite direction of the *qibla*. The executioner and the officers backed away from it, leaving it hanging on the gallows until the next day so that it would be a lesson of deterrence. The young Imam did not know where they took it and where they buried it.

He noticed that none of the city's inhabitants took the deterrent lesson seriously nor did they seem to be effected by the terrifying scene. As for Fethullah, he witnessed the scene minute by minute and to him this experience was a deterrent lesson and what a deterrent! Whenever he looked at the man he would know that he would die in an hour, then in half an hour, then in fifteen minutes, then in a few minutes, then in a few seconds. Then, he witnessed his breath being stopped forever! Witnessing this tragedy progressing to its pinnacle was so different from hearing or reading about it in a newspaper; for being informed is totally different from an existential experience. Therefore, this event remained in his heart as a funeral which he would never forget! It made him fully aware of man's terror of death which he would experience without doubt. Thus, Fethullah never became heedless of realizing the human's incapacity to stop destiny.

As he was watching the rope around the man's neck, he saw, through his spiritual eyes, the same rope hung around all the necks of all those who were witnessing the execution and how for each of them there would come a day when their breath would be cut. As the poet said, "Whoever does not die by the sword will die by something else. Causes may differ but death is one."

How many a judge had delivered the verdict to execute tens of people justly or unjustly but one day, the judge's neck would also be hung on the gallows and he would taste the same death he decreed on others many times: *"Indeed, Allah enforces His own Verdict but most people do not know"* (Surah Yusuf 12:21).

Fethullah dreaded that he would be known in the city as the spiritual cleric for those who were waiting on death row and that his efforts would be hindered negatively because of this reputation. His worries increased when he was called one more time to counsel another man who was to be executed. His burden was lightened when a new law, which prevented executing criminals publically, was issued.

The name of the man to be executed was Mehmed but he was simply called as Memo in short. The official physician appointed for the duty was a man originally from the Balkans from the city of Sophia. Fethullah sat in the backyard of the court and in front of him sat the judge, the General Attorney and the Chief of the military police. When the official physician arrived, he foolishly asked, "Is there a priest here?" even though he saw Fethullah wearing the Imam's traditional attire. The Imam felt a stab in his heart but he kept his pain within and did not show any emotion in front of them. Then, they all went to the prison.

Fethullah looked at the defendant with his luminous insight, and to him the young man appeared to be pure and his eyes appeared innocent. The young Imam was not convinced that the man was a murderer. When the defendant saw the judge and the two other men, his legs started to shake violently and he collapsed on the ground. One of them helped him to sit on a couch and the Imam approached him saying, "Oh Mehmed, such is Allah's decree! The parliament approved your death sentence. There is no escape from the Divine decree, so let your death be for Allah's sake if Allah so wills. Oh Mehmed! Put your trust in Allah! Do not turn your attention to anyone or to anything else except Him; for all roads, except the Path towards Him, are blocked." He then asked him with tender mercy, "Would you like to perform ablution?" The man said, "Yes." The poor man started to perform the ablution until he started to wash his feet and then he collapsed and could not finish the ablution.

Fethullah's heart was burned by watching this horrifying scene that was engraved in his memory and he would remember it for the rest of his life. He immediately started to urge the man to profess the *shahada* and say, "I believe in Allah, His Angels, His Books, etc." The man tried to repeat the words but they would stop in his throat as if the words were rapidly disappearing from his memory. Then, he started to repeat, "Please, send me to the hospital again."

Fethullah thought of what the poor defendant was asking and wondered within himself, what the benefit of sending him to the hospital would be. His execution could be postponed just for a short period of time and he would live for one or two weeks more. Such thoughts made Fethullah realize the preciousness of life and how it would be a great loss to waste its countable days in vain. He lived these moments of spiritual realization in pain that was tearing down the core of his being as if he were the one sentenced to death and not that young man. He really imagined that he would be executed in a few moments!

Thus, in spite of the years that have passed since that sad event took place, Fethullah still feels it as an open wound whenever he remembers it. His empathetic wing was lowered with immense tenderness towards the defendant, Mehmed. It was claimed that he had killed a shepherd and that was the only accusation that was hung around his neck before the execution. Fethullah did not see the traits of a criminal in his face.

The executioner was drunk to the extent that he could not stand straight and when he tried to approach the accused to execute the verdict he fell on the floor. At this moment, the physician jumped up and performed the executioner's role. Mehmed was looking to the people around him with eyes full of terror and sadness which tore down the core being of Fethullah as if Mehmed's gazes were arrows piercing through his skin one after another!

When the physician hung the rope around Mehmed's neck and was about to move the chair to execute the verdict, Mehmed seemed to move his legs to help him do it quicker. His body seemed to shake a couple of times then he passed away. The physician was a strange man. He performed the execution process as if it were a lesson he had learned in the college of medicine! He hung the rope around the defendant with mastery and he quickly fastened it and pushed the chair away with one kick of his foot in conformity with the rules of execution! How strange! What type of a physician was he?

The Eighth Obstacle:
Doubts on the Fire of Purification

The intellects of the genius follow them! On the other side, there are minds that lead their possessors to ruin! The speed by which thoughts flow and the power by which it can fold distance and space enable the intellect to stop at the threshold of the impossible! There, the affliction of the mind is intensified and the intellectual suffering is ignited! Nonetheless, the genius refuses to stop and the steps collapse as one tries to cross the ocean of the impossible! Whoever tried to cross the ocean of the impossible was drowned in the dungeons of madness or repulsed by wrathful waves that struck and pushed him forcibly to the shore's rocks which break his ribs. He then remembers that he is no more than a drop of water in a jar of mud! How can the drop ever comprehend the ocean's kingdom with its hidden treasures?

Doubt is the curse of the proud hardened minds. Their skulls get crushed under the hammer of insinuations until they are totally ruined! As for the faithful believers who are navigating their way towards Allah there is their share from the portions of mercy and it is lightning that strikes them to realize the gift they have. It is the nectar of the beating heart of the devotee which motivates him to walk in accordance with His Beloved's compass!

After mastering the ancient sciences, Fethullah's mind opened to explore philosophy and literature books and he emerged into a new adventure. He continued to accompany the philosophers and the pundits in his retreats, crossing stages of history and folding time at a rapid speed! He would examine the face of each philosopher under the light of his small candle, listening to the lesson of a scholar or discussing a philosopher's theory until his intellectual storage contained what is equivalent to a large library full of books on every inch of its shelves and corners.

Through his journey of navigating books he continued to ascend the stations of knowing life, knowing the human being and knowing the universe. This expanded his horizon of knowledge to the extent that he was able to refute many philosophical speculations and rebut their false sophistry.

His philosophical navigation was not paved and it was full of thorns. Why would it not be full of thorns if the devotee is jealous for his Beloved? Lightning had struck his spiritual ascent and his tracks went in violent commotion. However, the navigator of the way towards the Truly Real continued to steady his feet for months out of fear that he might fall until the clouds rained drops of peace and then his pain was soothed!

As soon as the young Imam finished reading one of the philosophical books by one of the Turkish writers he felt his heart beating rapidly within his chest and about to jump out! This was because the book had adopted the Darwin perspective concerning the existence of the human being. Its author was talented in a way that would make the reader drink the contents of the book dose after dose until its end. By the end of the book, the reader finds his heart drunk by its intoxication which awakens within him the insinuation of doubts.

Thus, Fethullah entered into a bitter battle with the Devil, but this time it was not through spiritual navigation but through intellectual argumentation and logical evidence which comes in the form of consecutive questioning, where each question does not give birth but to another question!

The influence of Darwin's theory in this era was very intense and many young people and thinkers had fallen prey to its argument. The currents of atheism confused them and they could not find a way out. Some of the Muslim scholars even tried to argue that it had roots in the Qur'an and the Sunnah. The youth suffered tremendously from these currents. This was the first intellectual commotion and the second earthquake came during his service in the military in the city of Iskenderun in the southern part of Anatolia near the Syrian border. There, the books of philosophy accompanied him for some time and caused him to inherit deadly insinuations and perplexing questions concerning the concerns of Lordship. In any case, the intellectual commotion he experienced weather in Edirne or in Iskenderun did not shake the roots of faith within him, which remained deeply rooted in spite of his intellectual suffering.

Thus, he kept praying, performing the practice of *dhikr*, or remembrance of Allah, and invoking his supplications.

The Devil used many tricks to cause his suffering! Whenever he would announce the first glorification to pray, the accursed one would come to him from all directions, throwing within him a series of insinuations to the extent that he would think to leave the Prayer in quest of being saved from his intellectual suffering and spiritual pain. His affliction intensified to the extent that he once thought to strike himself with an electric current so that he could completely cut his connection with the entire past!

Fethullah did not give up nor lose hope but he continued to drown himself in supplications, begging Allah until mercy was disclosed to him with the light of tranquility and the beauty of contentment and only then was the cloud lifted and the young man came out of the battle victorious by the leave of Allah. He saw the Devil falling thunderstruck on the ground wallowing in the dust, lamenting his horrible defeat.

Out of this trial, the young man received a strong vaccine that immunized him with a certitude which continued to feed him his whole life! Whenever the Devil would try to awaken his doubts he found his roots burnt! Fethullah would then laugh at him saying, "Do not tire yourself oh accursed one; for I have closed these doors in your face forever." Thus, the accursed would leave him disappointed and defeated.

The great victory which Fethullah achieved in these psychological trials gave him abundance of bounties. In addition to the firmly established faith in the intellectual realm and the certitude that came from witnessing in the spiritual realm, Allah gave him an extra prize in return for the struggles he endured and the patience he held. The prize was knowledge of the atheistic philosophy and its many internal contradictions. He gained experience in how to rebut and refute its confused concepts. Later, he came to be known as one of the most knowledgeable scholars of this philosophy. His experience produced much fruit in the form of several books and epistles that refuted the incoherence, the unfounded speculations and the illusory thinking. In this way he warned the coming generation from surrendering to its misleading ideas. He established for the youth a precious foundation in how to treat doubts and not to indulge deeply in its insinuations. This foundation was based on experience and was the result of practical scientific methodology.

This shows that doubtful insinuations must be buried in a grave while they are in their infancy and they should not be given the chance to grow and thrive or they would become a disease like an obsessive-compulsive disorder. The faithful believer must gain an intuitive vaccine against them and must bury them while they are still a passing ghost!

After he survived this experience, Fethullah realized that faith in reality is a gift from Allah that He bestows upon the person and that the human being is unable to earn it through either his intellectual or spiritual efforts, and the person who has faith is also not capable of maintaining it by himself. Allah made available for humanity the intellectual way and the spiritual path as initial steps. Whoever knocks on these doors while being in a state of poverty and need for Allah, the doors open for him. Otherwise, he becomes one of the deprived. Such gifts Allah does not bestow except on those whom He loves! Fethullah witnessed his incapacity and poverty existentially. He found out that his spiritual practices and inner struggles and all the knowledge he gained had evaporated and could not help him push away doubts. Thus, he realized the deep meaning of the truth, "There is no refuge from Allah but in Him" and that, "The heart that Allah does not steady, there is no steadiness for it with anything else." He found out that his salvation was in crying out to Allah, in weeping to Him and in begging Him.

The Ninth Obstacle:
Following the Way of Celibate Scholars

If marriage is destined so is celibacy and even though marriage is not one of the religious obligations it is the natural way which Allah created for His servants and it is the way of our Prophet Muhammad, upon him be peace and blessings. Some scholars claimed that living a celibate life is permitted for the sake of attaining self-perfection. In doing so they did not follow the way of the Noble Prophet and lived a monastic life that Allah did not prescribe for them. Nonetheless, many of the prominent scholars from among the Muslim communities did not marry and they were widely respected and given the title, "The Celibate Scholars."

The purpose and motives behind actions play a role in judging the actions. These scholars were the scholars at the time of hardship and persecution. Most of them preferred celibacy because of the difficult lives they had and due to the mission they had to carry. Time passed and the nation became in desperate need to rebuild the pillars of the sciences and some scholars dedicated their lives for this purpose. They would spend their nights writing and reviewing the ancient reference works. They tired their feet in long trips after their quest. They took risks and endangered themselves by crossing deserts and wastelands in order to collect the precious heritage of the nation and preserve it. Their lives were consumed in this struggle so they had no time for marriage and it was simply not their fate. In this way, many prominent scholars were celibates such as the

Grand Shaikh of the Qur'an commentators Abu Ja'far at-Tabari, Imam az-Zamakhshari, and Imam an-Nawawi.

The time of the affliction came and during this time Imam ibn Taymiyya led a celibate life even though he was a strict Hanbali jurist. His celibacy was forced upon him by the circumstances he found himself in. How could he have married in the darkness of the prisons he was thrown in? How could he have married while he was in exile? There was no spare time in his life to have a comfortable house. How could Bediuzzaman have married at the time of gallows and burning ovens? His destiny was to live lonely and exiled and homeless on top of the mountains. The martyr, Ustadh Sayyid Qutb, is another example of a scholar who lived a celibate life. He refused to allow the tyrants a single drop of weakness that they could use against him, even though he was a sensitive poet full of emotions. He did not want to give them a way to twist his arm. How could he have married a wife that could have been assaulted by the tyrants to make him surrender to them? How could he have brought daughters whose innocence could have been kidnapped by the beasts? He chose to face them alone bare chested, confronting them with flaming words until he was martyred.

From the beginning Fethullah did not think at all of leading a celibate life but he did not busy himself with thinking about it either. When his mother's cousin, Huseyin Top opened the subject with him, he was hesitant but then he shyly accepted the idea. So, Huseyin Top Hoja mentioned to him one of the rich families in Edirne who was known for their piousness and informed him that the father expressed his desire to wed his daughter to Fethullah.

When both men went to propose to the family, it was Eid day. When they entered the house and sat on the couch, Fethullah was sweating out of his shyness. He sat there lowering his head and could not lift his head to look around the room until they left! He did not remember seeing anything around him at all. He was shocked later to know that he had been rejected. There was an apology that the rumor about the father's desire was not true or was a misunderstanding from his uncle's side.

Thus, the young man turned his thoughts and emotions away from the idea of marrying. It was not the result of the rejection but it was the result of a contemplation that was growing within his mind little by little. He started to think about his difficult life and the condition of his time and people. That led him to decide to give up the idea of having a wife. He decided to dedicate his whole life to serve the religion and to invite people to Islam. From that moment on, that became the answer he gave to anyone who suggested marriage to him.

When he returned to Erzurum after finishing his military service, his whole family surrounded him: his father, his mother, his uncle and his older sister and they all argued that marriage was a necessary step. None of them was able to shake his firm position. His mother told him a popular Turkish saying, "My son, we need to tie your head while we are still alive." He answered her, "Mother, my feet are tied by the call to faith and in service of Islam. If you would tie my head as well, how would I be able to move?" The family's sorrow was intense; for their love for Fethullah was like a green tree with roots deeply established within their hearts. At the end of the conversation, his uncle told him, "Fethullah, contemplate the issue further. We are not going to insist on you marrying while you are only twenty-two years old, but you should expect that we will try to convince you again when you are thirty. After that we will never bother you about it again for the rest of your life."

His uncle kept his word; when Fethullah was thirty years old and he lived in Izmir, Ustadh Yaşar Hoja visited him and suggested marriage to a lady whom he had chosen for him. When he informed him that he was not thinking of marriage at all, Yaşar Hoja tried hard to convince him. He found himself in a position where he had to be strong and firm in rejecting his teacher's suggestion and to do so in a gentle and polite way at the same time. He held his position to lead a celibate life until Ustadh Yaşar left him feeling really sad. His last words for him were, "If you will not listen to me, then to whom will you listen?" His eyes watered and both of them wept.

At that point, Fethullah remembered his uncle's words and he knew that this would be a last chance for him to get married but again he contemplated the condition of his time and people and chose to live a celibate life; for great affliction was taking place in Anatolia. The gates of dark prisons were opened ready to swallow those in quest of the Light and those who were inviting people to Allah! Fethullah preferred not to disturb a woman's life with a marriage where she would not find any tranquility, where she might experience her husband getting snatched from her and her children becoming hungry and terrified from the persecutions and harassments of the police when they knocked on the door in the middle of the night or when they broke in with gunshots. Although Fethullah was a fearless lion in facing the enemies, he was very gentle, affectionate and compassionate towards those whom he loved.

The man entered the trial of celibacy! Indeed, for a strong man like him who was full of vigor and energy, celibacy was a hard trial. When he was forty the thought crossed his mind once while he was washing his clothes and house duties were burdening him. He said to himself, "Would not it have been better for me if I had gotten married?" But the next day, a friend visited him in the morning and said to him, "I saw the Messenger of Allah, upon him be peace and blessings, yesterday in a dream and he told me something about you. He sent his greeting of peace to you and said, 'Tell Fethullah that he will die on the day he gets married and I will not attend his funeral.'" Fethullah was not one of those who believed that one should base his religious affairs or life's essential decisions on dreams but this vision was clear and it was in conformity with what he had chosen to do. Thus, it cleared his doubts and encouraged him to safely cross the Path.

It became even clearer to him later that had he gotten married he would have truly died; for his life was about a great cause and it was a life of devoted service and upon his shoulders the faithful believers built their schools and dormitories all over Anatolia and atop the emerald dome they built their cultural dialogue and retreat centers and tents. He became the leader and guide of their children and wives. Had he gotten married everything that took place would have been ruined and if one window was broken, he would have collapsed and died!

Such were the nine obstacles that Fethullah had to overcome, or rather his journey of nine ascending pathways to be crossed, in the city of Edirne. He left Edirne safe from its fire by Allah's leave. Thus, in his life it was only a preparatory school that qualified him spiritually to enter the fire storms in the midst of the smoke. He was in need of this preparation, these spiritual, physical and psychological earthquakes which enabled him to lead the battle of deliverance!

When he was struggling in his third year in Edirne he received the order for the obligatory military service from the highest military counsel in Ankara. There, in his window chamber he sat for a few minutes thinking of the bitter displacement he had experienced on his path and the never-ending road of his emigration. There was nothing more difficult for him than saying farewell to his favorite mosque with its elegant three balconied minaret and leaving his friends and the gatherings he used to hold to invite people to Allah which was his spiritual ascent in Edirne. Everything has its term. Thus Fethullah realized that the summoning for military service was Divine Permission for him to enter a new experience and to overcome another obstacle on the Path and become qualified for the station that requires the greatest permission of all!

Fethullah left Edirne carrying his small suitcase without any of his family discovering its secret! He left Edirne as a concealed treasure just as he entered it; for the time of revealing the secret had not yet come!

Fethullah had a secret that the whole world was waiting for but he could not reveal it to anyone! Fethullah carried within his heart what it could not contain and that was why he still wept until tears were perplexed at its funeral! Fethullah inherited a secret which if the highest mountain inherited, the rocks at its top would fall and the mountain's foundations would crumble out of awe!

Chapter 5
Enduring the Mandatory Military Service

Farewell to the Spectra of Love

*B*eing enlisted in military service during the time of confusion meant diving into the depth of a rotten pot! Fethullah was not afraid of anyone except Allah. If anything was worrying him at that time, it was rather how he would be able to preserve his secret in the military camp. His deep faith quickly dispelled all worries away and calmed the ocean of his thoughts; for indeed Allah would not forsake a servant, but keep and preserve his secret!

The young man left the window chamber alone and continued to walk alone on the Path of his everlasting migration! He carried his limited luggage with him and walked with firm steps towards the train station. His destination was Ankara; there he was supposed to submit himself for the mandatory military service. As he was standing there waiting for the train to arrive, he saw a group of prominent scholars in Edirne led by the Grand Jurist Yaşar Tunagür coming to say farewell. Among them was his uncle, Huseyin Top, and Imam Salim Arıcı who served at the Üç Şerefi Mosque with him. He used to deliver the *khutba*s every Friday and Fethullah used to lead the Daily Prayers. Imam Salim was not comfortable having the young man in his mosque because of how he exceeded him in knowledge and how he was more eloquent in speech. He was worried that the young man would someday take his position or compete with him in some way and that is why he never granted the young man his request to deliver any Friday sermon instead of him. But it seemed that he regretted this decision when he observed how the people in Edirne loved Fethullah. When he became assured that the young man was sincere in serving the religion and that he did not have any desire for the lower realm and its pleasures he came to pay him farewell. He carried with him come biscuits and deserts wrapped in a large handkerchief. When he embraced the young man to say farewell, he gave the gift to him saying, "When you finish the military service, return to Edirne so that we can work together." Fethullah rejoiced in the gentleness and affection he found in his friend towards him because it was not usual and he accepted his unexpected gift! He kept the handkerchief for many years!

When the Grand Jurist, Yaşar Hoja, embraced the young man to say farewell he could not hold himself and in spite of his high revered status he could not hold back his tears. He knew what type of man Edirne was losing that day! The truth is that Yaşar loved the promising young man and saw in him, a successor to himself!

Fethullah left Edirne in tears and with a sad heart. Once the train moved he felt a sense of loss for the things he held dear in his heart: the familiar window, the favorite ancient mosque, the café in which he invited people to Allah, the secret gatherings with the students, and the love of ordinary and special people. All of it was turning to a memory of the heart but a few minutes ago it was a visible life he lived! How cruel the nature of this world! There is no pleasure in it, but disturbances from separation!

In Ankara, before he surrendered to the military life, he sought his close friend, Salih Özcan. He used to visit him all five days he was there. To him he was a source of solace and provided him good company as he was preparing himself to enter into a strange realm and a new experience in his life which would be utterly different from his previous life and from what he was raised in and used to, especially at this challenging historical time!

The Captive

To graduate from the military of Mehmed the Conqueror and be involved in a different path means that the earth had lost its balance and that time had turned upside down and that the sun was rising from the west! There was no way for a cavalier who was coming from the time of Light to the era of darkness to be except a conqueror, a martyr, a captive or all of these together!

Fethullah was traveling in time in accordance to the secrets of Light he received! Since he received the *Epistles* of Bediuzzaman, he had enrolled in the "army" of Mehmed the Conqueror. Every night, he would go to the tents of Mehmed's camp and he would train the cavaliers in how to cross the ocean secretly. He taught them how to draw the maps for the coming conquest. He would then return with the rise of true dawn in order to lead the people in Prayer inside his niche.

Fethullah owns a map for the conquest of Rumiyya and how to invade the darkness! He has a plan of how to besiege Gog and Magog. He, alone, knows how to unsheathe the swords of glowing lightning from the scabbard of the angry cloud! He knows how to align the horses following the front lines. He knows how to regulate the heartbeat to the tone of its drivers! He, alone, knows how to prepare the sun's chandeliers well and how to send its rays to the whole world!

Fethullah has been polishing the mirrors with the tears of the dark night and each day he shows them to the youth who have lost their heritage! These youth are as lambs but he shows them their image in an existential experience that reminds them of their lineage from lions!

Fethullah is a shadow of the Substitutes in time (al-Abdal).[14] Who is able to know the secret of his technique? Who is able to see the spirit's waves flowing upon the shores of his chest? Who is able to see the sun rise within his eyes and by which he can see what others cannot see and then he illustrates its features for people?

Today, Fethullah is a cavalier enrolled in the "army" of Light and his rank is that of the highest leader! To the spiritual cavaliers, he is the best prince and what a prince! Nevertheless, he was led to a path in which he was held captive! All the niches and the platforms in Turkey's mosques wept out of sorrow! Fethullah remained in captivity longing for the conquest and hoping for a triumph soon. He embraced his secrets within his heart only and none knew what he was hiding for a day of severity!

---

[14] *Abdal* (plural of *badal*) the name given to a group of the highest ranking saints. The term is used to describe the "men of the Unseen" who have certain degrees of knowledge of Allah, who are supported by Allah, and who, with their refined hearts and purified souls, are open to Divine mysteries. According to Prophetic tradition, each time one of them dies he is replaced by another. (Ed.)

The District of Mamak:
The Factory of Military Coups

The Narrator of sorrows told me: In November 1961, Fethullah was enrolled in the military service and he was appointed
to one of the major military barracks in the district of Mamak in
Ankara. Mamak is a terrifying name in the Turkish military. It
was a large district that contained many military barracks and
schools which accommodated thousands of soldiers and military officers. It also contained countless weapons arsenals and
different types of ammunition. Mamak had a determinate historical role in most of the military coups that occurred in Turkey.

Mehmed Mutlu was a military member with the rank of
lieutenant. He was one of the young Imam's devotees. He was
also an old friend of Yılmaz Bey, the company commander of
the barracks that Fethullah stayed in. He gave a good recom-
mendation of Fethullah to Yılmaz. The young man also carried
a greeting of peace accompanied with a box of sweet almonds
from one of his relatives to another commander in the same
barracks. All of these were indications that he should have a
peaceful time and Fethullah received such assurance as he
enrolled in the army that was not like any other army! The
young man started his military training with his new fellows and
learned many techniques of fighting.

One day, the company commander, Yılmaz Bey, called him
and asked him, "Are you the Imam?" Fethullah answered, "Yes".
Yılmaz Bey said, "My wife is sick. Can you recite for her something that may cure her?" The Imam answered, "Sir, I am very
sorry but I am not a master in doing such things. If you believe
that a recitation upon her would cure her then read it for her
yourself. That would be better than my recitation." The commander admired his wise answer and appreciated him. Later,

he discovered that Yılmaz Bey was just testing him. Thus, he became responsible for the wireless radio. He stayed in the barracks for four additional months to finish his training on using the wireless instruments.

In spite of all the special care he received, Fethullah still suffered a great deal in the barracks of Ankara. On the spiritual level, he had the feeling that he was not performing his military service in the true meaning of the word. Thus, he believed that the military food was not rightful for him and even the military uniform, which was given to all soldiers for free. He did not wear it. Instead, he bought other older military clothes from retired soldiers. That year there was an abundance of snow in Ankara. On its white surface, the young man received his training. Many times, he was charged to guard the barracks and would stand behind the barbed wire in the middle of the wilderness in the deep snow. He would stay there for as long as eight consecutive hours. Most of the time, it would be snowing and extremely cold. This took place during the month of Ramadan but a man like Fethullah would never abandon his Prayer or fasting even though he would not find an opportunity to break his fast or to eat the pre-dawn meal. He would put some crackers in his pocket and eat them to break his fast and for his meal before dawn. A meeting sometimes coincided with sunset so the young man would carefully watch his commander and as soon as the commander's attention would turn away he would quickly throw a little bite in his mouth.

The bedrooms there were very cold; the novice soldiers were initially given only one blanket to use; half of it to lie on and half to cover themselves with. Most of them used to sleep with their shoes on all through the winter season so they could protect their feet from freezing.

When the soldiers were led to the baths to shower, Fethullah would not shower there, he would only wet his hair to give the impression to the commanders that he had just taken a shower. This was because most of the soldiers would not hide their naked bodies and did not have any etiquette concerning modesty. So the young man had to return to his old habit in Erzurum. Whenever he wanted to shower he would go to the restroom and would pour cold water on himself and as he did so his feet would get stuck in the frozen water underneath him.

Life in the military environment was impure and had so many trials and afflictions that none could escape their corruption and power. However, Allah protected the young man and supported him. One day there was a general medical exam. The soldiers were ordered to be naked for the exam. When Fethullah's turn came, the military physician told him, "Take off your pants." The young man responded, "Sir, since I became aware none have looked at my body from the knee up, even my mother who gave birth to me." The physician looked him in the eye and quickly said, "Go." This was a marvelous extraordinary gift which saved the young man from something he hated without being accused of military disobedience and facing its consequences even though such types of actions were considered a violation that warranted punishment, especially at that difficult time in Turkey's history.

A Military Coup

The Narrator said: After one month or a little longer after starting his service in the military, the young man found himself facing a difficult test and a horrifying experience. In December 1961, a great rebellion took place in many military schools and barracks and without realizing it, the young man found himself to be one of the rebels!

Talat Aydemir was one of those who participated in the coup of May 1960 against the government of Adnan Menderes. In fact, he had a determinate role in making the coup successful. At that time, he was the commander of the War Academy and it was his students who rushed in the streets of Ankara with other military students. They occupied the official radio station and they enforced a curfew until they secured success for the coup. However, the leaders of the coup disputed among themselves concerning the type of government that should rule and who should rule. The majority of the leaders believed that the government should be handed to İsmet İnönü, the president of the leftist Republican People's Party and wanted to execute the Democratic Party government's head, Adnan Menderes, and his group. Others believed that they should hold the government and establish a military government. Among the latter group was Talat Aydemir and others. The former group enforced their opinion so that Allah would have an action taken that had to be done! The government was then handed over to the leftist Republican People's Party and the members of the Democratic Party government were executed on a small island in the middle of the Marmara Sea!

Then all the officers who objected were exiled in the form of sending them as military representatives in Turkey's embassies abroad. However, the leader, Talat Aydemir, was acquitted and was not exiled. He continued to hide his grudge for a while until a year after the coup of 1960. The man then decided to lead another coup against his fellows!

In fact, Talat Aydemir was a dangerous man who had a terrifying anti-Islamic inclination! His circle of friends and supporters were exactly like him. They were all tyrants and transgressors. Their war against religion and its adherents was fierce and cruel. None of them knew any gentleness except one officer by the name of Alparslan Türkeş, who was more of a nationalist. He objected to the execution of the members of the government and for that he was exiled to New Delhi. When comparing these officers with each other one would reach only one conclusion: between the porcupines there was not a soft one!

In 1961, Talat Aydemir became the highest officer responsible for the Mamak military district. All of its officers, schools and barracks came under his leadership. Under his command was about fifteen thousand soldiers and officers. He led the coup with all of them and Fethullah found himself all of a sudden in a dangerous moment in the midst of a rebellious military!

A month before the military coup, the preparation stage had begun. The soldiers were given real ammunition and weapons and they were trained for real fighting.

The night before the coup, the barracks were in great agitation and in a state of alert. Armed military teams went ahead and occupied the official radio station at night. As soon as the news of the coup reached the officers who supported the government, they rushed to act and a major fight took place between the two armies. The building of the radio station became like a swing. At one point, the officers of the coup had power over it and would start to broadcast news of the fall of İsmet İnönü's government and the success of the coup and at another point, the government army would gain the upper hand and broadcast the news of the coup's failure and that the rebels were utterly defeated! Some brigades were with the government as well as the air force but the soldiers at Mamak barracks had no knowledge of all of this. They were executing the commands of their leaders thinking that the entire military was involved in this coup. The planes of the air force started to circle above their heads moving from one barracks to another in a ready state to fight. The leaders inside the barracks then understood that the air force was threatening to destroy the whole Mamak district, erasing it from the face of the earth! Thus, they found no choice but for all of their soldiers to surrender to the other army.

It was a terrifying night the like of which Fethullah had never experienced before! As soon as the morning arrived, high ranking officers entered Fethullah's barracks. They summoned everyone and asked the soldiers to remove the firing mechanisms from their weapons and to give them to them. The soldiers carried out the orders immediately. Nothing remained in their hands except hollow iron tubes. Later, the leaders ordered the soldiers not to leave the barracks for two months and not to participate in any military training or missions and they later kept them busy with basic training and communication devices. Because of this, the soldiers found themselves having plenty of spare time. Fethullah took this precious chance and entered a new spiritual cycle. He would retreat into the barracks' mosque and devote himself to spiritual practices on the long winter nights, intimately invoking his Lord until he felt that his spiritual life was completely rejuvenated.

One day, the officers summoned everyone again and they told the soldiers, "We have good news for all of you." The soldiers were all ears for the good news. When they were informed that their weapons would be returned to them they were shocked! This was not good news for them. Besides having to clean them daily, they felt that weapons were a bad omen in the hands of soldiers whose fate is in the hands of officers of the coup!

New Mission

The Narrator sighed and looked at the far horizon and said: In the military picking up telegraph signals was not something anyone could master. But Fethullah had a story about it! His knowledge of deciphering spiritual signals had allowed him in the military to master deciphering telegraph signals in a way that impressed his commanders and perplexed them! But to him, deciphering the audio signals was minor compared to deciphering the code of Light from spiritual signals! It is not strange that lightning precedes thunder in unveiling the secrets of heaven; for only the seer can read the signals of sparks in the time of rebellion!

The Narrator of sorrows said: After four months of general training, the soldier Fethullah was appointed a post in the Department of Emergency Communication after he succeeded in the test. Then, he was enrolled in another four month training program. He learned how to type on a typewriter. He also learned how to tap out a message by telegraph. He reached an advanced level in his training and was considered quite skillful. He was faster than the soldiers who did similar jobs in mail offices before they joined the military. He was the fastest among them in receiving the signals and decoding them into the spoken language. He was relatively slow in typing but he was quick in picking up the signals and decoding them without missing anything at all. This was due to his high intellect, the fact that he did not get bored or tired, and also due to his sharp memory of sounds. This allowed him to decode the signals in a precise and accurate way so that he was eventually able to write five hundred letters in three minutes. Why not when Fethullah was skilled in reading the signals of the Unseen and he was quick in decoding their spiritual meaning? How could he have been slow in reading something easier than that, like the clicks which are transferred through the realm of the senses?

It is true that sending coded signals is very essential and important in the military but receiving coded messages and decoding them quickly is even more important. This is because missing one sound means missing all the news or changing its meaning or giving the opposite meaning. In the military, a mistake in receiving a code or decoding it can lead to a disaster. The soldier Fethullah had achieved success in an unprecedented way in the skill of receiving signals and decoding them quickly. Thus, his commanders decided to keep him in the Department of Emergency Communication until the end of his second period of training.

Painful Memories

The Narrator noticed that the signs of happiness appeared on my face so he promptly said in a sad voice: But in spite of all of this, the military period in Ankara engraved sad memories on the young man's memory. During the eight months which he spent in the terrifying military district of Mamak, Fethullah experienced hurt and insults. Many a time he was beaten up because he was late because he took a few minutes to pray. Most of the military meetings interfered with Prayer times and there was no one praying the five Prayers in the barracks except two persons: Fethullah and another young man from eastern Anatolia. Fethullah used to sneak into the prayer hall and race with the time of the meeting in his Prayer. If he was late even for a minute or two they would beat his hands until they poured blood or they would curse him and his religion and everything holy in Islam. He had no power or relief except in being patient and leaving the reckoning to Allah.

At this point, the eyes of my companion were drowned in tears so he retreated to silence until he got hold of himself. I asked if they really beat Fethullah. He told me the decree of the vicegerents of Allah, my friend, is to walk the path of the Prophets carrying their message and enduring everything else. However, they are still human beings and the afflictions that befall them cause the bodies to become chilled. How many a Prophet got beaten and how many a Prophet got killed? If Fethullah had been beaten a thousand times, it would have been easier for him to endure than listening to insults directed at his religion and at his Prophet, upon him be peace and blessings! I asked why he did not escape from the military service. The Narrator said: Fethullah does not escape! And if he had escaped they would have arrested him. In addition, he fully realized that to understand this environment one must experience it and examine it. One must live the life of the weakened in order to taste the bitterness of oppression and tyranny so that he may know how to illustrate the path to the Light to all the migrating birds inside the realm of darkness!

Many times an officer would issue an order to deny the soldiers the joy of having a weekend and they became prisoners inside their barracks for many weeks. The young man experienced this constraint and his soul yearned to inhale the life of faith in a civilized society. Thus, sometimes he would sneak among those who would sneak outside the barracks to visit one of his brothers in Allah such as Salih Özcan or to pray in one of the city's mosques.

The Narrator held a deep breath then he exhaled it slowly and said: One day he was in the company of some of the religious soldiers walking in a street across from a mosque when the military police surprised them. An officer rushed and punched him hard and he immediately fell on the ground. The officers tied the soldiers together in chains and led them to the detention compound at the military police center. They put in front of the detained soldiers some old containers and plates that were very dirty and asked them to wash them. The poor ones had to endure their punishment and obey the order. Fethullah, due to his serious attitude, started to wash the dishes really well with dedication until he made them very clean, and this caught the attention of the officer in charge who used his authority to release him and to erase his name from among the detainees while sending the names of the rest of the soldiers to their particular battalion to receive further punishment. Fethullah was saved from further insults that could have been severer and crueler. Such was his military life in Ankara, full of sad memories!

Departing to Iskenderun

Migration is Fethullah's eternal fate; for even during the period of his military service he had to depart. Migration is the way decreed for him to navigate the Way to Allah and therein is his retreat and his disclosure. It is his way to the farthest future. Fethullah used to observe the migrating birds crowded on the towering minarets taking shelter in them. They were waiting for a signal from him to direct them to spread their wings in the wind and fly freely to the earth of darkness, carrying between their small beaks the seeds of Light!

After eight months of tiring training, the soldier Fethullah was nominated to be appointed to a location outside Ankara. Usually, appointments of soldiers were done by drawing lots. The young man drew one of the arrows and it revealed the city of Erzurum! But the officer said to him, "Oh no, Imam. You are from Erzurum and your military service should not be done there so draw another arrow." The young man did and once more it was Erzurum. The officers nullified the result again and he then drew a third arrow and it was Diyarbakır. The officers said, "We do not want to oppress you either so you need to draw a forth arrow." This was because Diyarbakır was located in the farthest eastern part of Anatolia and had a severe rough nature. In addition, it was a location of occasional fighting because of the multi-ethnic groups that lived there such as Turks, Arabs and Kurds. Thus, living there was not easy and most officers considered it to be exile.

When Fethullah drew the forth arrow it was İskenderun and the officers clapped their hands congratulating him. One of them said to him, "You are such a lucky young man." This was because İskenderun was located on the shore of the Mediterranean Sea in the middle of southern Anatolia spread across from the boundaries with Syria. Sometimes hot winds blew there and at other times gentle cool winds blew. It has a beautiful environment and is distinguished by its beautiful gardens and abundant water. It has historical sites that are as ancient as the Roman era and some of its historical sites go back to the Abbasid era. It has been the target for many tourists from across the world. Nonetheless, the real reason behind the officers' congratulations was due to the liberal nature of the city that took off the veil of modesty like many other tourist cities across the world. This was the cause of the Imam's sadness. He left with a broken heart and wounded soul!

After a long journey, Fethullah entered the city and surrendered himself to its military barracks and in his mind he feared being tested like how Prophet Joseph was tested, and as it happened in Edirne! But after he met some of the soldiers they informed him that the closest neighborhood to them was known for its pious and religious inhabitants. Thus, his sadness turned to happiness and his fears transformed into tranquility and peace of mind in hope that he would find among those pious people those who share similar spiritual feelings. His happiness was increased when he discovered that the military camp there was different than the one in Ankara; for here the soldiers were treated better.

For the first two months he was treated as any ordinary soldier. He was sometimes ordered to guard and do other ordinary jobs in spite of the fact that he was a sergeant who should have been in charge of ten soldiers. When he was later appointed to do this he failed miserably to do it. This was due to the military style of leading which depended mostly on cursing and ridicule and he never knew such language. His way depended on guiding one's conscience and disciplining the hearts, but the military men were not raised in that way at all. Thus, to help them surrender to the spiritual authority would have taken months and maybe years. Fethullah could not make the soldiers follow him and firmly obey the military rules such as standing in front of him and saluting him or following the orders for the day and reporting to him the duties they had accomplished. His extreme politeness prevented him from scolding the disobedient soldiers and punishing them. When his commanders noticed this they thought about him because this was not something they saw in the military or even outside the military; for it was normal for them to love authority and control. So moving him to other jobs was a sign of relative sympathy for him; for they did not want to embarrass him.

A Different Type of Window

Fethullah was fond of seclusion. Whenever the opportunity allowed him to be alone he would rush to dwell in his spiritual ascent. The days he spent in Edirne in the window chamber fed his soul by the fuel of longing for the states of unveiling and visions. He did not expect to find a similar chamber in a military barracks in which he could devote himself to contemplation and to spiritual and intellectual practices. Thus, it was a great surprise to him to find that place inside a military truck he was charged to guard. It was located in a fixed place to receive the telegraph signals and he had another story with it!

Arif was an officer in the barracks who was the direct commander of Fethullah's brigade. He had the rank of master sergeant. He was very kind to Fethullah and that is why he relieved him from many difficult and embarrassing duties and appointed him to work in the telegraph department. Then, he put a military truck under his charge that was fully equipped with the latest communication instruments at the time. The car was large enough to contain a bed. Fethullah made it his private room. He used to work there, eat there, and sleep there. He even was able to bring a small camping stove to boil potatoes on and then hide it. He also used to bring bread and olives and eat inside the truck. But more importantly he used the truck as his private chamber for his spiritual retreats.

Because he was charged with telegraph communications he was relieved from all meetings and guarding shifts and that was to him an opportunity more precious than gold. He resumed his spiritual retreats, and his relationship with books. There, he read a large number of books on different subjects from literature, to history and philosophy. It was a great opportunity to explore Western philosophy in depth.

Once, one of the officers saw the books he hid inside the truck. He explored the titles and found most of them related to philosophy and literature so he said to him, "Good for you! This is how all young men should begin to explore universal cultures." What the officer feared was the possibility that the young Imam was reading religious books but Fethullah was too smart to bring religious books to the barracks; for he knew that for every situation there is a wise attitude just as for every particular retreat there is a special ascent!

The truck's communication instruments had good reception and Fethullah was able to tune in to many radio stations across the world. He even used to secretly listen to Qur'an recitation that was broadcast from radio stations in Muslim countries. Beside his truck, there was another truck parked for the same purpose and fortunately his fellow soldier was also a religious young man and so both of them used to cooperate in concealing their secret and pursuing the way of the pious.

Fethullah was madly in love with reading! Reading was the university he graduated from. He was never limited to a school curriculum and he used to read books in all fields. People might look at books, but Fethullah would eat them and digest them. Out of his big library he graduated as an imam, a scholar, a thinker, an author and a prominent poet! All the retreats he went to whether by choice or by force enabled him to travel far away and ascend through the books to other times and places. He attended the circles of scholars and jurists and all of the revivers of the spirit throughout history. He listened to the lessons delivered by the wise, the purified ones and the philosophers during long nights. He would drink from each what suited his nature and fulfill his need and meet the demand of his time and era. He would return from his retreats more experienced with life and all of its ways. He participated in conflicts between civilizations in ways that neither regular universities nor the popular social and intellectual leaders nor the political and media leaders had access to. Thus, Fethullah surpassed the possessors of degrees with his existential visions!

The Military Preacher

Fethullah started to meet the people in İskenderun during weekends and gradually became close to them until he had strong relations with some who discovered his great gift. They asked him to start to teach on Fridays at the central mosque in the city as a civilian not as a military soldier. In spite of his lack of knowledge of how that would be possible in this difficult historical time, he quickly accepted the offer knowing how it would feed the spiritual longing within him. Longing for the mosques and for the teaching gatherings was like flames within his burning chest and it was pushing him further to its crowded meadows!

Thus, the soldier took the risk and preached at İskenderun's mosque a few times under the disguise of his civilian clothes; for who would have been able to rein in a passionate horse when he became untied? Later, Fethullah took another risk with a daring attitude when he established a small mosque inside the military barracks. He found a small hall there and covered it with sand then he planted a hedge around it like a fence with the help of other pious soldiers, who were rare to find. He led six or seven soldiers in Prayer. Some of those soldiers had never prayed before in their lives and they started to pray there. The brigade contained about two hundred soldiers. To have thirty soldiers praying there was relatively a large number considering the critical situation at that time. They used to pray in the open hall and the sight of them invoked awe and spread beauty. On one single Friday Fethullah was able to lead them in Prayer in the hall that was dedicated to watching movies.

However, the officers who were anti-religion could not tolerate the Prayer so they went and planted the prayer hall with flowers and transformed it into a garden!

A Sudden Break

The young man could not endure the type of food forced upon him in the barracks and be abstained from eating it. Thus, for the second time in his life he fell sick due to malnutrition. He experienced continuous fatigue until he was unable to stand. People started to tell him, "Your eyes look as if you are jaundiced!" The first time he visited the barracks physician, he did not give him any treatment and he told him, "There is nothing wrong with you." But a few days later, his whole body was yellow and when he visited the physician for the second time, the physician was shocked and informed him that he had a dangerous disease. He immediately sent him to the hospital. There, he stayed for several days under continuous care and he was treated. He was then given three month sick leave to rest in his house in Erzurum until he fully recovered and regained his strength. He was overjoyed and he forgot all of his pain and illness. Four years had passed since he left his family and village and went to Edirne and then enrolled in the military. Then, all of a sudden, Fethullah found himself returning to Erzurum.

The Silent Messiah

The Narrator of sorrows told me a marvelous story! He said: When the train was leaving the İskenderun station, the young man was living in an intermediate realm between longing to arrive at the place of the beloved and being sad for the long separation and how it affected his heart with pain and how it also pained his parents' hearts and all of his siblings' hearts as well! Only Allah knows how many bandages were made of sighs and moaning that his mother exhaled with a heart wounded by separation from her beloved son. When longing for him would overcome her, she would weep, wounding the hearts of the rest of the family members with sympathy.

Fethullah was in the middle between all of his siblings and their family bond was like the tie between the body and the soul; for the relationship between the young man and his siblings was not only a blood tie that pushed them to appreciate each other, care for each other and meet their obligations towards one another, but it was something deeper. The spiritual bond between them was strengthened across circumstances of contractions and expansions and in circumstances of sadness and separations they went through together.

The siblings exemplified the names they carried and the spiritual states they lived as if they were one heartbeat and one breath. What one of them felt beat alive in the others' hearts. Ramiz Efendi made of the names of his children tracks through which he navigated the way to Allah. Thus, Allah provided him with offspring that did not feed except with spiritual nectar and did not drink but from the fountain of abundant love. Their main food was abstinence and their clothes were piety.

Nurhayat (or Noor al-Hayat, meaning "life's light") was the oldest sister. Next, was Fazilet (or Fadeelah, meaning "the pious" then Fethullah (Allah's conquest) then Sıbgatullah (or Sibghat Allah, meaning "Allah's dye") then Mesih (or al-Masih, meaning "the messiah") then Fakrullah (or Faqeer Allah, meaning "the poor for Allah") then Hasbi (enough for me) then Salih (the righteous) then Fazilet (the pious) who was named after the first Fazilet then Nizameddin (or Nizam ad-Din, meaning "the constructor of religion") then Kutbeddin (or Qutb ad-Din, meaning "the pole of religion") who was the youngest.

If one immersed himself into the deep meanings of these noble names, he would taste their realities! He would unveil their anguish and their hopes in a time like their time! He would find himself, without even being conscious of it, of ascending in the stations of sorrows!

The first Fazilet passed away at an early age. Fakrullah and Nizameddin also passed away during their childhood but the rest of the siblings lived longer. Whenever a younger sibling died, the rest would feel as if their hearts were snatched out of their chests. They would barely feel life's pulse for a while until many months had passed. Fethullah still remembers when his young brother passed away; how he would visit his grave when he himself was still a child and he would raise his hands to the heavens and supplicate Allah, "Oh Lord, would you please let me die so I can see my brother?"

As the Gülen children grew, this marvelous spirit grew with them. When Fethullah left Erzurum, all the brothers and sisters felt how separation had another meaning; for even if he comes back it would be just for a visit. They realized that he had left Erzurum for good and would never go back to live there!

Once his brother departed ascending in his path of migration, Mesih was powerfully attracted to the state of silence. He found himself continuously traveling as well through spiritual states caused by the pain of separation. It was beyond his emotional capacity. He tried to express how he felt in words or through weeping but once the words were about to flow over his tongue, he would feel the burning in his throat and tongue and he would not be able to utter a single word! It was a strange state that perplexed all physicians and had no cure. He stayed secluded in his silence for four years. This was the period when Fethullah was away from Erzurum, which was the first stage of his eternal travel. At this point, the whole family was awaiting the arrival of Joseph's shirt. Thus, as soon as Fethullah knocked on the door, Mesih spoke!

The main door of the family house in Erzurum was on a closed road. Once Fethullah stepped on it with his military uniform the children started to sing, "The soldier came, the soldier came!" The young man knocked on the door, which was opened by the dearest of all—his mother, the mother of his longing and dreams!

Refia Hanim stood there overtaken by the surprise! She almost stepped back and closed the door but then she smelled the fragrance of her beloved son, remembering the image of his childhood he had departed from four years ago. She exclaimed, "Are you truly Fethullah? Yes, indeed you are Fethullah."

A rain storm visited all the gardens in the city! The lightning was striking the core of the trees with a glowing flame! The rain wiped the leaves, weeping from the long separation! All the birds wept in their nests out of their intense love! Lightning has an explosive thunder upon the shields of the chests! Oh sea gulls, be silent! Oh gardens, bear witness! The mother threw herself in the arms of her son, embracing him weeping deeply. Fethullah could not help it and he too wept for the weeping of his mother and this weeping continued since then without giving his eyes a chance to dry!

The period in which he was away from Erzurum was a stage of biological growth and now his physical features changed to the extent that his mother could not recognize him with the first glance especially because he arrived unexpectedly. He was also wearing his military uniform which she was not used to seeing him wear. His mother realized how much he had grown and he also realized how much his siblings had grown and changed. They all exchanged gazes that marveled at the speed of time!

The Preacher and the Movie Theater

The Narrator continued his sentimental narration: Then, Fethullah quickly immersed himself in the social and religious life of Erzurum. He visited all of its old schools and filled mosques. He visited his elders and friends and renewed his connection with the seekers of Light. He would hurry to attend the gatherings of *dhikr* here and there until the three months sick leave came to an end. He went to present himself to the military administration but he was informed that the officers in charge of his case had extended his holiday one more month. Thus, the month of Ramadan came while he was still off duty. He made use of it, spiritually speaking, boosting his joyful state in a way he would not have been able to achieve if he were alienated in İskenderun.

Ramadan was an occasion when Fethullah resumed delivering lessons at mosques. His lessons at that time were not without surprises and adventures! One of the people at the mosque informed Fethullah about a movie that was going to be shown in the movie theater about the early stages of Islam where the Prophet's Companions and his wife 'Aisha, may Allah be pleased with them all, would be portrayed by actors. The movie was advertised one week before it was to be shown and some people bought their tickets in advance. Fethullah criticized the movie in his lessons; for he knew that the scenario would not be intended to serve religion at this time in Turkey's history. He realized that it would mock all the Islamic creeds and would provide worldly explanations for all the incidents that took place at the Prophet's time. This would portray the incidents without their spiritual meanings and their sacredness. If it was a positive movie, it would not have been allowed to be shown in movie theaters at that time in Turkey.

Fethullah based his criticism on arguing that things can only be simulated by their equivalents and a person who has no respect for religion cannot play the role of a revered Companion. He also argued that an indecent actress who has no religion or morality cannot play the role of Lady 'Aisha, may Allah be pleased with her, who is the mother of all the faithful believers. His criticism for the movie was limited and gentle and would discourage people from watching it. On the day the movie was to be shown, Fethullah's emotions were agitated and his heart exploded during his speech after the Afternoon Prayer. The lava of sorrow within his heart was gushing out announcing the death of people's hearts who would not try to prevent this abhorrent act. He screamed in people's faces while weeping, "Oh People! Woe to you! Can't you see how they will mock your religion and your Prophet, upon him be peace and blessings, tonight? They are insulting the souls of our noble master guides? How are you sitting like that in a state of submission to them? Where is your dignity? Where is your Islam?"

Fethullah did not mean to provoke people but he just wanted to awaken people's critical thinking so that they could carry their objection to the local authority to prevent the show. But because of his powerful words, people were agitated and they took off in the streets shouting and threatening. In fact, he tried his utmost to prevent people from doing so, but all of his efforts were in vain. The flow of people marched forward and was supplied by sources here and there. Some started to speak about the detailed scenario of the movie and its bad portrayal and evil intention. The news spread across Erzurum and within a few minutes, the movie theater was besieged by a large crowd of angry people! Even the Bloody Fuad was there as well. He was a man thirsty for blood as his name suggests. He had nothing to do with religion or its people; he was a rebellious young

man who was always subjected to mood swings and bad tem-
perament. He had a strong build and it was said that he could
beat anyone who fought him and shed his blood. He always got
involved in fights and he was incapable of abiding by the religious teachings and limits. Nonetheless, in spite of his weakness, he had a deep respect for religious people and for the values that religion promotes.

The angry crowd attacked the movie theater and broke the
projector. The owner of the theater was terrified and once he
saw the Bloody Fuad moving among the people he felt good; for
Fuad used to drink wine in his place from time to time. Thus,
he rushed to him and he started to complain to him about what
was being done to his theater. He said, "People mentioned that
Fethullah had criticized the movie but there is nothing wrong
with the movie; for it was approved by the Jurist of the city,
Imam Sakıp Efendi." As soon as the theater owner finished
his statement, Fuad jumped and shouted at him, "You said that
Fethullah Hoja criticized this movie? It must be an evil movie
then." He then started to beat the theater owner until he started to bleed.

Fethullah witnessed how powerful words can be, more powerful than pictures!

The Story of the False Messiah

The Narrator said: During that period, the young man announced
that he was going to deliver a speech about the imposter, the
false messiah. The mentioning of the imposter was highly disturbing to the authorities at that time! But the young preacher postponed the speech until the end of Ramadan for fear he
might get arrested and thus deprived from delivering his speech-

es. He thought if he were arrested, it would be better to get arrested at the end of Ramadan not at its beginning.

When the time of delivering the speech came the mosque was full of people who gave him their full attention. Everyone wanted to hear the speech about the imposter. People were looking in the direction of the platform where the preacher was sitting with their eyes wide open staring at the young preacher.

As usual, Vahdeddin Bey sat in the front row. He was a strange man who used to experience spiritual states with heightened emotions! Thus, whenever the preacher would start, Vahdeddin Bey would start weeping. His deep moaning would sometimes be intensified to the extent that the echo of his exhaling would fill the whole mosque. His weeping would affect the young preacher deeply and would kindle his enthusiasm. His weeping was like spiritual fuel and an important source of inspiration!

The young preacher spoke about the imposter while members of the government Secret Service were recording every word he uttered. Nothing happened right away. By the end of Ramadan, Fethullah as usual went to the mosque to deliver his last lesson. He chose to speak about the Prophet's Farewell Pilgrimage. At the end of the speech, he raised his voice ending it with the Noble Messenger's words, "Have not I conveyed the message? Oh Allah! Bear witness!" He then repeated it, meaning himself. At that moment, the weeping man, Vahdeddin Bey, raised his voice saying, "Allah the Almighty is our Witness that you have conveyed the message and completed it." His words were so sincere and glorious that they moved Fethullah who started to weep.

The young man was then informed that the police were waiting for him outside the mosque to arrest him. But, due to the magnitude of the crowd inside the mosque they decided to wait, at least for a while!

Organized Activism

Fethullah was not like any other imam; for his time was a time of confrontation with the ghosts of darkness! In the line of candles there were only a few lit! And what a sorrow! The storm was so intense! The inflamed longing within the young Imam's soul was enough to kindle the tip of longing for sunrise everywhere! His piercing certainty of a coming triumph was a secret that chests could not contain! Thus, Fethullah did not divulge the secret to anyone!

The young man made another use of his vacation. He used to visit an organization called Halk Evi (People's House) which was affiliated with the Republican People's Party which mostly served its secular goals. However, whenever a few pious members would be in charge of its activities, they would offer useful services. The members who were in charge of Erzurum's branch were religious people even though secularism was the modern cultural fashion of the new generation.

One time, Fethullah was invited to go to the organization to deliver a speech about the great Sufi, Jalaluddin Rumi. Before him, many prominent scholars and academic professors spoke and he was the last to speak because he was the youngest among all of them. As usual, he spoke from his heart not from something he prepared beforehand. He recited some Persian verses of poetry and simultaneously translated them into Turkish. The audience was impressed! He voiced his disagreement with the majority of the speakers before him who tried to misuse Jalaluddin Rumi to change the core of the Islamic creed, but the young Imam succeeded in planting the authentic creed of Islam within the minds of his audience.

So Fethullah's image was implanted in the attendees' minds, especially in the minds of the members of the People's House organization. When the next term came to elect the new administration of the organization he was elected as an official member. He therefore immersed himself with his friends in offering distinguished services to the youth, besieging the communist ideology.

Later, he took a further step and established an association with his friends with the goal of confronting communism. Fethullah announced the idea publically in the mosque after he delivered one of his lessons. Some of his friends from the Nur (or Noor) Movement became worried about this strange step. They advised him to only teach Nursi's *Epistles of Light*. In addition, one of Fethullah's relatives, who was an expert on forming organizations and clubs, also warned him against challenging some of the established laws and regulations that he must follow in order to form this association. The young Imam and his friends were ignorant of these laws. In all of Turkey, there was no similar association except one. It was in Izmir which was very far from Erzurum. But in spite of the far distance and the tiring trip, Fethullah sent one of his friends to Izmir to have direct contact with the members of the Komünizmle Mücadele Derneği (The Association for Fighting Communism). He requested to have their bylaws in order to make use of them in establishing a similar club in Erzurum.

The association was established and became very active and its activities soon became fruitful. It was one of the best means to limit the influence of atheism and it spread the *Epistles of Light* among the youth. Thus, the students of the Nur Movement who objected to the idea at the beginning got involved in the association!

Even though this period in Fethullah's life was short, it was a blessed period and full of intense activities that were extremely effective. He spread the *Epistles of Light* collection and distributed it everywhere. His feelings were kindled by his great enthusiasm. Thus, he did not leave any club but invaded it with his speeches and he did not leave any mosque but energized its domes with his call and supplication.

Returning to Iskenderun

Fethullah's spiritual findings reached lofty windows! Many clear visions came to him so much so that he was about to divulge his secret! He could not endure his military uniform further. He could not hold his rebellious soul from invading the fortress of darkness. He set out to purify the hooves of evil on the city's roads! If he hadn't needed to walk further, he would have destroyed the snake burrows everywhere! But revealing the secret had an appointed time and the wise should not rush. This is why Fethullah would weep!

The Narrator continued: When his sick leave came to an end, the preacher soldier was forced to return to his barracks in İskenderun. There, he continued to preach enthusiastically. He almost forgot that he was a soldier subjected to obey the rules and military traditions. He used to deliver a sermon every Friday at the city's central mosque. The mosque used to be full of people who were thirsty for religion in a country where religion was not practiced except secretly and its books were not exchanged without fear.

Every Friday, the crowd kept growing around the mosque until it extended to the street parallel to the mosque, blocking traffic. Fethullah used to wear the Imam's traditional garment on top of his military uniform, violating all the military traditions and rules. Some of the officers in his barracks sympathized with him and they would act as his protectors. However, the crowded place around the mosque would put them in a critical position. In addition, his enthusiastic words would weaken their ability to defend him in front of his enemies among the officers.

The Interrogation

Ramiz Efendi used to visit Fethullah in İskenderun from time to time. On one of those visits, it was the time of Eid (feast). Fethullah arrived at the mosque to deliver one of his lessons and the mosque was crowded but his father was not there in the place he used to sit. Fethullah also noticed that he did not see any of the Nur students in the mosque. Thus, he felt worried and after finishing the Eid Prayer someone came to him and informed him that his father had been arrested the night before along with some of the Nur students.

Immediately, the young man hurried to the office of the General Attorney. There, he was informed that the Nur students had gathered to celebrate the Eid by doing *dhikr* together at the house of Vahdeddin Bey of İskenderun. Suddenly, the police stormed the place thinking they would find Fethullah among them which would have allowed them to charge him with the crime of gathering people without obtaining permission. However, Fethullah did not go because he was preparing for the speech he was going to deliver for Eid. At the same time, Fethullah's father left the uncle's house feeling upset at the immodesty of the uncle's daughters and he went to seek protection at Vahdeddin's house where he could find tranquility in a house full of faith. So he was arrested.

From behind the interrogator's desk, Fethullah heard the interrogator asking his father, "So where does this Light come from?"

The father confidently answered, "From the Qur'an."

"Where does the Qur'an exist?" the interrogator further asked.

"Allah is the Light of the Heavens and the Earth."

After a few minutes, the father was released. As they were going back home, he turned to his son, and wittily commented on the incident saying they had escaped from the rain and fallen into the hands of coldness! He was pointing out his escape from the uncle's house! After the incident, the father stayed a few days in İskenderun then he returned to Erzurum.

Even though, neither Fethullah nor his father got hurt in that incident, he was deeply pained by what happened to his great friends Vahdeddin Bey and Nihad Karakum, who were fired from their jobs for their contact with Fethullah and the gatherings of Light.

Anger for a Pious Cause

Feeling angry for a pious cause is a virtue and a sign of manhood. The one who feels angry for a pious cause never regrets this. This is why the young preacher still remembers it! One time, his father visited him in summer time and Fethullah searched for a decent hotel for his father, but his search was in vain! All hotels there were indecent places with bars. The young man found it very hard to let his father stay at one of these rotten hotels. Thus, in the next lesson at the mosque, Fethullah strongly criticized the hotels which provoked the people to destroy their signs. He also criticized the police for turning a blind eye when it came to fighting reeking crimes of immoral corruption. As a military soldier he was going against the law preaching for religion. After this speech, his sympathizers among the officers could not protect him. One of them suggested that he say a few words of praise for Cemal Tural so they would be able to use that to defend him. They kept trying to convince him until he finally agreed.

Thus, in the following lesson, he tried to overcome his own feelings and said in a cold voice, "They say that our commander, Tural Pasha, is a patriotic man, so what about the Turkish military? May Allah prolong the life of those who defend their nation!"

That evening Fethullah fell down when he was getting in the military truck and he broke his ribs. He passed out and when he became conscious he found his head on sergeant Arif's lap. The young Imam said to the sergeant in a voice full of pain, "You have done this to me! You pushed me to praise those people from the platform of the Messenger of Allah, upon him be peace and blessings, and Allah did not approve of what I did!"

He continued to suffer for two months from his broken ribs. The physicians in the hospital could not do anything to help him. A chiropractor came to him and stretched his ribs until Fethullah passed out! Once he started to feel better, Fethullah resumed delivering his lessons. But the situation became harder; for all the officers that used to protect him were transferred to other places and there was no one to protect his back. Thus, Satan was released and he set out to step upon all the gardens of the city with his harsh hooves, destroying with his evil trunk the nests of all birds!

Military Detention

One of the stations of Divine Trials is to strip the callers from all support except that of Allah! No servant can attain his special place with his Master, unless no one handles his affairs except Allah directly. For whoever fails this test, veils are dropped and walls are raised between him and his Lord! He is stripped of his visions and secret epiphanies.

The Narrator of sorrows who has a marvelous radiation told me: On the first Friday in which Fethullah sat to preach after his ribs were broken, he delivered his lesson calmly using wise words so as not to give a chance for his enemies to arrest him. Nonetheless, he knew that as a soldier, he was violating the law by delivering a religious lesson without obtaining official permission which was in itself enough reason to arrest him.

When people left the mosque, they heard soldiers besieging the mosque and one of them was shouting, "Look for the scoundrel and if he tries to escape do not hesitate to shoot him." People could not contain themselves and they started to shout against the soldiers and the situation was inflamed by mutual anger. When Fethullah knew that he was the one pursued, he hurried to the officer and saluted him and surrendered himself to him. The soldiers intended to provoke people in order to find a good excuse to arrest religious people. Fethullah's quick surrender and smart decision succeeded in frustrating their plot and they had to leave the place. The next day all the newspapers published this news.

The commander was a wise man so he detained Fethullah along with the people who committed crimes that had nothing to do with politics. He was taken with all of them to the officers' center. There, he saw the commander of the military police who held the highest rank in the center. The officer who arrested Fethullah saluted the commander and said to him, "Sir! Once the soldier Fethullah saw me he came to me and saluted me and surrendered himself to me." He was trying to help the military preacher! The commander was arrogant and he started to insult and abuse them. Fethullah stayed that night in the detention center. But he was released the next day!

When his friends heard about his situation, they extended their white hands to him from afar and rescued him.

Fethullah returned to his barracks. When his commander saw him, and he loved him deeply, he slapped him and yelled at him, "Why did you deliver your speech when you knew you were being watched by them?" Later, in one of the meetings, the commander confessed to his colleagues, "I slapped Fethullah as a father slaps his son; for I love him a lot!" He said that and wept.

Other people in authority insisted on taking Fethullah to military court. The night before appearing in military court, Fethullah was worried and he had a sleepless night! In the middle of the night, he went and performed ablution then he prayed. He would never forget how when he had immersed himself deeply in Prayer, a light illuminated the place all of a sudden and that happened twice as if it were lightning, but it was not!

A Military Trial

The young soldier stood in front of the judges of the military court. The judge was a general and was angry at religion and its people. He started the trial with curses and insults. Fethullah had just washed his uniform and did not put the sign of his rank on the shoulder. The judge claimed that to be another violation of the rules and he yelled at him, "Oh outlaw! Where is the sign of your rank? Are you a soldier or a vagabond? Go then and spread your blanket in a minaret!" He then ordered him to be detained.

There was a captain in his barracks who was almost always drunk. He took the young man's salary by force twice to buy wine. The court summoned him as a witness in Fethullah's case. When the judge asked him, the captain answered, "Are you asking me about Fethullah? He is the only pious man in the barracks. It is rare to find the like of him." The tyrannical judge did not know what to say and he ordered Fethullah to still be detained and ended the court session.

Soon, the news spread and many people tried to interfere on behalf of the young man. Some of the elites who often visited the mosque went to the general of the barracks. The general was a patriotic man so they said to him, "Sir, Fethullah has been a patriotic and sincere citizen and he is not like what others accuse him to be. Through him, we came to love our nation, our history and our knowledge." Some of the elites traveled to the capital, Ankara, to meet high military officers in the central military center to intercede on Fethullah's behalf.

A Lieutenant Colonel in the Army Salutes Fethullah

There was a physician in the army who held the rank of lieutenant colonel. He saw in Fethullah what other people did not see! He could have gotten a glimpse of his radiant secret! Who knows? When the soul polishes its mirror with sincerity, the luminosity of Divine Love in the hearts of others is disclosed to it! Indeed, souls are ranked in troops and those who have the same longings recognize each other and those who have similar tastes know each other!

Necdet Bey was a brave man; for in spite of the prohibition to visit the detained soldier, he climbed the fence while in his official uniform and crossed the barbed wire and entered the building that was the prison. When the soldiers saw him they saluted him and opened the cell door so he could visit Fethullah. When he saw Fethullah, he embraced him and before he left he handed him ten liras. The soldiers marveled at the insignificant detainee who was visited by a high ranking officer! They started to revere Fethullah and treat him well and they would not even hurt his feelings with any offensive words.

However, the hostile officers did not forget what the military physician did and they later asked him how he could have embraced an ordinary soldier when military tradition demands the lower ranking soldier to salute him out of respect for his higher rank. He answered them, "But Fethullah is not an ordinary person. If I could, I would even kiss his feet. So, yes indeed I have no problem embracing him." Allah saved the high ranking physician and he was not harmed.

The Call inside the Prison

There were two young men with him in the prison cell. One of them was disturbed psychologically and was thinking of committing suicide. The other tried many times to escape military service but he was captured every time and he had a bitter story.

As soon as Fethullah met the former and recognized his psychological state he tried to heal him and converse with him, reminding him of Allah and helping him to accept the Divine Destiny and Decree and have faith in His Judgment. Hope started to find its way to the man's horizon. One time, he laid down his bed cover for Fethullah and insisted he use it. He would sit and listen to his beautiful teaching, which healed the deep wounds in his soul. He would inhale from Allah's spirit hope for a better life. Sometimes he would say to the young preacher, "Oh Fethullah! If Allah decrees that we be released I hope you will visit me in my town someday. I would accommodate you in a way that I've never done for anyone else." The young man felt happy hearing this; it was glad tidings that the man was healed from his psychological disturbance and that he had succeeded in helping him. It meant that the man was not thinking of suicide anymore. He found rest in being imprisoned with Fethullah. Fethullah felt that Allah had sent him to that prison to meet the man and undertake this noble duty of healing him.

Regarding the other man, he was summoned to serve the ordinary military service which should not exceed two years. Nonetheless, he stayed in service for nineteen years! He was impatient in enduring hurt and he could not bear the insults of the officers to the soldiers. He tried to be patient until the last month of his service then he could not endure it anymore so he tried to escape but he was captured and detained and the judge would order him to repeat his military service. This scenario kept repeating itself and every time he would try to escape he would be captured and the judge would order him to restart his military service again. They would capture him before he would arrive to his family and he would not be able to calm the fire of longing and nostalgia in his heart. He spent nineteen years suffering in that way.

One day, he received a letter from his daughter. She wrote, "My father, I am now a bride and you still have not finished your military service?" Fethullah engaged him in a deep conversation and taught him how a human being can survive hardships by the beauty of being intimate with Allah, even if he is all alone in a prison cell!

Ultimate Release

Interceding on Fethullah's behalf never ceased to exist and the pressure from many civilian organizations and military personnel continued until a letter arrived from the highest military leadership in the capital which instructed the barracks commander to release Fethullah. The letter mentioned, "If this soldier is patriotic why would you insist on hurting him to this extent?" Fethullah was surprised to find the officer who had treated him the worst coming to release him himself. He accompanied him to the administrative office and started to type a new report, changing the words that were said against Fethullah in the previous report. Other officers helped him choose words that would acquit Fethullah of all the crimes he was accused of. For example, they deleted a sentence that said, "He was trying to lead a coup and provoke people to revolt against the government."

At this point, Fethullah realized the dangerous situation he was in. But when the new report was done, one of the officers said, "So there is no reason to detain him. He should be released." They transferred him to the disciplinary prison for a few days with a mild accusation of violating the rules. This was in preparation to release him from the prison for good. There, he found a book of poetry written by the Turkish Islamic scholar and poet, Mehmed Akif, who wrote the nation's official anthem. The young man read the book several times before he was released.

A newspaper named *Yeni İstiklal* (*New Independence*) published the news in a positive way under the title "The Grandson of Mehmed the Conqueror: Muhammad Fethullah." On the other hand, other secular newspapers published the news with provocative criticism for releasing him.

The greatest surprise of all to the young man was the fact that captain Mahmud Mardin had visited him. He was the highest commander of the second largest battalion in İskenderun. He surprised Fethullah by praising him, saying, "Indeed, you are a great man! I used to attend your classes in the mosque secretly. So, now I am going to release you from your military service even though more than a month is left to finish your term. I am going to sign the document of release for you and you can return to your family."

Memorable Sentiments

The Narrator said: When Fethullah was released from the military service he felt a sense of relief and remembered the suffering of the two years he spent there. He remembered how he got sick because of malnutrition as he did not want to eat the military food, believing that it was not his right because he was not involved in actual military service. He used to buy his military uniform with his own money. He remembered how he did not use any of the military equipment not even paper and pens for personal purposes in spite of the fact that tons of these items where in his hands. He never used a paper to write any of his personal thoughts or lessons. He did not use any of the pens to write any single word or even a dot.

The two years were like a nightmare in which he even lived through a military coup. He received many insults and passed many afflictions but Allah made him resilient and helped him to endure patiently. The secret of his ability to endure with patience was due to His Lord's support and his daily recitation of supplications and prayers which provided him with a special ability to transcend time! He used to fold the years and transfer himself into the future and live an event before it occurred. He would see through his imagination what his life would be like when he finished his military service. He would convince himself that it was only a passing affliction or that it was a nightmare that he would soon wake up from and return to his place and time, serving in the army of Mehmed the Conqueror. This was how he gave solace to himself until the intense nightmare was over! Fethullah graduated as a hero from his affliction!

After his release from military service, the young man stayed in İskenderun for a few days to say farewell to his friends and devotees. One of the people who visited him to say farewell was a rich man who owned a big transportation company. Once he knew that the young man was released from the military service he offered him a job in his company as a general manager but the young man did not hesitate to politely refuse the offer. He was not thinking of material gains at all. He never imagined himself working for something else than inviting people to Allah. He only imagined himself teaching and delivering speeches at mosques. From the early stage of his youthful years he had dedicated himself to that purpose. Even his military service did not slow his determination or dedication to serve in that way in spite of his suffering the consequences he had to face.

After saying farewell to his friends, Fethullah returned to Erzurum; for it was his favorite airport from where he would take off and migrate to his next destination. Only there could he find his new direction. When he entered the city it was Ramadan and he went straight to the Jurist of the city (*mufti*) in order to request a license that would allow him to teach in the mosques during the noble month. But the Jurist, Sakıp Efendi, had not forgotten the incident that happened in the movie theater the previous year so he refused Fethullah's request. Fethullah went home sad with a broken heart. When people heard the news they gathered in front of the Religious Administration building in protest. They shouted strong criticism against the Jurist. One of them said, "The one who could prevent Fethullah from teaching is not born."

The young preacher did not know that this was happening until he was informed that the Jurist changed his mind under the protesters' pressure. Fethullah taught everyday of Ramadan without any problems until the end of the month.

Longing for Migration Blown Again

Fethullah's heart is a forest full of secrets! When the wind of longing blew therein, the birds and trees were agitated! Fethullah has a secret that he does not tell anyone! Fethullah has a secret that the whole world is waiting for but he cannot tell anyone! Fethullah carries within his heart that which he cannot endure and that is why he has been weeping until tears were perplexed at its death! Fethullah is the inheritor of a secret which if the mountain carried it, its rocky top would fall and its foundations would crumble!

Longing for migration was kindled again in his heart; for migration is a living doctrine for Fethullah and a way to walk towards Allah. It is an eternal journey in the way of reviving the religion and serving the realities of faith. The Light that inhabited his heart did not permit him to be satisfied just by being among family and relatives. Since he heard the Spirit's call he kept migrating until his feet were cut!

His longing was for Edirne, the sad city which soothed his wounds and he soothed her wounds. Its longing was united with his longing until they became one essence suffering one disaster. Fethullah's mother was deeply affected by his absence between Edirne and the military service and she was very sad for the separation. She desired that he would stay in Erzurum beside her. She tried to convince him with her warm feelings and he stayed for some time to satisfy her. Indeed, she had more children but Fethullah had a special place in her heart;

for he was always gentle and noble with her. This is why she insisted on him marrying and living in Erzurum. She knew that marriage was the cage that could keep the flying bird in. It is what reigns a running horse but Fethullah was not a running horse or a flying bird but he was a devoted one who fell in love with migrating for Allah's sake. He never felt annoyed with his family or village but rather he loved Erzurum and its surroundings. On its land he was born and grew up and there he buried the best of his memories and loved ones like his grandparents and spiritual masters. However, longing to migrate for Allah's sake was more powerful in his heart. Long ago, he had realized his purpose in life; to invite people to Allah and he has a great sense of this duty. The glowing light of his longing to fulfill the duty of his time was shining clear on the horizon of his whole youthful life. It did not allow him to rest in the warmness of being at home and doing what was familiar. For whoever carries the same secret that Fethullah carries, no city or town can contain him! So, horses march from journey to journey!

Chapter 6
Returning to the Rural Areas of Thrace

More of Edirne's Pain

$\mathcal{L}$adies and gentlemen, I am really tired; for I am ill. My search for Fethullah's roads is taking long and I am awaiting a moment of unveiling or a spark of lightning at which the young man would reveal his secret recipe for the elixir of life! I am waiting so that I may receive his concealed secret or receive his old keys! My sorrow spoke to me revealing that under Cordoba's Mosque there is a hidden pharmacy kept in a concealed box! My remedy is in one of its ancient scrolls which is still buried underneath one of the pillars of the Farthest Mosque (al-Masjid al-Aqsa). A trustworthy one had informed me that the map to both treasures is kept someplace close to the treasuries of the High Gate in Istanbul!

I said that this is a third treasure. Whoever misses it is going to miss the road to the Farthest Mosque and he would also miss the passageway of Tariq ibn Ziyad across Gibraltar!

The trustworthy person told me: Certainly, Fethullah knows the location of the map and is keeping the keys of the ancient gates! But no one knows how to stretch his hand inside his small case to reveal to the world the secret of the Arrival at the Treasure's Presence!

I ran after his footsteps so that I may find in his footprints an illustration, a mark, or an indication! I spent a long time traveling here and there until my sadness swelled in vain! I am not going to lose hope! Whoever is able to do so must keep running after the flowing Light.

I felt a great need to rest. My illness got worse and my insight was not able to find a way out! I then decided to return home and to contemplate the matter for a while!

After I arrived at the city of Meknes, I rested a little then I started to frequently visit the house of the Last Cavalier, trying to open the passage of his ascent; for who knows I might be able to find the way towards the new era or I might be able to find the map of the road towards Fethullah's orbit and know his resting place!

I then stopped at one chapter of the *Akhir al-Fursan's* (*Last of the Cavaliers*) chapters and I wrote what was decreed for me to write except of one flashing indication when I saw Mehmed the Conqueror standing beside Tariq ibn Ziyad, Bediuzzaman Said Nursi and Muhammad Fethullah together and many others with them, but I could not recognize them but I saw all of them looking at the earth from heaven, from the same orbit, and then I understood that they were all one person!

At that moment, I was longing for the Mediterranean Sea and I felt glad tidings that I might receive there at the end of my story! Why not, for the sea is one that extends from under the feet of Ayyub al-Ansari in the strait of Bosporus to the Strait of Gibraltar.

So a few hours later, I found myself mounting my horse and galloping the distance between Tangier and the boundaries of as-Salibah. I was looking across the horizon at the Andalus of sadness! The echo of the moaning in the depth of my being was broken on the opposite bank. I looked and there was Gibraltar! And here is Granada, the ancient center of Moorish civilization, and behind them lies the graves of Muslims! But to the conquerors imperishable trees are erected high and a forest full of wild flowers are stretched in front of them. Its fragrance fills the lungs of time!

Here, I remembered Edirne and the Selimiye Mosque and the mosque with the elegant three-balconied minaret and it seems that the time between Cordoba and Edirne was a distance of two bows' length or less! Then, all tragedies and pains manifested to me and I heard the wind weeping between the two straits! It occurred to my heart that I was going to see him there and if I could not find him, I would at least find his traces or a clue that would lead me in the direction that could take me to join the fellows' horses! The longing for departing called me and so I carried my luggage and followed the cause!

Between Istanbul and Edirne is sadness similar to that between Cordoba and Granada. The car was folding the history that once was! The glorification of the conquerors and the neighing of the horses filled my ears across the European section of Turkey. The driver was playing a tape that had one of Fethullah's lessons. From time to time, his voice would crack; crying. On the windshield in front of me, rain drops were falling in a sad flow. The driver insisted on not using the wipers unless visibility became absolutely impossible.

My companion was talking with me about the Selimiye Mosque, the mosque with the three-balconied minaret and about Edirne, the city where Mehmed the Conqueror was born. He was telling me the story of glory as if he were living it now. It augmented my longing to visit the conquest's base! But indeed, my longing to find traces of Fethullah there was stronger. The car was speeding and in spite of that I found myself unconsciously pressing on the floor as if I wanted to increase its speed even more so that I might see road marks in Fethullah's window!

A few minutes later the four minarets of the Selimiye Mosque appeared standing high in the sky. Their agile position had an extraordinary beauty! They looked like beautiful necks getting taller by the minute without stopping! What a marvel! They were like trees growing with time! As for the large dome, it looked from afar as if it were the rock of the ascent to heaven! I witnessed the spirit's breezes blowing its flowery breath between the domes and minarets emitting a beautiful fragrance illustrating the road towards heaven's gates!

When I entered the Selimiye Mosque, eons of time crashed into its rocks and I fell on the ground thunderstruck! I then heard Fethullah weeping– Ah! I joined him and we cried deeply. Who can endure witnessing the Selimiye dome with its sentimental calling without being shaken to his core with reverence? There is nothing in the entire world equal to the Selimiye dome! If all the architects in the world designed beautiful domes and monasteries, their designs would not be equal to the dome of dignity and authority which still crowns the heads of all conquerors until the Day of Judgment!

These are my ancestors so bring to me the like of them
If you would gather us, Oh Jarir[15] of the councils!

The Selimiye still brings the Light which escaped the marching reckless storms in the Andalus of sorrows! The Selimiye still embraces the emigrants with its nostalgia and it still embraces the dreamers of a return! Here is Cordoba keeping its ancient marble! And here Granada where its secrets are buried under the pillars with scripts engraved, speaking to its visitors! All

---

[15] A famous Arab poet (653-728) (Ed.)

the calligraphy and the decorations, all the colors, the intricate curves, the plait-like patterns hanging from the ceiling from underneath the sentimental letters as if they were bowing down or prostrating to their Lord. I could hear its hidden weeping flowing as cries of little birds: Oh Lord! Forgive me! Oh Lord! Forgive me! Oh Lord! Forgive me!

The Narrator of sorrows said to me: When Fethullah finished the military service he longed to go to Edirne. Its hills across the boundaries of the Balkans were strongly pulling him and its mosques with their historical minarets looking upon the European boundary, powerfully shaking its soul! The mosque with the three-balconied minaret was the dearest to his heart. Its window which embraced him for three years was longing for him! An intense nostalgia had been awakened within his soul and he yearned to sit in the space of the glorious historical mosque which was designed by the great architect Hayreddin. He loved the mosque with the three-balconied minaret more than the Selimiye, which was located close to it even though the Selimiye Mosque with its glorious dome, four towering minarets and beautiful architecture is the pride of all Turks. It is the greatest edifice of the bright Ottoman era!

Fethullah always felt a similarity between the mosque with the three-balconied minaret and the giant at the time of afflictions, Ustadh Bediuzzaman Nursi! He saw how that mosque was united with the lordly Sultan Murad the Second, the father of striving Sultan Mehmed the Conqueror. It is as if the mosque and the Sultan completed each other!

Fethullah decided to go to Edirne and chose it to become the goal of his migration! The mosque with the three-balconied minaret became the point of attraction to resume his spiritual ascent and his striving to teach, to educate and to invite people to Allah.

It was July 4, 1964 when Ustadh Muhammad Fethullah arrived in Edirne, the land of his first migration. He went directly to his beloved mosque in hope that he could return to being its imam where he could speak to people. But he found out that a new Imam was hired. After a few gentle trials with the new Imam and the office of the Religious Affairs, Fethullah failed to get his past position. Thus, he soothed his wound and accepted Allah's decree. He then remembered he still held a valid certificate that qualified him to work as a religious preacher and guide so he went and showed it to the Religious Affairs Department in Edirne. They hired him as a teacher of the Qur'an in one of the religious schools. This was the only window through which he could enter the arena of guiding and teaching.

He was surprised by how popular he had become and how his popularity had grown by what many newspapers and magazines wrote about him at the time of his military trial. What made his life difficult was that one of the secular magazines started to publish hostile essays about him once they became aware of his return to Edirne and his new job. The essays were presenting the old accusations against him at the time of the military trial. The title of the magazine article was written in big letters, "How Can Someone like Him Hold an Official Position?" So his arrival in Edirne became a media target and a political problem. A few days in Edirne passed and he found security personnel watching him and following his footsteps from place to place whether he went to the mosque or to a friend's house or to the club of the devotees. He felt he was being watched all the time by the security forces as if they were his shadows.

At the same time, many officials at the Department of Qur'an Education did not tolerate him. They tried to marginalize him and to strip him of all authority; for they did not like to have an effective active man like him who truly invites people to Allah. This is because many of them were followers of a specific religious doctrine and they could not compete with the young preacher and they disliked the influence he had on the students. Some of them openly admitted this to Fethullah while others alluded to it. In addition, he was a suspicious person in the eyes of the security forces who was to be chased forever! He was more devastated by the hostility shown towards him by those who were supposed to be close to him. It certainly saddened his heart and hurt him deeply more than the hostility he received from the secular community!

Allah's plan was more powerful than all of their plots! By Allah's favor, Fethullah found a new place for his cause. Thus, he made the Imam's room a place for him to rest and at the same time he made it a school in which he would educate students. There was nothing dearer to his heart and more enjoyable than teaching. Thus, he actively began to teach with great enthusiasm and strength but at the same time with caution; for he understood that many eyes were watching him waiting for a mistake. He spent some of his most enjoyable days in Edirne which was full of secrets and blessings!

At this time, Ustadh Suad Yildirim was hired as the General Jurist of Edirne. He was a close friend of Fethullah. The General Jurist at that time was responsible for all the employees in the Department of Religious Affairs and its affiliates such as the imams, the speakers, the teachers of the noble Qur'an, and so on. The administrators rented a private house for him. At that time, Fethullah had to leave the Imam's room at the Daru'l-Hadith (House of Hadith) Mosque and rented a house for himself but the house was really old and in very bad condition.

One day, Fethullah visited his friend, the General Jurist Suad Yildirim in his house after dawn so no one could see him.

To his surprise, the house in which the General Jurist lived was worse than his house. Once he sat with the General Jurist, the man started to complain to him concerning the situation, "This house is infested by fleas and I cannot sleep because of their bites." His friend, the young Imam, said to him, "My situation is similar to yours. So if you wish we can both rent a better house together that has two rooms, one for each of us." The General Jurist immediately agreed.

After a tiring search the two men found a house that had two empty rooms on the ground floor, and on the second floor the landlord lived with his family. His daughters and wife were immodest as were many women in Edirne. This was disturbing to the two righteous men. In addition, they had no kitchen in their house but they managed to set up a small kitchen-like space under the stairs. They were relieved from flea bites and the constant urge to itch that they had suffered from!

More importantly they were happy to find their precious chance to study the *Epistles of Light*. Fethullah was able to copy whatever he liked to use in his lessons and speeches in the mosque. Fethullah used to put his prepared points for the class between the pages of a book titled *The Abridged Authentic Hadiths (at-Tajrid as-Sarih)*. This was a brief summary of *Sahih al-Bukhari* in the Turkish language which was published by the Department of Religious Affairs in Turkey. Sometimes, he would write a few words in coded language so that nobody could read them except him, being aware of how the secret service from the police were always watching him. They used to attend his classes and would not leave the mosque until all the people had left first. The secular government in Turkey did not want the religious preacher to give people the slightest hope of the possibility of returning the Light to the nation of Allah's vicegerency! In this way, the small gathering which

Fethullah used to hold in the mosque was like a meadow in a desert that was drowning in deep darkness!

A Beautiful Dream

Dreams are the ethereal threads that connect the human being with the invisible realm! When the mirror of the faithful believer's heart is polished, the soul yearns and his love of Allah rises opening the door for him to witness the heavens and he sees! The possessor of vision lives in continuous joyful intimacy with the angels and the Prophets' spirits!

The Narrator said: One day, one of those who used to attend Fethullah's gatherings came to him running. He was carrying good news from a dream he saw. He was a faithful, sincere and pious man. When Fethullah permitted him to speak he told him that he saw the Prophet, upon him be peace and blessings, in their mosque while Khadija, the Mother of the Believers, was standing at the door. She asked the Prophet, upon him be peace and blessings, "Oh Messenger of Allah! These youth are asking if you are satisfied with them (she was pointing to Fethullah and his companions)." The Messenger of Allah, upon him be peace and blessings, said, "Yes, I am satisfied with all of them but I am especially happy with one of them." While the young man was telling his dream, the listeners started to weep out of reverence and happiness! Because the Messenger of Allah, upon him be peace and blessings, did not reveal the name of the person whom he was extra happy with, it made each one of them wish and hope that he was the one. This increased their love for the classes, their longing for its time and their studies of the lessons.

Until now, when they remember that dream they feel humbled and they weep. They all became active in inviting other youth to the gathering and a few days after the dream the number attending reached thirty young men. The room could not contain them so they sat in the prayer area. This agitated the worries of the Secret Service who told Fethullah that they were going to attack the mosque and arrest the youth. Fethullah replied, "If you do, I am going to expose you to the public and reveal all of your plots to the people." When they found such strength and determination in Fethullah they wisely chose to leave the place in peace.

On the day of Eid al-Fitr, the Feast of breaking the fast of Ramadan, Fethullah invented an effective way to awaken faith in people and to give their miserable souls some hope. He printed a card for an Eid greeting. The card had two sides. On one side, he wrote the greeting and on the other side he wrote a translation of one hadith of the Prophet and his advice. The hadith was narrated by Khabbab ibn al-Arat and it asked people not to rush things and at the same time assured them of the final victory of Islam.

The owner of the printing press company sent a copy of the greeting card to the General Attorney following the law of the time. This caused great havoc in the Police Department and in the Justice Department in the city. It was night time and snow was calmly falling. Fethullah was in his room when he suddenly heard noise outside so he looked from the window and saw the head of the Police Department himself, Resul Bey, with a small security force. Fethullah realized that they were going to invade the house so he threw tens of books behind the bookshelf. As soon as he did, they stormed into the room and searched it but they could not find anything forbidden and could not find evidence that would allow them to prosecute him. They then said, "Let us search the next room." But Fethullah immediately said, "This is the Grand Jurist's room and I do not use it at all." Nonetheless, they insisted on searching it and then they took him to the police station.

Fethullah had a good relationship with Resul Bey who rescued him before from being arrested. Nonetheless, Resul's boss issued an order to bring Fethullah to the police station. Resul Bey wanted to do it by himself since he knew how cruel and arrogant his boss was and what bad manners he had. In the beginning Fethullah thought that the reason behind his arrest was the greeting card, but he soon realized that it was because of something different. The real reason was that some of his colleagues in the Department of Qur'an Education had complained to the police chief concerning his activism in gathering the students and training them to become activists themselves. This complaint was because of their jealousy and inability to compete with him in attracting the students to their circles. They were jealous of his success. After some questioning at the police station, the chief told him, "Fethullah! For the last time I am warning you! From now on, do not get involved in the students' affairs. If I receive any complaints against you again, not only will I arrest you but I am also going to punish you in a way that no one can imagine!"

However, Fethullah was not a coward nor was he a weak man. He had responded before to those who were higher in rank and position among the army. Thus, he immediately said, "Yes, I know that you may have the power in this world to do whatever pleases you with me but know that someday you are going to die and be buried under the dust! There I am going to bring you to a fair reckoning."

The young man would never forget how the General Jurist, Suad Yildirim stood up against the behavior of the police chief who wanted to bring him to the police station. The chief called him and arrogantly said, "Oh General Jurist! We want you here and we are waiting for you to come." Ustadh Suad Yildi-rim replied in a strong manner, "I am now in my office so if you need anything I do not mind you visiting me here at my work place!"

The police chief swallowed his wounded pride and fell silent. Fethullah's love and reverence for the General Jurist increased and he wished he would allow him to kiss his head as a gesture of gratitude for taking such a manly stand and annoying the arrogant chief who was used to ordering all employees of the Religious Affairs Department, including the highest jurists, to come to his office. He deliberately wanted to insult them and bring them whenever he wanted for whatever he wanted! It was Ustadh Suad Yildirim who cut this habit by confronting him and taking a strong stand and forcing him not to cross his boundaries.

In the police station there was a drunken officer who was almost never sober day or night. He was the one who interrogated Fethullah. He described the greeting card which Fethullah printed as treachery. One of the issues he kept asking about was why after the Laylat al-Qadr, the Night of Power, his friends embrace each other while crying? What is the cause of such extraordinary love between them? Why do you weep a lot during the Salat at-Tahajjud—the Night Vigil, on the Night of Power?

After some time, many judges and even the General Attorney started to frequently visit the Daru'l-Hadith Mosque where Fethullah was hired as the Imam and would teach there. The reason behind such visits was to monitor him themselves. The name of the General Attorney was Selçuk and he was originally from Erzincan close to Erzurum, Fethullah's hometown.

After one Friday Prayer, the Imam was informed that the General Attorney was waiting for him outside the mosque. Fethullah did not expect good from him so he did not leave the mosque. After a long period of waiting, the General Attorney sent a guard to Fethullah to inform him that he must go to the court to meet the General Attorney there. Fethullah felt he had to go. The General Attorney asked him again about the greeting card and about other allusions or words that Fethullah made. In the end, he said to him, "Fethullah! You are a terrible enemy to the authorities even though you do not mention the names of the rulers directly during your classes, but you do mention their qualities directly so that the audience is able to identify them. You always praise the past and strongly criticize the present with your powerful expressions. You do not read your speeches but your random expressions are very influencing and terrifying! Be reasonable, for it is in your capacity to praise some of the people from your platform while you are sitting and delivering your speeches." He continued to try to convince the Imam in many different ways to join the secular authority. He would sometimes try to tempt him with worldly gains and at other times he would threaten him, but all of his efforts were in vain!

After a preacher named Huseyin Efendi insisted, Fethullah started to teach ladies every Tuesday instead of him. The ladies used to stare at him and examine his handsome face for a long time! This used to disturb him. Thus, one time he said to them, "If you would look at the spot where you perform your prostration while listening to me it would be better than looking at my face." This sentence flew to the General Attorney who later asked him about it. This confirmed to Fethullah that even some from among the women were hired in the Secret Service.

On the day of Eid, Fethullah delivered a speech in the ancient mosque in response to Ustadh Suad Yildirim's request. He was cautious not to agitate the authorities so he only used a few words to criticize the over use of intoxicants and to criticize the general ethical corruption. He also criticized how many young men and women stood beside the mosque windows and exchanged kisses. He criticized how drinking was so widespread that there was even drinking behind the courtyard walls of mosques. He mentioned how the Justice Department and Educational Department were trying to remedy the situation. This speech resulted in further interrogation in courts and police stations where Fethullah was questioned about every single word he said and was accused of many kinds of political crimes.

One of the strange issues that Fethullah discovered during his interrogations was that fifteen witnesses came voluntarily to testify against him. There was one man who pretended to testify on his behalf but later Fethullah discovered that he too belonged to the Secret Service and was one of the people who wrote reports against him.

But the strangest testimony issued against him was the testimony of the principal of the high school of arts. He claimed that he had heard Fethullah telling people, "We have to attack such and such place. Let us attack such and such person." After he finished his lies, Fethullah requested the judge to allow him to speak and when he was permitted he said, "I would like to ask this man in front of you did I not tell people to preserve the country's security and not to hurt anyone? Did I not tell them that social stability is important to maintain and that they must follow the law? People heard me saying these words. Why did you not testify that I said these words?"

The principal did not know what to say except to make an excuse, "The microphone was not working well and I did not hear every word you said." Fethullah said, "How strange you are! The microphone works well when you want to hear something and does not work well when you do not want to hear something! What is happening to this microphone? It seems to work well for the words that can lead to my prosecution and does not work well for words that can be used to defend me!" Fethullah looked at the judges and said, "Oh respected gentlemen! When a person has contradictions in his testimony he cannot be considered a reliable witness. His credibility should be questioned and his testimony should be rejected." The face of the lying principal was darkened and he resorted to silence trying to hide his feeling of shame.

There was even a stranger testimony that was delivered by a lawyer who was supposed to be well-informed of the law. He worked for the government's Treasury Department. He used to pray regularly at the mosque where Fethullah served. He even prayed the Tarawih Prayer behind him for many nights. In addition, he invited him for breakfast one time and let him sit with his close circle of friends. He sat with Fethullah for tea many times before Ramadan with other well-educated people in Edirne. When the head judge asked him about Fethullah saying, "Do you know this man?" The man answered, "No!" In his strange testimony he said, "I once entered the mosque and felt a terrifying feeling as if I were attending a military coup! This Imam was strongly criticizing the authorities and provoking people. The top of his turban was shaking out of anger and people were agitated with anger because of the influence of his words."

One more time, Fethullah requested permission to speak but this time the head judge denied him the chance to speak. But Fethullah kept insisting on speaking until the head judge permitted it. The Imam looked the man in the eyes and then at the judges and said, "Oh respected gentlemen! This man who claims he does not know me is one of the people who know me well. He prayed behind me the Tarawih Prayer this year except for a few nights and Ramadan just finished a few days ago. So did you forget me that fast? This man invited me to have breakfast at his house with a few friends who can testify to this. I wonder if he also forgot that we had tea together at such and such café with so and so and so and so. If he has forgotten all of that, how can he remember the things that he said against me?"

Hearing the Imam's words, the lawyer was greatly disturbed and he said, "Yes I know him." Then he took his coat and immediately left the court room without looking back.

There was a person named Rifat Bey who was one of the very few who testified on behalf of Fethullah. He was honest and sincere and strongly defended Fethullah. His defense was nobler and stronger than any other attorney who could have defended Fethullah. He was one of the elites of the city and was one of the most honorable people there. His testimony had a great influence on the judges. Rifat Bey used to socialize with many of the elites in society, including the judges themselves and the prosecutors as well. He looked at the judges and said, "Oh gentlemen! You all know me very well. I used to drink wine until I got drunk and go in the city streets and scream. Many people used to be afraid of me. But when I met this great Imam and witnessed his sincerity I revered him and sat in his classes. I paid farewell to my bad past and started to pray in the mosque. I found myself there." Everyone attending the court session was looking at him with great admiration. The man was tall and his voice was loud. He had a strong personality and people respected him.

In spite of the fact that the court sessions seemed to be going in favor of Fethullah, the Imam was prevented from teaching during the entire period his case was in court. The authorities held his license which qualified him to preach and teach. They prepared a fake report full of lies in order to put him in prison for a period not less than ten years. In spite of this conspiracy, Allah protected him and they did not succeed in achieving their goal. They were forced to change their minds at least for a while.

Later, Fethullah knew that all of these plots were planned by Edirne's Governor Ferid Kubat who was stubborn and a racist. An anti-Islamic secularist stance was running within him like his blood. He used to hate seeing religious scholars, preachers and speakers. He was very annoyed and angry seeing them doing their jobs. He became the Minister of the Interior after the military coup that occurred in Turkey on the 12th of March, 1971.

This envious man was the one responsible for Fethullah's suffering during that time. The Imam knew that his license to preach was in Ferid Kubat's drawer. Fethullah would not forget the day when Ferid Kubat called all religious scholars for a meeting and spoke strongly to them and everyone felt that Fethullah was the real target in that speech. He looked straight at him saying, "Among you today there are those who commit treachery who are lowly and varmints. They deserve to be crushed and annihilated!"

That man spent the latter years of his life suffering bitterness and facing hostility even from among members of his party who accompanied him for years. He died lonely and bitter!

Migration to Kırklareli Province

There was nothing more difficult on Fethullah than confiscating his vocal ability, arresting his tongue and preventing him from teaching and preaching. Suffocating him would have been easier on him than doing this. His heart was attached to the ancient mosque domes and their lofty minarets. Whenever he would sit underneath the domes and minarets, flocks of doves and hoopoes would land listening to him chanting the spring's hymns. When they comprehended the lesson well they flew towards many cities in the world. They would then return to him holding branches of olive trees between their beaks and some grains as evidence that they had arrived at the land of peace!

The siege set around Fethullah had intensified shaking the birds' nests and destroying their dreams. The snipers were looking for the moment the birds would land on the mosques so that they could shoot the birds. Fethullah foresaw that and wept and wept!

Edirne became a horrifying nightmare for him, which deprived him of sleep at night and made him worry in the morning. Here, the Head of the Security Department was terrifying him continuously. He prevented him from teaching the noble Qur'an to the students. And the city's Governor held his teaching license, preventing him from preaching in the mosques. He was forced to argue with them all the time. Thus, he started to think of migrating to another place.

After a few days, he traveled to the capital, Ankara. There he coincidently met with his intimate friend Ustadh Yaşar Tunagür. At that time he was an employee in Izmir in the western coast of Turkey. He was in Ankara for a personal reason. They both sat together and Fethullah told Yaşar about his problem with the authority in Edirne. Yaşar advised him, "Listen my brother, Fethullah! No one in the Religious Affairs Department will listen to you now and they will not listen to your complaint about this difficult situation."

Fethullah was fed up with the situation in Edirne and could not stay there with tied feet and hands and with an arrested tongue. Thus, he went to the Head of the Religious Affairs Department in Ankara and told him his story, asking him to help transfer him to another province. But the Head Administrator insisted that Fethullah should continue working at Edirne. Fethullah did not give up and tried to persuade the man to transfer him to any other city even to one close to Edirne. Finally, under Fethullah's pressure the Head Administrator agreed. He issued him a document which stated that his work in Edirne had ended and another document that stated he was hired to work in the province of Kırklareli which is across from Edirne on the European side of Turkey across from the Balkans border. Fethullah took both documents and returned happily to Edirne.

As soon as he returned to Edirne, he was informed that the angry Governor, Ferid Kubat, had been transferred to another place and that his assistant would be in charge for a while. The assistant's name was Nail Memik. He was a conservative man to some extent. He used to at least pray the Friday Prayer. He was soft and gentle. He was the one who signed the document that Fethullah brought with him from Ankara which would cut his relations with Edirne. The man immediately gave Fethullah the document as if he wanted to get rid of a problem. And in spite of the fact that his preaching license was taken from him, this did not pose a problem for the Assistant Governor; for what was important to him was to get rid of the problem by getting rid of Fethullah.

It was so ironic that the miserable man was hired later to be the governor of Kırklareli which was the same city that Fethullah was transferred to. Thus, Nail Memik had to face his destiny in dealing with this strange preacher!

Fethullah entered Kırklareli on the 23rd of July, 1965 and he stayed there for six months until the 11th of March, 1966, after which he migrated to Izmir in the southwest part of Turkey.

Kırklareli was a city like any other city! It has an old military barracks and shelter which protected the heart of Constantinople. The mountains of Kırklareli face the western cities close by, raising a challenging flag to confront the fog, a reminder of the struggle which once took place in the past!

Necip Fazıl, the Dean of Turkish Literature, Answers Fethullah's Invitation

Even though Fethullah stayed only a short time in Kırklareli, he still filled it with activism and energy as usual. In addition to being the Imam of the mosque there and his continuous preaching, he gathered a group of youth in private meetings for teaching and spiritual training. In a few days, he succeeded in planting a seed of good in that strategically critical city. They took a particular house to be a place for meetings, teaching and spreading the message of Light.

At that time, Fethullah succeeded in convincing the Turkish poet, Necip Fazıl to deliver a lecture in the city. The poet came and it was a historical event for the young people and for the whole city. Necip Fazıl was not only a poet, but he was a thinker, a masterful scholar, and a wise preacher. He was the legend of modern Turkish literature and Turkey's first poet. He deservingly gained the title "The Sultan of Poets" and became "The Dean of Turkish Literature" without any equal competitor. He excelled in writing poems, novels, short stories, plays and he was also a great journalist. His articles were highly regarded in political circles. He published a newspaper called *The Great East* (*Büyük Doğu*) which became a school for a whole generation of deprived youth. It was a meadow in which one can inhale the fragrance of religion at a time when religion had been confiscated!

Necip Fazıl lived his whole life moving from city to city, delivering lectures, and renewing determination and destroying the illusion of despair in the youth. He strongly refuted the irreligious philosophy and fiercely resisted the current of alienation. His pen was like a diamond sword piercing through time in all directions. The ink of his pen was bleeding from the deep wound that split the head of the Islamic civilization.

Being able to accommodate Necip Fazıl while being chased everywhere sent many messages about Fethullah. On one of the nights, the youth met with Necip Fazıl in one of the houses and sat around the same table eating dinner. It was there that Necip Fazıl felt close to Fethullah Gülen and gave him special attention. He praised the thoughts that Fethullah represented during the meeting. Necip Fazıl was staring at the face that perplexed people and disturbed the tyrants as he spoke openly and bravely. Newspapers had called him "the grandson of Mehmed the Conqueror." The poet Necip Fazıl was able to read the sad story on Fethullah's face. He knew that this story would change the current of history!

Fethullah's name was not unknown at that time. News of court sessions and what was published by the secular media at the time made him famous. This could have been the reason why Necip Fazıl accepted Fethullah's invitation. But on that particular night, Necip Fazıl became certain that Fethullah is the revival of Light in Turkey. He was the heir of the secret of the Last Cavalier.

After leaving the city, Necip Fazıl started to write a series of essays in *The Great East* about the importance of spreading the *Epistles of Light* and its necessity for Turkish society.

There was a local newspaper named *Ata Yolu* that was continuously publishing essays against Fethullah. It published an essay against Necip Fazıl. Fethullah sent Necip a copy of the newspaper. In response, Necip Fazıl published a sarcastic caricature of a big dog and beside him a very small dog. Under the illustration he wrote, "We are facing this big one so from where did this small one appear?"

A New Eclipse

The situation in Turkey at that time was difficult and darkness had intensified. The attack on the radiant rays was renewed. The ghosts of darkness hijacked everything beautiful. The birds felt so suffocated in their tears that they could not chant for a while! The voices of the *muezzins* calling for the Prayer were cracked as they tried to suppress their tears.

Since the terrible 1960 coup and the execution of Prime Minister Adnan Menderes and some of his faithful ministers, their grasp of people was tightened and they became furious until İsmet İnönü became the Prime Minister again.

İsmet İnönü was Ataturk's companion. During Atatürk's time he served as the Chief of Staff. Then, he became the second Turkish President after the death of Atatürk in 1938. In the same year he became the head of the Republican People's Party which was ruling Turkey. Then, he became the Prime Minister a few times. He also became the Minister for Foreigner Affairs one time. He played a great role in erasing the Islamic color of Turkey. He was a furious dictator. He came from the heart of the military and ruled the Turkish people with an iron fist.

İsmet İnönü criticized Ataturk for being slack in diminishing all the traces of Light inside schools and mosques. He changed Turkish money by erasing Atatürk's picture and printing his own picture instead.

When the army let him rule Turkey after the 1960 coup, the whole country was transformed into hell. Trees were burnt and the nests were transformed to ashes! There was no place to chant! The sound of death was heard on the streets and roads. 1960 was the year of sadness in the modern history of Turkey. In that year the reviver of religion, Bediuzzaman Said Nursi, passed away. In that year the bloody coup occurred and destroyed the civilian government. Gallows were erected everywhere. The ordinary people of Turkey felt that they were truly orphaned and opposite the beaches and gulfs, weeping voices were issued from all lighthouses!

Fethullah's Role Had to Come

The young Imam felt that the time of revealing the secret was approaching! It was time to prepare the cavaliers; for the horses had arrived at the city walls. He was twenty-six years old and realizedhow great his responsibility was that he had to carry on his shoulders.

The tree of secrets was quickly growing within Fethullah's heart. Its branches were extending vigorously into his arteries. Every morning his eyes were opened by the walnut roses! His spiritual findings extended across the European part of Turkey until Thrace's gardens could not contain his lofty branches anymore. The shadow of his branches spread between Edirne and Kırklareli until there was no more room to contain his fruit. His great trunk was vibrating knowing that he must depart! He kept weeping and weeping!

Fethullah has a secret he does not divulge! Fethullah has a secret the whole world is waiting for! But he is not revealing it to anyone. Fethullah is enduring that which no heart can bear! This is why he continuously weeps until tears become perplexed at its death! Fethullah is the heir of a secret which if it were revealed to a high mountain, the rocks at its very top would fall and its foundations would crumble!

The Narrator said: After the military coup Imam Fethullah had the annual break of forty days. He took the opportunity to visit many Turkish cities to renew his connection with his brothers and companions on the path. In the capital Ankara he met his close friend Ustadh Yaşar Tunagür who was appointed as the Vice-President of the Religious Affairs Department in Ankara. Fethullah explained to him his dire situation and how he was besieged. Ustadh Yaşar suggested that he migrate to Izmir in the far west of the country. Fethullah thought that such a move would be very difficult, wondering how a young preacher could be accepted as a preacher in a big city like Izmir. Nevertheless, Ustadh Yaşar insisted that Fethullah should submit an application to the Religious Affairs Department. When Fethullah refused, Ustadh Yaşar instructed one of his employees to fill out the application on his behalf and he insisted that Fethullah sign it. He then sent the application to the office of the Head of the Religious Affairs Department, Ustadh Muhammad Hamdi Yazir to sign it.

Ustadh Yaşar used to be the principal of the religious school in Izmir. He used to work as a preacher in the mosque affiliated with it. He was loved because of his honesty and devotion and when he was hired as the Vice-President for the Religious Affairs Department in Ankara people were very sad so he promised to send them a young, strong, honest and devoted preacher to replace himself and he had no one in mind except his friend Muhammad Fethullah Gülen.

When Fethullah returned to Kırklareli to collect his small suitcase and to pay farewell to his brothers before departing to Izmir, his friends were shocked and they wept when he was leaving. On the morning of the 11th of March, 1966 they said farewell to him by glorifying Allah and testifying to His Oneness and they accompanied him to Edirne where he said farewell to his other friends there. He then took the train towards the big city of Izmir in the western part of Anatolia.

It was His decree! When we look at the marvelous coincidences in his life we can clearly see the signs of the beginning of a new era! He was born in 1938 which was the same year which Kamal Ataturk passed away. The time at which he was able to reveal his concealed secret was in Izmir which is the same city where İsmet İnönü was born. Izmir was then the base of ultra-secularists and their resilient fortress until Fethullah arrived!

Fethullah's life was full of signs and coincidences. If the Narrator of sentimental memories had permitted us to reveal them, we would have disclosed the extraordinary gifts he was given in this chapter! But, Oh my heart! Be patient on your difficult walk; for you still have some pages before you include from the treasury of secrets what would fully delight you! Everything there was alright as long as there was a spring but suddenly darkness crept upon the houses!

Chapter 7

The Main Migration to Izmir: The First Union with the Horses of Conquest

A City on the Shore of Alienation

The full secret was in Izmir! And what a secret! The waves of the Mediterranean Sea were going back and forth between Izmir and Gibraltar uniting Granada and Izmir as twins in sorrow. With the same rhythm, the two cities lamented the diminishing Light. Everything was alright as long as there was a spring but all of a sudden, darkness crept upon the houses.

On one of the difficult days, the creeping waves of Greek gulfs attacked Izmir's shores and it drowned all of its ports! The walls of the city were defenseless and the agitated water filled all the roads so much that the whole city of Izmir was about to be drowned in the Mediterranean Sea as Granada drowned and it almost became the news of a history that once was!

When the Romans invaded Izmir in a heedless moment they found a lost Ottoman princess, searching across the sea shore for her murdered father. Therefore, they captured her! What a sorrow! She was young with beads made of Light. If she would have revealed her hidden pearl, she would have impressively stopped the deer in their green meadows and silenced the chanting of birds; for she would be the only melody and the only poem worthy of listening to! Ah! Who is going to free the captive and heal the wounded honor? Who can stand on behalf of the princess of a wounded country?

Fethullah entered Izmir with caution and watchfulness! He was cautious enough not to let anyone discover his secret before he arrived at the fortress gate. He carried on his shoulders the responsibility of opening the city gates for the conquerors' horses. He carried his heart full of seeds of Light and a map showing him how to free the captive princess. For the first time he started to use the keys of the secrets; for Fethullah has a secret that he does not reveal to anyone! Fethullah has a secret that the whole world is waiting for but he does not divulge it to anyone! Fethullah carries within his heart that which he cannot bear! This is why he has been weeping until tears were perplexed at its death! Fethullah is the heir of a secret. If a high mountain would inherit it, its top would fall down and its foundation would crumble out of reverence and awe!

A Principal of Kestanepazarı School

Kestanepazarı (Chestnut Market) is a place in the middle of Izmir that has a Roman style of architecture and people. There, the pillars of the religious school were erected in a modest style. The school was supervised by the Department of Religious Affairs. After a few months of pain and suffering, this place had a deep spiritual impact upon Fethullah that filled his whole life.

The Narrator of sentimental memories said to me: When Fethullah arrived at the mosque in Kestanepazarı he found Mr. Ismail Türe waiting for him and the man immediately carried his bag. He also found a group of people anxiously waiting for him at the mosque door. The mosque was an ancient historical mosque and in its main hall, there was a student dorm. There, a new stage of Fethullah's call was going to start. This stage was going to be very different from the previous stages concerning its magnitude and its quality.

Fethullah put his small bag in the room that was given to him in the student dorm. He arranged his stuff in a closet that had a glass door. There was one couch that could be made into a bed at night. When he got to work, he observed the necessity of taking care and watching over the students day and night to rectify their affairs. It then became his duty to stop by their rooms every day and night. He also had to carefully watch the other rooms of service and the bathrooms. From the first moment it became clear to him that the students were not convinced that their principal could be that young. Moreover, all the teachers did not believe it as well. Fethullah heard some of the teachers saying to the students, "Could not Ustadh Yaşar have found an older teacher instead of sending us this young man to be our principal?" This hurt Fethullah's feelings and it made the students take him lightly and this made his mission even more difficult.

The teacher, who previously held the managing position of the student dorm, introduced Fethullah saying, "O students, this young man is going to be your principal or someone like a principal." This was how the young man received his duty with absolute low morale.

But this was the beginning in the school of Kestanepazarı in Izmir. The students remained the same until the President of the Organization and his high ranking assistants intervened. The President's name was Ali Rıza Güven. He was a highly respected man in Izmir. He was very intelligent, observant and he could quickly and accurately evaluate men and realize their true substance. After a few days he realized the greatness of Fethullah. Ali Rıza used to stop by the student dorm and observe their affairs. After Fethullah's arrival, he noticed how Fethullah was always available and how he was performing his duties in the best possible way. One time, he entered the place while Fethullah was performing his duties and he said to him, "Oh honorable one, Ustadh Fethullah! This dorm is fully under your control and I think there is no reason for me to stop by from now on." Indeed, Ali Rıza Güven stopped visiting the dorm from that moment on. Instead, he held a meeting with all the administrators and the teachers in the school and said to them, "Fethullah Bey is a great man and I have observed how he is serious about his work. He is performing all of his duties in the best possible way. I also noticed that he does not eat from the students' food, not even one morsel. He is worthy of respect and reverence. If I ever hear that any of you have dared to disrespect him in any way I will not hesitate to fire you." This was the beginning of changing their attitude towards Fethullah and how they looked at their young principal.

The Beginning Was from a Wooden Hut

After six months, Fethullah's personality became more apparent and all rebellious souls surrendered to him willingly or unwillingly. They all discovered that he is a masterful preacher and has a personality of leadership that is characterized by a degree of strength and honesty that they had never witnessed before.

The school's administrators decided to provide him with private lodging. They built him a small room on the side on the mosque hall. It was only two meters square and made of wood. It looked more like a cave but Fethullah loved his room; for it witnessed many important meetings, many enthusiastic initiatives concerning the call and many decisive plans. There, he laid the first cornerstone for his call in a new format which contained all of the Turkish people and extended across the world.

In his wooden hut, Fethullah met his new friends who carried his call later and assisted him in spreading it. Some of those friends were: Mr. Ali Rıza Güven, Mr. Sacid Çayköylü, Mr. Saffet Solak and many others. They used to meet there and listen to his deep conversations with all due respect. They were feeding their souls. Fethullah would make them tea and serve them himself. Ali Rıza was one of the people who was greatly influenced by him; for he was a man ready to serve and contribute his efforts for a good cause. He was a pious man and was revered as one of *awliya'*, or Allah's friends.

Fethullah obtained a license to preach in the entire Aegean region. It was a chance to visit all of the different cities and towns and get to know people there. He used to travel to Anatolia, Aydın, Denizli, Isparta, Tire, Ödemiş, Simav, Salihli, Turgutlu, Gediz and many other places. In addition, he entered many mosques in Izmir. On some Sundays, he would preach outside of Izmir and therefore travel at night to be on time for the students on Monday mornings to deliver his lesson at the Kestanepazarı Boarding Qur'anic School! He had an intensive work program and he used to move everywhere in all directions. In the beginning, he used to use public transportation but after he met his friends, Yusuf Pekmezci and Mr. Köse Mahmud, they donated the use of their car for the call and they would accompany him wherever he went. Mr. Mustafa Birlik and his family also devoted themselves to serve Ustadh Fethullah and his call. They would open their houses for meetings. Fethullah used to hold educational meetings every Tuesday and Saturday.

Izmir's condition was different at that time and it did not have many students interested in religious sciences. Most of the students were from the Kestanepazarı Boarding Qur'anic School. They were underdeveloped spiritually speaking. This is why Ustadh Fethullah organized two trips for them to Edirne and Istanbul in order to introduce them to the Cavaliers of Light and so they could learn from their ethics and spiritual lessons.

In the beginning the security condition was slightly better even though Fethullah knew that he was secretly being watched. Luckily, the policeman who was charged with watching Fethullah was from Erzurum and a graduate from the religious institute there. This meant that he could be closer to the imams and the preachers. He had gentle manners and would hold long conversations with Fethullah. He only wrote positive reports regarding Fethullah. At that time, Fethullah did not know that reporting about him was the man's job. He only found that out later from one of the reports that was given to the Department of Religious Affairs.

One time, Fethullah was called for investigational purposes to the office of Public Persecution. This was because a female judge had been hired in Edirne in place of the judge that handled Fethullah's case when he lived there. A person wrote an insulting letter to this judge and he signed it as if he were Fethullah Gülen. This was why he was called to go to be questioned. It was fortunate that the letter had been handwritten and it was easy to realize that it was not Fethullah's handwriting and this is why they released him immediately.

Fethullah was able to go beyond the walls of the university in Izmir through the Institution of Islamic Sciences. He used to participate in the symposiums held there. In one of those symposiums he delivered a lecture about Islamic financing and another time he spoke about *tasawwuf*—the spiritual aspect of Islam. In this way he was able to correct many misconceptions concerning Islam. He also provided the religious students great spiritual support to face the spread of secularism.

The communists used to write anti-Islamic statements on the walls and young Muslims used to write their responses in the same style. Fethullah advised them that such efforts were in vain and instead he became involved in lecturing around the city. His interactions used to attract people's attention and they became the subject of conversations among young people. He also delivered several lectures about the Qur'an and its doctrines that explain physical phenomenon and affirm scientific facts. When he intensified his efforts, his efforts led to establishing a legal organization that embraced his teaching. The name of the organization was "Revival Foundation." Its members were university students and pious people and of course Ustadh Fethullah. The organization did not continue for long because its vision was not clear and its members did not share the same perspective. It eventually turned out to be meetings and talks without being fruitful. Thus, Fethullah made the decision, with some close friends, to dissolve it.

Fethullah turned his attention towards reconstructing the official high school for imams and preachers. He aimed towards constructing a new Islamic institution that would be affiliated with the university. This was because he noticed how the government neglected all religious institutions and provided buildings that were in bad condition. For the graduate institutions for Islamic Studies, the Educational Department did not provide them a building at all. They were usually given a few classrooms or one floor within another college. Fethullah used to go every day, along with Ustadh Ali Rıza and Dr. Dursun Aksoy, looking for a good location until they found a suitable piece of land and they purchased it. They had to visit many businessmen and merchants to solicit donations. He went through many bitter experiences from which he learned many lessons which made him develop a way in which to address wealthy people. This helped to serve his call.

He still remembers the owner of one of the big factories who donated fifty liras only. At that point, he realized that this way was not effective in collecting donations and that he must invite them to a certain place at a certain time rather than visiting them at their work places.

The first meeting of that kind was organized in a room above a shop owned by Hajji Ahmed Tatari. There were a few merchants there and the first to speak was Fethullah. After him, Ali Rıza Güven spoke. Then they started to solicit donations. Mr. Tatari gave one hundred thousand liras and Ali Rıza gave half of that amount. Then every person in the room gave in accordance to their capacity. What perplexed Fethullah was the fact that the richest person among them gave only two thousand five hundred liras. Thus, Fethullah said, "Each person gives in accordance to his faith."

Fethullah learned that the most important issue in this kind of meeting was to convince the audience of the importance of serving the Islamic cause and the importance of spreading the message of Islam. This became the foundation of every speech from that time on. All efforts continued under the care of Fethullah until the high school for imams and preachers was opened and until the Islamic Institution for undergraduate students was established in a new building especially designated for it. This was the first strategic step towards educating a new generation within Turkey that had been held captive for so long!

A Step towards the Media

Media and education are one and the same job and two faces for one reality. Thus, Fethullah published a weekly newspaper with his friends in Izmir called *Vahdet* (*Union*). Salih Özcan, the old friend, used to visit Izmir often and with his help and the help of the older brother, the student of Bediuzzaman Nursi, Zübeyir Gündüzalp, the newspaper started to be issued weekly. For the Hajj occasion in 1968 a larger issue was published and the students of Light sold it in Mecca and Medina. This was a fruitful year for the newspaper.

The editor of the newspaper was Mr. Mustafa Polat, who had been a close friend to Fethullah since childhood. He was from Erzurum as well and he was an expert journalist and loved journalism. Before meeting him, Fethullah thought that there was no such journalist in Turkey. He was an expert in designing newspaper pages and at the same time he was a great writer. Nobody ever saw him writing a draft for his articles; he would spontaneously write them. When he would write he would be totally absorbed by what he was writing. He would sweat even if he were writing during winter time. He would be deeply immersed in writing in a marvelous way. He would put his feet in cold water and put the typewriter in front of him and would continue to write without stopping until he had finished. He would then tell his assistant, "Take this to be published in this issue." He would not feel the need to edit or correct anything. Mustafa Polat was a talented and clever journalist and writer. He inherited his talent from being raised in a house of journalists. His father was the owner of a newspaper called *Hürsöz* (*Free Word*) which used to be published in Erzurum. Mustafa Polat used to write his diary when he was a young child in a secret language so that no one else could read it. Because of his talent and expertise *Vahdet* was a high quality newspaper.

At that time, Mehmed Şevket Eygi used to publish a newspaper called *Bugün* (*Today*) from Istanbul. It was a truly successful newspaper. More than a hundred thousand issues of the newspaper used to be sold daily. This was an exceptional number at that time. Later, *Vahdet* started to gradually excel its distribution. This alarmed some of the administrators of the *Bugün* newspaper and it stimulated their envy. This was because they thought *Bugün* was the only representative of the Islamic current. Thus, disputes began to happen here and there which led to confrontation on the pages of the two newspapers. Writers from both newspapers exchanged accusations and criticism. This angered Fethullah so he called his friend, Mustafa Polat, and told him, "My brother, why do you attack those people? I cannot agree with your approach at all; for how can I reconcile your approach with that of Bediuzzaman's approach?" The editor said, "Oh Sir, they attack us as well." Fethullah said in a firm tone, "Even if they attacked us ten times if we attack them once, then we would be the transgressors because we are the people who invite people to Allah, which means we should apply all the values we call people for and that these principles should be illuminating our way. Oh Mr. Polat, if you insist on following this approach, I will find another way to solve this problem." He said these words in an angry tone and he hung up. Fethullah did not see his friend, Mustafa Polat, after this incident; for the man passed away shortly after that in a horrible accident. Fethullah regretted how he ended the last phone call with him with such a rough tone, but Allah knows that he never gets angry except for His sake. Fethullah has a tender heart and he felt really sad for losing his beloved friend Mustafa Polat, and he wished that his last words with him were not the words he said to him but anyway, that was Allah's decree after all.

The dispute between the *Vahdet* and *the Bugün* newspapers intensified after that and this disturbed Fethullah immensely. He saw a bitter quarrel heating up between the companions of the same path and how can the call to Islam be successful in such an environment? Thus, he took the decision to stay away from participating in the newspaper out of care for his main mission.

Constructing the University Dorm

Fethullah found Izmir's Grand Jurist, Ahmed Karakullukçu, with one of the imams waiting for him when he arrived in Ankara after he performed the pilgrimage to Mecca in 1968. At this time in Ankara there was a dorm for the religious students who were enrolled in the university. Forty students gathered that night in one of the rooms and invited Fethullah and the Grand Jurist. The Grand Jurist was impressed by their devotion to their religion. When he left with Fethullah to return to Izmir he said, "We should also open dorms like this in our city. You should open any number of dorms you want and house all the religious students. I will bring the rental price of the buildings from the İlim Yayma Cemiyeti (Organization of Spreading Knowledge)."

Indeed this took place, as the Grand Jurist came up with the rental fee for a whole year and this was the initial seed for a great good which served the Turkish society and became a center for inviting people to Allah. Fethullah established the first dorm for the students in Izmir. The area where the house was rented was not so good but the student dorm was like a green meadow in the middle of an arid desert. There, students used to gather for remembrance (*dhikr*), and to study issues related to faith. Fethullah used to attend many of the student gatherings. He wished he could live with them and he used to stay with them until the middle of the night and then he would hurry to his work place to perform the duties of his administrative job in the school of Kestanepazarı.

Fethullah would never forget the night when he read with the students Bediuzzaman Said Nursi's book *Isharatu'l I'jaz* (*Signs of Miraculousness*). They stayed up most of the night until many students fell asleep except one of them, Mr. Muazzam who spent the night studying the section on the Day of Resurrection from the book with Fethullah. When Fethullah reached a sentence that stated, "Oh Merciful Beloved! Oh Beloved of Mercy!" his voice started to crack and the student could hear a sound issuing from the wall accompanied by moaning, "Ah!.. Ah!" as if the wall was moaning from the intensity of its longing to meet the Beloved. Fethullah heard the sound repeated five times while his friend heard it three times!

Before the March 12th coup, Fethullah opened two more dorms. One of them was in an area called Buca while the other was in Bornova. Mr. Mustafa Birlik was the one who purchased the one in Bornova. He bought it with the money he got from selling the shops he inherited from his father. The price of the shops was eighty-five thousand liras. Other friends added about fifteen thousand liras to it. They purchased the house for one hundred thousand liras. It is worthy to mention that Mr. Mustafa Birlik himself did not have a house at that time!

The brothers bought more houses for the students at that time in many areas across Izmir. All the dorms became places to gather to discuss issues pertaining to faith and to hold schools from which faithful believers graduated and dispersed across Turkey's cities carrying the same invitation to many others. In this way, they rescued the country from irreligiosity.

The Stage of Camping

The Narrator said: The summer of 1968 was not an ordinary summer in the life of the Islamic Call in Turkey. It witnessed the first step in establishing camps where students retreat to serene havens for the sake of spiritual refreshment. The first challenge that faced the establishment of such camps was funding the project. Fethullah remembered how the military borrowed large amounts of money from people after the military coup that occurred on the 27th of May, 1960. In return, the military gave the lenders securities and checks that could be cashed from the nation's Treasury Department at its due time. So Fethullah traveled to Izmir and met many people he knew and convinced them of the project he was seeking to fund and he collected about 3,000 liras from securities and checks that were due at that time. He returned to Izmir with the money and gave everything to the organization that ran the Kestane-pazarı Qur'anic Boarding School. Fethullah then immediately started setting up the tents for camping with the help of some of his friends. He organized many youth camps in the mountains and in the middle of natural forests that were far away.

These camps characterized that time, which Fethullah still remembers when he looks at how he invited people to Allah. These camps had a great impact on the youth that they would not forget. There the students were given a boost of faith and learned the realities and meanings of having faith. This was something they never learned the whole year in the regular educational system. This stage of organizing youth camps continued for three consecutive years. One of the faithful supporters of these camps was Mr. Ali Rıza Güven.

Nobody can explain the spiritual ecstasy that Fethullah felt with his friends as they lived a true natural godly life amongst the trees and the mountains. Each moment would pass as a spring cloud raining on them the beauty of having spiritual intimacy with Allah, filling their innermost being with great hope in the future, illuminating their hearts with the light of beautiful green visions where they live in the glorious past seeing the sun rising again in the horizon of a delightful future. They could see that future with their own eyes in a spiritual vision. They could see its intricate carving with its vivid colors so delightful and so wonderful!

The youth would wake up before dawn listening to the waterfalls, to the rustle of tree leaves and to the chirping birds. At this time, the breeze would blow equal to the flow of longing within the hearts of devotees. It would fold the edges of the rugs here and there responding to the moaning of those who were prostrating, embracing the shadows of the devoted youth who were standing between Allah's Hands, blowing their garments to match the flow of their heated yearning, carrying them with the wind in a spiritual ascent.

The scene of the devotees waking up before dawn, leaving their beds in the middle of the darkness was like seeing the deceased running out of their graves after the blow of the trumpet on the Day of Resurrection. They still had to sooth their painful fear, holding it in hope through praying and remembrance. They would continue to prostrate and bow until the call of the Dawn Prayer was heard. After the youth finished their Prayer, they would join the circle of the remembrance of God waiting for the sun to rise in order to pray two more units of Supererogatory Prayer.

They lived time moment by moment, observing everything in their beautiful camp. The sun's heat would intensify at noon, reminding them of Allah's words concerning the story of the defeated hypocrites who had abandoned their duty for struggling against their egos. "*They said, 'Do not leave your houses during hot weather'*" (Surah at-Tawbah 9:81). The faithful believers would hear the answer coming from the Divine Voice as Allah says, "*Say: The heat of the gloomy hell is more intense if they would comprehend*" (at-Tawbah 9:81). In this way, the souls were becoming purified, the determination was strengthened, and the spiritual yearning would rise to lofty states.

In this atmosphere, the companions of the camp were standing behind Prophet Ibrahim, upon him be peace, contemplating with him the dominion of the heavens and the earth. They would declare Allah's Oneness at every sunset as they witnessed the truth, declaring, "*I do not like that which sets*" (Surah al-An'am 6:76). They would live the longing expressed in Prophet Ibrahim's saying: "*Indeed, I turn my face towards the One Who originated the heavens and the earth, with my pure innate nature and I am not one of those who associate partners with Allah*" (al-An'am 6:79).

The youth would enjoy the spiritually nutritious tables on this beautiful path. They would converse with each other saying, "If the road to Paradise is as delightful as this, what will Paradise, in itself, then be?"

In the darkness of night, imagination can mix with reality and the camp family who were navigating their way towards Allah would ascent towards intimacy with Allah to the extent of becoming almost purely spiritual beings or luminous shadows. The beautiful blue light would flow within them and they would drink a fragrant tea from its cups which would be poured to them from the pitchers of the Spirit!

Whenever they would gather to pray or to join in a circle of remembrance of Allah, they would feel marvelous spiritual delightful intimacy and they would be touched by subtle spiritual touches that would overwhelm their hearts with happiness that words cannot describe! They would feel as if angels' wings were tapping their shoulders or touching their faces or were wiping their heads with their soft gentleness!

At the beginning and the ending of the day, they would perform their duties with an active and energetic attitude as if they were swarms of honeybees taking care of their hive, or sucking the nectar of roses or the drops of dew, secreting delicious and sweet honey! This was how the youth performed their daily duties in the camps moving between trees, waterfalls, and refined flowers and between their tents, their prayer area, their classrooms, their kitchen and their sport games. They would arrange trail trips and walk to different nearby villages or to the sources of water or to explore the surrounding woods or hills.

The people of the villages, the forests and the mountains loved the youth and they would devote themselves to serving them and showing them generosity. Sometimes the students would walk at night. They would also wrestle, jog, climb hills or organize other sport contests.

Until now those who lived the early stages of camping feel the taste of the sweet wild honey on their tongues. Until now the camps open in every season producing flowers carrying the fragrance of Paradise.

As much as such camps were established to teach the youth about the past and its spiritual sciences and the struggle their ancestors lived, they also gave a chance to read the future's maps and to receive the first guided steps from the intermediate realm of faith through direct Divine Provision.

Until now the sentimental recitations echo within the hearts of those who attended the camps and tears are shed as they miss the warm nights they experienced there. The echo of the students' chants, the rhythm of remembrance and the expression of the souls where sadness is mixed with joy is knocking on the hearts' doors, bringing them out of lethargy and rejuvenating their vigor and boosting their energy to pursue the major Islamic renewal.

It is not strange then that the days of the camps hold within Fethullah's heart a special place; for he lived some of the most marvelous moments of his blessed life in those days. He wished that he could carry with him forever some of the beautiful moments he lived in the camps.

Fethullah realized through direct experience how camping can be an effective way to have a spiritual impact on the new generations in order to bring out the dormant energy within the youth and discover their talents and genius and prepare personalities to be capable of leadership and to become faithful citizens inspired by Allah's Guidance.

For Fethullah the first camp was the most difficult to organize and in the amount of effort he exerted to start it. Nonetheless, it was the most beloved to his heart. It had two big tents for the students and a small tent for him. There was a building closer to the tents which they could use as a kitchen. Ali Rıza served them with his motorcycle. Their provisions and equipment were very limited. Sometimes a storm would blow at night and the students would have to form groups and cover themselves with mats or sit underneath an area they had covered with straw to study the books given to them in the camp.

Most of the services needed in the first camp were performed by Fethullah from setting up the tents to teaching, to preparing the food, to fixing any tool or machine that stopped working. He used to sit on a small chair and put some pots in front of him while students would line up holding their cups in which Fethullah poured their share, and he would cheerfully say to each student, "Here is a ladle of blessed milk! Thus, pray upon the Beloved Prophet, upon him be peace and blessings."

The electric generator was very old and so it used to stop every day and need to be fixed. Fethullah was the one in charge of this duty. He became an expert at fixing electric generators for he had to work on it many times.

When the well water was low, Fethullah felt that he needed to dig further and so he did so by himself. He built toilets for the camp. Students would never forget how they saw their teacher digging with his shovel the locations for the toilets, while one of the new students was standing watching him. The student pointed to the teacher saying, "Oh hoja, would you dig here as well." The teacher gladly responded, "Yes, yes." The student would continue, "Would you dig here further?" And the teacher would respond, "OK! Sure!" And he would walk to where the student had pointed and dig. The teacher enjoyed digging, knowing that the pure water of the coming time would gush fourth. He would find in the strikes of his shovel an ecstasy that the resting student would not feel. In every strike he would witness the treasures of Persian Chosroes falling into his hands and he would see Caesar's dominion coming to him by force.

Because nobody else was capable of driving a car, Fethullah had to drive. He used to drive the small truck they borrowed from the Jurisprudence Department to transport the students from Buca to the camp site. One time, the truck rolled over on one of the sharp curves on the wild road. Until now, he does not know how he came out of it safe and sound even though the front of the car was completely damaged. The cost of fixing it was about four thousand liras. Some of the students were injured. One of those who were injured was Sacid, the son of Mevlud Bey, the Jurist's secretary. The young man was injured on his head and he bled a lot. Fethullah called his father right away and he would never forget how the father answered him, "May my son be a ransom for you! May a hundred others be ransomed for you as long as you stay well!" This was similar to the responses that many women gave to the Messenger of Allah, upon him be peace and blessings, after they were informed of the martyrdom of their husbands, fathers and sons.

In the third year, the brothers bought a car which Fethullah used to transport the students to the camp. He also used it to serve other needs of the camp. One time, he was going to Buca to pick up one of the university students to drive him to the camp. Beside him sat Mr. Isa Saraç. Fethullah tried to play a Qur'an recitation tape. He did not feel how he lost control of the steering wheel and the car rolled over. Allah protected them and they did not get hurt. But the car was damaged and fixing it cost a lot of money. When Fethullah later played a recorder that was in the car, he found out that it had recorded the accident and the echo of Fethullah calling for help, "Oh Allah!" When he heard the tape, Fethullah wept. He said to his friend, "When Bediuzzaman's foot slipped when he was standing on a high roof in the citadel of Van, he called his Lord, 'Oh what about the Call?' He did not worry about his death but was worried about calling people to Allah but I was concerned about myself."

The days of camping were full of joy and even the tiring work was enjoyable. This is why, Fethullah would not leave the camp for the entire trip, which was three whole months, except to deliver the Friday speech in Izmir, after which he would immediately return to his beloved camp.

All the visitors to the camp were impressed by his excellent organizational skills and his lofty manners. In the beginning, Mr. Ali Rıza visited the first camp and offered great help and also the merchant, Ahmed Tatari and Mr. Mustafa Birlik and the two great preachers who were Bediuzzaman's prominent students, Hulusi Yahyagil and Mustafa Sungur. This camp became very popular in Izmir and its news was widely spread among the circle of those who were concerned with the Islamic call in Turkey. Some sent their students from the far east of Turkey to Izmir in the far west of Turkey to attend the camp. Some students came from Urfa and from Diyarbakır. Thus, faith-based camps were reproduced across Turkey, between its seas and mountains and its beautiful wild forests.

The number of students in the first camp was seventy but the next year it reached two hundred and in the third year it reached three hundred. In the third year, the water level in the well decreased so much that Fethullah had to transport water from a far place, but this did not interfere with his ability to educate and discipline.

The camp programs were focused on preparing the students spiritually by purifying their faith and at the same time by giving them practical lessons and books to read. This was geared towards allowing them to confront the communist and anti-Islamic ideologies which had heavily invaded Turkey and the rest of the Muslim world at that time. The second aspect the camp focused on was how to purify the self and the third aspect was how to discipline the self. These three balanced aspects: the intellectual, the spiritual and the practical was not known in Turkey's educational system. This comprehensive approach had a great impact on facing the Marxist ideology in the country. Many faith-based activists emerged from these camps and established branches in every town and every province.

Extraordinary Gifts of the First Pilgrimage

This was in 1968 while Fethullah was thirty years old. His longing for pilgrimage was immense but he understood that he had no means to do it. He did not have the money to even reach half the distance to Mecca. He almost had what was enough to feed himself daily. He would spend some of his money to serve the call and many nights he would sleep hungry. How can someone like him hope to perform the pilgrimage to Mecca when it costs what it costs? Thus, he used to look at the pilgrims with eyes full of tears and his heart was yearning to visit the Mosque of the Prophet, upon him be peace and blessings, and the Rawda.

In 1968 at the pilgrimage time, there was a random lottery drawing across Turkey to select pilgrims. Fethullah aspired to be able to enter the lottery someday and he was soothing his sadness with tears. One day, he was teaching one of his lessons at the Kestanepazarı Qur'anic Boarding School when one of the students asked him, "Oh master, do you not wish to go for hajj?" Fethullah felt as if someone had put salt on his deep wound and he said to the student, "But who am I to earn this honor to go on the hajj?" He said his words with eyes full of tears. He immediately left the classroom and went to his office and closed the door behind him and stayed alone for a while. He sat on his chair and put his head between his hands and his elbows on the desk. He burst into tears. Under the glass on his desk was a photo of the Mosque of the Prophet, upon him be peace and blessings, and the Rawda. He looked at it through his tears and his yearning grew. He wept loudly as if he were complaining to the photo concerning his state.

He does not remember how long he stayed in this condition, but he remembers that one of the administrators eventually entered the office and found him this way. He said, "'Oh master, I am sorry but there is a phone call for you from Ankara, the capital." Fethullah hurried to the phone and found Mr. Lütfi Doğan, the Assistant of the Head of the Religious Affairs Department, on the other end of the line. After greeting him, he surprised him by saying, "Fethullah Bey, we have decided in the counsel of the Religious Affairs Department to send three qualified teachers with the pilgrims. The first one is Mr. Ibrahim Değirmenci the Jurist of Denizli, and the second person we have chosen is Mr. Ahmed Baltacı the Jurist of Eskişehir province, and the third person we have chosen is you!"

Fethullah could not believe what he had just heard. He wanted to make sure he was really awake and that he was hearing the speaker's voice, for fear that he was just dreaming! This was the first year that the counsel of the Religious Affairs Department in Ankara decided to send some teachers with the Turkish pilgrim group. The young man later learned that his friend, the past Jurist of Edirne, Yaşar Tunagür, the Vice-President of the Religious Affairs Department was behind nominating him to accompany the pilgrims. Fethullah prayed for him a lot. This was the first pilgrimage trip in Fethullah's life. It had a great effect upon his heart which he would never forget.

When the Ustadh arrived at Mecca, he did not leave the Masjid al-Haram, the Sanctuary Mosque, except for a necessity. He retreated and stayed in front of the Ka'bah day and night. When hunger would overwhelm him, he would eat some cookies, fruits or biscuits then he would return to pray and make invocations.

It then occurred to him to perform *'umra*, or minor pilgrimage, on behalf of those whom had rights upon him in Islam. So he did perform minor pilgrimage on behalf of the Messenger of Allah, upon him be peace and blessings, then he performed one on behalf of the Rightly-Guided Caliphs. He did not think how authentic this was; for he saw himself as an insignificant man that cannot be compared in any way to those men, but he was driven by his love for the Prophet, upon him be peace and blessings, and for his Companions. He did it as a thankful gesture to show appreciation for them. After that, he performed another minor pilgrimage on behalf of his relatives, starting with his teacher and the initiator of his work, Ustadh Bediuzzaman Said Nursi, may Allah bestow His Mercy upon him, then he did minor pilgrimages for his mother, father, then for his grandparents. He used to perform minor pilgrimages once or even three times a day on behalf of his loved ones, his family members, spiritual guides and friends.

Fethullah had a strong build and he did not know tiredness or experience fatigue especially when he was deeply immersed in spiritual practices such as performing 'umra or hajj. When he was striding back and forth between the hillocks of as-Safa and al-Marwa (i.e. doing *sa'y*) on behalf of his grandfather Şamil Agha, he felt a strange feeling! He felt as if he were flying! He felt his feet were above the ground as he was running. His entire body shivered and all his limbs started to shake. He then found himself sweating abundantly and he went into a state of intense sentimental longing that nobody knows its extent except Allah!

The spiritual illumination and the witnessing of the heart which the human being experiences in such states cannot easily be experienced in each moment. Fethullah remembers how at times, longing was so intense that he was completely pulled into the spiritual realm. Nonetheless, the state he experienced when he was performing the *'umra* on behalf of his grandfather Şamil Agha cannot be fully described; for he cannot express it in words. History recorded that day upon his memory and he would never forget it.

When he returned from the pilgrimage, the Jurist of Izmir was waiting for him in Ankara's airport accompanied by one of the imams. They all went to Izmir and after a few days, Fethullah decided to visit his family in Erzurum. There, his mother told him about a dream she had seen when Fethullah was performing his pilgrimage. She saw Fethullah's grandfather, Şamil Agha, flying above the clouds like the angels! When Fethullah investigated the date she saw that dream, he found that it was the very same day he had performed the minor pilgrimage on behalf of his grandfather. He remembered how he himself felt as if he were flying between the two hillocks of as-Safa and al-Marwa. Such spiritual experiences were among the subtle extraordinary gifts. It was a type of union of the innermost beings or a direct spiritual connection between him and his grandfather, may Allah bestow His Mercy upon him. You can also say it was a harmony between vibrations or etheric waves between the grandchild in the lower realm and his grandfather in the intermediate realm on the threshold of the Final Abode. This was due to the deep love and the spiritual tie between them. It could have been a sign from Allah to Fethullah to assure him that his gift to his grandfather had reached him. This was a demonstration of leaving "a pious child who prays for him."

Fethullah did not forget his students in the Kestanepazarı School in Izmir; for his connection with them was deep. He looked at them as the seed of salvation for the Muslim world. Thus, he took a list of their names with him when he went to the pilgrimage and prayed for them one by one. He also bought a small gift for each of them: a few dates, a small bottle of Zamzam water and a small silver ring!

During the pilgrimage, Fethullah was impressed by seeing the multi-ethnic groups circumambulating the House of Allah weeping, invoking Allah, supplicating and begging in many different languages but with the same heartfelt sentiment, with the same longing and with the same desires. They would line up in parallel lines, bow and prostrate as if they were one form. There, his certainty increased in the fact that in spite of the many wounds of the global Muslim community there was still some goodness. The more crowded the Masjid al-Haram was with those who were praying and circumambulating, the more it looked like a garden full of a diversity of roses and flowers with all colors and shapes!

Fethullah would not forget the accursed devil's envy. He had a story about him at the Masjid al-Haram! One day, Fethullah went to the second floor of the mosque to pray the Dawn Prayer there. After the Prayer, he sat close to the balcony reciting his *dhikr* and he heard a voice firmly instructing him, "Fethullah, throw yourself over the edge. Throw yourself down." The voice kept repeating its demand. Fethullah answered, "What would be the benefit of throwing myself from here?" The voice said to him, "Just throw yourself.'" Fethullah asked again, "But what would be the benefit?" The voice answered, "It would not harm you. Throw yourself." Fethullah realized that this voice was that of the Devil's. He sought refuge in Allah and immediately stepped back away from the edge of the balcony. When he was retreating backward, he saw his friend, Hajji Kemal, retreating backward with him at the very same time. There were about fifty meters between them and when they met later, Fethullah asked him what had caused him to retreat backward. He answered that it was because he heard the devil instructing him to throw himself from the balcony. He described to Fethullah the very same experience and they both heard the Devil's voice at the very same moment, may Allah curse him! The two men realized that it was the Devil who had come to them at the same location and at the same moment, wanting to take advantage of their intense longing and their stimulated passion to destroy them and get rid of them considering who they were in the way of summoning people to Allah and renewing the religion. If they had had no knowledge from Allah they would have been ruined. Thus, they did not separate for the rest of the pilgrimage days and they did not separate during any ritual or rite.

Painful Separation

At the end of the fifth year of Fethullah's work at the Kesta-nepazarı Boarding School, he started to get some harassment from the organization that used to supervise the school. It intensified with time and grew into a firm position against him. They hired a man in a higher position than him and withdrew from him all of his administrative powers. They asked him to only deliver his lesson. They also hired some of those who were hostile towards him to work with him. As for the man who was hired to supervise him, he was a sincere man and he did not have any knowledge of the bad intentions of the organiza-tion's members. His name was Sıdkı Şenbaba. Fethullah loved him a lot. Their relationship was very good. Sıdkı Hoja accom-modated Fethullah's father in his house once when he stayed in Izmir. As for the members of the organization, they were pressured by the Secret Intelligence Department, and the jeal-ousy some of them felt went beyond simple dislike. They hated to see Fethullah succeeding in gaining trust and popularity in Izmir, especially among students, either those enrolled in the Kestanepazarı Boarding School or enrolled in the universities of Izmir. They also hated to see him gaining the trust and sup-port of merchants and businessmen.

In that year, an earthquake hit Gediz and people in Izmir started to solicit donations to help the victims. Fethullah was one of the people who volunteered for this noble and humane work. He left the city for a while and went to distribute the donations in the areas that were damaged. While he was busy in such noble and humane work outside Izmir, the students attacked the new principal, Mr. Sıdkı Şenbaba. They insulted him in ways he could not bear so he left his position and never returned to school. The members of the organization thought that Fethullah was the one behind the incident, but he was innocent and was deeply pained by the students' bad behavior and attitude towards their new principal. The members decided to hire another principal but the relationship between Fethullah and them was made worse because of their bad speculations.

Fethullah realized that he had no more future in the Kestanepazarı Boarding School, especially because of how the administrators had separated him from his students. The direct connection between him and the students was the spirit by which he lived. Many teachers had envied him and would always criticize him and treat him badly, but he had endured it all and kept his hurt inside himself as if he were chewing bitter alloy leaves. He eventually decided to leave the school in hope that Allah would bring ease with the hardship!

When Fethullah started to move his luggage out of the Kestanepazarı Boarding School at night, the students came to his help with sad and broken hearts. The features on their faces were asking in silence, "Master, where are you going? Why are you leaving us?" His tears were running down his cheeks; for those students were part of his being and his small wooden cave was like one of his limbs and here he was, forced to leave them! He felt as if some of his organs were being cut from his body.

The small wooden hut had witnessed many beginnings for the new type of faith-inspired activities. From there, many graduated and had a great impact upon the activities of Islamic revival across Turkey. There many meetings were held on many nights to plan how to invite people to Allah and how to organize youth camps. Other important meetings were held there to discuss educational methods and curricula and how to prepare groups of students to carry the faith-based message across Turkey.

Hajji Ahmed Tatari was one of the members of the organization and he loved Fethullah a lot and could not understand why the organization wanted to separate Fethullah from his students. This shows how the whole issue was a conspiracy plotted by a few members who were affiliated with the Secret Service Department. Fethullah rented a big house with some of his devotees in Güzelyalı County. It had many facilities and could accommodate about forty students. They divided it into classrooms and a dorm room. At that point, the President of the organization, Mr. Ali Rıza Güven, realized the grave mistake that the organization's members had fallen into. The organization was dragged down in a cunning way. Upon realizing this, Mr. Ali Rıza Güven visited Fethullah and asked him to return to the Kestanepazarı Boarding School, promising to give him all of his administrative powers back. He asked him to forget the past but the arrow had been shot from the bow and struck whom it struck. Fethullah could not return to the school. A few days later, Fethullah's new school was filled with students and the Kestanepazarı Boarding School became empty except for its pillars. The members of the Kestanepazarı Organization regretted what they had done; for they all knew that Fethullah was honest and sincere in his work. He had a high level of piety in the way he administered the school. He never ate a morsel from the school food and never used a single sheet of its paper. He did not even touch the soap in the restroom which was available for everyone, but instead he would buy his own soap and everything he needed from his salary no matter how little it was. How miserable then were those who let Fethullah leave! What a loss they lost and what a blessing they let go from their hands!

Fethullah's popularity was increasing. Pious and righteous people in Izmir and its surroundings supported him. Some of the political parties tried to offer him high positions so he would join their parties, but Fethullah knew he was not created for that; for his only joy was sitting with his students, revealing to them his melting heart and his innermost being and spirit. His wish was to be buried in the graveyard near the Kestanepazarı Boarding School so he could hear the voices of the students while they were learning while he would be lying in his grave!

The Fire of Disorder

Fethullah dedicated his efforts in three main directions. The first was focusing on educating students in the religious sciences. The second was preaching in mosques and the third was organizing faith-based meetings and gatherings in private houses. University students formed the majority who attended these meetings in both mosques and private houses. In his spare time, Fethullah would immerse himself in reading books as was his usual habit.

Most Islamic organizations at that time were afflicted by a disorder that stemmed from their separation and disputes to a degree that became unbearable. Fethullah's main concern was to limit such disputes and prevent the disorder that was based on focusing on differences.

Some Islamic groups aspired to political goals and they would be easily triggered into violence whenever someone provoked them. They were impulsive and reactive and lacked wisdom.

After the death of the founder of the group who followed the *Epistles of Light* in 1960, the group tried to maintain its peaceful quiet work and separate itself from politics and its people, but eventually dispute started to occur within the group itself. This had a negative effect on the Islamic activities in the country.

A few years after Nursi's death, may Allah bestow His Mercy upon him, the disorder turned into hostility that was ready to ignite at any moment into a fight. Conflicts between parties and organizations intensified regardless of their affiliations and ideologies. Many hidden hands were igniting the fire of disorder between the Islamists, the right-wing ultra nationalists, and between them and the communists.

Many walls on the roads had graffiti drawn by parties accusing each other and cursing each other or supporting this party or that party or writing slogans showing support to this group or that ideology. The matter became worse when assassinations started to be one of the methods used. The whole environment was polluted by blood and the desire for revenge. The situation became very dangerous.

Fethullah was one of the few people who was against all of this violence. He was sure that provoking people with slogans was useless. In all of his public and private teachings he would call for self-restraint, wisdom, balance and beautiful contemplation. History recorded that the students of Light, regardless of the distress they faced, had stayed away from such violent movements and did not indulge in these fights.

Those who read the situation correctly knew that everything was leading up to a military coup. The language that was dominant at that time in the political arena, in all parties regardless of their ideology, and the way they handled the political dialogue between themselves using threatening tones, accusations and even assassinations was like a fire prepared and lit by those who were plotting for a military coup.

A Second Military Coup
Opens the Gates of Prisons

The second military coup happened ten full years after the first military coup that occurred in 1960. Regardless of its causes, it was a powerful strike to the Islamic movement in Turkey. Nonetheless, this strike, which first caused the Islamic movement to fade, later motivated it to have a clearer perspective and stronger vision.

The Narrator said: On a Friday in 1971 about one o'clock in the afternoon, a radio broadcast the announcement that the army had gained control of the government and declared a state of emergency in the whole country. This was followed by the mass arrest of many people from among the liberal wing and the Islamic groups and many other prominent activists from both sides. Arrests continued until prisons were filled with men and women.

Many Islamic countries were suffering under Western colonization at that time, just as when in the past Allah put them under the power of Genghis Khan, Timur the Lame and Hulagu. He put them under the Western power in order to awaken them from their heedlessness, and unconscious state of indulging in the lower desires and whims so they may return to their roots. Such is the Divine Way in dealing with Muslim countries everywhere and that was the case in Turkey at that time.

Backbiting was terribly widespread in the Islamic groups and even within a single group. Suspicion became the rule in dealing with those who held different opinions even though they were known for their righteousness. Separation was becoming wider and wider and the abyss was increasing in depth!

Backbiting was one of the bad behaviors which Islam came to fight and focused on abolishing from the Muslim communities. The Qur'an compares backbiting to eating the flesh of one's brother. At that stage in Turkey's history, talking was reckless. Criticism was furious and critics used strong words against each other which poisoned both the political and the Islamic environments.

This led to the interference of the military in politics by plotting a military coup claiming that there was a need to establish security and stop the chaotic environment. The army suffocated the whole country and each citizen endured his share of harm as a result of such suffocation.

In this situation Ramiz Efendi came to visit his son, Fethullah, in Izmir. The first of May, 1971 was the day when he was supposed to return to Erzurum. It was night and Fethullah prepared his father's bag and after a while his friend, Mustafa Asutay, arrived and drove them to the train station. After saying farewell to his father, Fethullah returned with his friend to his house but they stopped by some students' houses. Fethullah warned them that the security forces might storm their houses at any time and might arrest them and confiscate their books.

As the two men were on their way the car hit a black dog and the dog immediately died. Fethullah took it as a sign that they were about to collide with something extremely dangerous. They then drove towards Mustafa Birlik's house and when they were about two hundred meters from the house Fethullah asked Mr. Mustafa Asutay to stop the car. Asutay's son, Rıdvan, was with them and he was still a child in elementary school so Fethullah asked him to go to Mustafa's house and see what was going on. When the boy returned, he informed them that he saw men searching the house. Fethullah knew that the police had arrested Mr. Mustafa Birlik.

Fethullah asked Mustafa Asutay to take him to his house, but on the way the car hit another black dog. Fethullah expected that the police were waiting by his house and this turned out to be true. When he entered his house he noticed how the security personnel had searched the house inch by inch and they had collected many items from the house. He found one of the students, Sabahattin Atalay, who used to visit him once a week and sleep for the night, waiting for him. On that day, the student had prepared his teacher a rice dish. Fethullah heard one of the policemen speaking from inside one of the rooms saying, "Welcome back." They then continued their search.

A time had passed in Turkey when the mere recitation of the Qur'an was considered a felony punishable by law. Studying and exchanging the *Epistles of Light* was also prohibited. Fethullah was aware of all of these laws and he was careful enough not to leave any trace of evidence that he was involved in such activities. He did not even leave a single paper of the *Epistles of Light* that could be used against him. There was only one book by al-Mawdudi on his desk which he noticed and gently put his garment on it and picked it up. He then went to the restroom and then crept into another area of the house and hid it.

By the time the police ended their search they had collected forty books but there was nothing in the books that could be used against him. During the search, Fethullah asked them if they would mind if he ate. The policeman answered in a sarcastic tone, "Eat a lot; for it is unknown when you will return to your house."

At the military detention center, they put him in a room after they shaved his moustache and hair and took a profile photo, a front photo and a photo of his back. Fethullah asked the policeman if he could perform the ablution. He brought him a small amount of water in a dirty container and gave it to him in a rough way. The detained Imam performed his ablution and prayed the Night Prayer (Salat al-'Isha') there. Afterwards, they moved him to a big cell. He was surprised to find Mr. Mustafa Birlik, Imam Şaban Düz and Mr. Harun Tüylü and some of the youth activists there. They all seemed depressed and sad; for who would not feel that way in this situation. They all had their moustaches, beards and hair shaved even Imam Şaban who used to have a long beard.

When Fethullah noticed how his brothers were feeling, he tried to lighten their mood and transform the environment in the prison to that of an intimate joyful time with friends. He succeeded in his goal because of his wit, gentleness and intelligence. This night turned out to be one of the best nights of their lives that they would never forget.

When they put them in the cell they took everything from them: the Qur'ans, the *Jawshan* and all the other books of prayer and supplications. Because Fethullah had memorized Allah's Book by heart, he started to recite it night and day. However, he could not recite the Jawshan and the other supplications from the voluminous prayer book of *al-Jawshan al-Kabir* because he had not memorized it, which he regretted not doing.

They brought two more men in the next day and they belonged to the nationalist movements. Then, they brought some of the religious teachers and some of the administrators of mosques and the assistants to the imams. Two of them were Nizameddin and Recep, the math teacher. Recep Bey was one of the members who supported Fethullah in resisting communism. Nizameddin Bey had a nervous breakdown because of his detention and he was shaking. He suffered from heart disease as well. His daughter was very sad when he was arrested and she tried to commit suicide. This increased the man's anxiety and illness. Fethullah and the other brothers tried their best to support him emotionally and they had empathy for him.

On another day, they brought a physician named Dr. Kahid Bey and the cell could not contain all of them comfortably. They were moved to a place that resembled a kitchen. Fethullah sent a secret message to his friend Ismail Çelebi asking for the *Jaw-*

shan al-Kabir. The *Jawshan* came to him secretly in the evening of that very same day! Fethullah opened it and started to recite it and weep.

The group stayed in detention without a trial. There was a short lazy policeman who had a temper. He used to curse and revile them. He used to address Mr. Mustafa Birlik, who was the age of his father, "Oh scoundrel! How can you speak to an officer like me while you are sitting? Have you not done your obligatory military service? Have they not taught you there how an insignificant man like you should talk to a leader like me?"

In spite of detention, the prison cell was transformed into a godly place of worship and prayers. The scene of the faithful believers lining up to perform the Prayers was worthy of reverence and awe. It stimulated the innate nature of faith and fed the souls to the extent that two people who belonged to the nationalist movement started to come closer to the brothers until they eventually joined the Prayer. This annoyed the rest of the nationalists.

In the first court session, all the nationalists were released as well as Recep, the math teacher, and Nizameddin Bey who had heart disease. Fethullah was returned to his cell with Mr. Kahid Bey, Mustafa Birlik, and Harun Reşid Tüylü. In the first trial, the brothers saw their brother Osman Kara in the court and they understood that he came to testify in that session but at the end of the court session he was arrested.

In another court session, they were sentenced to be jailed for different periods. Harun Reşid, Mustafa Birlik, Dr. Kahid Bey and Imam Şaban Düz were all sentenced to be imprisoned. Later, Ustadh Fethullah was called and he had already predicted a similar fate to that of his brothers. He did not speak in front of the General Attorney for too long and the General Attorney was holding many greeting cards which Fethullah used to receive from his family over many seasons. Their abundance was the subject of the interrogation. There were reports concerning the contents of his lessons in the mosques and in every other gathering. Many of the brothers who were arrested had claimed that Fethullah was the source of all their teachings and put him in the front of the canon. The General Attorney looked at him and said, "So what do you say about all of this?" Fethullah said in a cold and sarcastic tone, "The Secret Service needed to work so they wrote all of that out of their big imaginations."

His words angered the General Attorney and he started to read every document out loud. While he was doing so, Fethullah's thoughts were in another realm contemplating the Day of Judgment. When the General Attorney finished reading, Fethullah was alerted and heard the summary and he was aware of the fact that it did not have anything that could be used against him in spite of all the false accusations they forged against him. He realized that only the confessions of his brothers against him could be used; for it was what could be weighed. He wondered if they were forced under threat to sign what was presented to them as their testimony.

At that time, Fethullah remembered a strange vision he had a few months before which he could not interpret then. It was right after he left the Kestanepazarı Boarding School. He had just started giving a class in hadith to the students of the Islamic Institute which many imams and high school students used to attend, as well as in a mosque in Güzelyalı. In his dream, he saw that he was leading the people in Prayer in that particular mosque and when he looked to his right side and performed the greeting he saw the Prophet, upon him be peace and blessings, looking at him with eyes full of tears. Fethullah was wondering why the Noble Prophet had that look on his face. Later, he realized that it was the last day he would deliver the lesson at that mosque. He could not resume the class later because the military coup occurred and many brothers were arrested. He realized why the Prophet, upon him be peace and blessings, looked sad in the vision.

After finding Fethullah guilty, they returned him to the first cell he was detained in and they later transported him from one prison to another. In the beginning the religious prisoners used to be detained in the same cells with the prisoners who belonged to the left-wing but when the number of religious prisoners increased they separated the two groups in different cells. The religious prisoners increased until there were fifty.

Later, they released Dr. Kahid Bey who was originally from Jordan. He used to help the ambassadors of his country in some matters. Fethullah testified that the man was patient and submitted his case to Allah; for in spite of being detained in a foreign country and although his wife had a miscarriage because the police terrifyingly stormed into her house, no single hair of his head moved but he showed resilience and determination.

Mr. Harun Reşid Tüylü was a wise man who continuously smiled and made jokes. He once said to Fethullah, "Oh Ustadh, we could not agree outside the prison about even a little bit of the plenty we have in common and so Allah put us under the military's control and made us agree about everything!"

Imam Şaban fell sick in the prison and fell from his bed and Dr. Kahid Bey took care of him. The reason they arrested him was that they found a few papers of the *Epistles of Light* in his house.

Ustadh Bekir Berk was a skillful attorney. He used to prepare his defense strategy inside the prison at night. He would not sleep until he had finished it. During the court sessions, he would sleep for an hour or less. His main concern was to find proof and form logical arguments. When he would find proof, he would wake Fethullah up and say to him, "Ustadh Fethullah! Listen to this proof! I will defeat them with this." When he would read a book, he would underline the same sentences ten times. He was an active man, highly intellectual and full of spiritual energy. He loved the Prophet's Companions, may Allah be pleased with them all, and he used to ask Fethullah a strange question, "Oh Ustadh, you know best the state of the Companions, so please tell me, by Allah, which Companion do I resemble? When you look at me, which Companion do I remind you of?"

During this bitter experience in prison, Fethullah realized that one could only know the reality of a human being when he is tried. He said, "Allah's Caliph, 'Umar ibn al-Khattab, identified a measurement by which we can evaluate the human being: to really know someone you have to travel with him or to have financial dealings with him, but I am going to add one more measurement to these measurements – to live with him inside a prison."

Fethullah was an inspired man with pure intuition, gifted in reading Divine Signs. One day, Şaban was called to go to a court session. Fethullah was lying on his back in the cell. He noticed a white butterfly falling on Şaban Bey's head and it went outside the cell with him, then it flew away. Fethullah felt optimistic by the sign as he interpreted it to mean that his friend was going to be released. This was exactly what happened. After the court session, Şaban Bey came, gathered his clothes and left the prison.

On another day, Fethullah was called to a court session. Before being called, he was lying on his back inside the cell, thinking whether they would release him or not. He noticed a brown butterfly on the ceiling. He kept looking at it to see if it would fly out of the window. He waited a long time and the butterfly did not move. This was it! Many religious prisoners were released except him and a few of his devotees. They put all of them in the same cell with those who belonged to the left-wing.

The number of communists who were in the cell exceeded the number of religious prisoners. No matter how the religious people tried to be gentle and treat them nicely, the communists would respond to them with a rude and rough attitude.

Fethullah started to escape to his books which he used to read secretly. He used to hide his books under a removable piece of wood in the cell floor. The restrooms were located in a small hall outside the cell. The doors of the cells used to be closed from nine o'clock at night until seven in the morning. This used to cause hardship and embarrassment to the prisoners but necessity can make a man creative. Some prisoners could not hold on until the morning and so they would urinate inside bottles they used to put on the edge of the high window in the cell. The bottles would line up like bottles on a shelf in a pharmacy in a funny and embarrassing scene.

Fethullah would not drink any tea or fluids starting from the afternoon so that he would not be forced to urinate in a bottle which would have been very embarrassing to him. Allah protected him from such an urge during the time he spent inside the prison.

The prison warden was a colonel and he tried to prevent the prisoners from urinating into the bottles but necessity had its own rules so they did not obey him. Regarding taking baths, the prisoners were allowed to take a bath only once per week.

One day, Fethullah ate an egg that was offered in the meal and it caused him a severe allergic reaction that could have caused him his life. He got many sores on his skin and had difficulty breathing. He was left to meet his fate and they did not bother to bring a physician to see him. In addition, they took all of his medicines from him when he was arrested. At the same time, one of the communists had the same allergic reaction like that of Fethullah's. They allowed him to go out of the cell to breath. When Fethullah's state got worse, they took him to the military physician who turned out to be one who knew Fethullah. Fethullah was happy to see him and when the physician examined him he wrote his name among those who should be checked by a physician weekly.

Throwing away the garbage was the prisoners' responsibility. They would take turns doing it. They used to eagerly wait for their turns because it was their only chance to see open space and to breathe fresh air even if it was for only a few minutes.

One day, it was Bekir Bey's turn and when the garbage carriers were called he was asleep and no one noticed. He became very sad about losing his turn; for it meant losing the chance to breathe fresh air.

The prisoners suffered from mosquito bites, especially during summer. If they closed the windows they would feel the intense heat as if they were inside a lit oven. If they opened the windows, the cell would be invaded by swarms of mosquitoes and flies. Whenever Gültekin Bey would go to the restroom, he would spray mosquito repellent but if he stayed long a new swarm of mosquitoes would attack him as if they were getting revenge. He would not move until his skin was torn from scratching. Every morning, the prisoners would wake up with swollen faces and limbs because of the hundreds of bites they got at night.

Dialogue with the Ensnared

After three months, a group of the ensnared ones (*majdhubs*) were brought into the cell. There was a group of ensnared people in Turkey who deviated from the true path of religion. They claimed the love of the Prophet, upon him be peace and blessings, but they put their desires and whims as the foundation of religion. They used to gather around a person whom they considered to be their Imam or the Shaikh of their religious order. They used to hate others who differed with them and thought that they were the only one following the Straight Path. Living with them in the same cell became a huge problem. No matter how hard Fethullah and his followers tried to approach them, they would repulse them; for they would not even consider Fethullah and his group as Muslims. They would not accept to be led in Prayers except by one of them and they would not eat from any food that was brought to someone else outside their group. To minimize the gap, Fethullah instructed his beloved group to pray behind them, but their Imam turned out to be ignorant and he did not recite even the shortest Qur'anic chapter of al-Kawthar correctly. Moreover, they would not perform the Prayer in conformity with its rules. Thus, the brothers used to pray behind them then repeat the Prayers afterwards to minimize the chance of fighting inside the prison. Some brothers refused to pray behind the ensnared; they preferred to pray in a separate group. This created tension inside the cell.

Fethullah tried to open dialogues with the ensnared ones (*majdhubs*) to make them familiar with Islamic teachings, but in spite of his skills and knowledge he could not succeed with them. Whenever he would present evidence from the Qur'an or the Sunnah, they would turn it to a different context and they would seek proof in the jinn's sayings and actions. This was the main issue of their conversations day and night. Blind ignorance was the basis of their thinking and Fethullah could not achieve any intellectual results with them.

A Fight with the Ensnared

One day, an intense argument occurred between Ustadh Bekir and one of the ensnared. The argument developed into a fight. The ensnared ones were observing the situation until the fight started, six of them attacked Bekir Bey. One of them hit him on the head with a chair. Some brothers also got involved in the fight and the matter became confusing and dangerous. Fethullah and others tried to calm the situation and put an end to the fight but they were beaten and kicked. The situation in the cell became war like and Fethullah rushed towards the window and started to call the guard who violently opened the door. As soon as he did, all the ensnared ones ran and sat in their corners. The guard looked angrily at everyone and said in denial, "Is this how Muslims behave?" The ensnared ones did not care about what he said, but Fethullah felt as if someone had stabbed him in the heart. This sentence pained him for a long time and his only solace was the fact that he had prevented a murder from taking place by calling the guard.

After the fight, they were secluded in individual cells even though they were not the ones who started the fight. At that time, Fethullah felt that he was experiencing the same situation which the whole Muslim world had been experiencing for four centuries. He was telling himself, truly, history repeats itself!

Among the ensnared ones, was a man named Arif. He was gentle to some extent. After they left the prison he met Fethullah on the road one day. He said to him, "Oh Ustadh, please forgive us, for we hurt you." He said it and quickly left on his way. His fellows were not as gentle; they were very rigid and almost cruel.

With the Communists in the Prison

Only a few of them had sound reasoning! Most of them were envious and used to threaten the brothers from time to time. They would try to provoke the brothers day and night. They used to forge complaints against the faithful believers like claiming that the ground shook as if there were an earthquake when the faithful believers prostrated. Others would complain about the Dawn Prayer (Fajr) or about the night vigil (Salat at-Tahajj-ud) or about ablution, and so on. Nonetheless, Fethullah would try his hardest to live peacefully with them. Sometimes the two groups would confront each other. For example, he heard one of them curse Allah, glory to Him, and curse the Prophet, upon him be peace and blessings. The attorney, Bekir, also heard the man and he went and complained against him to the prison administrator. The communist denied what he said and the attorney asked Fethullah to testify and Fethullah did testify to the truth in front of the administrators.

The faithful believers were put in a separate cell whenever they would pray, and when the Imam would start to recite the Qur'an, the communists would loudly knock on the wall from their neighboring cell even though they never ceased to play their music and sing loudly during the day. They would not stop cursing the religion, the country and everything sacred.

One day, the prisoners were given permission to go out in the prison yard to get some fresh air. The brothers heard the news that the right-wing in Indonesia had defeated the left-wing in the elections, so Bekir Bey commented, "We will defeat them here too, when Allah wills." Some of them heard him and the environment became extremely intense. They were about to attack the entire religious group but Allah granted them safety and frustrated their plan. If they had, the administrators would not have interfered except at the end of the fight and would not have brought them to reckoning. The atmosphere was charged and ready to be ignited with fire at any moment. It seemed that the hostility might result in death on both sides. To prevent this possibility, Fethullah used to exert his utmost effort, for those who would win any fight would be the communists!

Dangerous Prisoner

In the last days inside the prison, one man was brought to the religious cell. His name was Kadir Kaymaz. He was very dangerous. He belonged to a gang that used to break into banks. He stole more than forty million liras. To avoid his evil, the prisoners put his bed beside Fethullah's, especially because they saw how easily he could be provoked and that he needed special treatment. Fethullah befriended him and cut the way for the communists who were trying to attract the man to their group. Fethullah discovered that the man was ready to accept religion and so he started to explain to him little by little the concepts of religion until the man went and performed the ablution and started to pray and he had not done that before in his life! He felt remorse for all of the wrongdoing he had committed in his life. He confessed to Fethullah some of the plots of the left-wing which he knew of.

In the Prison of the White House

The prisoners spent most of the last days in Bademli Prison and then they were transported to a military prison that was located in Şirinyer. The prison building was painted white. This is why the prisoners would jokingly call it "The White House."

From the outside, the building looked like a beautiful modern building but from inside it was just a narrow passage that had no access to the sunlight except at noon time when the sun lit the place for a few minutes and then disappeared again. It was built to imprison people in individual cells. The guards used to give the prisoners their food from underneath the door. Restrooms were inside the cells and there was little water. It had an offensive odor and there was no hope of going out and smelling fresh air.

No one remained in the prison except two, Muhammad Fethullah and Mustafa Birlik. This is why they put them in the same cell with Kadir Kaymaz and another man from the left-wing. It was Ramadan and the two men used to fast and then Kadir started to fast with them. His communist friends found out and they cut off their relationship with him. Kadir had a Jewish girlfriend who used to come visit him every day, and one day she discovered that he was fasting so she cut off her relationship with him. This affected him emotionally and shocked him. Fethullah was the one who gave him solace. Even after leaving the prison, Fethullah did not forget his friend, Kadir, and he visited him twice, and carried gifts to him.

The Communists' Sadness

One day, the communists were very sad and their weeping could be heard from time to time. When the prison guard entered the cell they kicked him out and closed the door behind him then blocked it by putting a bed in front of it. Their tension towards Fethullah and Mustafa Birlik intensified. Mustafa said to his friend, "I am worried that they may take us hostage."

Fethullah said, "There is no use in taking us hostage, for they know that we are of no value to the administration." After a few days, the two brothers understood why the communists were weeping.

There were two leaders among them, Nedim and Ibrahim, who were pillars for the left-wing movement in Turkey. The police were searching for them. Ibrahim was killed during a violent confrontation with the police in Istanbul. They thought that Nedim was killed as well during this confrontation, so they wept. After a few days, Nedim was arrested in Izmir and was brought to Bademli Prison. Nedim was a rebellious man who did not care about the law and did not follow any rules. He was tortured during interrogation but he was a strong resilient man and he did not speak a single word. They used to put salt on his wounds to increase his pain but all of their efforts were in vain. After two or three months, he was unable to speak because of his injuries and infections. He used to jump like a frog. Fethullah felt sympathy for him in spite of the extreme difference in their beliefs. He was sorry to see him tortured like that.

The Farce of Trials

At that time trials were nerve wracking. A new type of pseudo-hero appeared. There were brothers who testified against their brothers to get revenge on them because of old personal conflicts. There were also brothers who would readily accept anything that would be offered to them just as the left-wingers did. This meant that they accepted to be secret agents in exchange for their release. When Fethullah's trials started there were many secret agents and voluntary witnesses who testified against him. For Fethullah, this was the most hurtful experience. Some lawyers volunteered to defend Fethullah for free.

On the other hand, some cunning people volunteered to testify against him with made up stories about him.

The ensnared ones (*majdhub*s) were the most harmful; for they testified against the religious prisoners and made up stories against them during the trials. They accused some men who had not even gotten involved in the Islamic call at all. They only used to attend the classes and listen to the spiritual guidance and did no more than that.

Fethullah would never forget the bitterness he tasted when many members of the organization that was managing the Kestanepazarı Boarding School testified against him during the trials.

There were two particular ensnared ones who used to watch every move of the religious group inside the cell. They would report everything to the prison administrators thinking that in doing so, they would score some beneficial points for themselves. Nevertheless, they eventually got a heavy sentence from the court. They remained for many years inside the prison.

Whenever the brothers would go to the court sessions, they would be shocked by the false testimonies of the ensnared ones. It became a nightmare disturbing them everywhere they went. The brothers felt helpless and did not know how to defeat the plot by the ensnared ones.

Courageous Supplication

In court, there was a retired colonel. His name was Mehmed Çatalkaya. He was a member of the organization that managed the Kestanepazarı Boarding School. When the court staff asked him to testify about what used to happen inside the youth camps he delivered a speech that made Fethullah and his beloved group cry. He spoke with truthfulness and sincerity. He said,

"The camps were under our organization and the teacher was just an employee. I did visit the camps a few times and I did not see anything suspicious considering the imam or the muezzin."

Before his testimony, the prosecutors showed him some pictures from the camps where turbans were worn and they asked for an explanation. The man told them that only the imam and the muezzin were wearing them inside the camp. His testimony matched the testimony of Fethullah without any previous conversation between them. The retired military commander continued his testimony, saying, "Since Ustadh Fethullah came to Izmir to teach, I have sat between his hands and benefited from his teachings a lot. I ask Allah to release him from the prison soon so that I can listen to more of his lessons." Fethullah would never forget the testimony of that man who was a retired colonel.

He had exposed himself to a serious vulnerability considering his position of security. The man delivered his testimony with courage that was rarely seen among religious people.

The Death of Uncle Enver

When Fethullah was in Bademli Prison, his father, Ramiz Efendi, visited him and stayed a month in Izmir in hope that his son would be released before he returned to Erzurum. He witnessed four court sessions and when they did not release his son, he was forced to return to Erzurum sad and depressed.

His first visit to Fethullah was full of emotions of sorrow and deep sadness. He cried a lot after his father left. He could not even touch his father or kiss his hand; for there was a high wire fence that separated them. He asked him, "How are you my father? How is my mother?" He could barely hear his answer because the place was crowded with other prisoners and was full of noise. His father said, "Your mother traveled to the city." Fethullah asked, "Why? What happened there?" His father answered, "Your uncle Enver is very sick." He said this and his eyes were filled with tears. Fethullah immediately understood that his beloved uncle had passed away so he wept a lot with his father. Fethullah loved his uncle deeply. The uncle was younger than his father by eight years and he passed away at the age of sixty. Later, Fethullah understood that his uncle fell sick out of his sorrow when Fethullah was arrested; for to him Fethullah was like his dearest son. Fethullah returned to his cell and the image of his father crying did not leave him and he could not stop crying. His brothers sincerely tried to give him solace and comfort him. Mesih, Fethullah's brother, used to visit him frequently. Many of Fethullah's other relatives and friends visited him as well.

The Last Lamp

One day in July, it was the twenty-sixth day of the blessed month of Ramadan, the brothers were taken to attend a court session again. At this time something significant happened that no one expected. The Judge stood and all of a sudden said, "If all others were released, then there is no reason not to release Fethullah and Mustafa Birlik as well." The two men were very surprised and they learned that the court decided to release them.

During these days, Fethullah saw Said Nursi in a dream. He was wearing a black garment and standing in front of the prison! Nursi started to take out his devotees and threw them one by one into a place that resembled a stronghold. In another dream after that, he saw that they were freed from a high summit sliding safely down its steep slopes to the Ka'bah.

After the trials came to an end the two brothers were taken to "the White House," into their cell to gather their luggage. Their faces were shining with delight. Guards and other prisoners congratulated them and they quickly gathered their luggage and peacefully left. It was the Laylatul Qadr of the blessed month of Ramadan.

Sadık Bey was waiting for them with his car outside the prison to drive them to their houses. When Fethullah sat inside the car, he wondered where he should go. He did not have any place in Izmir to go to; for after this long time of not paying the rent for his small house, he anticipated that the landlord would not allow him to stay there. The only place he could go to was Mustafa's house. Fethullah was a highly sensitive and considerate man and he preferred to leave his friend to have private time with his family so he decided not to go and stay with him. The image of his weeping mother and wounded father appeared in his mind and he decided to go straight to the train station. He spent the night on the train going to Erzurum. The man left Izmir as he entered it, carrying nothing except his small suitcase and wounded heart!

The day they released Fethullah, his older sister, Nur Hayat, was in front of her house standing sadly and she heard two passing persons speaking. One of them said to the other, "They were released today." She took it as a sign of Fethullah's release. She hurried to her mother and gave her the good news which turned out to be true!

After a long day of traveling, the whole family was surprised to see their son Fethullah standing in front of them. Joy was mixed with confusion and tears with laughter and they all cried. Eid al-Fitr—the Feast of Breaking the Fast, that year was one of the most joyful occasions for the family and was full of sentimental emotions and spirituality which Fethullah would never forget!

Chapter 8

Opening up to the World and the Cavaliers' Victory

A Return Stronger than Steeds

*F*ethullah is a man who would not dismount his horse except when he was victorious. Fethullah is a spiritual leader who would not stop his efforts until the sun of the spirit rises. His concealed secret would not allow him to surrender to the bats of darkness. As he was crossing the storms of the terrible night he witnessed the striking lightning of the conquest coming from the near horizon! He saw the treasures of Persian Chosroes thrown between his hands, and the dominion of Caesar coming to him by force. Whenever his pain was intensified and he was besieged from all directions, the major conquest manifested to him emerging from the West from all directions, opening the windows for the sunrise there. He saw the horses melting the Siberian snow with their hot panting, warming the hearts of the distressed across Transoxiana—the land behind the two rivers!

He saw the horses lined up as if they were a structured building, facing the Atlantic Ocean with bare chests, swimming swiftly as if they were magnificent whales and they would continue to swim until they reached the new Roman land! They would enter the cities raising the flags of love and peace! They would also go to African jungles to distribute the loaf of Light upon the poor everywhere! The spirits would reveal the pure at heart and fill their hearts with merciful peace that would overwhelm all of their peoples. They would listen to the spiritual call flowing from the depth of the forests and all the trees would become minarets and its branches would form domes and prayer halls.

Fethullah saw all the continents join together in his hands like one garden! He would read the Prophet's glad tidings as an instruction to the generations and weep![16]

The Narrator said: After releasing him on the ninth of November, 1971, Ustadh Fethullah tried to mount his desire to migrate! He wrote to the Department of Religious Affairs to resume his preaching activities again and to return to his job to perform his duty in inviting people to Allah with official permission from the Department so that he could return to Izmir; for that city was embracing the new sprouts of the call. He really wanted to return to Izmir so he could care for such sprouts, and help them to grow and flourish. The Department's response was taking a long time so he stayed in Erzurum teaching without a license.

One day he was called to go to the Department of Religious Affairs in Ankara. There, the man in charge of employment told

---

[16] This was included in a sentimental lesson which Fethullah delivered on the Fifth Floor about the following hadiths of the Prophet, upon him be peace and blessings: "My name will reach every house on Earth whether it is made up of earth or canvas tent" (Hakim, Mustadrak, 4:476; Ibn Hanbal, Musnad, 4:103). "The Earth was laid out before me, and I was shown its remotest corners in the east and west. My Muslim community will extend over whatever was laid out before me" (Muslim, Fitan, 19; Abu Dawud, Fitan, 1; Tirmidhi, Fitan, 14; Ibn Maja, Fitan, 9; Ibn Hanbal, Musnad, 4:123). Such hadiths call for duty and instructs believers to convey theDivine Message to everyone. (Ed.)

him that the army had been pressuring the administration concerning him. They wanted him to leave Izmir and to be hired in another place. Thus, Fethullah was hired in a city called Edremit very far from Izmir and that was on the 23rd of February, 1972.

Although he had embraced his first students in Izmir, he succeeded in planting new seeds in this rural city. What he had done in Izmir became an inspiring provision that supplied him over there. After two years and four months, he was transferred to another city called Manisa to work as a preacher in its main center. This was a great relief for him considering his service in calling people to Allah. Manisa was not too far from Izmir. Therefore, he was able to resume his connection with his first students there. He actively resumed his constructive teaching. From Manisa to Izmir, Fethullah revived life in the faith-based services. He improved educational methods and increased his inviting meetings. Youth camps were resumed and increased in number. Activities in schools were developed. In brief, the Islamic call was developed in quality and intensity in a very short time.

The Death of the Father

The spiritual connection between Fethullah and his father was very deep. Losing his father through death was not an easy event for the young man. This took place on the 20th of September, 1974. Fethullah named this year "The Year of Sadness." One month before his father died, Fethullah's close friend Necmeddin Güvenli passed away. Before that happened, Fethullah saw in a dream two airplanes flying vertically and rising gradually to the sky until they completely disappeared from sight. He saw that same dream a few times. Then, both his father and his close friend passed away in the very same year!

The difficulty of separation continued to burn Fethullah's heart. When he was informed that he was hired in Manisa he kissed his father's hand as he was taking his permission to accept the job. The father was sick and asked his son not to leave until Thursday. Fethullah kept silent but the father, who understood the nature of Fethullah's job, gave in. He exhaled deeply and said to Fethullah, "Oh my son, go! Here, there are only two eyes waiting for you (pointing to his eyes) but over there, there are thousands of eyes waiting for you."

Fethullah traveled to his work place and after one week he received the news of the death of his noble father. He was informed that his father had passed away on the very Thursday that he had asked him to wait for. He immediately returned to Erzurum folding the long distance with a bleeding heart because he had not waited until Thursday. He did not have an opportunity to say farewell to his father and his life companion.

Another Arbitrary Transfer

The tyrannical authority was keen on making Fethullah live an unsettled life. One of the ways to do so was to arbitrarily transfer him from one place to another all of a sudden after a short period of time so that his efforts to invite people to Allah would not be completed in any place. Whenever the watchers felt that the warmness of faith-inspired relations had started to extend from his heart to the inhabitants of the place they would rush to cut the rope of affection by moving him to a new place far away from the area he was in.

Fethullah would frustrate their cunning plans; for he would be faster than what they thought. His words were like fish eggs that migrate into the oceans. He would put them into corals before he departed! Soon, the eggs would open and the new embryos would emerge to the realm of life and grow and then join the first schools of fish no matter where they were! Fethullah continued to receive new provision from one exile to another and from one migration to another, leaving each place he went to as a home for supporting his movement.

Fethullah was arbitrarily transferred from Manisa to Bornova. This did not harm his call nor did it stop or sever it. On the contrary, his move to Bornova was a new opportunity to plant new roots for his call and greatly extend his efforts. The new city was not far away from Izmir. In fact, it was a province of it.

In the middle of moving here and there, Fethullah started to deliver lectures outside the mosques in hope of reaching gatherings that did not pray. He never neglected to speak in coffee shops. Wherever he would be, he would answer the youths' questions and engage them in spiritual discussions concerning how the enemies of Islam make it appear evil. At the same time the irreligious philosophy continued to spread and overwhelm the country especially among the elite, the educated, the students and university professors. Fethullah, who studied the modern Western philosophy and all of its schools of thoughts, was able to answer the challenging questions of the era and confront the attacks on religion and its followers. He was able to defeat the theories of anti-Islamic philosophy by demonstrating intellectual arguments and logical evidence. The "revealed book"—the Holy Qur'an was his main source of provision and the "created books" of the universe and man—Allah's Signs within the souls and on the horizons, would manifest to him as clear books of which he could read their words and letters. He would read the Signs directly and his knowledge would impress the audiences in both mosques and lecture halls.

Thus, he used to receive many invitations to deliver lectures and speeches about such and such issue from all around the country to the extent that he gave a lecture in almost every major province in the country. In 1977, he traveled abroad to speak to the Turkish who lived and worked in Germany. He toured many of the known cities and delivered his speeches to the people of his nation, renewing within them the connection to their original roots and to the religion and civilization they belonged to.

Locally, he became well-known because of the essays he used to write for many journals and magazines which his students published in many fields and levels. Out of these essays and the speeches he delivered, he formed the books that he later published and they were translated into many world languages.

From Schools to Forests

Izmir was the first incubation for the school of the new Light. The school which Fethullah founded there in the beginning of the 1970s was not an ordinary school! It had both middle and high school grades. Outwardly, it followed the national educational system, excelling the curricula of the Ministry of Education, but inwardly it differed from the public schools in an essential aspect. The major difference was in the "teacher." This is the essential aspect; in Fethullah's schools they had a true teacher. The governmental forced curricula with its official books did not allow any mention of the word "religion" at all and teachers could not utter that word in their classrooms. Otherwise, they would close the whole school and confiscate all books. Nonetheless, the teachers who graduated from Fethullah's academy and were transferred from place to place used to teach by example and provide role models for others. They mastered speaking the heart's language and the Light's rays which they received from their great teacher who had a piercing glare. Whenever they would look at the eyes of the students, children and youth, they would awaken their souls to look at the lofty windows of the spirit. They would directly raise their heads towards heaven and see the clusters of Paradise hanging down upon their hearts. They would passionately fall in love with the images of the Truly Real and the Divine Beauty. Their hearts would hang on the lamps of Light.

Thus, Fethullah's schools, in spite of the rigid curriculum and harsh laws, would be waterfalls of goodness flowing with thousands of spiritual beings who had graduated and who would be dispersed everywhere and start to share in constructing the new era!

From Izmir, the Gülen-inspired schools spread everywhere. It became a fluid of love and epistles of good news embraced by the students and sponsored by his devotees among businessmen who competed to buy buildings and rent places until there was a school in every city across the country.

Ankara, the challenging capital of the country, was one of the first cities in which the Gülen-inspired schools were established after Izmir. There, side by side with the forests of hell, were the waterfalls of peace flowing across the city forming spiritual oceans that are inexhaustible. Ankara was transformed from a city that people feared to a city radiating spiritual rays, releasing doves of love and peace and within a few years flowers were grown across Anatolia.

The Fifth Floor

The fifth floor originally means floor number five in any building that has five floors or more. But in the terminology of

Fethullah's students it was an allusion to a meaning full of faith-inspired treasures and spiritual realities that have educational and disciplinary dimensions. It was the treasury and the depository of Fethullah's secret invitation to the spiritual realm. It was a social and communal center of his *Hizmet*, or benevolent services. The services which Fethullah fulfiled to revive religion, were all issued from the "Fifth Floor"!

The schools, which Fethullah inspired and encouraged his supporters to build, used to be constructed as high buildings with departments and classrooms for official and private education, except the Fifth Floor.[17] It was so subtle and awe inspiring as if it were the lion's den, the magnificent lion, Muhammad Fethullah Gülen, let them be in Izmir, in Ankara or in Istanbul.

On the Fifth Floor, Fethullah used to give his lessons for his specially selected students. He would teach them Qur'an exegesis, the science of the Noble Prophet's traditions, the Arabic language, Islamic jurisprudence and many other spiritual sciences. He used to do so even though he was always chased, kicked out and exiled.

The Fifth Floor had a special position in Fethullah's heart and a great deep bond was always formed with it. It was a station from which the spiritual light manifests. Thus, the man would never leave the Fifth Floor except for the necessity of safety. To him, the Fifth Floor was like the Cave of Hira or the House of ibn Arqam or the valley of Abu Talib—a refugee camp

---

[17] The term "Fifth Floor" originally referred to the top floor of the dormitory of a prep school where Gülen resided in Istanbul in the 1980s. Indeed, the number "five" in itself is not significant as Gülen states that it could be, for instance, the fifteenth floor. The Fifth Floor is rather a symbol of an elevated, sacred space which is both a personal spiritual retreat of Gülen and a social and communal center of his philanthrophic services. (Ed.)

of sorts outside of Mecca where the Noble Prophet's uncle Abu Talib provided what protection he could during the three year tribulation. Therein he found retreat and revelation, his exile and prison, his companions and gatherings. Month after month he would stay there in his sacred space and not leave it except to go to one of his other small rooms if he received a sign, an indication or a warning that it was necessary for him to leave or go to another place.

Out of the Fifth Floor, Fethullah served to revive religion in Turkey. From the Fifth Floor he opened its doors to the world, to the whole world! When Fethullah sat there, he delivered his highly influential speeches to his faithful students, businessmen and people from all walks of life. It would be enough for him just to point in order for school trees to grow here and there and for classrooms to be filled with children's and youths' chants, as they drew on the green boards masterpieces of new hope! With one word from Fethullah, school and university buildings were erected as well as hospitals of lofty services that embraced the sick and weak everywhere. With his word, media companies would be built and media equipment would be supplied to broadcast good, pure and beautiful images which would push away the images of evil!

Fethullah's call continued for twenty some years and established powerful financial organizations and strong media tools and groups of faithful men who are devoted to their cause. They excel in every field and exist there as pillars constructing the nation's edifice for the new era!

Fethullah's movement formed a powerful force that has affected the entire society while its members have never actively participated in political parties. Nonetheless, they influence the socio-political direction of the nation. This is why, all the political parties started to try to gain their empathy and support. During all the election periods, Fethullah would be visited by many political leaders so that they might gain one word of approval from him or at least gain a good reputation that they are not enemies to Fethullah or for his call!

A Third Military Coup That Ruins Public Safety

An observer of the history of military coups in modern Turkey notices that they occured approximately every ten years. The military would intervene with a bloody coup to remind the society and the politicians that the top word in this nation is for the army and that there is no room for any better change.

The Narrator said: That was what happened on the 12th of September, 1980. At that time, the Prime Minister was President Süleyman Demirel. The one who led the military coup was General Kenan Evren. It was a random chaotic coup. It demanded the arrest of 1,000,683 people! 650,000 were arrested and 230,000 were sentenced to long jail terms. 517 were sentenced to death, and 50 among them were executed.[18]

Fethullah realized that the atmosphere that overwhelmed the country before the coup was a sign that it would happen. The reader of social events and their development can clearly see that the army was plotting something and that the moment to seize public freedom and suffocate people so they would not be able to breathe was at hand!

The conflict between the right-wing and the left-wing was intense and Marxist and Lenin slogans were raised everywhere and it became clear that the real indirect conflict was between the United States of America and the Soviet Union. It was a

---

[18] Numbers taken from a Turkish daily called *Zaman*, published on Sept 12, 2009.

battle that the Turkish people were paying the price for regardless of which ideology they supported. The slogan of madness and destruction was raised, "Let us first destroy and later think how to reconstruct." This is the familiar slogan in any civil war in third world countries. This makes it easy for the hidden hands to play with the youths' emotions in the streets and universities in order to prepare the way for the tyrannical military coup to take over. This coup destroyed both green lands and arid deserts!

Fethullah was aware of this fate and used to warn his friends and the youths who belonged to other Islamic ideologies of the possibility of its occurrence and from the danger of getting burnt by its fire!

The Fugitive Preacher

Directly after the military coup, the security forces in Izmir started to continuously chase the preacher until he felt suffocated and annoyed. He asked the Department of Religious Affairs to transfer him out of Izmir. He was hired in Çanakkale. Nonetheless, everything became worse when those who initiated the coup enforced martial law and started to arrest people. Fethullah became one of the first people wanted by the Secret Service and his picture was posted everywhere as if he were a dangerous criminal. His picture was posted in all of the military barracks everywhere.

Fethullah sank himself into the depth of the society. He kept moving from hiding place to hiding place and from one shelter to another. He lived as a refugee and could not publically continue his cause or in sharing his faith-inspired services which he was sincerely devoted to. His students used to secretly visit him and they would retreat together for a few months in one place, studying the sciences of the Qur'an and contemplating how to invite people to Allah until a warning sign would come to them from those who were charged with observing the security of the meeting and the location they would meet in. They would creep out quietly and move to another county or to another city.

Signals

One day, Ustadh Fethullah was looking from behind the tainted glass across the horizon through the Fifth Floor's wide windows in Istanbul. He saw birds flying above the roof, going back and forth and they then circumambulated the building in a strange way! He contemplated the scene for a few moments then he immediately called his students saying, "Let us leave this place now." They crept out of the place and secretly moved to another location. A few minutes later, the police stormed the Fifth Floor and searched everywhere but could not find anything.

In another incident, the chased Ustadh was suffering from painful ulcers on his skin that almost paralyzed him and he could not sit to deliver a lesson for pain was emanating from his body. A warning came from his students that they should immediately leave the location but the teacher was too sick to be able to move quickly. He instructed his students to disperse inside the rooms of the Fifth Floor and he stayed alone in the big main hall, hiding behind a curtain. He stayed there for a time that felt like years to him and he was in great pain, sweating from the tip of his head to the bottom of his toes. After a few minutes, the police stormed the place. They looked everywhere and stormed every room and found a couple of students here and there. They were looking for Fethullah and

did not care about the young students. They looked everywhere
back and forth, wondering among themselves where the man
could have hidden himself! They had definite information that
he was in this location at this hour. Fethullah could hear them
from behind his veil. He could hear their loud footsteps. If
one of them would have looked down, he would have seen his
feet or if he would have lifted part of the curtain he would have
found Fethullah who was squatting there. The search took very
long and he sweated until his clothes were all wet and glued
to his body!

Allah blinded the policemen's sight and none of them paid
attention to what was behind the veil! When they eventually
gave up, they left disappointed and defeated. Fethullah left
his hiding place and walked to the living room and was amazed
at the ease he felt. All of his pain from his ulcers had completely disappeared!

Fethullah would never forget the Divine Intervention that
protected him and how he was once saved by a tiny insect!
This took place at one of the camps. Fethullah was delivering
a lesson to his students about knowing Allah. The study circle
was held in the middle of the forest surrounded by trees. While
he was focused on his explanations and logical demonstrations,
he was inspired to make an example of some of the realities
of Lordship to make the concepts more accessible to the students. As soon as he started to utter the first words, a strange
insect appeared. It had wings and claws and it emerged from
among the trees and started to circle above the gathering as if it
were searching for something. In a few seconds, it went directly
to Fethullah and landed on his mouth, grasping with its legs
and claws his lower and upper lips closing them together and
preventing him from talking. The man tried to remove it quickly but it seemed as if it were glued to his lips, holding onto

them. He had to grab it with his fingers and throw it away. He resumed his teaching as if nothing had happened until he reached the very same sentence he was about to say before, the strange insect came circling again in the space around them. The students became worried that the insect would harm their teacher again and what they feared quickly happened. The insect went like an arrow towards Fethullah's face and landed on his mouth, grasping his lips together with its claws. At this time, Fethullah read the signal and realized that the sentence he was about to utter was not fitting for the state of Lordship. He burst into tears and sought Allah's forgiveness, declaring his repentance. He sought refuge in Allah from being one of the ignorant!

These were two subtle stories in Fethullah's life which were full of intimate communication with his Lord and special supplications. He would weep a lot between the hands of his Guardian Protector. He would spend the whole night devoting himself fully to his Lord. In the morning, he would ride his horse and gallop in the dust, dispersing musk, leading the way of striving in inviting people to Allah.

Fethullah has a lofty station of devotion. He has always been cautious of minor doubtful actions so he tried to avoid some of the permissible actions if they were not necessary; so much so that he would harm himself at times. He did not feed himself or heal his body but with that which is permissible. His close friends would never forget how one day while he was teaching them on the Fifth Floor, he had an excruciating chest pain, which used to occur to him from time to time. He leaned to his side and almost passed out. The students ran at the speed of lightning to his room to bring his heart medicine but they realized that the medicine had run out. They did not know what to do. At that time, the teacher was following the movement of his students while he was almost passing out. One of the students

brought him a paper of the medicine he should be taking. The
teacher noticed that the students were coming from a direction different than the direction of his room so when the student put the medicine in his hand, Fethullah asked him in a
weak voice, "From where did you bring this medicine?" They
answered that they brought it from the pharmacy on the fifth
floor which had a small depository. The teacher refused to take
the medicine in spite of his critical situation. How can he take
it when he had lived his whole life feeding himself from his own
salary not from the donated money from which the medicine
in the depository had been bought? He felt that he had no right
to use it. He remained in this critical condition between life
and death until Allah relieved his distress.

Fethullah in Moses' Basket

When Fethullah used to leave the Fifth Floor, only a few of
his close students would know where he would hide. This was
after the coup in 1980. He could be in an empty apartment
or in another school or in any other location. One time he hid
in the family house of one of his faithful devotees. They were
brothers and businessmen. They had a great mother who treated Fethullah as one of her sons. She used to treat him kindly,
care for him and serve him. He stayed in the room prepared
for him for quite a while until Allah permitted him to leave.

One day, Fethullah hid in an unknown place away from the
Fifth Floor. The situation was really very difficult. It was night
and there was an emergency situation the cause of which could
not be resolved except by arranging a meeting with his close
students to consult with them and to make sure that the news
he had heard was correct. He was determined to meet them
but they were on the Fifth Floor and he was in the secret shel-

ter and the meeting could not be held in this shelter. Thus, he decided to take the risk of meeting them on the Fifth Floor.

In the middle of the night, a small truck stopped in front of the secret shelter and three students whom he trusted to keep secrets entered his place. There was one couch that could be opened into a bed. Fethullah opened it and underneath it there was a large drawer in which pillows and blankets could be stored. It was as wide as the bed. Fethullah took everything out and lay inside the drawer on his side and instructed his students to close the drawer. They turned it back into a couch. Fethullah lay inside the couch and his students carried the couch on their shoulders. They put it inside the truck and sat on it and their teacher was lying underneath them. The truck crossed Istanbul's streets passing by many security check points without raising any suspicion until they arrived at the gate of the Fifth Floor where the meeting was supposed to be held. The students carried the couch on their shoulders and entered the building. When they arrived at the private elevator they opened it and opened the couch. Fethullah left it quickly and they ascended to the Fifth Floor to surprise everyone with what they could not imagine happening; meeting Fethullah guarded by Allah's security!

Escape Lesson and Arresting Fethullah

What was really marvelous in the middle of all of this was the teacher's persistence in delivering his lessons no matter what the situation was. Many times, the escaping car that would carry Fethullah and his students to his hiding place became the classroom in which he would deliver his lesson. One student would be driving and the rest would be listening while he explained to them his lessons calmly as if he were in the middle of the mosque or in his own place on the Fifth Floor. The struggling teacher continued to be in this marvelous situation until he was arrested in a city called Burdur on January 12, 1986. After a long interrogation, he was taken to Izmir, the center of his activities, to be tried there. However, a Merciful Divine Intervention led to his release!

Through such rough years, the army declared a new democratic era. It submitted authority to civilians and a general election was held. President Turgut Özal was elected and charged with forming the government.

Turgut Özal was a man who carried a heart beating with goodness. Fethullah had a connection with him before. The President had drunk from the cups of Fethullah's lessons and accompanied him to some gatherings. He received from him admonishing wafts of spiritual insights that made his heart feel the hidden faith which accompanied him during his political life when he was the Prime Minister and when he became the President. He was the first President to pray Friday Prayer publically and officially. With his political experience he succeeded in forming relations with Western nations and to pressure the army and to relatively force them to stay inside their barracks. He achieved many gains in granting general freedom that was unprecedented in the Turkish society. His political ruling period had a positive impact on the freedom of Islamic activism. Goodness spread everywhere. Then, all of a sudden he died a mysterious death. May Allah bestow His Mercy upon him!

President Turgut Özal knew of Fethullah's arrest once it took place. In the middle of the very same night, the President gathered all of his ministers at his office. He issued a governmental announcement that acquitted Fethullah of all of the accusations forged against him. Immediately, Izmir's security force released him.

Fethullah took advantage of that temporary release and started to tour the country, moving from one city to another, checking on his friends and empowering his men and enhancing the quality of faith-inspired services to make it hard to be broken or be swallowed by any other ideology. This continued until the sixth of June of the same year when Fethullah went to perform the pilgrimage for the second time. During his stay in Hijaz, political unrest took place in Turkey and a few of the Muslim activists were involved. The security forces, who were always ready to take an action against Fethullah, wanted to accuse him of being involved in this unrest even though Fethullah was clearly innocent of it. A new order to arrest him was issued.

Although Fethullah's companions and students advised him to stay in Medina, he refused to do so and decided to go back to Turkey. He went to it secretly through the Syrian border. Then, he secretly traveled to Izmir in the western side of the country. There, he surrendered himself to the security force. Soon, the court acquitted him once more and he was released. He freely resumed his lessons of admonishment in mosques.

His call at this stage was deeply established in the Turkish society to the extent that it became impossible to annihilate it. Its scientific, economical and media organizations became very well established and took hold of almost the whole arena. The Ustadh used to see with the eye of his insight, the black octopus legs extending to him little by little waiting for any excuse to arrest him once more. He continued to be very cautious even when time sleeps!

The Poet of Heroism and Grief

At that difficult stage, Fethullah used to retreat a lot in seclusion. He would contemplate the condition of his nation and observe what was happening. He would remember the Ottoman legacy and the hostility it faced from inner and outer enemies. He would reflect on the many calamities that the Turkish people were afflicted with one after the other. He would pick the pearls of wisdom and weep. Much of Fethullah's poetry reflects that stage.

During one of the retreats, with spiritual sentiment Fethullah remembered the bloody days. He would sooth his wound through writing his inflammatory poems with his blood mixed with his tears. He wrote about the Ottoman Vice-Regency (*Khilafah*) and about the hero who opened Europe until he reached Central Europe beyond Hungary and Islam found a home there and delivered it from darkness to Light. The forces of deception continued to watch him from behind their fences. Once they saw him falling into slumber they crept to him and assassinated him in the middle of his den and a period of stagnation and regression started, ending with the collapse of the Vice-Regency.

People's nostalgia for religion was awakened by free men among the Turkish people who strove to recapture the lost treasure. When they were at the beginning of the road, the military coup of 1960 took place and ruined people's dreams. Fethullah wept a lot. About all of this, he wrote his heated poem "The Nation's Spirit." He said, encouraging his assassinated knight:

There was a hero buried on the near slope of the mountain.
They stripped him of his shirt and ripped open his coffin.
In fear of him rising again, they heaped stones upon him.
There was a hero buried on the near slope of the mountain.

Oh my brave one! Would you tell me what happened?
Your soul is sad, the country is distressed.

Sit up and cry with me and let our hearts be burnt by fire.
Oh my brave one! Would you tell me what happened?

Cannot you hear me? Send me an inspiration!
For I have been soothing my hope with you for too many years.
May be you would come tomorrow.
Cannot you hear me? Send me an inspiration!

A shirt of shame on my back, laden with the burden of years
My heart is longing in hope to see you again.
At times it ascends to lofty heavens; it crawls out of weakness at times.
A shirt of shame on my back, laden with the burden of years.

Everywhere is in ruin, a festival for owls!
Bridges have fallen one by one and the roads are without travelers.
No one stops by anymore, the fountains have run dry!
Everywhere is in ruin, a festival for owls!

Willpowers are hesitant, souls shocked.
A dozen unfortunate ones hijacked history's testimony.
Ethics turned upside down, sacred values unowned!
Willpowers are hesitant, souls shocked.

Oh my knight! Arise and come just like in dreams!
Come with the new dawn, riding your white horse.
Now, I shut my eyes and see you with the spirit's eyes.
Oh my knight! Arise and come just like in dreams![19]

Opening the Doors of Central Asia

At this time the Soviet Union was torn down and its inner most core was torn and many independent Republics with Muslim

---

[19]   From his poetry collection, titled *Kırık Mızrap* (The Broken Plectrum). (Ed.)

majority populations emerged in Central Asia. The suffering for eons of these Turkic Republics under the Soviet Union's chains was not easy. The Republics were perplexed and disturbed. This caught Fethullah's attention and he delivered a historical speech in the Suleymaniye Mosque in Istanbul in November, 1989. He encouraged the Turkish men who were devoted to the call to transport their faith-inspired services to these different Republics such as Kazakhstan, Azerbaijan, Turkmenistan and others, especially that these countries had relations with the Ottoman Empire in the past. In a short time many Turkish schools and companies were established in many of the countries in that region. It even reached the depth of the Soviet heart! Schools were established in Moscow and other cities across the world.

A New Year of Sadness

On the eighth of April, 1993, Fethullah was leaning on his bed in his room on the Fifth Floor. He was looking for a moment to rest from the long tiring path so that he might be able to restore the strength he lost in preparing what must be prepared for the future.

As he was lying down, he heard a light knocking on his window. In the beginning he thought the children of the servant were playing with their small toys close to his window. But the knocking continued with a regular rhythm. Fethullah raised his head and looked at the window. He saw a white dove tapping on the glass with its beak. He looked at her and she looked at him then she flew away. He quickly picked up the phone. He called a friend and he informed him that President Turgut Özal had passed away. Fethullah sent a telegram of condolence expressing his sadness and pain. To Fethullah, no one was as faithful to the country as the President!

On the twenty-eighth of June in the same year, Fethullah's mother, Refia Hanim, passed away in Izmir where she lived with some of her children. Fethullah led the funeral prayer of his mother. As it was very hard for him to lose his father, the excellent teacher, it was similarly hard on him to lose his mother, who inhabited his heart and filled it with the spirit of the Qur'an. It is enough to hear how Fethullah described his feelings to understand the depth of his sadness; he felt orphaned. That year was truly another year of sadness in his life.

The Conquest of Istanbul

Istanbul is the mother of all cities. Whoever possesses it possesses the whole earth! Whoever loses it loses the whole earth! When Mehmed the Conqueror besieged it, his siege had stages of striving and difficulties. Then, Allah's triumph and conquest were granted to him. Before him, the Prophet's Companions and the followers strove as well for centuries but Allah decreed a time for it. When the era of darkness arrived, Istanbul was in need of a gasp of Light.

The only weeping person at this time was Muhammad Fethullah Gülen! His weeping was not a lamentation out of despair or inability but it had its own language! A language that kindled Light in the rocks that were looking down at the world from the top of the lofty mountains! Birds twittered the good news of lifting the dark era!

It was the twenty-sixth of August, 1977 when the first spark of lightning struck Istanbul! The doves had a date with Fethullah's weeping in a mosque called Yeni Camii, or the New Mosque, in the historical peninsula of Istanbul. There, on the shore of

the Bosporus behind tens of old minarets and domes embracing ancient pain, there Fethullah threw the first flash of Light
in the latest era of darkness! As soon as he did, the gulls received
its shimmer as a delighting glare that agitated history's sadness!
The lightning had struck all of Istanbul's horizons, terrifying
all the bats of darkness everywhere!

This was the first dose. After that Fethullah returned to his
first incubation in Izmir. But Istanbul had tasted the beauty
of the Light and so its minarets and domes shook their wings
longing for the tasty weeping. Fethullah is a compassionate person who is shaken by the moaning of the weakened and he cannot but respond to every call of prayer that pierced the hearts'
walls: Oh, horses of Allah, march!

Fethullah had ridden the terror of the night and departed
to Istanbul again! He stayed as a guest in the halls of the majestic Sultanate mosques like the Sultanahmed Mosque, Suleymaniye Mosque and the Sultan's Mother Mosque. He found
the faithful people thirsty stretching their hands crowded around
the platform were he sat waiting for the flow of the Light's
faucet, pouring Fethullah's exhalations in all of Istanbul's mosques
until no dove or seagull remained, but it knew the beautiful melody of his noble weeping! The trees of Fethullah's call had flour-
ished all over Istanbul and all branches joined embracing the
schools of goodness in the princes' city. Thus, a new Light extended to Anatolia until there was no place inhabited without the
longing for the birth of a new dawn. All cities and villages cor-
responded together concerning their findings which echoed
everywhere, exchanged between shores and mountains from
east to west and from north to south.

Istanbul became a real capital and the new prince conquered
it and opened the High Gate all anew. The spirit's storm
embraced the throne of leadership that overlooks faith-inspired

services across the whole country. In 1996 Ustadh Fethullah came from Izmir to Istanbul and stayed there for good. He sat on the throne of teaching in his favorite settlement on the Fifth Floor. From there, all groups and organizations emerged to conquer every place in Istanbul. Which city could be more capable of making the dawn's light reach the world?

Dialogue Activities

Fethullah became a prominent national figure so it was not easy for anyone to harm or to limit his freedom even though the enemies did not give up and continued to plot and conspire against him. Since 1996, Fethullah succeeded in initiating a broad national dialogue across Turkey. He started to communicate with minorities of other religious backgrounds such as the Catholics, the Protestants, the Orthodox, the Armenians, the Greeks and others. His relationships extended to include leaders of all political parties from the right and the left. The dialogues had a great effect on lessening the pressure on the Islamic call in Turkey and on Hizmet's faith-inspired services that were spreading everywhere. At this stage, the Ustadh established what he called Journalists and Writers Foundation (GYV) which was behind organizing many conferences aimed towards national dialogues and exchanging ideas and presenting different points of view. The foundation became a wide umbrella under which many prominent educated Turkish thinkers and writers from all directions and different political parties gathered. It became a way of letting people from all walks of life meet who would not have met otherwise.

It was the first initiative of its kind in Turkey's history. Fethullah has to be credited for his remarkable ability to unite people from everywhere to bring together those who were very distant from each other. He formed a co-existing peaceful atmosphere between fighting groups in the socio-political arena, in the ideological arena and in the religious arena. It is a great accomplishment that Fethullah will be remembered for across the country and in sociopolitical and intellectual circles.

Fethullah's image was broadcast across the media through interviews with him and publishing news about the dialogues and the conferences he held across Turkey or outside it, especially across Europe.

Betrayal of Those Who Are Near

Fethullah is a cavalier who is skilled in piercing through the believing self and he is skilled in opening up to the whole of humanity. The dialogues which he initiated locally and abroad became strong pillars that preserved his faith in Turkey in spite of receiving many wounds and cruel hits. They opened for the call new doors that used to be closed to faith locally and abroad. Only a few people at that time understood him and he was criticized by many people who belonged to Islamic activism and from the Islamist parties and groups and even from some of the sufi shaikhs. They attacked him and criticized him viciously in magazines and in gatherings. When he met with Pope John Paul II, and engaged him in a historical fruitful dialogue they accused him of preaching Christianity as they accused him of reconciling with secularism and surrendering to those who oppressed him. Later, when he traveled to the USA they accused him of being a traitor and working for the CIA.

Regarding his public meeting with the Pope it was a key to great goodness for faith-inspired services in many European countries and in America. It was a strong shield against ultra secularism that fought against religion locally and abroad. Fethullah was an innocent man and he was oppressed from two sides: from the tyrants' side and from his brethren who worked in other Islamic organizations. The most hurtful oppression was that which he received from his brethren. His pain can be expressed in the words of the Arabic poets who wrote:

The oppression of those who are near has a bitter taste
On the soul from the strike of a sharp sword!

February's Storm: The Postmodern Military Coup Burning All Air

The twenty-eighth of February, 1997 was not an ordinary day in Turkey's history. It was the day of a terrible political storm that destroyed that which was green and that which was arid. The storm was led by the military caste. A comprehensive coup of a different nature was directed at the elected government and forced it to sign laws and issue decisions by which the army gained the upper hand to besiege Islamic activism from all directions. It suffocated religious people in the Turkish society which led to the destruction of the many gains that the religious people had achieved during a long period of sacrificing and struggle.

The President at that time was Süleyman Demirel, the previous leader of the Democratic Party. The Prime Minister was the prominent professor and Islamist leader, Necmeddin Erbakan. Süleyman Demirel was allied with the military and was involved in the postmodern military coup. Necmeddin Erbakan was forced to pay for his ideological beliefs. Under the threat of the coming fourth coup, he was forced to sign oppressive laws against the country and religion. The laws prohibited any religious manifestations inside official and private organizations. According to these laws, many army officers were fired because they were accused of praying! Some of them were accused of allowing their wives or mothers to wear the headscarf or for anything else that showed any religious gesture even if it was subtle.

Many families suffered from such arbitrary firings. It was prohibited to hire any woman who wore the headscarf and men who showed any religious gesture in governmental positions. Girls wearing headscarves were prohibited from pursuing their college education. The young ladies were given the choice, either to remove the headscarf or to pursue their education. In other words they had to choose between following their religious beliefs or continuing their education.

Many physicians, lawyers, and university professors lost their jobs. Many administrators in many governmental departments were also fired. The Islamic Welfare Party (RP) was dissolved and the sufis were prohibited from their activities. The fire of the storm extended to the educational curricula and to school and university rules, burning any green leaf that remained there! Living in Turkey became like living in unbearable hellfire. As a result many Turkish scholars, teachers and spiritual activists migrated as they were forced to exile themselves or burn in the firestorm. Courts opened their doors against many people, and many Islamic activists from all groups and ideologies were arrested.

Turkey lost a great deal due to this horrifying storm. The results of the storm continued for many years and caused many chaotic practices from some Islamists. They raised provocative slogans against cruel ultra-secularism and issued aggressive statements that warned that what they saw was a dangerous enemy. An enemy that was like an octopus that extended its legs locally and abroad and they had no power to resist it even for an hour! Thus, some of the Islamists were involved in unwise activities that led to the ultra-secularist coup allowing them to rule the country for a short time and use such slogans as an excuse to prohibit any religious activities.

Fethullah's activities were also besieged everywhere and searching his schools became a regular routine. Due to his heart disease, Fethullah went to America for treatment. He departed the country in June, 1997. He stayed in America for seven months. When he felt a little relief he returned to his country to continue his struggle and he saw how the services he had organized were attacked and disturbed. The bats of darkness continued to chase him all over again and they opened the file of his past trials. There were many indications that the man was in danger and under a threat that would annihilate his life either by assassination or by forging false accusations that could lead to his execution as had already happened to many spiritual leaders and politicians.

Many warnings and indications came to Fethullah showing him that this time the threat was very serious and he was in danger. Because the plot of assassination was two-bow lengths away or nearer, Fethullah decided to exile himself to America. He left the country under the pretext of needing treatment for his heart again. On the twenty-first of March, 1999 Fethullah left Turkey and never returned.

The Fifth Floor in Exile

From atop a faraway mountain, in his lofty exile in the USA, in Golden Generation Retreat Center among the trees of Pennsylvania, Fethullah was not only looking at Anatolia but to all the continents of the world! His perspective extended to faraway locations. The conscious birds would migrate to different locations and the striving groups would race with their longing and attain Paradise!

The Pennsylvania camp had a Fifth Floor as usual even though the building had only three floors. The Fifth Floor had become an allusion whose meaning was known to the students and their teacher. Wherever Fethullah goes, there is a Fifth Floor even if it is a small cave. This is because all of the functions of the Fifth Floor are carried out in it. From there, the Light dispersed into the whole world. To there, groups would travel, be they teachers or students or those who offer different services to the faith-inspired activities such as businessmen. Many groups would travel for one goal; to meet the educator, the teacher. The groups became like honeybees that migrate and build new hives, crossing the Atlantic Ocean back and forth. The Ustadh remained as active as always, delivering his lessons in the sciences of the Qur'an to his elite students.

The preacher's relationships extended to the scientific institutes and American universities. He held gatherings and meetings and initiated dialogues with academic researchers and university professors there. His academic students established an Institute for Islamic Studies which was named after Bediuzzaman Nursi under the University of John Carol in a city called Cleveland. Through this institute, MA and Ph.D research programs were developed and many conferences and symposiums were organized.

Fethullah would not leave his small place in exile except to go to the hospital to receive treatment for his coronary artery stent. Inside his place of exile, he would receive many groups, prominent academic professors, and some Christian scholars and priests. They all admired his personality, the depth of his intellectual reasoning, and his spiritual refinement.

In the beginning, staying in America was not easy. He was an undesired person there. The authorities were forced to accept his need to visit the USA for treatment. He was given an official permit to stay in the country after a long period of post-ponement and excuses. He would pressure them with his simple tool and they would renew his visa for a short time in order to force him to eventually leave the country. It was not a secret that this attitude of the Immigration Department was affected by pressure from the Turks who were fighting him from behind their fences! The arms of the dark octopus continued to extend and chase him everywhere.

But the experienced preacher started to meet the Turks who were coming to the USA to work or study and he would also meet with the emigrants among businessmen and encourage them to start schools everywhere across America. He guided them in establishing connections with the scientific and academic institutes as well as with intellectuals, writers, religious scholars and other prominent figures in the civilized circle of people in America in order to break the barrier between Muslims and the Turks and to release from its siege the call that is based on civilized and peaceful dialogues. This is the way adopted by Muhammad Fethullah Gülen.

Many symposiums were held to discuss his thoughts and to provide exegesis of his doctrine in understanding religion and in leading dialogues with others. Many Turkish scholars and American academic professors participated in these symposiums. But in spite of this, the envious entities in Turkey continued to practice their old habits, preparing files for trials against Fethullah to persecute him and find him guilty of something even while he was suffering from living in exile; alienated from his own country! They cut his hope of being able to return to his home country someday. Nonetheless, the man returned long ago but they did not feel it! His spectrum is crossing the streets of Anatolia but they cannot see it! His voice is in the midst of every gathering in Turkish meetings. How can the bat of darkness ever be able to besiege a man like Fethullah?

The Greatest Opening:
The Divulging of the Concealed Secret
A Void Grew in the Heart of Moses' Mother

It was not easy for Fethullah's students in Istanbul and across Anatolia to swallow their teacher's departure. It was very hard on them and its effect shook them like an earthquake in the beginning. However, the edifice of the call was strong enough not to collapse or be destroyed by this event. All of Istanbul's domes were shaken but they did not fall! This is because Fethullah had established his faith-inspired services by constructing organizations. His call was preserved in the hearts that beat with the Love of Allah and who know Him. He tied the hearts with a rope from heaven then departed. It is true that his personality was the cornerstone in serving the call and was a source of spiritual provision that is gushing with longing that quenches the thirst of millions of hearts. But because of his awareness that people do not persist in existence except by Allah, he tied his call to Allah and lived the ecstasy of being present in the pain of being absent!

From Istanbul to the rest of Anatolia, Fethullah Gülen Hocaefendi's tapes were released everywhere. "Hocaefendi" is the favorite title that the Turkish people chose for Muhammad Fethullah Gülen. It is a title that means "The Esteemed Teacher." His tapes traveled across roads and streets, glowing on the shelves of libraries and houses. You cannot enter a single house or shop without finding the inflamed longing kindled in between its ribs!

The echoes of his admonishing lessons exploded everywhere under the domes of the majestic Sultanate mosques and in many other places. All of his speeches since he started offering his faith-inspired teaching until his forced exile filled every space in the country.

Oh ladies and gentlemen I marvel how his words, even from old lessons and admonishments emerged alive once again as if they had just been delivered from the platform of this or that mosque. I saw people flowing to the gates of the major mosques while birds line up in a marvelous way on the minarets and domes.

Fethullah has thousands of spectrums and his lessons became loafs by which millions of the Turkish poor and needy were fed across the world. The cowards became helpless and the bats of darkness withdrew to their caves terrified from the overflowing Light!

His lessons were not mere admonishments but because of the sentiments of its author, the lessons became mirrors of the ancient time flowing powerfully into the wakeful presence! History became a garden producing flowers within the hearts of thousands of audiences crowded around the sources of the echoing birds that are continuously chanting hymns of remembrances! The weeping of the preacher Fethullah stimulates the inhalation of the authentic horses and the neigh of glorification rises everywhere! The Prince lines them up one line after the other!

Here they are standing between his hands, giving him the salutation of peace, declaring their submission, waiting for the order to dispatch throughout the vastness of Allah's earth! This is the time of conquering the cities by opening the hearts! History is now pouring good news into the rising future!

Fethullah glorified Allah – Allah is the All-Great! And the authentic horses are dispatched everywhere! They have pure white blazes on their foreheads owing to the water of ablution dripping from their body and they are longing to smell the fragrance of Paradise! Groups are dispatched with permission one after the other! I saw it, ladies and gentlemen, I saw! I saw groups, each led by a highly energetic cavalier, with a glow on his forehead. I saw them dispatched towards every continent. One group is led by Khalid ibn al-Walid. Another led by 'Ali ibn Abi Talib. One led by al-Qa'qa'a ibn Amr at-Tamimi while another is led by 'Amr ibn al-'As. I also saw the group led by Abi 'Ubayda ibn al-Jarrah and the one led by Sa'd ibn Abi Waqqas and many other groups of the first generation of Light! Nothing veiled them from me except the intensity of the Light!

I then saw the group led by 'Uqba ibn Nafi' and I heard the neigh of his noble horse crossing the ocean waves! I witnessed the horses of Tariq ibn Ziyad and saw his ships reaching the port of Andalus burning the rays of defeat and withdrawal. I saw triumph advancing in the new era, spreading peace and security across the world.

I then saw Salah ad-Din's group and Palestine's youth were between his hands, pouring the calf's ashes in the sea and putting an end to the nightmare. I also saw Mehmed the Conqueror's group declaring the accomplishment of the Muhammadan promise! I witnessed the Light dispersing everywhere on earth in all directions. There was no house, no land, no island but the Light entered it!

Then I Saw!

I saw Fethullah in the midst of the crowd, pointing with his finger upward towards the source of all the secrets! His tears were shining in delight, happy with the rise of the new era! He was holding his old keys and his small suitcase. He dismounted his horse and walked slowly among the lines until he reached his platform. He announced to the people the unity of all sunrises from all directions! Fethullah declared his secret to the world!

The Narrator of sorrows said to me: In one of the meetings on the Fifth Floor that looks upon the whole lower realm, Fethullah was asked,

"Sir, how were you able to see what you saw?"

"When the tear is purified from all distress, and it longs solely for its Initiator, the veils are lifted and the Light is manifested. Then, the Path's landmarks become disclosed to the travelers!"